ALSO BY TED MOONEY

*Easy Travel to Other Planets*

*Traffic and Laughter*

*Singing into the Piano*

# THE SAME RIVER TWICE

# THE SAME

# RIVER TWICE

## Ted Mooney

 ALFRED A. KNOPF · NEW YORK · 2010

THIS IS A BORZOI BOOK
PUBLISHED BY ALFRED A. KNOPF

Copyright © 2010 by Ted Mooney
All rights reserved. Published in the United States by Alfred A. Knopf,
a division of Random House, Inc., New York, and in Canada by
Random House of Canada Limited, Toronto.
www.aaknopf.com
Library of Congress Cataloging-in-Publication Data
Mooney, Ted.
The same river twice / by Ted Mooney. — 1st ed.
p. cm.
ISBN 978-0-307-27273-7
I. Title.
PS3563.O567S36 2010
813'.54—dc22          2009041691
Manufactured in the United States of America
Published May 13, 2010
Second Printing, December 2010

*For Gema Alava*

The first thing one notices is that violence has been done.

GORDON MATTA-CLARK
(1943–1978)

# THE SAME RIVER TWICE

# CHAPTER 1

THE PALE RUSSIAN youth whom Odile had engaged as her driver displayed neither fear nor pity as he sent his battered panel truck hurtling through the streets of north Moscow, and he now assailed her additionally with the plot development of a movie in which he seemed to be inviting her to invest. Odile spoke no Russian and he no French, so he framed these imaginings in an imperfect English that from time to time required him to take both hands off the wheel and, for her benefit, shape the vectors of his desire in the air before them. It was a slate-gray afternoon in March that threatened snow.

Odile, having been in Moscow for three days, found herself quite ready to leave. Assuming the success of the present outing, her fifth of the day, she and her partner, Thierry Colin, would in less than three hours be boarding the train that would return them to Paris. Though she had no regrets about agreeing to this venture, all was not well at home, and only her driver's studied recklessness kept her from brooding over her troubles.

In due course, they arrived intact at an open cobblestone square off Tsvetnoy Bulvar, not far from the Circus and the old Central Market, now padlocked. Along the square's eastern periphery ran a row of dilapidated kiosks, only one of which, lit feebly within, might conceivably be open for commerce. Her driver stopped a short distance away, executed a brisk three-point turn, and backed his vehicle up to the mouth of the scorched-looking structure. The day's business had taught them that it was impolitic to leave the engine running, as prudence might otherwise dictate, and he hastened now to shut it off.

After taking a moment to collect herself, Odile got out of the truck and headed with as much aplomb as she could muster to a spot behind the kiosk where three men stood smoking in the frigid air. They didn't look particularly surprised or happy to see her.

"Good afternoon," she said in English. "I am told you are well stocked with the merchandise I require today. Perhaps we can discuss it."

The spokesman for the group, a compact, muscular youth barely out of his teens, considered her carefully. "You like drugs, sweet-pie? Hash from Afghanistan?" He smiled accommodatingly. "Or maybe you like big American refrigerator? Anything you need, gorgeous, we fix you up."

Odile had left Paris somewhat impulsively and hadn't thought to pack for the weather. She had been cold since Warsaw, her pleated plaid overcoat was self-evidently French, and the offer of refrigerators struck her as an insult of some kind. She shrugged and said nothing.

As if they had been waiting for just this signal, the other two men approached a steel storage bin appended to the kiosk. One produced a key and, cursing immoderately, set about unlocking it.

"We have also souvenirs, patriotic mementos. Maybe this is what you come for? Very good merchandise. Kick-ass."

In fact it was what she'd come for, and she was annoyed to realize that the men had known this from the start. Russia more and more impressed her as a place of thundering redundancies, and in the spirit of this recognition she had learned to state her purpose clearly.

"I'm looking for May Day flags of the Soviet years. If they are the right kind, I will buy them all from you immediately in dollars." She waited a beat while they inspected her person thoughtfully. "The money is in the truck with my driver. If I like them, he will pay you. He has a gun."

These words had an instant and enlivening effect, and shortly four grandly oversized Soviet banners, perhaps nine feet on their longer side and made of red velvet, lay spread out on the cobblestones for Odile's consideration. Fringed extravagantly with fine gold braid, they bore across their faces, along with the lately defunct hammer and sickle, a multitude of meticulously appliquéd decorations in satin, cotton, and lightweight wool. Each flag was unique, depicting the several architects and contractors of Soviet communism grouped together in attitudes of slightly pained farsightedness. Different periods were represented, and the personnel varied accordingly. One flag featured a likeness of Stalin, who, by a quirk of handicraft, gazed slyly at the viewer with an expression of robust good humor. He seemed to be sharing a joke.

"Very interesting," she said after examining the merchandise. "How do I know they're real?"

A small silence ensued as all present pondered the question.

"I will tell you," her interlocutor finally said. "Straight up, no bullshit. In all of Moscow you do not find flags like these. Handmade by Russian factory workers to be entered in May Day competition for whole Soviet Union. These are objects of . . ." He turned to the man who had unlocked the bin. "What is English word, Leonya? Cultural . . ."

"Patrimony," the man pronounced with satisfaction. "Highly illegal."

"To take them out of Russia is a crime, but we do not take them out of Russia because we are not criminals. Our business is business—this is obvious to everyone. So enough stupidities." He blew into his fists a couple of times for warmth and calculated. "I will sell you these four very fine artistical objects at the price of"—his ice-blue eyes scanning the sky for counsel—"at the exclusive price of eighteen hundred American dollars cash, no tax. Almost a gift."

Odile sniffed. As it happened, she'd been given standing instructions to pay whatever was asked, and though mildly shocked by such intemperance she had purchased twenty-six flags over the past three days, never parting with more than three thousand for any single one. Her employer had given her a fifty-thousand-dollar stake to work with, and this would be the last of it. "Okay," she said at last. "Pack them up, and we have a deal."


BACK AT THE HOTEL, Thierry Colin was pacing the parquet floors in a state of some perturbation. A girl he'd met in the bar downstairs had contrived to separate him from his wallet and what remained of his hard currency while keeping up her end of a lively conversation about Russian literature. Thierry was an assistant professor at the Sorbonne.

"It's the unreality of the place that offends me," he said. "Nothing here is what it seems. A thief's not a thief, the police aren't police."

"At least the girl was a girl, I hope," Odile said, checking her watch.

Open on the bed lay the five suitcases in which they intended to transport the flags, now piled against a wall in smoldering array. It was apparent at a glance that space would be a problem.

Thierry ran a hand vexedly through his hair. "I wonder," he mused. "Do we try to conceal them, or just stuff them in?"

"I'm sure it makes no difference." She shook out one of the flags. "Here, help me."

Odile had been put in touch with Thierry by the friend of someone she didn't really know, a social acquaintance who'd guessed or been told about her current situation. Thierry, for his part, had been brought in by a cousin who happened to play squash with the scheme's American sponsor, an appraiser for the Paris office of a celebrated auction house. Since Odile and Thierry would each be paid thirty thousand francs on delivery of the contraband flags, it seemed safe to infer that the American intended to make a good deal of money.

"What's our plan for customs?" she asked as they packed the flags.

"I told you: our employer's taken care of all the details. When we get to Brest, we just give customs our declaration forms and passports, then *merci, bon voyage*, we're on our way."

"Let's hope so. With your money gone we have almost nothing left for bribes, fines, whatever they call them. Do we even have a clue what the penalty is for what we're doing?"

"You don't want to know, Odile. What's more, it's irrelevant. Customs has been paid to take our interests to heart."

At the train station, a massive beaux arts fortress painted verdigris and cream, Odile ran ahead to claim their compartment and Thierry followed with the baggage cart. All westbound trains originated or terminated here, and as the passengers jostled past one another, conferring in the languages of Europe, Odile felt her spirits lift. She located their assigned compartment without difficulty—a two-berth cabin just far enough from the overburdened toilet—and when Thierry appeared on the platform outside, she threw the window open and took the suitcases from him. Ten minutes later he settled into the seat opposite her, and the train pulled off into an occluded sunset.

THE FROZEN RIVER, the enclosing highway, suburban housing blocks of unfaced concrete, ranks of rental garages built into the railroad embankment and guarded by dogs: they watched the landscape unspool until darkness was complete and nothing could be seen at the window except their own reflections.

"It's a catastrophe, this country," Thierry said.

Odile shrugged. There was no disputing his assessment.

The train picked up speed, its horn erupting at intervals that suggested frustrations incompletely contained. Balalaika music issued from unseen speakers, and after awhile Odile recognized it as an American pop song that had been popular when she was at lycée.

"When we first arrived," she said, "I expected something marvelous. Something you could see on people's faces, a wakefulness after all those years. It was unfair of me, but I thought they would be drunk with freedom."

Thierry was unimpressed. "Drunk, yes. But not with freedom."

"Now what seems strange is that I had any expectations at all. My ideas about this place came from nowhere, really. They weren't even ideas."

Watching her, Thierry took a cigarette from his coat pocket. "You say expectations, but that's not what you mean."

"Isn't it?" she said. And then, with sudden irritation, "I wonder why not."

From the corridor came a smell of socks, sweat, and pickled cabbage. The *provodnitsa*, an imperious, moon-faced woman in her late twenties, had locked all the windows before departure, and the air in the carriage had quickly gone stale.

"You're describing longings, not expectations," Thierry said. "And you're hardly the only one. People want to believe a new life is possible, even if not for them. They still have faith in the fresh approach, the original act, all that. Yet this is a world in which everything of consequence is already known." He frowned, turning the cigarette slowly over in his fingers as if examining it for fine print. "What to do in this painful situation?"

She pulled her sweater close about her shoulders. "I really don't want to hear this, Thierry."

"No?"

"And you can't smoke that in here." Rummaging through her bag, she produced a brush and ran it repeatedly through her auburn hair.

Thierry watched and said, after awhile, in a different voice, "Don't worry. I know you're a serious woman."

In the dining car they had to wait for a table, clinging to the safety rail as the carriage shimmied and bucked. Most of their fellow passengers had changed into loose-fitting clothes for the trip—sweatsuits, gym shoes that were more like slippers—and the mood was markedly more festive than it had been five days ago, traveling in the other direction.

They shared their table with an American student who'd come to Moscow from Beijing. The boy had changed all his yuan—five hundred dollars' worth—into rubles on entry and had just now discovered that the rubles, which couldn't be taken out of the country, could only be changed back into yuan, of which there were naturally none to be had. Rather than surrender his net worth at the border, he had decided to spend it all at the next stop with worthwhile goods for sale. Odile was worried by this boy—he would arrive in Paris without any money at all—but the thought brought with it a kind of pique. Someone else would have to take care of him.

After dinner, Thierry stayed behind to play chess with a Pole he'd befriended and Odile returned to their compartment alone. She rented sheets and blankets from the *provodnitsa,* made up both couchettes, and lay down without undressing. The music program had been changed to Tchaikovsky. Moonlight fell intermittently into the compartment. The rails chattered.

Odile hadn't considered herself committed to this trip until Thierry received their train tickets from the American, an hour before departure, and in her rush to reach the Gare du Nord a number of practical matters had gone untended. In particular, she'd failed to get a phone call through to her husband, Max, who was in New York visiting his daughter from his first marriage. After trying twice to phone him from Paris, she realized that her return ticket would get her home before Max anyway, and she set aside the idea of the call without ever quite meaning to abandon it. This lapse now unnerved her. Although it was not their habit to give daily account of themselves, Odile was troubled by her negligence, and she wondered what it might portend. At a time like this, she told herself, I can't take anything for granted.

She woke hours later to the sound of Russian voices raised in song. When she switched on her reading lamp, she saw that Thierry's berth was undisturbed, and after a moment's thought she got up and left the compartment.

Their dinner companion had succeeded in spending his rubles at the Smolensk station and now, at one end of the carriage, spilling into the corridor, a party was in progress. Open cases of vodka and Georgian champagne, jars of Caspian caviar, smoked sturgeon in folds of brown paper: the boy had resolved that if he was to arrive in Paris destitute he might as well make the most of it. Half a dozen passengers had joined him in a mood of dutiful excess.

She found Thierry sequestered between cars, a champagne bottle in one hand, a cigarette in the other. There was a glow about him, a halation that went beyond the ordinary flush of someone drinking alone on a homebound train. Fleetingly, Odile was confused. This very scene, she realized, had played out before her eyes on some other occasion, in some other place.

"Do you know," asked Thierry, "what they say here about someone who goes after things methodically, searching out the facts one by one?"

She accepted the bottle he offered and took a cautious sip. Her sense of déjà vu, if that's what it was, shimmered out.

"They say, 'He stalks the shit, but not the bear.'" Thierry nodded gravely. "The shit, but not the bear. This is incredible."

Though realizing that he was less than sober, she put a hand on his shoulder to steady herself as the train lurched violently to one side. "Come back to the compartment with me, Thierry. It's late."

"Ah, Odile." His gaze settled on hers, amusement flitting across his thin features. "Tell me, did you ever get through to your husband?"

"Yes, yes. Everything's fine." The ease with which she produced this lie troubled her, but she couldn't think about it now. "Thierry, please. Come get some sleep."

"He's jealous, of course. I expected that."

Odile rolled her eyes but said nothing. Outside, fifteen feet away on a parallel track, the Moscow-bound train roared by, its horn blaring in a Doppler slur, and for several seconds the din engulfed them.

When next he could make himself heard, Thierry said, "About customs, Odile. I've been thinking: why put us both at risk?"

She stared at him. "What happened to *merci, bon voyage,* we're on our way?"

"All that still holds. I have total faith in whatever has been set up, okay? But if there are other precautions one can take . . ."

Watching him raise the bottle to his lips, she began to doubt that it was his first. "I'm listening," she said.

"When we fill out the customs declarations, why not have one of us claim all five bags, the other just personal effects. We tell them we are traveling separately, for baggage inspection we split up. So in the event—the very unlikely event—that something goes wrong, they have only one of us to execute."

Odile flared her lips unhappily. "This is new. I don't like it."

"If you don't like it, we won't do it. But you do see the logic?"

"No," she said. "Which one of us claims the bags?"

His eyebrows raised, Thierry drew deeply on his cigarette and flipped it away. "Obviously a man is better suited to the situation, so by good sense and natural law I am selected."

She had to conceal her surprise. Five days with him had led her to the opinion that Thierry rarely strayed far from the precincts of self-interest.

Where he could, she believed, he avoided his share of hazard, and Odile now grew wary of both him and his proposal. "I don't understand," she said. "Are you going to get all the money, too, since you're taking all the risk?"

"Don't insult the hero, my dear. Duty requires concentration." He seemed to be taunting her, and laughed. The train slid into a curve that sent him staggering, but he caught himself on the handrail. "We'll split the money as before, naturally."

"Macho posturing. That's all this is."

"I told you: if you don't like it, we won't do it." Bracing himself against the door to the next carriage, he suddenly grew formal. "Now," he said, "a toast."

"No more toasts, Thierry. Come on."

"To the bear!" he proposed, lifting his bottle to her. "To the bear and not the shit!"

In the end, Odile had to enlist the help of the Russian vocalists in getting him back to the cabin, where, with a final declamatory snort, he toppled onto his couchette and passed decisively from consciousness.


THE TRAIN MADE STOPS irregularly throughout the rest of the night, sometimes at stations attached to towns but also at others set seemingly alone amid low, rolling hills. Later the terrain flattened out into floodplain laced with streams, luminous in moonlight, and later still the plain gave way to marshland.

At daybreak, wide awake in her seat by the window, Odile washed her face with bottled water, brushed her hair and pinned it up. Watching Thierry sleep made her own wakefulness painfully acute, and she examined him now with the pinpoint attention of someone given only minutes to construct a life-saving device from common kitchen utensils. In fact, her husband's first feature film contained exactly such a scene, flashes of which now fired off unbidden in her mind. Her earlier episode of déjà vu, riding between cars with Thierry, had left her unpleasantly quickened.

When the train entered the outskirts of Brest, she woke him up. He was wretched and poisoned, ill-disposed to talk. She put on lipstick and perfume. He changed his socks. Ten minutes later they rolled to a grinding stop at the Brest station, just a river's width from Poland, and they descended with their bags and all their fellow passengers into the frigid morning.

Built in the Stalinist style of the 1950s, the station was more mausoleum than depot, with a big arched entryway and a cavernous hall into which they now passed unspeaking. Here was ruin. The chandeliers that had once lit the hall today hung twisted and dark from the blistered ceiling. Plaster peeled away from the walls in sheets, doorways were boarded up. But as their eyes adjusted to the dim light, Odile and Thierry saw that the hall also held a large crowd of would-be passengers, elbowing one another and pushing forward in quiet struggle while militiamen with pistols looked on.

"Stay here with the bags," she told him. "I'll be right back." He shook his head in disgust and seated himself on the suitcases, now grouped in shadow just inside the hall.

Edging into the crowd, Odile was surprised and then dismayed by the vehemence with which these people besieged the ticket window. When she saw the object of their maneuverings—a lone gray-haired woman writing out each ticket by hand—she changed course, cutting across the throng to enter an adjacent hall, as large and dim as the first.

Here two lines of passengers waited mutely before tables on which X-ray machines sat idle for want of electricity. These were the customs officers' stations. Behind one, a uniformed man sat reading a newspaper; behind the other, his colleague stared off into space. They were waiting to be relieved, and neither gave any sign of noticing Odile as she took two declaration forms from a third table and started back.

In her absence, Thierry had willed himself to life and with unsound energy was loading the suitcases onto a flat-bed trolley. Odile had no idea what he hoped to gain by claiming them as his own at customs.

"Listen, Thierry," she said as he heaved the last of the bags into place, "it would really be much better if I were the one to take them through."

He blinked, said nothing.

"A woman attracts less suspicion, especially when the inspectors are men. And of course there's always the insultingly simple male ego to work with."

A smile flickered across his face and was gone. "We could flip a coin."

"No need. I've already made up my mind."

He seemed about to protest but instead gave her a long, appraising look that made her flush. In the end he shrugged. "If you like," he said.

They filled out their customs forms accordingly. She took the trolley, and they split up without ado. Just as she was about to plunge into the crowd, some stray instinct made her look back over her shoulder. Thierry was smiling a real smile then, a private smile marking a private victory.

She would have plenty of time to think about it.

# CHAPTER 2

ON WEDNESDAY MORNING, two days ahead of schedule, Max Colby flew into Charles de Gaulle. The visit with his daughter had not gone smoothly, and a project of his, now come unexpectedly to crisis, required his attention at home.

He took the RER into town, sharing a car near the back of the train with some Algerian youths. None of them was older than fourteen, and they were dressed international style, in baggy pants, logo warm-up jackets, and loose-laced sneakers. Glancing at Max uneasily, the oldest-looking boy produced a plastic freezer bag. One of his friends squeezed a tube of rubber cement into it. As they passed the bag around, each fitting it over his nose and mouth for a couple of breaths, the boys grew animated. Their lustrous eyes were the color of ripe olives.

From the Gare du Nord, Max took the métro under the Seine and southeast to the thirteenth arrondissement, where he and Odile lived in a small pocket of winding streets and cul-de-sacs that had inexplicably escaped urban renewal's clean sweep of the area in the 1950s and '60s. Made with materials recycled from the Paris Expo of 1900, their building was a two-and-a-half-story mews, laid out so that twelve ground-floor studios, each with an interior staircase leading to living quarters above, faced one another across a narrow cobblestone courtyard, at either end of which stood century-old chestnut and maple trees. Designed as low-income housing for artisans and artists, the mews remained a modest place, with almost half the studios retaining their original dirt floors. Max and Odile rented two lightly renovated units on opposite sides and ends of the cobblestone walk. They lived together in one of them; in the other Max maintained a film studio. Inexpensive though this arrangement was, they sometimes had trouble paying the rent.

"Odile?" he called once he let himself in. Upstairs, the bathtub faucet was running full force.

Most of the ground floor was set up as a workspace for Odile, who designed clothes for a limited but adventurous clientele. She worked alone by preference, doing all the sewing herself, and sometimes months elapsed between completed designs.

As he climbed the stairs Max called out to her again, but the pounding sound of water continued unabated. In the kitchen he poured himself a glass of vegetable juice and flipped through his mail, absurdly hoping that a note from his daughter—some conciliatory token—had managed to precede him across the Atlantic. His visit had been an ordeal for them both. Adolescence had lately descended on Allegra like a malevolent wind, stripping her of her childish clarities and swathing her instead in furious black silences that he was not invited to understand. She avoided his eyes, shrank from his touch, and found excuses to remove herself from his company. Toward the end of his stay, when he asked her to a friend's screening, she'd actually stomped her foot at him in rage. "Movies are just another kind of *lie!*" she had shrieked, shocking him thoroughly. He had always been truthful with her about the divorce. It shamed and angered him now to have imagined that the truth alone would suffice.

The water in the bathroom stopped. Max stood by the window skimming the previous day's *Le Monde* for stray items of the sort that sometimes ended up in his films—a butterfly scourge in the Dordogne, a ballerina poisoned by her dentist, illegal immigrants arriving by parcel post—but today there was nothing for him, and he tossed the paper aside.

Simultaneously the bathroom door burst open, and in strode a tall, rangy woman in her twenties, naked and oblivious, shedding water athletically in all directions as she toweled dry her tangled ink-black hair. Rachel, an American expat and frequent guest of the household, stood six feet tall in bare feet.

"Rachel, it's me," he said so as not to startle her. "Max."

"What?" She snatched her glasses from the kitchen counter and peered through them, her eyes dark blue and fathomless. "Yikes! It *is* you."

"I finished up a couple days early."

"Well, way to go, Daddyo!" She pranced over to deliver a welcoming embrace, then, recalling that she was naked, wrapped herself somewhat belatedly in the towel. "Have a good time?"

"Ah, you know. *Comme çi, comme ça.* Where's Odile?"

"Haven't seen her. I'm just here for hygiene and such." She lived with her Dutch boyfriend, Groot, on a decrepit houseboat docked nearby on the Seine. Odile had extended them bathing privileges within an hour of meeting Rachel, almost a year ago. "You get your mail?"

Deciding to defer the phone messages, he wrote a short note for Odile, nodded goodbye to Rachel, and left.

Max had long had it in mind to film Rachel. She was all limbs and unexpected angles, and she moved with a recklessness that might have been merely awkward were it not for her scale. With it, though, she was an event. He half expected her, on some sunny afternoon, to take a long, straight run and lift up into the air like a late-developing seabird. The right scenario in which to explore these kinetic rarities hadn't yet revealed itself, so his demeanor with her was frequently one of irritated speculation. Maybe she had to be her own film.

Walking the length of the courtyard, he paused midway to retrieve two cobblestones from in front of a neighboring studio and replace them in the walkway. The anarchist collective housed there, students and ex-students, sometimes used the stones to prop their front door open on warm days, and it was understood that Max would put them back. He enjoyed the exchange and looked forward with interest to the day when the stones would, in someone's moment of need, be used as projectiles. In Paris such things always came to pass, sooner or later.

He found the studio unlocked and his assistant, Jacques Bollinger, in the editing room, sitting in front of a computer screen. Hip-hop issued from a boom box at low volume. The air smelled of espresso and hot plastic.

"You'll be really glad you came back early," Jacques said, keeping his eyes on the screen while he worked the mouse. "Everybody and his dog have been asking for you."

"Let them bark. I'm still in New York."

"Ouah, ouah!" said Jacques absently. "Bow-wow. Woof."

Max paused before a bulletin board onto which his protégé had tacked some inspirational images. A sequence of black-and-white stills depicted two monocled gentlemen in turn-of-the-century dress attempting to subdue an apparently hysterical female patient. Beneath the pictures Jacques had stapled two squares of yellow poster board; on one of them, written in block letters, was the word MISÈRE, on the other MYSTÈRE. Max valued his assistant highly and prided himself on having snatched him from the jaws of commercial TV. He was ten years younger, a true child of the image age.

Dragging a red plastic chair over to the editing deck, Max straddled it, facing him. "Now, in plain, low-impact language tell me where we stand."

Jacques sighed and saved to disk. "Part of it you already know. Our backers are having a crisis of faith, okay? But with more emotion than usual. They want to see a revised script."

"Fine, we'll give them one. It's not as if we're planning to use it."

"I think they've started to realize that, Max."

"Fuck them. We'll handle it just like we did with *White Room/Black Room.*"

A short silence followed while they both reviewed the somewhat unorthodox means by which Max had kept the backers of his last film from withdrawing their support at a crucial moment. The truth had been bent quite far, and possibly the law as well, but in the end the film got made. It had been well received critically and even earned a small profit. For the most part, Max's films tended to fall into the category of *succès d'estime.*

"Hopefully it won't come to that," Jacques said soberly.

"We'll give them a revised script by next week," Max assured him. "What else?"

His assistant shrugged and blew air from his cheeks in a pantomime of disavowal. "Isabelle is very upset. She says she won't work in natural light—it's too anonymous and unpredictable. Either you let her bring in her own lighting stylist for her scenes or it's finished. She won't do the part, end of discussion."

"Think she's serious?"

"One has to assume it, yes. She's Isabelle."

Max sprang to his feet and began pacing the room. "Actors—more trouble than they're worth. Half the time you'd do better just picking out someone on the street."

"Before you pursue that thought, Max, let me remind you that without Isabelle our distribution deal is null and void. And our investors—"

"I get it, okay? Christ!" Max kicked the red plastic chair across the room. "How can I work if my principals won't trust me?"

They listened for awhile to the music: gunfire and police sirens spattered across bass and drum, voices syncopated in rhyme. It was masterfully mixed and suggested a place not unlike the real world, but much clearer.

"You could recast," Jacques said finally.

"No, I don't think so." Max wandered back to the bulletin board and gloomily looked it over. "Maybe this one just wasn't meant to be."

He spent the rest of the afternoon upstairs in the screening room, watching miscellaneous footage he'd shot at various times and places. Some of it he hadn't seen in years: a foundering sailboat that he had planned to use in a memory sequence, twelve minutes of Odile strolling through a pear orchard, two old Marseillais staging a knife fight that had somehow turned into the real thing. Even unedited, these snippets might, to the discerning eye, be recognizable as his own. Any one of them held enough visual force to provide the kernel for a full-length film, yet viewing them left him strangely restive. They no longer offered what he needed.

At dusk he closed up shop and walked back across the courtyard. Rachel had decamped, and there was no sign of Odile. He unpacked and showered. When at last he checked the answering machine, he found fourteen new messages waiting, the earliest of them delivered nearly a week ago, none of them from Odile.

After dining alone on asparagus and broiled chicken, he poured himself a Calvados and took it into the living room. He had met Odile six years ago in New York, some months after his divorce. At the time, his ambitions for the films he intended to make absorbed him completely, and, though he hadn't realized it, he was in retreat from the world. The only people he saw were those he needed in order to work—his actors, crew, producers, backers. When not with them, he looked at film. Sometimes, when he couldn't sleep, he took long walks through the half-night of Manhattan.

Late one such evening, as the downtown clubs were starting to disgorge their patrons, Max heard the quickened staccato of a woman's high heels coming up behind him in the street. A female voice, lightly accented, seemed to greet him delightedly with a name not his own. Before he could turn around to correct the error, the speaker caught up with him and slipped an arm through his. "Please," she said, "there is a man following me. I will walk with you."

Without looking back, Max took her to a nearby bar and bought her a drink. The night was warm, they sat outside. After they'd chatted for fifteen or twenty minutes, just as Max was deciding that there had been no man, no pursuer, the woman leaned forward and said, "I'm sorry about this, okay? But that man coming toward us is the one who followed me. He is a very bad person. You will have to hit him." And an altercation had in fact ensued, though the man was quite drunk and the violence mostly pro forma. Afterward, once he staggered off into the night, the woman wept a little. Max used a napkin dipped in ice water to clean up and ordered another round of drinks. When it arrived, Odile lit a cigarette and introduced herself. She was twenty-eight. So from this encounter, of which they did not speak again, Max and Odile had fallen by degrees into a relation-ship. Trust had preceded intimacy, it had preceded knowing anything at all about each other, yet neither of them wished to question that trust, prefer-ring to treat it more like an appointment than an accident. Instead they had slowly built upon it, revealing themselves bit by bit over the course of that spring and summer.

A few hurried footsteps, a rejected lover, the instinct to protect: in that first night lay the seeds of all that was to follow. Max and Odile married a year later, and a year after that they moved to Paris. He had never felt espe-cially at home in his native land, and she, from the first, had intended to return eventually to France. It seemed to him now, sitting by the window, looking out at the dark, that they had made the right decisions.

Around ten thirty he got up and poured another Calvados. After review-ing his options, he decided to call Odile's father, Sebastien, whose house in Brittany had long been her retreat of first resort. The line was busy. Max relaxed. Since Sebastien spent much of his time away on business and famously hated the phone, it was almost certainly Odile tying up the other end.

Taking his drink with him, Max retired to the bedroom and lay down without undressing. The problem, as he saw it, was this: that while he had, at forty-two, accomplished much of what he'd set out to do, had made the films he wanted to make and done so mostly on his own terms, he lately had begun looking for something more, from both himself and the world. His dissatisfaction wasn't with film, whose capacities he had never doubted, nor even with the subsidiary pursuits, demeaning and distasteful though they were, that filmmaking inevitably entailed—the endless whoring after money, the petty despotism and psychologizing, the deceptions large and small. What disquieted him, rather, was the suspicion, shading more and more toward certainty, that he had come unexpectedly to the end of something—a part of his life, a habit of thinking, he didn't know.

Five feature films in theatrical release on both sides of the Atlantic; seven shorter ones screened at festivals, universities, and museum pro-grams; videos, a handful of them aired on European TV. Considering them together, half a lifetime's work, Max felt a mix of pride, consternation, melancholy, and the beginnings of detachment.

His work to date, it seemed to him, cohered to a degree that ought to be apparent to the attentive viewer. He had tried to make light yield up a few human secrets before darkness snatched them back again, and the visible world, in his films, danced deceitfully close to sense.

But just a step beyond coherence completion lay, and he knew better than to hold on to what was finished; he'd already let it go. The intuitions he'd had about the world, intuitions he'd spent his youth putting to the test, had brought him this far and no farther. He hadn't foreseen their exhaustion, he hadn't made provisions. So now, having reached the horizon of his ambitions and longing for something more, he found himself separated from past achievements, lacking momentum and even clear direction. He was adrift in the world, floating with the tide, at the mercy of the passing breeze.

All this he would have to address. Opportunity would present itself, and he would have to be ready. Yet for the first time in a long while he was unsure of his resources, uncertain even of what resources he might be asked to draw upon. It was like starting over, and he began to feel he'd put himself at risk. He had never worried about his age before. He recognized the warning signal. And though the feeling that now flickered over him, insinuating and perverse, seemed only distantly familiar, he knew quite well what it must be.

Max lay a little longer with the feeling, then undressed and took a tranquilizer and drank a beer and waited, stretched out in the dark again, for sleep to smear his thoughts away.

# CHAPTER 3

THE AMERICAN NAMED Turner lived in an airy fourth-floor apartment in the quartier Bastille, and when Odile arrived the next morning with the suitcases she found him in the hall, very close to losing his temper. Two Corsicans, sweaty and unshaven, were maneuvering a large boulle-work cabinet through his doorway, banging it against the jamb at every opportunity and showering it with cigarette ash. Finally, when they succeeded in wrestling the intricately inlaid piece out to the elevator, Turner sighed and looked round to discover Odile and her bags.

"You are who, please?" he said in brisk French.

"The other Moscow courier. You talked before with my partner."

"Ah." He eyed the suitcases appraisingly. "Yes, of course. Come in."

His living room was high ceilinged and sunny, painted linen white and furnished sparely with objects from other times and places: the marble buttocks of a Greek *kouros,* a leather stool from Africa, a Régence chair set against a Japanese screen, a Cibachrome image of brightly colored toothbrushes tumbled together. Odile took a slow circuit of the room, leaving Turner to bring in the bags.

"Everything go all right?" he said over his shoulder.

But his tone wasn't interrogative; he didn't even seem to be addressing her, and she ignored the question. Instead she said, "The train was filthy. I'd like to use your bathroom, please."

"Down the hall and to the left," he told her.

As she went, she heard him unzip the first of the suitcases.

The trip's last leg, Warsaw to Paris via Prague, had left her wary and on edge. Although she had cleared Belorussian customs as promised, without anyone so much as mentioning baggage inspection, she afterward could find no trace at all of Thierry Colin. He had, as far as she could tell, simply disappeared. She looked for him everywhere, even venturing, as their train's departure grew imminent, to ask a security officer for directions to the station's lockup. But the man spoke only Russian, and in the end she had had no choice but to leave Thierry to his own devices.

Inspecting her image in the mirror, Odile now began to feel the strangeness of her situation. The events of the past week, which she'd half imagined casually recounting for Max over dinner, were already receding, breaking up, and she felt as if she were emerging from a fever dream to which she'd momentarily surrendered. Thierry's disappearance, whether scripted or not, continued to alarm her, but now her concern carried an element of resentment. *I can't involve myself in this,* she thought.

She removed her sweater and blouse, washed her face, neck, and arms, then dried herself with a guest towel and tossed it into the hamper. Fresh lipstick, a little perfume. She'd never had to work much on her looks. After surveying herself in the mirror, she put her blouse and sweater back on, flushed the toilet, and returned to complete her business.

"There are how many all told?" Turner asked, still in French. He had opened all the suitcases, and three or four of the banners lay spread out on the floor.

"Thirty in all. The most expensive was three thousand, and the cheapest was four hundred something, I think. You said not to bargain."

"So I did." He circled the flags, lingering over one from whose crimson field Brezhnev glowered, the famous eyebrows rendered in astrakhan. "Extraordinary. Better than I could have hoped."

She sniffed. "What will you do with them now?"

Catching her tone, he looked up and for the first time seemed fully aware of her presence.

Turner was a man of medium build, erect in carriage but also agile, his movements light and understated. He had a slightly elongated face, black hair cropped close, and large rawboned hands that were strikingly at odds with the rest of him. Odile guessed he was about fifty.

"I didn't get your name," he said.

"My name is Odile."

"Look, Odile. Do you know how these things would have ended up if somebody hadn't intervened? They'd have been cut up to patch blue jeans and line motorcycle jackets. Made into scarves and curtains and dishrags. You saw what it was like over there. We're doing these people a favor. They'll thank us for it someday, I promise you."

The passion behind these words—but she wasn't sure it was passion—caught her off guard. Before she could stop herself she said, "And in the meantime you make a pile of money."

"Well." He inclined his head tolerantly. "If this weren't a profit-making enterprise you wouldn't be here, would you?"

In another room the phone rang, the answering machine picked up, a voice spoke in French and English.

"But it is," Turner continued, walking over to his desk, "and you are." He took a set of keys from his pocket, unlocked the top drawer, and removed two brown envelopes. "What about your partner? Are you picking up for him too?"

"No," she said quickly. "He's . . ." But she hadn't prepared this speech, and now saw that she'd been waiting for Thierry's disappearance to be revealed as merely a misunderstanding on her part, a trick of perspective that Turner might instantly correct. This was not to be. "He couldn't make it this morning," she decided to say. "But he'll be in touch."

Turner nodded, tossed one of the envelopes back into the drawer, and handed her the other. Inside were sixty five-hundred-franc notes, which she flip-counted and put in her purse, giving him back the envelope.

"Happy?"

She shrugged. "Why not?"

"Good. So am I." He produced a business card and wrote a phone number on the back. "Maybe we can work together again sometime."

"No, I think that would be difficult," she replied, accepting the card without looking at it. "Impossible, more or less." But Turner smiled as if she'd given him an altogether different answer, and she said no more.

As she was leaving, she stopped to admire a display she hadn't noticed earlier. Arranged on a plain white pedestal and illuminated by pin lights were five tiny Egyptian heads, antiquities in stone. Their sparely carved faces radiated an unsettling power.

"Those," Turner said, "are my soul's delight. I could look at them forever." Seeing her hesitate, he waved her forward. "Go ahead, it's okay to touch."

She reached out and took one of the heads carefully in her hand. Carved from pink limestone, it was about the size of her two bent thumbs pressed together, weightier than it looked but easily held in one palm. Beneath a helmet of stylized hair, the oval face was distant and impassive, its full mouth and languid blank eyes touched with just the faintest trace of a smile. Odile had never before held anything so anguishingly beautiful. "Are they very old?"

"Fourth Dynasty," said Turner. "The one you're holding probably dates from around 2600 BC. That one and the one in basalt"—he pointed to a similar piece—"are real. The other three are fakes."

She replaced the head among the others. "Why do you keep them if they're fakes?"

"They're good fakes. Unique pieces in their own right." He let his gaze linger a moment longer over the objects. "Anyway," he said, looking up brightly, "I do keep them."

In the hallway, waiting for the elevator, she took Turner's card from her coat pocket and tore it up.

As trying as the last few days had been, on balance the trip had to be counted as a success. Experiences had been had, and money made. That, after all, was the point. She checked her watch, then dropped the scraps of card through the elevator shaft's wrought-iron fretwork and took the stairs five flights down to the street.


THAT AFTERNOON, Max met with his business manager, Eddie Bouvier, at a country-and-western-themed brasserie near the Place de la République. The sky had brightened, and they took a table outside.

"It's normal," Eddie was saying. "Absolutely. My own daughter, when she turned thirteen, suddenly everything was the fault of the 'patriarchy.' Sexist this, chauvinist that. It was horrible while it lasted. Worse than being in America."

"How long did she keep it up?"

"Six months, a year."

"With Allegra it's more personal. She blames me for the divorce, I think."

"And is she right?"

"In effect. I suppose so, yes."

"So why be upset? When she starts going out with boys, that's the time to worry. Then I will be sympathetic." Eddie tossed back his espresso and cast a moody eye over the pedestrian traffic. "Bastards," he added darkly.

Max had gotten to know him in the course of an all-night poker game at

Cannes the spring he and Odile had moved to Paris. At the time, a business manager was the last thing Max thought he needed—another salary to pay—but as he listened to Eddie deconstruct the financing of each of the films they'd seen at the festival that day, independent efforts all, he found himself enthralled. Eddie knew how to make the numbers dance, how to play his cards. The next day over lunch Max had retained his services and begun a friendship that had survived both disappointment and triumph, professional and personal. It was an alliance that seemed to comment on the folly of men and their plans, men like themselves.

"So," Eddie said, signaling the waiter and offering Max a cigar, "are you going to tell me what's on your mind, or should I guess? You want to know whether the divinely unobtainable Isabelle H. can be detached from the deal I risked my health to put together for you. Correct?"

"Something like that." Max spoke around the cigar as he lit it.

"Are you sure she won't do the picture? It is possible, don't you think, that she's waiting for you to put her at ease."

"Out of the question. To put her at ease I'd have to light her up like a Botticelli. I told everyone right from the start that I'm going to shoot this film in natural light. If she can't live with that, why didn't she say so then?"

"You wouldn't have listened."

"True. But she would've gotten it out of her system."

Eddie was amused. From inside the brasserie came the voice of Hank Williams, singing of whiskey and women and lonesome death. The waiter delivered two more espressos.

"Let me ask you this then, Max. Are you sure this is the film you want to make right now? Maybe you have another project in the back of your mind, something more suitable to the circumstances."

"More suitable to Isabelle, you mean?"

With an equivocating shrug, the Frenchman seemed to invite Max to speak his mind.

"I don't know, Eddie. Lately I've been rethinking things. I mean, why not get rid of some of the artifice? Shooting in natural light is a step in the right direction. But what about actors? Can anything be done about them? Who the fuck knows?"

Chewing on his cigar, Eddie stared hard at his friend and associate. "So you're in transition, creatively speaking."

"What I need you to tell me is, one, can we keep our financing without Isabelle, and, two, do I have to make the film I said I would?"

They smoked in silence while Eddie pondered. Once he'd thought it through he said, "The answer to your second question is no. These guys should understand how you work by now, but if they want to be difficult we've got a letter of intent with their signatures on it and language I can work with." He pursed his lips and expelled a puff of air. "Unfortunately, it makes no difference, because the answer to your first question is also no. No star, no financing. Maybe they would accept a substitute, someone with the same box-office draw, but I wouldn't want to bet on it. Investors are like children: they remember only what they were promised."

"You know what?" Max said after a moment. "I don't want their money. Tell them the deal's off."

Eddie looked at him evenly. "You're sure?"

"Certainly. I'll go to video before I let those morons tell me how to make films." He dropped his cigar to the pavement and ground it out with his heel.

"Your decision," Eddie said, picking up the check.

"I need to reassess, take a fresh look at things. Maybe I will shoot some video."

"Do what you need to, Max. Just don't fall off the map. *White Room/Black Room* gave us a touch of box-office credibility, and people want to know what you're doing next. Your name's in the air. It would be a pity to let that go to waste."

"Thanks, Eddie. Point taken."

They stood, shook hands, and as they parted company Max felt his head grow clear. It was like a reward. And he wondered, as he walked, if there would be more of that to come.

NORTH BY NORTHWEST was playing on the television, with the soundtrack turned up very loud. Books, videotapes, and DVDs had been pulled from their shelves, furniture upended, drawers and their contents strewn across the floor. One wall was badly stained where a bottle of burgundy had been hurled against it, and the room stank of scotch and cigarette smoke.

Odile put her groceries on the kitchen table. Scanning the damage, she felt sick to her stomach.

"Cocktail before dinner?" asked the dining-car steward.

"Yes, please," Cary Grant said, as the train rounded a bend. "A Gibson."

She switched off the TV. In the next room Max's voice was saying, "No, I finally got through . . . Right . . . Well, you know Bastien, the usual *connerie:* 'I'm her father, not her concierge.' Meaning he hasn't heard from her either."

Standing in the doorway, Odile watched Max approach the window, the phone pressed to his ear, his body in profile. The light changed around him—it became a glow, a luminous haze, and she realized she'd been through all of this before, the same scene in every particular. Max turned around, just as he had the other time, his eyes widening at the sight of her, just as she remembered them doing.

"Wait, Rachel, she just walked in. I'll call you later, okay? . . . Thanks, you too. *Ciao.*"

A beep as he turned off the phone.

"You're here!" He stared at Odile. "Thank God! What happened? Are you all right?"

Odile stepped forward uncertainly. "Yes, yes, I'm . . . I'm fine." She'd unbuttoned her plaid overcoat without taking it off. "You're home early."

He came forward and, slipping his hands inside her coat, pressed her to him. "Christ, Odile! Where have you been? I was starting to get seriously worried."

"I'm sorry. There was a courier job, one just too good to turn down. I thought I'd be back before you even—" He kissed her on the neck, and for an instant she felt the sting of tears rise in her throat. This was her husband. This was her home. This was her life.

"And then when I saw this," Max said, releasing her and waving his hand vaguely around the room: a cherrywood dresser with its drawers yanked out, a shattered mirror, clothes scattered in heaps. "I thought, well, you can imagine."

She was shaking her head.

"Whoever did it must have been watching the house," he went on, forcing himself to calm down. "I was only gone for a couple of hours."

Drifting across the room, Odile picked her jewelry box off the floor, the earrings, bracelets, and rings all untouched. "What did they take?"

He grimaced, waving the question off.

She stared with growing unhappiness at the chaos visited upon them. "Very nice. We'll call the police, no?"

Max sighed. "The police are likely to be more trouble than they're worth. Let's see what's missing first." Then, looking her over once more, he seemed freshly troubled. "Where did you say you were?"

"Just picking up some packages and delivering them." She grimaced. "How did it go with Allegra?"

"Not too well. I'll tell you about it."

Odile's sense of déjà vu dissipated, things shed their luminosity, her dismay mounted. "And now?" she said, leaving him to decide what she meant.

"Now we put everything back," he replied.

So, working methodically, Max in the living room, Odile in the bedroom, they began setting the place to rights. And while the actual damage proved to be less than they'd feared—the china was intact, the upholstery unharmed, only the one wall defaced—they felt reduced by the violation, which charged the air still, and they didn't speak as they straightened up.

One of the intruders had left a large black turd in the toilet bowl, and Odile gagged as she flushed it away. There were other leavings: cigarette butts, candy wrappers, a scorched spoon that Max discarded. He righted the furniture, she hung their clothes back up, order was restored. Yet once they had sorted through everything and taken a mental inventory, separately and together, of the apartment's contents—even, in their distraction, starting to count the silverware—neither of them could find anything missing. There had been no burglary.

"Vandalism?" said Max. "Hard to believe anyone would go to the trouble."

"But what else could it be?" Odile said.

"Maybe someone's trying to send us a message."

Odile recognized his dry, half-sarcastic tone of voice. Puzzled, she dismissed it. "We'll both feel better when we've eaten," she said, moving to unpack the groceries.

As Max and Odile made dinner together, each maneuvering around the other by habit and cooking by rote, the rhythms of domesticity gradually reasserted themselves. On the radio: the music of Bebel Gilberto. Max poured Odile a glass of wine, another for himself. By the time they sat down to eat, they'd finished the bottle.

She listened sympathetically as Max told her about his difficulties with Allegra. The girl had a stubborn streak and, in Odile's estimation, had suffered more over the divorce than Max allowed himself to know. Making friends with her had required diligence and stamina. Still, she had managed it, and Odile now suggested to Max that they arrange with Diana, Allegra's mother, for the girl to spend the summer with them in Paris. He frowned, he said he would think it over, but Odile could see that he was pleased. And so, bit by bit, the oppressive mood brought on by the break-in began to lift.

"Tell me about your courier job," said Max, spearing the last piece of pear with his fork. "Go anyplace interesting?"

"I went to Moscow."

"Moscow! Really? What for?"

"The job was to pick up some flags—big folk-art things from the Soviet years. Some Americans are going to sell them at auction, I think." She paused, reaching out to straighten a candle before it dripped. "Moscow, though—it's extraordinary. Unreal, I want to say. Everything for sale. Ordinary people seemed to lack basic things, but the mafia cowboys, it was almost comical, you know? If one paid with hard currency, anything was possible. Armored . . . how do you call them? Like tanks, but not so many guns?"

"Personnel carriers?"

"Yes. A man was selling them. I saw one in traffic, like a car." Odile had encountered the APC early on the first day, before she had registered the full extent of the disorder surrounding her, and she had been shocked. Now all that seemed far away.

Max wiped his mouth and put his napkin on the table. "Poor Russia," he said.

"It wasn't what I expected," she agreed.

"How long were you there?"

"Not long. Just long enough to pick up the flags."

Max nodded. "Coffee?"

"No, thanks."

He traced her jawline gently with his fingertips. "You're tired, Odile. Go have a bath. I'll finish up in here."

"What about the police?"

He seemed to consider. "I don't know. What do you think?"

Odile looked the apartment over skeptically, then let her glance be drawn to his. "As you said," she replied. "Just another kind of trouble."

In her bath, amid clouds of steam, Odile closed her eyes and systematically willed herself to relax. She heard the phone ring. Max answered. She did not listen to his words.

Some months ago, at her father's house in Brittany, she was alone one evening—Bastien away on business, Max en route from Paris—when an unusually violent thunderstorm knocked out all electric power in the region. Odile tried the phone, but the lines were down. For a time, lightning flashes provided jagged instants of illumination, but the storm passed on and soon she was sitting in a darkness so complete that her only reference point was the chair beneath her. She seemed to remember that her father kept candles and a flashlight on a shelf in the cellar. Once she worked out the route in her mind, she stood, took a few steps, stumbled, and was immediately disoriented. Feeling for a wall, she traced the room's perimeter to a connecting corridor, continued through the dining room to the kitchen, and stopped at the cellar door, her hand on the latch. The rain, while it lasted, had been torrential, and it dimly came back to her that the cellar was prone to flooding. Abruptly she was seized by a neck-prickling animal fear for which she could find no cause, fear that had a life of its own, fear of darkness, certainly, but also of something pre-human to which darkness only alluded. For perhaps three minutes she stood there frozen, unable or unwilling to lift the latch. "This must be what it's like to be blind," she said aloud. Then she opened the door. A series of sickening thumps sounded on the wooden stairs, followed by a small skittering. She cried out softly, immobilized before a wall of blackness within blackness, but heard nothing more. When her heart ceased pounding, some time later, she forced herself down the stairs, and, wading through ankle-deep water, located both flashlight and candles. She fumbled the flashlight on. A heavy plastic bucket floated near the foot of the stairs, surrounded by hundreds of polystyrene packing pellets, clearly its contents until a moment ago. But if this accounted for what she'd heard, what had knocked the bucket down the steps? She hadn't touched anything, and the cellar door opened outward, into the kitchen. She hurried back up the staircase, eager to leave her speculations behind.

Now, nodding down into her drowsiness, Odile jerked awake. She was still herself. The bathwater had gone cold. She pulled the plug and got out.

*What's done is done,* she thought. But at once she doubted the truth of this ancient tautology and saw any number of reasons why what's done would be done over and over. Very possibly—or so it seemed to her for a second—nothing happened at all until it happened again. She toweled herself dry, put on her dressing gown, and let these strange thoughts pass from her mind.

She was asleep when Max came to bed but woke at his touch. Turning to him, she pressed her forehead to his and, in the bedside lamplight, let herself be held. "I missed you," she told him.

"I missed you too," he murmured. "I always miss you."

She wriggled closer to him. "No regrets? You know you could pick up your New York life in a minute, if you wanted to. Even now."

"But I don't want to. I want to be here with you. You know that."

After a small silence she said, "Tonight scared me. What do you think they were after?"

"Ah, it was probably just some punks with nothing to do, no place to do it. I wouldn't worry." He slipped one strap of her negligee off her shoulder.

"So it's over now?"

"Definitely. What possible reason would they have to come back?" He ran a hand down her side, over her hip and back again. She shivered. They kissed. When he reached out to turn off the bedside lamp, she intercepted him.

"Leave it," she said.

Sitting up, she pulled the nightgown off over her head. With this unveiling her breasts became the forwardmost part of her body, the nipples stalks from which all that was about to happen would bloom. She tilted her head back and shook her hair out to confirm this sensation. Once again it was true. When she opened her eyes, they met Max's, blue and unblinking. "Does Madame still please Monsieur?" she asked.

"Very much. More all the time."

Her lips swelled, she saw him see them swell, and all at once Odile and Max were avid for each other, giddy with appetite. "I want everything," she said as he pulled her to him. "All of it."

He drew the inside edge of his hand, wrist to thumb to forefinger, up between her legs. She moved sideways to be beneath him and a moment later guided him in.

"We both do," he said into her ear.

And it was as if they were home free.

# CHAPTER 4

THE AUCTION HOUSE where Turner worked had its physical premises in a restored Second Empire building just off the Champs-Élysées, and he was allotted a small, rather cluttered office on the third floor, overlooking the courtyard. Standing there now with the phone pressed to his ear, he switched on the lightbox he kept in one corner. A red glow suffused the air.

"Believe me, Ron. Schedules are not the issue. As soon as you see these you'll *make* room. Plus, I can guarantee the show will sell out. I've got buyers lined up for you, and, as I said, I'm discounting my usual fee." He had a Manhattan art dealer by the name of Ronald Balakian on the line. In the two years since Balakian had opened his gallery on West 24th Street, it had become the exhibition venue of choice for rising young art stars, and the man himself a minor celebrity.

"How many would I show?" Balakian asked, affecting puzzlement and indecision. "I mean, I don't even know what size these things are."

"The size is jumbo. Heroic-statement size. And I've picked out seven I think you'll like." Turner contemplated the color transparencies he'd laid out on the lightbox. It was helpful, he thought, that the flags photographed so well.

"Seven big red flags that I'd like," mused Balakian. "Not totally impossible, I guess. And, let's see, you're doing me this favor because . . ."

"Because I want them positioned as artworks, not historical curiosities.

For this, Ron, your gallery is perfect—a true no-context space. It's the only setting that will let people see what's really there."

Appearing just then in the doorway, Turner's assistant regarded him neutrally, her arms folded across her chest. Disapproval barely contained was Gabriella's natural expression, but she was fiercely loyal and Turner often relied on her judgment. He waved languidly at her. She frowned—message received—and disappeared.

"I'd have to look them over," Balakian was saying. "The real thing, of course—not photo repros."

"Say no more," Turner told him cheerfully. "In your hands by this time tomorrow."

"I'll be waiting. Oh, and Turner?"

"Yes?"

"Let's keep the paperwork on this one to a minimum. In case people get the wrong idea."

Turner spent the next hour on the phone, making the necessary arrangements. The buyers he had in mind were all first-time clients, unaware of their role in developing the objects' worth, and in such cases Turner had learned that a modicum of personal attention at the outset made the whole process exponentially easier. After speaking with each of them, he communed briefly with his calculator, had the seven flags insured at thirty thousand dollars each, and turned them over to Gabriella to pack up and ship to New York.

He left the auction house at three o'clock, walking east on Saint-Honoré. Businessmen, shoppers, and tourists filtered onto the sidewalks for lunch. Small winds gusted.

In the five days since Odile had appeared at his door, Turner had again and again found himself replaying her visit in his mind. Her ironic manner, the casual arrogance with which she'd moved around his apartment, even the care with which she cradled the Egyptian head in her palm—all this had inexplicably put him on the alert, so that well before she left he thought, *She's not to be trusted, this girl.* And, a moment later: *She's all but telling me so herself.*

Though he concealed his misgivings, waiting for her to reveal more, she evaded his probes and refused his invitations. Now he wondered if he'd overreacted. Sending in the Corsican brothers to search her apartment—he knew how much these thugs and clowns enjoyed their errands—had then seemed the logical thing to do. Had she kept one or two flags for herself, it would have compromised his ability to price the rest. Inventory control was everything in this business. Yet when the Corsicans told him that he'd been mistaken, that she'd withheld nothing, Turner felt no relief, quite the contrary; it was like a further betrayal, and he was forced to question his insight.

Turning now down rue de Castiglione, he walked the length of the chilly sidewalk arcade, crossed Rivoli, and entered the open ground of the Tuileries. The April light held color and new warmth. He passed a couple changing their infant's diapers on a stone bench. A boy with a remote was sailing a white model boat across one of the reflecting pools.

It was strange, he thought, that such a woman should have involved herself in the Moscow venture. Usually his couriers were students, proofreaders, interim dropouts—people still buffered by youth and inexperience who took the jobs as much for the small adventure as for the money. But Odile was a candidate of a different order. She'd seen something of life and didn't trouble to hide it. She handled herself with aplomb and understood the value of the unspoken. At the very least, it seemed to Turner, you had to wonder where she had learned it all.

And there was this that was also strange: as Odile increasingly occupied his thoughts, Turner developed the impression, faint at first but already difficult to dismiss, that they'd met before—somewhere else, in another context, he couldn't say how. When he tried actively to place her, to recall the specifics of a previous encounter, this feeling of familiarity evaporated and he would turn his mind to other things. Then, like water returning to its customary level, the feeling would seep back into place, growing gradually to a conviction, until he was once again driven to ransack his memory in search of a time and locale, and once again it would seem obvious to him that no prior meeting could possibly have occurred.

He crossed the Seine at the Pont des Arts. As he looked out over the water, cocoa brown and swollen with spring runoff, a Dutch barge piloted by a housewife in slippers eased out from under the bridge.

On the Left Bank he stepped up his pace, continuing east to the Latin Quarter. Here the narrow, mazy streets were clogged with students as well as tourists, and Turner was repeatedly obliged to sidestep both as he hurried along, navigating by blind habit until, on a backstreet that was more like an alley, he stopped before an inconspicuous pair of wooden doors painted green. Punching in the entry code, he let himself into the building's courtyard, a shady, quiet place crisscrossed by laundry lines and presided over by a single stunted lime tree.

He unlocked the semiprivate entrance at the courtyard's far end, then climbed three flights of stairs to the top apartment. The door had been left ajar. He went in without knocking.

"Céleste!" he called. And, a moment later: "It's me."

Receiving no answer, he proceeded into the long rectangular front room, sunny and underfurnished, that offered an unimpeded view of rooftop Paris. Placed informally here and there, as if they might be rearranged at any time, were a pair of halogen floor lamps, a cordless telephone, some filing cabinets, three easy chairs losing their stuffing, a mahogany coffee table, a distressed armoire, and, at dead center, facing the windows at an angle, an antique sofa upholstered in maroon satin. Turner stood beside it and took in the view—terra-cotta tile roofs and chimney pots, TV aerials and balconies—and then, after glancing at his watch, began to undress.

"You're late, my dear," the woman he had come to see called in French from the back of the apartment. "I hope you're not planning to make yourself interesting today."

He stretched out naked on the sofa and sighed. Sunlight poured over him. "Anything you want," he called back, and she replied with something not quite intelligible from where he lay.

Already the sunlight was making him drowsy. Turner closed his eyes and let his thoughts drop down a level. He saw himself on a boat, a white boat cruising fog-shrouded waters. There were other people on board, and, in the distance, sirens. Because this daydream—if that's what it was—belonged to him, he knew he could alter it at will, so he now added a little music, settling on a small Biber sonata. Then he decided to take the fog away, but he must not have been concentrating because instead it just grew thicker—a dazzling, pearlescent white that matched the boat and enveloped everything—and he no longer could tell up from down or locate himself in space at all. He felt that an event long anticipated by everyone was finally about to unfold, and he was grateful in a distant, almost paternal way to be part of it. So this was what it was going to be like! A woman whispered something definitive in his ear. He realized it was Odile but couldn't understand what she was telling him. Then there was a plunging splash, and the incandescent whiteness went dark. The music stopped. He opened his eyes.

Céleste kissed him on the cheek. "Goat, bastard, pirate. Have you at least cleared your schedule for me this time? I want what's left of the afternoon, all of it." Fleetingly the whiteness of her still-abundant hair reminded him of the boat and the fog. A wave of regret passed over him as he relinquished the daydream and in the next instant forgot about it completely. "I told you, Céleste. Whatever you want." He stifled a yawn. "And please don't call me pirate."

A petite woman in her mid-seventies, she had startlingly large, cornflower-blue eyes whose effect was compounded by the frankness of her gaze. Inspecting Turner's naked body, she furrowed her brow. "But what is this? You've gained at least one kilo since last week."

"A kilo?" he said. "Impossible. I don't gain weight."

She shook her head in reproof. "No, you absolutely cannot get fat until I'm done with you. Promise this to me."

"You're worse than a wife," he said, capitulating.

Céleste trailed a hand across his bare chest, then went over to a corner where an art deco screen created a small, private space within the larger one. She disappeared behind the screen and emerged a few moments later with a wooden easel, a medium-sized canvas on stretchers, and a pushcart loaded with paints and brushes. While she set up in front of him, Turner rearranged himself on the sofa so he was seated mostly upright, legs extended, head tilted to rest on the knuckles of one hand. This was the pose she'd coaxed from him at his first sitting, three weeks ago. Céleste mixed her paints, studied him, and began to work.

For some time she painted in silence, her eyes darting from Turner to the canvas and back again. Twice before she had done his portrait. He'd been the cocky American in the first one, arms folded across his chest and expectation in his eyes. The other showed him two years later, in personal disarray. Both paintings, as it turned out, had captured him at the end of one phase of his life, on the threshold of another, and neither had been kind. Turner hadn't expected them to be.

Pausing to change brushes, Céleste stared at him.

The completeness of her attention, pitiless and cleansing, laid bare Turner's vanities and unleashed in him a sudden longing to be known. He was certain that such a thing was possible. He seemed to remember a time when it had been routine.

"What is it?" said Céleste, seeing the look on his face.

He let his gaze drift past her to the window. Three buildings away a woman stood on her balcony shaking out a rug. Dust exploded into the air.

"I think," he said, "I've found someone you should meet."

THE WEATHER WAS UNSEASONABLY MILD—the warmest spring in thirty years, the newspapers said—and on Saturday afternoon Odile, Max, and

Rachel installed themselves topside on the *Nachtvlinder*, basking in the sunlight. The houseboat was tied up just downstream from the Pont de Sully, in the center of Paris. Diesel fumes, mildew, and sewage scented the air. Below, Groot hammered at the vessel's engine mounts and swore intermittently in Dutch.

"Does he really think he can rebuild those engines?" Odile asked.

"Oh, he can for sure." Rachel pushed her glasses back up her nose and sipped her beer. "But there's more to it than that. He has, like, a vision."

Her six-foot frame was hypnotizingly out of scale with the boat. Max zoomed in slowly. "Vision?" he repeated.

"That's my word, not his. He's going to clean her up totally, stem to stern. And when he's done—when *we're* done, I mean—she'll be running under her own power for the first time in, like, fifty years." She grinned and gave the camera an enthusiastic thumbs-up.

"That's great, Rachel." He checked the time code. "Could you tell us a little about the boat?"

"Sure. The *Nachtvlinder* started out life as an admiral's gig at the turn of the last century. She's made of Burmese teak and British hardware, measures fifty-four feet long, thirteen wide, and she displaces an even thirty tons. After World War II somebody turned her into a motor yacht, with two diesel engines of the kind you used to find in London taxis. Those are the babies Groot's going to rebuild this spring. Getting parts will probably be the main problem."

Running behind Rachel's head was a long window box of brilliant red geraniums that now came into focus. Max panned slowly along these flowers until Odile's head entered the frame and the shot included both women, Odile squinting into the sun.

"What happened to the boat after that?" asked Max. The vidcam, a beta-built HD digital, was on loan from a Japanese company that Jacques had been badgering for days. Something had been said about product endorsement, but Max had no intention of providing any such thing.

"Basically she was worked to death," Rachel explained, "then left to rot. When Groot found her in Utrecht, she was sunk up to her wheelhouse in sludge and looked much worse than she does now. He raised her and patched her up, then had her towed here by barge. We've been working on her and living on board ever since." She appeared thoughtful. "Two years now."

"So thanks to you, the *Nachtvlinder* will have a whole new life," Max suggested.

"Um. We don't think of it like that, not really." Rachel gathered her lustrous black hair in her hands, gave it a twist, and held it up off her neck. "She has her history. All we're doing is giving her a little rehab. Right, Odile?"

Max kept both women in the viewfinder as they looked at each other.

"Yes and no," Odile answered after a moment. "It's a question, I suppose, of how much of a thing can be replaced before it becomes another thing altogether."

Rachel cocked her head. "You're kidding, right?"

Reaching out across the frame, Odile squeezed her friend's hand. Then, looking straight into the camera, she said, "Enough for today, Max. It's the weekend."

He lowered the vidcam. Rachel excused herself and, ducking into a low oaken doorway, went below to help Groot.

"Are you really going to use that footage?" Odile said when they were alone.

"No, that was just for posterity." He sat down beside her in the deck chair Rachel had vacated. "Anyway, according to Eddie, I'm in creative transition."

"But that's good, isn't it?"

"Neither good nor bad. Real, though." He put the camera down in the small shade cast by his chair. "I'm looking for something, so it goes without saying I'll find something else. I accept this now, even embrace it. Do you think I'm old?"

"Don't be morbid, Max," she told him. "You have no gift for it."

The two of them looked out over the Seine in companionable silence. Weekend pleasure craft—sailboats, ski boats, outboards, rowboats—plied the river in both directions, and the *bateau mouche* heading upstream now sent these lesser vessels scrambling. From its loudspeakers came a steady blast of tour commentary, and in its wake bobbed assorted flotsam—a shoe, a soccer ball, a hat, a bloated pig carcass.

"Oh, I've been meaning to ask you," Max said. "I saw from this month's bill that you paid off the back rent. Was that the fruit of your Moscow trip?"

She extended her lips in a pout of feigned boredom.

"Odile." Reaching out, he took her chin in his hand and turned her toward him. "My love. There's nothing to worry about. Raising money's a sport I play. I'll sell the Giacometti drawing."

"Why?"

"So that you don't have to—"

Brushing his hand aside, she put her own impatiently over his mouth. "Enough. When the time comes, you'll do what must be done. I require it, and you won't fail me." His breath in her palm was warm, and she held it for another beat before releasing him. His eyes shone. "I see that we understand each other," she said. "Good."

Around four o'clock, Rachel called for Max. Groot needed his help in cutting away the old oil storage tanks. Odile remained topside. Across the river a patrol boat of *la brigade fluviale* was ticketing a small outboard that had been sprinting up and down through traffic, leaving the other boats tossing in its wake. As Odile watched, a Welsh terrier jumped from the outboard into the police boat and viciously attacked the warrant officer's trouser cuff.

Since returning from Moscow, she had been visited repeatedly by an old notion, an idea about herself dating from adolescence. It had then been her private conviction that, under circumstances only marginally different from those in which she found herself, she would renounce the world and its ten thousand excruciations, she would retreat into solitude and live her life as an ascetic. Yet religion had held no interest for her then or now, she didn't even consider self-denial a virtue. She had only noted, with youth's cruel eye, that she possessed the capacity for it. It was a choice among many, and meant that another life was possible for her. But now she wondered whether she hadn't overestimated her own freedom to make such decisions. Perhaps it was just an illusion.

Below, Groot started his saw, and the shriek of metal cutting metal set the deck vibrating. A smell of burn wafted up. The air had grown chilly. She stood and gathered her things.

After calling down the companionway to tell the others she was leaving, Odile descended the *Nachtvlinder*'s gangplank to the packed-sand quai where the boat was docked. Stone steps led back up to the street. She decided to walk home.

Leather jackets in burgundy and black, pleated silk trousers, crocodile shoes and cowboy boots: Odile identified the two men waiting on the sidewalk as Russian even before she realized they were waiting for her. The burlier one, his head shaved and the rim of one ear studded with tiny gold rings, regarded her with an alertness that struck Odile as professional.

The other man was tall and finely featured, with a wolfish smile. "You are Odile Mével," he said to her in French. "True?"

She made a lunge, trying to get around them, but the burly one easily caught her.

"A most economical answer," said the taller man. "Unfortunately, certain events, developments, et cetera make it necessary we talk with you in private." He flashed a police badge at her. "Now is convenient?"

She inhaled deeply, but before she could call for help the other man clapped a thick hand across her mouth.

"Good. We talk in my car. Is more discreet."

Parked behind them, two wheels up on the curb, was a black sedan of Bavarian make. The burly man wrestled Odile into the backseat, and his employer, as she now judged him to be, slid in beside her. The door slammed shut, and the other man got behind the wheel, started up the car, and pulled out into traffic. At close quarters he smelled very bad.

"Okay, this is the deal," said the tall man. "You have involved yourself in transborder activities of highly criminal nature. The details are known. My office takes an interest. Maybe I find extenuating circumstances, maybe not. This is up to you."

Odile grabbed at the door handle on her side. It was locked. "Why do you pretend to be police?" she demanded. "Show me your badge again."

The man examined her closely for a moment, then laughed. "Police, fireman, garbage inspector—who gives a shit? Actually, I am in import-export business like you."

Odile sat facing forward, her arms folded across her chest.

"Understand: my interest in Soviet memorabilia is extremely limited—nonexistent, I would say. But in Russia to export such things is serious crime—life sentence recommended. You may find it more desirable to talk to me than Interpol, but I leave this decision also to you."

He produced a pack of cigarettes and lit one, holding it between his thumb and forefinger. After a couple of long, thoughtful drags, he turned to her. "My question is this: where and when, please, did you last see the man called Thierry Colin?"

Odile stared at him in surprise.

"Colin," he repeated, "Thierry. The man with whom you went to Moscow. Where is he, please?"

She left a little silence. "I don't know anyone by that name."

At these words her interlocutor grew mournful in aspect, nodding minutely to himself. Once again, he seemed to say, his small hopes had been defeated by the forces of fecklessness and obstinacy, everywhere abundant. "Why do you make trouble for yourself, *dushka*? This man is a dog. Don't get involved in his stupidities."

But already Odile's anxiety, her anger and resentment, had begun to shift in character, so that from being on the defensive, detained against her will to fend off questions and threats, she now became detached. "I told you," she said, "I've never heard of the person you're looking for. What else do you want from me?"

The man slapped the seat with the flat of his hand and cursed in Russian. He ordered his driver to pull over, and the locks popped open. "Consider carefully," he told Odile. "You are creating bad atmosphere. Our next meeting may not be so pleasant."

She got out, the car sped off.

Waiting at the taxi stand in the Place de la Bastille, watching the traffic swirl around the monument, Odile tried to recall when she had started lying for Thierry Colin, or about him, and why. None of the obvious answers satisfied her.

"A thief's not a thief," he had told her in Moscow. "The police aren't police."

In the taxi she allowed her thoughts to grow abstract. Bits of music passed through her mind, just phrases at first, but gradually filling out and cohering until she recognized the work, a small Biber sonata she hadn't heard in years.

## CHAPTER 5

MAX AND JACQUES SAT in the studio one rainy morning watching some footage of Rachel that Max had shot over the past few days. On the screen, Dorothy struck the Cowardly Lion on the nose and rebuked him for chasing Toto.

"An homage," said Jacques. "Who would have guessed?"

Max ignored him as the camera pulled back to reveal that the Oz sequence was playing on TV, and that a little girl of about five was seated on the floor watching raptly. The reverse zoom continued until it took in the nearby kitchenette, where Rachel was preparing dinner and talking nonstop, apparently to the child.

"She makes most of her money babysitting," Max explained, "so I asked if I could come along the other night. The little girl doesn't know a word of English, and Rachel's French is, shall we say, modest."

Here the soundtrack brought Rachel's monologue to the acoustic foreground. She was talking about her childhood in California.

"So whenever my parents got, like, really confused? We'd all pack up and go to Disneyland. It was their holy city, you know? People make pilgrimages to Jerusalem, Mecca, Oz, whatever, but my folks would go to Disneyland. I still don't know why. One thing, though: it definitely wasn't for me, it was for them. Whenever they needed spiritual guidance or reaffirmation or just some kind of emotional boost, boom, Disneyland here we come. This happened so many times, and I was so young, that I thought Disneyland was a real place, a city with extra-good zoning laws or something. Seriously impaired, right?"

As she spoke, the camera showed Rachel moving around the kitchenette, chopping vegetables, tending the stove, throwing a hand into the air for emphasis. The length of her limbs gave her movements an elastic, oddly centripetal grace that compelled the eye and engaged the mind. It was as if her physical presence in the frame reduced everything else to subtext.

Jacques was impressed. "I've never seen her like that before. Is she acting?"

"Hard to say," Max admitted. "But I don't think so. Watch this."

Again the camera showed the TV screen in frame-filling close-up. The Scarecrow, the Tin Man, and the Cowardly Lion were hiding outside the Wicked Witch's castle, mustering their courage to rescue Dorothy, when a column of the Witch's green-skinned sentinels, looking like Cossacks and singing their terrible dirge, marched into the scene. Here Max's camera reversed angles to show the little girl reacting to these events: her jaw dropped, her face turned crimson, she covered her ears, staggered to her feet, and, gasping for breath, emitted a prolonged wail of fear and outrage.

Immediately Rachel scooped the child up in her arms, seizing the remote control from the floor to mute the sound. Max's camera zoomed in until his subjects' faces filled the screen. Light from the TV played over them kaleidoscopically, bouncing off the white wall behind, ringing Rachel and her sobbing charge in an unearthly phosphorescence. Rachel pressed her cheek against the top of the little girl's head, and here Max froze the frame. After a short silence he said, "I could look at that for five seconds. Maybe more."

Jacques nodded. "It's good, Max. Verging on the numinous. How did you do it?"

"I don't know." He began to pace. "Maybe it's her. Somehow she affects the look of things around her. I can't put my finger on it."

Since withdrawing from the Isabelle project, Max had videotaped Rachel on five occasions—informal, spontaneous shoots whose only common element was the woman herself: cleaning the *Nachtvlinder*'s bilge pumps, dancing solo in a nightclub in Oberkampf, being fitted by Odile for a birthday dress. And although Max had no plans for this footage and no investment in it, professional or otherwise, he was growing mildly possessive of her, as if she really were his project.

That afternoon, at a small Left Bank theater where *Der blaue Engel* had premiered almost seventy years ago, Max attended a screening of his own first feature film, a tragicomic drama called *Fireflies*. It was being shown as part of a festival—a dozen debut films by independents who'd since made their names—and although Max disliked speaking in public about his work, he'd agreed to introduce the film and to take questions afterward. Sixteen years had passed since its release. He allowed himself to believe that there was something to be learned by revisiting it now, when he'd exhausted the vision that had made it possible.

Despite the rain, Max found the theater almost full when he arrived—the crowd a mix of film students, intellectuals, and others who he supposed just happened to be free at four o'clock in the afternoon. He'd sent Jacques ahead with the actual film cans, and when he spotted his assistant, waving to him from the balcony, he relaxed somewhat. Before him stood a short, bearded man in spectacles who had been addressing him continuously since his arrival.

". . . less a film than a conflagration of images," the man was saying. "What is seen is consumed, what is consumed is seen. In this way, one makes possible the new. A brilliant attack."

"Thank you," said Max. He stifled a sudden impulse to harm this man, who seemed to be the program director, and leave the theater, taking his film with him. Instead he said, "Let's keep it informal today. No need to introduce. Just let me know when, I'll say a few words, and we'll roll the film. Okay?"

"As you like," the man said. He looked unhappily at the speech he had prepared, then folded the pages lengthwise and put them in his jacket pocket. "You will take questions afterward? The audience—"

"Yes. I'll take questions."

"Thank you." He nodded his head in relief. "Please begin whenever you're ready."

A podium and microphone had been set up at the front of the theater, and as Max took up position behind them the audience fell silent. He hadn't prepared any remarks, thinking instead to take his inspiration from the moment. Apparently he would have to do without inspiration.

*"Mesdames, messieurs,"* he began, leaning over the microphone. *"Bonjour. Je vous remercie d'avoir bravé la pluie pour venir voir ce film, mon premier."*

A woman in the front row stood up, aiming a camera at him. The flash went off and she sat down again.

"When I made this film," Max continued, "I was twenty-six years old, working on a budget of nothing, more or less. We shot it in New York in thirteen days, averaging thirty-two setups—complete changes of camera and lighting—per day. The conditions were not ideal, but I can tell you that I have never again worked as freely and easily as I did making *Fireflies.* Maybe that's what first films are for."

Pausing to drink from the glass of water that had been set out for him, he recalled that at the time of *Fireflies*'s release he was still married to Diana, Allegra had yet to be conceived, and he spoke no French at all. His real life, in any sense that mattered, had barely begun.

"Well," he said, "it's easy to sentimentalize one's youth. So let me not waste more of your time. We'll see the film, and afterward, if you have questions, I'll try to answer them."

An usher with a flashlight hurried two last ticket holders to their seats. The lights went down.

*Movies,* Max thought, *are just another kind of lie.*


RAIN FELL IN SHEETS against the facades of buildings and rebounded off the pavement in bull's-eye splashes. Odile shook out her umbrella. She'd spent the morning inspecting the clothing boutiques of the first and second arrondissements to see what was selling and to catch up with the trade. Now she stood just outside the glass vestibule of a music-and-electronics emporium on the Champs-Élysées, waiting for the rain to let up. She stared into the downpour, half mesmerized by its fall and force.

Her run-in with the Russians had prompted her to make her own inquiries about Thierry. At the Sorbonne she was told that he was on emergency leave, attending to a family problem. His home phone was answered by a machine. His apartment intercom—twice she had tried it, once at night—brought no response. Even the friend of a friend who'd first put them in touch professed to know nothing of his whereabouts and seemed surprised to hear about his leave. Whatever the reason for Thierry's disappearance, Odile began to doubt that he would return anytime soon.

She checked her watch, then turned her back to the weather and passed through a set of glass doors into the megastore's tri-level atrium. Part of an international chain, the establishment had opened barely a year ago to uniformly hostile press. Since then it had become a sensation, as much a social draw as a retail outlet, and Odile now paused to take in the spectacle. The ground floor was packed with students, office workers on lunch break, and others, like herself, just waiting out the rain. They sorted impatiently through CD bins or stood at listening stations, pressing headphones to their ears while their eyes went wary. A marble staircase, centrally placed, ran to the upper floors, and Odile took it to the top.

Twice since returning to Paris, she had dreamed she was back at the

Brest train station, pushing through the crowd of people waiting to buy tickets, people she now understood to be desperate. All was as it had been—the dimness, the silence, the guards, the ruin—but now she, too, was desperate, no longer a traveler on an errand but another refugee, someone whose world had been erased by catastrophe and fate. Panic gripped her as she fought through the crowd, pushing and pleading and kicking until at last she reached the ticket window. But there, in place of the gray-haired matron, she found Thierry filling out the forms, and though he recognized her and spoke to her teasingly, in good humor, he wouldn't sell her a ticket. "Because you can't pay for it," he said when she demanded an explanation. "What's more, your seat has been given away." In the distance were sirens, growing louder as they approached.

She wandered among the floor samples, televisions, DVD players, personal stereos, cell phones. A salesman showed her a palm-sized computer that could download and display electronic books. "This," he confided, "is the quintessential Anglo-Saxon invention. I myself would never own one."

When she spotted Turner—he was at the computer-peripherals counter, trying to return a pocket scanner—her first thought was to slip downstairs and out to the street. But it was too late for that; she'd already taken a step in his direction, and with it committed herself to the whole encounter and whatever might follow.

She walked straight up to him, assuming nothing. "Remember me?" she said.

Turner looked at her in surprise, but not just surprise. "I do, Odile. Most definitely." His face struggled for a suitable expression.

"Because that job I did for you recently? There are problems."

"Excuse me?"

"Problems that don't belong to me, problems I don't want." She shrugged. "Who knows? Maybe they're your problems. Shall I tell you about them?"

"No," he said. "I'd really rather you didn't."

She tilted her head thoughtfully. "The police, then?"

"Wait." He cast an unhappy eye over the sales floor and the customers wandering across it. "There's a café next door."

Ten minutes later, when they were ensconced at a corner table amid dark wood, tourists, and immaculate linen, Odile began to be alarmed at what she'd set in motion. She had not planned for this meeting, didn't even know where to begin, and her earlier confidence threatened to desert her.

Their waiter deposited two espressos on the table in passing.

"So, Odile. You were saying?"

She let a small silence go by. "I am very curious to ask you, did the other courier, my partner, ever show up to collect his fee?"

"He didn't, now that you mention it. Why do you ask?"

"No reason," she said quickly. "I just wondered."

Turner leaned back in his chair and considered her, frankly and at length. She fidgeted with her coffee spoon, turning it over and over on the tabletop: concave, convex, concave again, convex. "Problems," he said finally. "The subject was problems, yes?"

"Okay." She forced herself to look at him. "I'm being threatened by two Russian guys—thugs, gangsters, I don't know. They pretended to be police at first, but it's not true. They know about the flags, and my part in getting them out of the country. I think they also wrecked my apartment, but to prove this would be difficult."

He was nodding slowly, as if to suggest a distant familiarity with unrelated but similar events. "And what is it that they want from you?"

She hesitated. "I don't know. They're not entirely rational."

"Did my name come up?"

"No. They know about the flags, but your name as such didn't come up."

"Then, in all candor, Odile, what do you expect me to do about it?"

She held the espresso cup a little away from her lips, steadying it with her left hand, and looked into his eyes. Dark as they were—brown almost to black, the pupils a darkness within darkness—she found herself quite able to negotiate their depths. He had told a lie to match hers, a lie of omission. It didn't matter what he thought he was concealing, or if he'd succeeded. What counted now, the only important thing, was what the two of them had recognized, each in the other.

"I was hoping we could talk about that," she said.


MAX STOOD at the back of the theater watching his film's final scenes.

It is dusk. The protagonist brings his battered sports car to a screeching halt on West Street, where a half-ruined pier juts nine hundred feet into the Hudson. At the end of the pier a woman stands silhouetted against the dying light, her back to him, her arms folded, her hair lifted in the wind. The man runs toward her at full speed. Here the camera reverses angles so he's seen from her point of view—she has turned to face him—and no longer in full motion but in a succession of stills, each held for two seconds, as he gets closer and closer to her, breathing hard, grimacing. The woman is now heard in voice-over, very near to the ear, with all else silent. "It isn't really love, it's the illusion of love . . . It ends badly . . . Well, no. Finally, it ends well . . . Or"—the last image of the man appears, he has yet to reach the woman—"it ends badly." Freeze frame and credits.

The applause was more than polite. As the lights came up, Max went back down the aisle to the podium, nodding his thanks and then speaking them into the microphone.

When *Fireflies* had premiered, in New York, at Lincoln Center, he'd sat rapt through the screening, as though he were watching someone else's film. By the time the credits rolled, he knew he'd succeeded in making, if not the film he'd set out to make, then another that was at least as good. There had been a podium on that occasion too, and when he stood behind it facing the audience, he had felt his whole life stretching out before him. Nothing had seemed beyond his reach.

The applause died away. He lit a small black cigar, then opened his hands to the audience, inviting questions.

"Did you give your actors any special guidance or exercises to prepare for their roles?" The speaker was a woman in her thirties wearing violet lipstick with a matching scarf tied close about her neck. "And if so, what did you intend?"

"In general I prefer my actors to sink or swim without my interference. For *Fireflies*, though, because my cast insisted on it, I did give them an exercise. I asked them to walk to the location each day, rather than take the subway or a taxi." Max began to enjoy himself a little. "And my intention? It was just to make them wonder what my intention might be. As a result they became more thoughtful, more alert to possibility. Also, they absorbed the city more deeply. New York's like a character in this film."

A tall man in a black turtleneck asked about the shooting ratio in *Fireflies*.

"I was very fast when I started out," said Max. "About three to one for *Fireflies*. But with my most recent film, *White Room/Black Room,* I shot close to ten feet for every foot that made the final cut. The more one learns, it seems, the more film one wastes. Or, alternatively: I've forgotten what I knew."

There was laughter, then an interval of silence. A woman in her twenties, her glossy hair hennaed red almost to magenta, stood up and smiled at him. She seemed to be referring to some private understanding between the two of them, and he smiled back.

"It is something of an open secret," the woman began, "at least among your more devoted admirers, that there exists an alternate ending to *Fire-*

*flies*. In that version a boat is tied up at the end of the pier, waiting for the two lovers. They argue about what to do, then board the boat. Something is thrown overboard, and the boat sets out. The lovers escape together. Obviously, this ending changes the meaning of the film radically. My question is: do you favor one ending over the other, and why did you choose this one today?"

The woman sat back down, looking pleased with herself. She seemed eager to hear his answer, and he was fleetingly sorry not to have one.

"Unfortunately, you've been misinformed. There is no alternative ending to *Fireflies*, because, among many other reasons, I didn't shoot one."

"But one does exist," she replied from her seat. "I've seen it with my own eyes!"

He hesitated. "Then you are ahead of me," he decided to say. "Thank you for your question, though. You've given me something to think about."

The woman acknowledged these words with a nod. She didn't seem the least bit discouraged; rather, it was as if her earlier air of complicity had been shown to be justified. And though Max had dealt before with unsound or misguided students of his work, people who felt personally addressed by his films and unduly intimate with him, their maker, this woman was not at all like them. It would be desirable, he thought, to avoid her on the way out.

He continued to take questions for the better part of an hour. His audience was intelligent and well informed; he tried to give them worthy answers. Yet the more he talked, summoning up and consulting his younger self, so confident, even arrogant, the more he wished to be rid of this and all his other films. By the time he cut off further questions, he was fatigued— if grateful for the applause.

"That was really super good," Jacques assured him as they walked back up the aisle together to the lobby. "And," he added, brandishing a fist-sized vidcam, "I've got it all on disk. You really have to publish it as an interview."

"What about the film?" Max asked. "Do you think it holds up?"

"You're joking, right? It's a classic." He eyed his employer suspiciously. "What is this, a test?"

In the lobby they found, to Max's discomfort, that a modest reception had been prepared for the occasion. The program director at once reattached himself to his distinguished guest and resumed his critical musings while Max pretended to listen, nodding thoughtfully from time to time. Several members of the audience waited politely to engage his attention, but at last he felt his patience exhausted.

"Jacques," he said, catching his assistant by the elbow, "this gentleman"—he pulled the program director firmly forward—"has quite a lot to say about film. You two really ought to get to know each other better."

Jacques shot him an indignant look, but already it was too late for protest.

This handoff effected, Max turned toward the exit but instead found himself face-to-face with the henna-haired young woman. He supposed the encounter had been inevitable.

"I'm sorry if I embarrassed you just now," she said. "That wasn't my intention."

"You didn't embarrass me," he replied.

She held out her hand. "Marie-Claire."

"Hello, Marie-Claire. Pleased to meet you."

She had the pasty white complexion of a film enthusiast and was modishly dressed in a black-and-white-print miniskirt, a tailored denim jacket buttoned to her neck, and red patent-leather pumps. Max scanned her oval face for signs of madness.

"I admire your work very much," she said. "I didn't know that the other version of *Fireflies* was . . . unauthorized, if that's the word. What happened? Did you have trouble with your backers?"

"I always have trouble with my backers," Max answered, looking belligerently around the room as if one or two might be present. "Tell me, Marie-Claire. Where did you see this other version of the film, with the ending you describe?"

"At university. In Bordeaux." She frowned. "But also it's in the video stores, though you can't tell from the packaging. You just get what you get. I've rented both."

"Really?" He looked at her anew. "So my films interest you?"

She blushed and with her fingertips hooked her hair back behind her ears. "Yes, very much. I am writing my thesis on you."

Max received this news as gracefully as he could. "Oh. Well, I'm honored. Prematurely, I hope, but definitely honored." After looking thoughtfully at her, he inspected his cigar, then let his gaze float away. "And who knows? Maybe you'll be the one to clear up this confusion over *Fireflies*. If that's what it is."

Encouraged, she started to ask another question, but he cut her off. "Look, Marie-Claire. There's only one version of *Fireflies*, and you just saw it. Anything else is horse manure, okay?"

She stared at him.

"If you're going to write about film, you have to start with the facts." His anger embarrassed him. The conversation was over. He left the theater.

Dusk had settled over Paris, and the rain had stopped, leaving the air fresh and cutting. He walked south on rue Claude Bernard past the technical schools for which the area was known, toward Gobelins. The streetlamps came on. Reflections from the rain-slick pavement twinned the passing traffic—headlights, taillights, white and red.

It annoyed and discouraged Max that already, at mid-career, he was the subject of an academic paper, let alone one written by somebody as demonstrably misguided, even disturbed, as the girl he'd just encountered.

A gloom settled over him, frustration at having wasted the day and its possibilities. He thought of his daughter, struggling to make a place for herself, and of Odile, never fully predictable but also, since the break-in, tense and preoccupied, inclined to brood. He felt keenly the fragility of their intermingled lives, of other people's lives. Something like pity welled up in him, so enveloping that it soon encompassed everything and was all he felt. Then, abruptly, it left him, and he knew only exhaustion.

Making a right on Glacière, just blocks from home, he noticed the local video store was still open. He glanced at the cardboard promotionals in the window—most of them for an American space-epic remake—but kept on walking.

The store didn't even stock his films.

# CHAPTER 6

BALAKIAN HAD HIRED a publicist for the opening, a Congo-born Belgian blonde who stood just inside the gallery entrance monitoring arrivals and pouncing triumphantly on those she believed useful to her. Young female journalists circled behind her, notepads in hand, while photographers jockeyed for position.

Turner's first impulse was to step back into the night, but the Belgian gleefully called out his name, kissed him hello, then asked loudly in French whether he still provided intimate services for his preferred clients. He knew what she was referring to, and though the incident, years past, had been largely her invention, considerable trouble had ensued from the brief account of it she had managed to place in the gossip pages of the New York tabloids. He was careful now to appease her before plunging ahead into the crowd.

It was largely an art-world crowd, ambitious people imaginatively dressed and coiffed, but there was also a scattering of foreign nationals, men in suits, demi-celebrities, and downtown hipsters—notables of the sort that routinely appeared at the Belgian's events. They milled around the soaring exhibition space, a former trucking depot whose interior had been gutted and elegantly refurbished, drinking wine from plastic cups, conversing in small groups, discreetly vigilant for company more desirable than their own.

The flags upstaged them all. Unframed, suspended from clear plastic clips high on the walls, the crimson banners charged the gallery with their presence. After inspecting the initial seven that Turner had sent him, Balakian had requested three more, and they now hung two or three to a wall, positioned so that each commanded enough surrounding space to be seen for itself without appearing isolated. Marx, Lenin, Stalin, Kosygin, Brezhnev—all looked perfectly at home in the quasi-industrial setting, as if they were reviewing yet another May Day rally. Taken as an ensemble, though, the blazing monochrome fields with their iconic figures—figures once recognizable to virtually anyone, anywhere—strongly resembled an Andy Warhol exhibition of the late 1960s or early '70s, the time of his Marilyns and Jackies and Maos. The same mix of adulation and irony, awe and indifference, suffused both bodies of work. Such had been the zeitgeist, big faces for impossible times, as much a force in the Soviet Union as in the U.S., and Turner rejoiced at his perspicacity. A serious man didn't become less so just because he was attempting to turn a profit.

Turner made the rounds, greeting clients, colleagues, acquaintances, and friends, taking care not to appear connected to the show, which was being presented as a Balakian production pure and simple, but when talking to critics or journalists he allowed himself to share his Warholian insight. These people would be writing about the exhibition, and it was only sound practice to point them in the correct direction. Positive reviews in the art press could double the price of the flags, and a magazine cover could do even more.

Quartz lights came on, a TV crew began taping. He dodged them and hurried on to Balakian's office in the back. There, variously disposed around a bowl of caviar, a plate of blinis, and two liter bottles of vodka on ice, were four men with whom he was well acquainted: Balakian himself; a Swiss collector named Wieselhoff; a corporate art consultant called Baxter; and Nikolai Kukushkin, known to his friends as Kolya, a Russian banker with a number of entrepreneurial sidelines, creatively incorporated and managed. A mood of relaxed complicity prevailed. Turner shut the door behind him.

"The man of the hour," announced Balakian, pouring drinks all around.

"Very good," Wieselhoff said to Turner. "Very provocative. Are there more?"

"Glad you like them, Horst. And Ron, the installation's superb. You were right about adding those extra three."

Balakian accepted the compliment with a nod. "It works, doesn't it."

Kukushkin, who had been grinning craftily at Turner since his arrival, now raised his glass in greeting. "We are all of us in new world," he pronounced. "We will wreck it like old world. Is scientific certainty. *Na zdorovie!*"

"*Na zdorovie!*" repeated the others. All drank.

"You know what I keep thinking?" said Baxter. "From a humanist point of view? Nothing's handmade anymore. On a daily basis you don't really notice it, or at least you get used to everything being manufactured or computer generated. But then you see something like these flags that just radiates the human touch, and it makes you want to weep. They're imperfect, they're poignant, they're beautiful. And, face it, they're rare, which is good for business."

Balakian smiled. "Watch out for this guy," he advised, helping himself to more caviar. "I think he just said that painting's the next big thing."

Everyone seemed amused. Turner poured himself another glass of vodka, raised it in toast, and drank it down.

"Excuse my bad manners," Wieselhoff told him, "but I am curious, and we are colleagues here together. How did you come into possession of these flags?"

Turner smiled and shook his head. "Sorry, Horst. Anyway, you know how it is. People bring me things. I facilitate."

"*Ja,* okay." The Swiss drummed his fingers on the arm of his chair. "But if more of them turn up, I would like to be informed. I am much excited by these objects."

Turner exchanged glances with Balakian. "Better talk to Ron about that," he said.

"And do watch the resale market," Baxter added drily. "I know I would."

As the talk turned to gossip—a dealer they all knew was said to have begun blacklisting collectors who put her artists' works up for auction—Turner's eye kept coming back to Kukushkin. Compactly built, dressed in a boxy British suit, oxford shirt, no tie, the Russian exuded an authority from which all visible signs of striving had been purged. Although Turner had known him for some time, they had done little business together, instead exchanging the occasional favor in token of their mutual regard and possible future association. When Turner sought to pay off Belarussian customs to get the flags through passport control, it was Kukushkin he'd called, and at once the necessary doors had opened. Secretly, though, and for these very reasons, Turner feared the man to an inconvenient degree.

As if guessing his thoughts, Kukushkin nodded sympathetically and refilled Turner's glass, then his own. "Business is good?" he asked.

The others went on talking.

"I can't complain," Turner replied. "We've got some first-rate antiquities coming to the block this spring. Not that we couldn't use a good death or divorce, as always. But that's the auction business: part salvage operation, part grief counseling."

"Is good, such business. Death and divorce never out of style. Same for beautiful objects." Again he raised his glass. *"Na zdorovie!"*

*"Na zdorovie!"* Turner was beginning to feel the liquor. "What about you, Kolya? Got anything big in the works, or do I have to read about it in the newspapers with everybody else?"

The Russian waved these words impatiently away. "My projects are of no interest, even to me. Maybe I make change."

"Really? What kind of change?"

But Kukushkin appeared not to have heard. Grimly he poured them yet another round. "In Russian we have expression, *smekh skvoz' slyovzy.* You know what is meaning, this expression? Least-bad translation: 'laughing through tears.' True Russian concept. Is saying in life tragedy and comedy exist always side by side. Is saying they are *inextricable,* okay? You believe me?"

"I believe you," said Turner.

"Hah! Excellent! *Na zdorovie!*"

*"Na zdorovie!"* Seeing that Wieselhoff, Baxter, and Balakian were still caught up in their own conversation, Turner leaned forward and said, in a quieter voice, "Kolya, I'd like your opinion on a small business matter."

The Russian widened his eyes.

"Ordinarily I don't involve myself in these things, but the case is special. One of the couriers I sent to pick up the flags tells me that since she got back from Moscow she has been followed by two Russian guys, a little coarse, maybe, who know about the flags and ask her questions she can't answer. They mention Interpol. This is troubling to her and, by extension, to me. As you can imagine."

"Yes, yes. Go on."

"Well, I'd like to put a stop to it, to be perfectly blunt. But I don't really know how. Who are these guys working for, I wonder. Is there someone to call?"

Kukushkin frowned. "Paris situation now is difficult. Too many amateurs, lousy communications. What is it these bastards want to know?"

"Nothing specific, as far as I can tell. But they're fishing in my waters. It's annoying."

"And you are sure she has nothing to tell them?"

"Close to certain."

"Okay. Then I will look into it." He shrugged and once more filled their glasses. "Always there is a way."

Turner thanked him, and they drank without toasting.

"But I will tell you frankly," the Russian added, his eyes now alive with Slavic mischief, "sometimes, also, the way is too far to go."


BACK AT HIS HOTEL, a postmodern study in pinpoint lighting and computer-generated curves, Turner took a seat at the bar and continued to drink. The clientele was young, sleekly good-looking, and, it seemed to him, mostly local. To his right, two women in black cocktail dresses were drinking cosmopolitans and planning a putsch at a well-known fashion magazine.

It had been several years since he'd lived full-time in Manhattan, and although he returned frequently on business, he no longer pretended to himself that he might one day come back for good. To him New York was like a dream of beauty ruined, but the dream had begun long before he'd set foot here, and the ruin had preceded the dream.

He had worked out of his loft in TriBeCa, dealing fitfully in objects that, though genuine in themselves, had unexplained gaps in their provenance, gaps that suggested they were stolen. While such irregularities hardly detracted from their artistic value, they did make resale difficult, and when talking to inexperienced buyers, people who often paid with cash of similarly doubtful origin, he wasn't always forthcoming about this drawback. One August night, he returned to the loft with his lover, a woman whose capacity for self-invention exceeded even his own, to find an unhappy customer ensconced in his Régence chair, pistol in hand. The man held the gun to Turner's head while Turner wrote him a check for the object in question—a Cycladic fertility figurine in limestone, circa second century BC. Seemingly appeased, the man pocketed his refund and left. Turner waited until he heard the street door slam shut, five stories down, then picked up the phone and stopped the check. The next afternoon, his lover, who didn't possess a driver's license, was involved in a single-vehicle traffic accident in Queens, where she never went. He was informed of her death by her sister, calling from the morgue. He waited then for the police to contact him, waited for their questions and, with his useless answers, for his own exposure as a careless trafficker in the rare and impossible. But no call came. And it was shortly after these events that the idea of moving to Paris suggested itself to him.

"Excuse me," said a woman hovering behind the barstool to his left. "Is this seat taken?" She was attractive, dressed in a backless dress split to mid-thigh, and when sitting down she allowed him a lengthy flash of leg. She was, he realized at once, a prostitute. Chagrined to be taken for an out-of-towner, particularly since that was what he was, he bought her a drink.

"Bad day?" she said, sipping her kir royale and searching his eyes. "You look maybe a little depressed."

"Do I? It's probably jet lag." He finished his drink and absently rattled the ice in his glass. "Because my day was good. I did business and tended friends, and tomorrow I'll be back in the City of Light. Where I make my home."

She raised an eyebrow. "But tonight you have a room here at the hotel, right?"

"Exactly." He realized he was drunk. "Would you like to come up for a nightcap?"

"That depends," she said. When she had recited her rates and ground rules he called for the check. They left the bar and together took the elevator to his room.

In bed she was professional but unhurried, and Turner found himself unexpectedly in tune with her, as if she really were someone he knew. Her movements anticipated his by half a beat, teasing him, luring him on, and he imagined himself pursuing her through the Tuileries, in dappled light. When he began to come, she gripped him tightly from inside, releasing the pressure only gradually, until he saw stars.

After she had showered, dressed, and left, he experienced a moment of plunging sorrow. It occurred to him that he'd mismanaged his life and would doubtless die alone in a place very much like this room, perhaps not so long from now. He was already half resigned to such a fate, and part of him even looked forward to it: what happened to other people would happen to him.

But there was also this—and it was like a glimpse of the world made good—that though he was cynical, even contemptuous, of people and their motives, although he was rarely disappointed because he seldom allowed himself to hope that there was more to things than met the eye, he'd lately come to imagine a scenario of deliverance, vague but encompassing, that seemed to promise him not just another chance but another existence, one in which everything that was counterfeit or used up would be swept away and a new order of being revealed. In his mind this deliverance was not for him alone, but whether it included everyone or not he was at a loss to say. Sometimes he thought it would have to.

He switched on the television, and watched a scarlet-haired woman in her twenties race frantically through the streets of Berlin. If she didn't raise a hundred thousand deutschmarks in the next twenty minutes, her boyfriend, who was supposed to deliver the money to his gangster boss, would be killed. Small obstacles in her path—a flock of nuns, a boy on a bicycle, some workmen carrying a sheet of plate glass—kept delaying her and made it seem certain that she would fail to get the money to him in time.

Turner watched without sympathy. Just before the woman arrived on the scene, the boyfriend panicked and pulled a gun. Already he was robbing a grocery store.

*"Smekh skvoz' slyovzy,"* Turner told the two of them, switching off the set in disgust.

# CHAPTER 7

LATE ON FRIDAY AFTERNOON, Max emerged from his studio to find his anarchist neighbors taking spring inventory *en plein air*. Spread out on the cobblestone courtyard in front of their apartment were quantities of scuffed motorcycle helmets, gas masks, police batons, shin guards, goggles, life vests, gloves—all the accoutrements of violent and total dissent. A pale blond girl he'd never seen before was noting the amount and condition of the equipment on a clipboard while her comrades brought out still more.

"Planning a major action?" Max asked.

She looked up sharply. "But of course! We're going to Maastricht for the trade summit!" Studying him, she appeared to take his measure, right down to his wedding ring. "You and your wife should come also."

"No doubt. What is it exactly you're protesting?" He guessed her to be eighteen, nineteen at most.

"We protest, but never exactly," she said. "Our struggle is against all that is the case. We oppose everything. To do less would be incorrect and shameful."

"Yes, I see your point." He shook his head in neighborly sympathy over the state of the world. *"Vive la lutte."*

*"La lutte,"* she said, returning to the clipboard.

At home, upstairs, Odile was preparing a lamb tagine for the party that Rachel and Groot were giving that night aboard the *Nachtvlinder*. A light sweat moistened her face and arms, and she seemed irritated.

"Our anarchists are mobilizing," Max said.

"I saw." She handed him a jar of pickled limes she'd been struggling with; he wrapped a dish towel around the lid, gave it a sudden twist, and returned the open container to her. "You have an e-mail from Allegra," she told him.

Surprised, pleased, apprehensive, Max poured himself a beer and sat down at the computer they kept in an alcove off the kitchen. When he had located his daughter's letter and printed it out, he brought it with him to the kitchen table.

*Hi, Dad,* it began. *I hope you're not still mad at me. Mom says I'm just as stubborn as you, so we've got to be friends, no choice. That's logical, I guess. Like logic has anything to do with it.*

Max winced and drank deeply of his beer. Lately Allegra's communiqués disturbed him only slightly less than her silences. She was dismayingly expert at manipulating him.

*The big news here is that Alison—remember Alison? my friend you liked so much?—she just got kicked out of school for drugs. What really sucks about it is that the pills weren't even hers. She was just keeping them in her locker for this odious guy she's been hanging out with all semester, and he didn't even get caught. Now we're going to have "drug awareness week." What a joke. I mean, hello? We're already "aware" of drugs, thank you. Most kids know ten times as much about psychoactives as the so-called experts who come in to lecture us. Really, adults can be so clueless.*

Max reread these words, compulsively examining them for lacunae and subtexts. The thought of Allegra on drugs, as she well knew, filled him with panic, even though by her age he himself had ingested every controlled substance that he could get his hands on. She was so vulnerable to the world, his daughter, but the days when he could hope to protect her from it were fast receding, possibly gone.

"What does she say?" Odile was cutting the lamb into cubes and dusting them with turmeric.

"I don't know yet. Adults are clueless."

*Anyway,* the e-mail went on, *I was thinking about this summer. Mom kind of hinted that you were going to invite me to spend it with you and Odile in Paris, which is really cool of you. But would it be okay if I don't come? Upper school starts in the fall, and I just really need to be with my friends.*

There was more, but the gist was clear: a summer in Paris would not only turn her into an instant social outcast but might conceivably ruin the rest of her life as well. Despite himself, Max was surprised and hurt. He tried to remember when she'd acquired veto power over his plans for her.

"It's completely normal," Odile said after he read her the e-mail. "At her age I was much worse."

"Worse?"

"More self-conscious."

"Really? You think that's what this is?" Max could barely contain himself. "She tells me straight off that her friends deal drugs, then she says she wants to spend the summer in New York so she can be with these punks full-time. Why is she punishing me?"

Odile blew a strand of hair out of her eyes. "Maybe she enjoys it."

Her tone of voice startled Max. He'd been expecting comfort, or at least comforting words, but this was something else. His features hardened. "You sound as if you know all about it."

"No. But you do make it easy for her." Odile gathered the cubes of meat in her hands and dropped them into the skillet, where they sizzled and popped and sent up a plume of yellow smoke. "Why don't you call her, Max?"

"That's exactly what I will do," he said. But he made no move toward the telephone, and he was no longer thinking particularly about his daughter.

THEY ARRIVED just after dark at the quai de la Tournelle, where the *Nachtvlinder* was docked. Strings of amber lights festooned the houseboat, and as Odile and Max hurried up the gangway—she with the tagine, he with his HD vidcam—the quavering tones of Algerian *raï* drifted up from belowdecks. Topside, half a dozen guests smoked and talked.

"We've already had a visit from *la fluviale*," Rachel told Odile and Max after kissing them hello, "but I bribed them with fresh sardines and a bottle of Sancerre. If they come back, I've got *tarte tatin*."

"Where's the skipper?" Max asked.

"Groot? Oh, he's just checking a fuse or something. Let's go below. I'm so glad you two are here."

They followed her through the companionway and down three steps to the main compartment, twenty feet long, where more guests stood in clusters, eating bouillabaisse from enameled metal bowls. Most of those present were in their thirties or younger, and several had been introduced to Max and Odile on previous occasions: a black performance artist from New Orleans, a Dutch photographer, a pair of Iranian journalists, an editor from a French publishing house. The conversation was animated and rose easily over the music.

"Are we going to film tonight?" Rachel asked.

Max looked her over. "I don't know yet." She was wearing the dress Odile had made for her, a green silk mini with mesh ribbon insets. Despite pantyhose and a shawl, she shivered in the dank river air. "How do you feel?"

"She feels older, Max. Less young. It's the nature of birthdays."

Rachel laughed. "No, I feel great. Really." She took the stew pot from Odile. "Come on, let's heat this up. I'm starving."

While she and Odile retired aft to the galley, Max stowed his camera in his hosts' cabin, thinking he could always retrieve it later, at a more advanced stage of the festivities. Then he returned to the main compartment, helped himself to a beer, and began prowling the party.

He spoke for awhile with Katje, the photographer. She had come to Paris to shoot a series of images documenting life on the Seine, but, present company excepted, her intended subjects had refused to cooperate. They viewed her as an interloper and nuisance, someone to be chased away with a marlinespike if necessary. Puzzled by this lack of *gezelligheid,* Katje quietly abandoned the project. Now she was shooting large-format portraits of transvestite hookers in the Bois de Boulogne, and life had regained its savor.

"To be what one is not," she told Max. "We all have this dream."

"When I was growing up," he replied, "the big dream was to become yourself. You had to work at it."

"Yes, the age of psychology." She smiled politely. "That must have been interesting."

"Not the way you might think. Anyway, it's all over now."

He excused himself. A passing *bateau mouche* threw spikes of light and amplified accordion music in through the open portholes. When the larger boat's wake reached the *Nachtvlinder,* she rolled hard, causing several guests to stagger a step, spill their soup, laugh. Meanwhile, running beneath everything—the conversation, the music, the bilge pumps' electric drone—the Seine could be heard in its many mutterings, a syntax of gurgles and splashes that lapped at the boat, tirelessly wheedling a path in through the fittings, offering at every moment to bear the vessel northwestward through Normandy and out to sea.

Max found Groot, as he'd known he would, alone in the engine room. The parts of one of the diesels lay spread out on tarps, and he was examining them by the light of a single safety-caged bulb that swung back and forth overhead, casting spiderweb shadows. In his straight blond hair was a stroke of engine grease.

"Couldn't tear yourself away, Captain?"

Groot stood solemnly, but as they shook hands he broke into a shy grin. "I had an idea about the exhaust manifold, a kind of workaround, so I thought I'd have a look. I'm not really hiding."

Fair-skinned and finely made, the Dutchman would have seemed delicate were it not for the breadth of his shoulders and his startlingly round face. The latter gave him an air of unflappability, which was well deserved, and of innocence, less so. Lately Max had been thinking of including him in some of the Rachel footage. Visually, they made a striking couple.

"So it's coming along?" asked Max, surveying the ranks of engine parts.

"I make progress, but slowly. These diesels are quite old. Everyone around here who ever worked on one is dead. Maybe I will go to England for parts or maybe I'll make them myself." He wiped his hands on a cloth. "It's a mystery, this boat."

Max said nothing. From a rack affixed to the bulkhead, Groot took a tape measure and a flashlight and, from his pocket, a carpenter's crayon, which he handed to Max. "Fifteen minutes," he said. "Twenty at most, I promise."


THE MUSIC HAD SWITCHED to techno—a maddeningly wistful piano figure floating above the beat—and though the *Nachtvlinder* wasn't spacious enough for actual dancing, Odile saw a number of people rearrange themselves subtly to the melody. A man she barely knew was explaining the placebo effect.

"In short," he concluded, "one gets something from nothing. Belief alone—misplaced belief, yes?—stimulates the immune system. It is better than Catholicism."

"I have no idea what you're talking about," she said. Catching sight of Rachel, Odile pointed to the companionway and made smoking gestures. Rachel nodded.

Topside, leaning on the foredeck rail, they shared a cigarette and gazed up at Nôtre Dame, its apse, steeple, and iconic twin towers dazzlingly floodlit, not six hundred yards away. The cathedral looked massive but somehow fragile, like a shop-window wedding cake.

"What's the matter, O? Aren't you having a good time?"

"Yes, of course I am."

"What, then?"

Odile took a long drag on the cigarette and passed it back. "Is it going well, the filming?"

"Oh, really excellent. Max makes me see things I'd never notice on my own, just by what he decides to shoot. It's eerie sometimes."

"Max is very talented," Odile replied. She spoke neutrally, stating a fact.

"The other day," Rachel continued, "he really surprised me. We were shooting at that Roman ruin in the fifth—the Arènes de Lutèce?—and he told me that all he wanted me to do was walk across the open space, the arena, that was it. So he set up, and I started out. When I was almost halfway across, suddenly, running toward me from under the trees, there were all these children, maybe twelve or fifteen of them. It was like when the Gypsy kids swarm you, but this wasn't about robbery. It was a kind of game where they ran up and touched me—my hips, arms, back, whatever—laughing and shouting the whole time. Then they ran a circle around me, really fast, and went back where they'd come from, all in different directions again. They just disappeared into the trees, and I finished walking across the arena. That was all." She laughed. "But it was enough, too."

"Were you scared?"

"A little. It all happened so fast."

For a time, neither of them spoke. The night smelled of diesel, tobacco smoke, and beauty products. A junked TV floated past.

"You don't mind, do you?" Rachel asked.

"Mind?"

"That he's filming me."

"Don't be silly, Rachel. I'm his wife." But even as she spoke these words Odile wondered why she had chosen them. It was as if she were addressing a third party, someone who'd asked a different question, and a spasm of doubt made her catch her breath.

"I knew it wasn't that," Rachel was saying. "It's just that you seem so tense lately."

"Do I?"

"Since you got back from your trip. I don't want to interfere, but is there anything I can do to help?"

Her pride, her will to win, her half-shaded fears and inadequacies . . . Odile failed to understand why she'd withheld from Max the details of her Moscow trip and its continuing consequences. She'd said nothing about the Russian thugs, or Turner, or what had happened in Brest, or Thierry and his disappearance. But now, from a different quarter, she was being offered a chance to rectify her silences, or at least to compensate for them, and she discovered it was the opportunity she'd been waiting for.

She took it.

BY ONE O'CLOCK, when the lights on the Eiffel Tower flicked out, the party had sorted down to an inner core of seven. They were seated in deck chairs on the quarterdeck, blankets draped over their shoulders, drinking poire. The man with whom Odile had been speaking earlier, the editor, said, "Gustave Eiffel—a true visionary. He designed the tower, yes, but his greatest achievement, for which he receives tragically little credit, was the invention of the garter belt. An essential cultural innovation, and, why not say it, an icon of modernity."

"Show us your legs, dear," the performance artist told Rachel.

"I think everyone has had enough of my legs for one night, Weston."

"Such a pretty dress, though," said Katje, who was drunk.

Max had spent a good deal longer than twenty minutes working with Groot but they now sat with the others, mildly fatigued and bound by the wordless comradery of labor. From his shirt pocket Groot produced a cigarette. He slit it open with a fingernail, mixed a dozen pellets of hashish into the tobacco, and rolled it back up again. After he had lit it and taken a drag, he passed it to Max.

Odile said, "That won't help anything." She and Rachel sat side by side, a little apart from the group.

"On the contrary," said Max, exhaling. He gave the cigarette to Katje, who drew on it hungrily. "Already I notice an improvement."

Weston looked pained.

"No need to be alarmed," the editor advised him. "We're all frivolous people here."

Both Rachel and Odile declined the cigarette. The editor, after a pantomime of inner debate, accepted it and took two long drags before surrendering it to Weston.

Then, wafting in on the breeze, there came a man's voice, conversational in tone but very distinct. It seemed to originate across the near branch of the river or beyond, on the Île Saint-Louis. "But my darling, of course we can start over. Why not?"

Putting his hands behind his head, Groot leaned back in his chair. "It's strange how voices carry over water." He spoke dreamily, as though to himself. "Listen."

"Don't be an imbecile! We can't start over!" A woman's voice this time, equally clear and distant, answering the first. "One can end many times but one can start only once. You and I started years ago. And since, we have ended many times. We end and end and end and end. That's all we can do. And then we can end some more. But to start again? This is impossible. Completely, utterly impossible. Don't you understand *anything?*"

"Listen to me, my sweet—"

And here, with a shift in the breeze or a change in the air pressure, the voices abruptly ceased to be audible.

Weston laughed softly and passed what was left of the cigarette back to Groot.

"Madame does have a point," the editor said with a shrug. "Though I myself would have suggested a more indirect approach."

Odile said, "But your opinion is irrelevant, isn't it?"

Raising an eyebrow, the editor glanced at Max. "If you like."

Katje leaned forward suddenly and, finding herself within reach of the poire, poured herself another drink.

"Living on the river," said Rachel, "you hear all kinds of things. The other day I was here repotting the geraniums, and there was, like, this *eruption* of singing from upstream. A man's voice, opera, something famous. At first I thought it was a recording, but then I wasn't sure. He sounded . . . maybe a little off. Anyway, when he finished, another man, closer to us and live, definitely live, shouted, 'Shit! Complete shit!' And then he, this second guy, sang the whole . . . aria, I guess, over again, the whole thing. And it was great, even I could tell. People applauded."

Groot nodded approvingly. "Rachel understands the river."

"And vice versa," added Max.

They sat in silence. Groot reengineered another cigarette, and it made the rounds.

Odile and Rachel's change of mood had unsettled Max, and now he felt a pang of anxiety that his camera's interim subject might be getting away from him. All the qualities that had led him to Rachel in the first place— her openness, her readiness to understand, her physical exoticism— seemed suddenly to conceal a deeper, more elusive self that he had failed utterly to penetrate, or even to appreciate, until now. This lapse was like an intimation of failure, and with it came the further realization, petty but impossible to ignore, that he and Odile had begun to vie for Rachel's attention like jealous schoolchildren. Foolish, even damaging behavior. And Max saw that he would have to rethink his approach.

"So maybe," Katje was saying, "in a past life, I too understood the river. But now . . ." Her attention seemed to waver. "Now what I understand . . ." She trailed off into a bewildered silence.

"Some things are best not put into words," said the editor firmly.

There were fireflies in the corners of Max's sight—phosphorescent lights flashing on and off in two-part synchrony. He blinked them away.

"But the boat!" Katje announced. She appeared agitated. "Will there be enough room?"

"Room?" said Odile.

"Don't worry," Groot assured Katje. "She's more spacious than she looks."

And with that the amber party lights, the lights below, the music, the bilge pumps, and everything else electrically powered aboard the *Nacht-vlinder* switched abruptly off.

"Max?" Odile called softly.

"I'm right here."

"It can't be another fuse," Rachel said. "Or can it?"

Already Groot was on his feet. He had taken a halogen flashlight from his pocket and was headed forward to the gangway.

"It's probably a short on board," Max told the others. "He's going to start at the quai-side hookup and work backward. I'll take a look below."

"Don't, Max," Odile said.

"Are there candles?" the editor asked.

"Candles?" Katje looked left and right in panic. "Is that what those are?"

Weston sighed. "Relax awhile, sweetie. Think of your skin."

Groot's footsteps sounded on the gangway. He hadn't yet switched on the flashlight, and halfway to the quai he was swallowed by darkness.

The others peered after him.

Max had heard the note of appeal in Odile's voice, the half-stifled distress, and he hesitated, trying to make sense of it. But sense wouldn't come, nor could he reconcile her sudden apprehension with the moodiness that had preceded it, and he was just making up his mind to go below when, on the quai, something small—a rag, a rolled-up newspaper, a sodden bit of sponge—ignited and lifted into the air, seeming at first to rise straight up. He heard the slap of shoe leather on packed sand—two people running. Someone laughed.

The bottle came toward them in a shallow arc, trailing flame, then struck the wheelhouse and exploded. Fire splashed up from the wheelhouse roof. More fire streamed down onto the foredeck. In seconds the *Nachtvlinder* was burning.

"The hose!" Rachel called into the dark. "Turn on the hose, Groot!" Then, to Max, "Quick! There's an extinguisher on the port side."

He found it at once but could not, for several long seconds, detach it from its bracket.

"The blankets! Use the blankets!" said Odile, undraping hers from her shoulders as she ran. The others followed her and began slapping at the fire with their moth-eaten lap robes.

Rachel laid out the garden hose to starboard and called again for Groot to turn it on. She moved swiftly, resolutely, without panic.

Cursing himself for not having the vidcam to hand, Max pulled the pin on the extinguisher, squeezed the lever, and directed the chemical blast at the base of the burning wheelhouse. It had little effect. He squeezed harder. The flames fell back.

"Smother, don't fan," counseled the editor. He had rolled his blanket into a tight tube with which he flogged the foredeck fire. The others did likewise.

When at last the water came on, Rachel stood one step from the top of an aluminum stepladder and, half choking on the oily smoke, systematically hosed down the wheelhouse roof. The fire had not eaten far into the wooden superstructure—mostly it was the gasoline from the hurled bottle that burned—and gradually the flames began to yield. Groot reappeared with a bucket on a chain; he and Max worked in relay, filling the bucket from the river, pitching the water across the deck. The others continued to beat at small patches of resurgent flame with their blankets. And working together like this, vigilant and unspeaking, they were able finally to extinguish the fire.

*La fluviale* arrived some minutes later. While the officers questioned Groot about what had happened—repeatedly referring to the bottle of gasoline as *"la bombe"*—Odile and Rachel stood a little to one side, whispering. No, Groot said, he could think of no one who wished him or Rachel harm. No, he was not politically active, he avoided social causes. No, there had been no warnings, no threats, nothing at all out of the ordinary.

Odile and Rachel ceased their whispering and now looked on with an air of stoic hauteur, their faces expressionless.

Max thought, *I've been paying the wrong kind of attention.*

## CHAPTER 8

THAT WEEKEND, obeying an impulse that she dared not examine too closely, Odile took the train to Nantes to visit her father. He met her at the station in a distressed-looking Italian sports car she'd not seen before. Like most of the objects with which he surrounded himself, it suited him.

"So," he said. "You've come."

"You knew I would." Embracing him, she wondered if he'd lost weight.

Sebastien lived some distance outside Nantes in a quiet town called Vertou, and as he drove them there, leaving behind the small bustle of the city, continuing past the shopping malls and suburban housing tracts that had sprung up on its outskirts, Odile saw the land open out into fields and vineyards and little towns with churches, and she began to feel something like relief. *Here,* she told herself, *I'll be able to think.*

Her father had just returned from a three-week stint in Africa, and he told her about it as he drove. A geographer by training, he had been hired by the government of Mali to assess the environmental impact of a hydroelectric plant it proposed to build on the Niger. The undertaking was quixotic and grandiose in the sub-Saharan manner, almost certain to come to nothing, but it appealed to Sebastien's sense of social betterment. He was an *engagé* and Trotskyist of the old school, a natural contrarian. This last trait Odile had inherited in full, but, without the politics to give it shape, it expressed itself unpredictably. She had learned to live with it.

"The case of Mali is special," Bastien told her as he drove, "and it would seem that now, despite my best efforts, I am a specialist." He had a toothy smoker's smile that had always captivated her.

At the house, a small nineteenth-century stone structure two stories tall and roofed in blue slate, Odile retired to her bedroom to change clothes. Although this was not the house of her childhood—Sebastien had moved here only after her mother's death, five years ago—she had come to feel unexpectedly at home in it. Nestled amid a tumult of magnolia trees, now in brick-red bloom, the house was for her a kind of refuge, a place to seek shelter, and she often came here when Sebastien was away. When he was in residence, things were sometimes less restful.

She emerged from the house to find Sebastien in the back property, leaning a ladder against the old oak that marked its limit. The tree had been struck by lightning while he was in Africa, and its upper half was now split and splintered with one massive limb hanging off the trunk, broken but not detached, reaching almost to the ground. Sebastien climbed the ladder, chain saw in hand. When he started up the saw and its howl obliterated thought, Odile went back into the house.

His self-certainty, his aversion to small talk, this retreat into physical activity: all of it was deeply familiar to her. Opening the refrigerator, she found a bag of coffee beans, a quart of milk, some leeks, and three eggs. This, too, was familiar, and she decided to take the car into town for groceries.

The church bells struck four. Thin white clouds scudded overhead as she drove.

One summer afternoon when Odile was thirteen, she was with her best friend, an imaginative girl almost a year her senior, window-shopping amid the clothing boutiques, *parfumeries,* and leather-goods stores of downtown Nantes. At the time, Odile's parents were professors at the university, and though their income met their expenses, not much money was left over for nonessentials, and compared with her contemporaries she felt poorly turned out, lacking even the smallest tokens of adolescent chic. Her friend was sympathetic, and together they set out to remedy the situation. They began with easily pocketable items—lipsticks, tortoiseshell combs, sunglasses—but as the summer wore on and they became more confident, their shoplifting grew more ambitious. On the afternoon in question, they hesitated outside a designer boutique, inspecting a red silk dress that Odile particularly coveted. When her friend judged the moment to be right, they entered the shop. The friend's role was to distract the shopkeeper, a sharp-faced middle-aged woman with glasses, while Odile looked casually through the racks. When, with four or five scarves laid out on the counter before her, the friend asked to see yet another, Odile quickly turned her back and stuffed the dress under her shirt. The friend chose a scarf and paid for it, and the two girls left the shop together. They'd gone scarcely half a block when the shopkeeper caught up with them, grabbed each girl by an ear, and dragged them back to the store. The police were called, then the girls' parents. Sebastien arrived. After paying for the dress, he put the girls in his car and drove the friend home, all without uttering a word. When he and Odile were finally alone in the car, she in the backseat, he asked her why she stole. Odile shrugged. She didn't know. Was it the thrill? he suggested. No, not that. Maybe she had some kind of grudge against the world and its injustices? Not that, either. No grudge. Was it the clothes? he persisted. It was the clothes, wasn't it? Yes, she answered wretchedly, it was the clothes. Sebastien lit a cigarette and drove for awhile in silence. "Then," he said at last, "you will learn to sew." His eyes met hers in the rearview mirror. "Your mother will teach you," he added. And Odile burst into tears.

Nobody, least of all herself, could have imagined that at that moment she had found her future vocation. It proved to be a turning point, and she wondered how many such moments a single life might afford.

Parking the car in front of the post office, Odile extracted a string bag from her purse and went shopping for dinner. She was by now a familiar figure in the local business establishments, and at each stop—the baker's, the butcher's, the greengrocer's, the wine merchant's—she lingered to exchange a few words with the proprietor. Sebastien was well liked in Vertou, and everyone with whom Odile spoke inquired after him respectfully. Before his first African sojourn, a year ago, there had even been talk of his running for mayor. He hadn't discouraged the idea, but neither had he troubled himself over it, and in the end the incumbent had been reelected.

Odile got back to the house around half past six. The oak's damaged limb had been cut up for firewood, now stacked neatly against the tool shed. When she took the groceries into the kitchen, Sebastien appeared. "And now," he announced, grinning his satyr's grin, "one will have an aperitif."

They took their drinks in the living room, sitting side by side on a sofa facing the fireplace.

"You look very well," he said once he'd studied her.

"So do you," she answered.

He dismissed her words with a wave. "In Mali everyone is sick. It's normal. I have a little bit of what they have, and as you can see I've lost some weight. But that's all. It is not yet necessary to flatter me about my health."

"Good," she said, and sipped her pastis. "I'm happy to hear that."

"What about Orson Welles? Going from one success to another, I suppose?"

"Max is fine. He sends his best."

"Yes? Is he working?"

"Always. He's like you in that respect, remember?"

Sebastien sniffed dismissively, as if at the very idea of such a comparison. "Your husband doesn't know what work is. One thing I will say, though. I'd trade him a month of Mali for a day of filming Isabelle H. An extraordinary woman, truly. Tell me, what's she like?"

"Actually," Odile said, "Max put that project on hold for the time being. He wants to work out some new lighting ideas. He's shooting video."

"Ah yes, of course. Lighting ideas." Sebastien took a swallow of port and grimaced. "I should have known."

"What is it with you?" Odile demanded. "Max is everything you believe in: independent, idealistic, driven. He never does the easy thing or follows the conventional wisdom. Money means nothing to him except what he needs to make his films. He thinks for himself, and he's uncompromising. Why can't you accept that?"

Sebastien shrugged. "I don't know. It's irrational, isn't it?"

"You don't like him because he's American."

"But I do like him. I just don't respect him."

"Well, believe me," she said, getting up to check on dinner, "sooner or later you'll learn to."

By the time they sat down to eat, they were laughing over a bit of village gossip she'd picked up at the wine merchant's, and it was as if a crisis had passed.

Her father went to bed at ten. Later, she put on one of his sweaters and sat out back beneath the stars, letting her mind run free. Flashes of herself as a little girl were interspersed with other, less familiar images that at times seemed to have nothing to do with her. Two men playing chess, one of them laying his king on its side in wordless defeat. Some Italians and a German model named Nico in an American car, a white convertible, deliberately crashing it into the gate of a villa to get to a party that was all but over. Another woman, much older, contemplating a painting on an easel until the painting burst into flames.

Whatever had led Odile to lie to the Russians about Thierry—and she knew so little about him or his motives, hardly enough to conceal—the firebombing of the *Nachtvlinder* had rendered moot. Now she would be obliged to confront what she had unleashed, determine its nature, and, with little but her native stubbornness to go on, extract from it what vindication she could. The prospect made her uneasy. Yet mixed with this anxiety was a deeper response that she couldn't quite put out of her mind. She felt as though she had been given an opportunity, as inexplicable as it was rare, to help break the impasse at which Max found himself, both as a filmmaker and as a man. He thrived on adversity, his occupation required no less, and as long as she'd known him he had done what was necessary, whether for her or his work. Viewed from this perspective, the troubles she'd brought upon herself in Moscow, however tawdry and destructive in themselves, might yet be turned to advantage, if one kept an open mind. The prospect filled her with dark surmise.

Max was the only man she'd ever come across who seemed to know, instinctively and without deliberation, how to anticipate her needs, needs she often didn't recognize herself and would have disavowed on principle even if she had. From the very outset—that night in SoHo when she'd sought his help and he'd provided it, no questions asked, then or later— he'd seen and understood her whole. A trust had been established, fierce, wordless, almost arrogant in its certainty. Now, in her love for him, Odile wanted a chance to reveal to Max a part of his character that he himself might have overlooked, an untended capacity that might offer him—and them—something new in their life together, another level of existence. That an element of pride underlay this desire could not be doubted. And while she knew her pride to be a dangerous thing, perverse and not fully under her control, there were times when she had no choice but to trust it. This, too, had to be lived with.

She grew drowsy, allowing her thoughts to scatter until they were no longer thoughts but mere traces, then not even that.

A shooting star passed across the sky. She waited for another, and when it came she went gratefully back into the house, up the stairs to bed and sleep.


WITH ODILE STILL at her father's, Max took his Sunday-afternoon meal in the company of Eddie Bouvier and his fourteen-year-old daughter, Dominique, at their apartment in the Marais. The building, an eighteenth-century stone town house, stood on a narrow, twisting street that channeled the sounds of foot traffic and conversation up to where they sat. A shaft of pale sunlight crept across the dining table. Dominique held out her hand for Max's inspection.

"It's a bluebird," she said. "Papa hates it." Neatly positioned between her thumb and forefinger was a small tattoo of a bird taking flight. Max thought it surprisingly well rendered.

"Cool," he said, spearing the last of his veal cutlet. "Did it hurt?"

She shook her head serenely.

"In point of fact," Eddie explained, "this is a prison tattoo, recognized wherever there are convicts. It signifies that the bearer is a thief."

"Maybe a hundred years ago it did," Dominique confided to Max, "but now it has no meaning. It means I have a tattoo."

"You see what I'm up against," said Eddie.

After salad and dessert, Dominique, who had tickets to a death-metal concert at La Villette, asked to be excused. Kissing Max goodbye, she told him to say hello to Allegra for her, and he was obliged to notice yet again how nearly adult she had become. He recalled with guilt that he hadn't yet responded to his daughter's e-mail.

"In the end," said Eddie, when he and Max were alone, "you have to allow them their concerts, their revolting boys . . ." He shrugged. "One suffers, of course."

The two men retired to the living room for cigars and Armagnac.

In the thirty-six hours since the gasoline bomb had smashed against the *Nachtvlinder*'s wheelhouse, Max had tried to imagine a scenario that would explain the attack, or at least make it less improbable in the light of day. And he had gone further, seeking to link the event with the break-in at the apartment. He'd put his speculations to Odile before she left for Vertou, inviting her response. But though she agreed that it was possible to see a connection between the two incidents and didn't contradict him when he spoke of intimidation and harassment, systematic or otherwise, she added nothing useful to his imaginings and he let the subject drop.

Eddie said, "Are you working?"

"I'm shooting video. Nothing scripted." Max swirled his drink and inhaled the fumes. "Maybe it's a documentary, I don't know."

"Do you want to talk about it?"

"Nah. Too soon. I'm still trying to get a handle on it."

"Of course. No problem. But when you *are* ready, Max, I'm eager to have a look. As always."

"Thanks. I appreciate it." A short silence ensued while Max relit his cigar. Then, when a cloud of blue smoke again billowed around him, he added, "One thing, though."

"Yes?"

"I'm shooting in natural light only—outdoors, beside windows, wherever I can get an image. Maybe I'll include ambient electric too. I'm not sure yet. But the point is, no staged lighting, nothing cosmetic."

Eddie nodded. "More reality."

"There's a look to it, yes. I start there." At the thought of reality, Max grew abruptly restless. Getting to his feet, he strode across the room to the french windows, which opened onto a small masonwork balcony. In the street below, two Hasids were arguing in Yiddish. He watched as they lunged forward, knocking each other's hats off, yanking each other's temple locks.

He returned to his seat, his impatience only exacerbated by what he'd seen. "By the way, Eddie, did I tell you that there was a screening of *Fireflies* at Studio des Ursulines? Part of their first-film series."

"But this is good, Max, very good. They run an exceptional program. Useful people pay attention. Everything went well, I assume?"

"People seemed to like it," Max told him. "Anyway, I met a girl there, a film student. She said she had seen another version of *Fireflies,* one with a different ending. She said it was in rental distribution on video." He stubbed out his cigar. "That's not possible, is it?"

Eddie seemed genuinely shocked. "How could it be? It's out of the question. You didn't shoot a different ending, did you?"

"No, but these days, with digital this and that . . ."

"I'll call the distributors first thing tomorrow morning," Eddie assured him. "I promise you, it's nothing."

"Thanks, Eddie. I know I'm being stupid, but I can't get it out of my mind."

"Forget about it. Besides, you must realize it's a kind of compliment when rumors like that start circulating. People are impatient for more of your work, Max. In the absence of product, they fantasize."

"Don't we all," Max replied.

They had a laugh together.

After taking his leave, Max walked three blocks south to the Place des Vosges, found a bench, and sat for awhile in the dying amber light. Some young black men—Malian, by accent—were playing pickup soccer beside the equestrian statue of Louis XIII, his famous smirk frozen forever in stone. Two elderly ladies sat together knitting. Toddlers, pursued by their mothers, ran stubby legged across the lawn. And, cruising right by Max, three skinny white boys in their teens recited rap lyrics in unison: *Anutha day, anutha niggaz name in da newz.*

When it occurred to Max that he was putting off going home, he consulted his watch. Odile was due back on the eight-o'clock train from Nantes. Suddenly he longed for her company, wanted her to be at the apartment when he arrived. After a moment's thought, he abandoned his bench and the little park and headed east to the métro stop at Bastille. The music-and-electronics megastore on the Champs-Élysées stayed open till midnight, he recalled, and, at least in principle, carried cassettes or DVDs of all his films.

# CHAPTER 9

GABRIELLA SAT in Turner's office with an advance copy of next month's *ARTnews* in her lap. On the cover was a detail of one of the May Day flags, reproduced in a super-saturated red, with the appliquéd images of Marx, Lenin, and Andropov gazing stolidly heaven-ward. Yellow display type running across the lower right quadrant read: *The Return of the Unique Object? 20 Artists and Critics Respond.*

"Incredible!" Gabriella said. "How did you do it?"

"I didn't," Turner told her. "That's the beauty of the art world, so responsive when money's involved. And it almost always is."

She flipped through the magazine, chose an article at random, and began to read aloud. " 'After almost two decades in which contemporary art has been dominated by video, photography, film, computer code, and other infinitely reproducible mediums, the unique art object has been given a much-needed boost from a most unlikely quarter.' "

"Not at all bad," Turner observed, settling back in his chair. "Very old school and respectful, don't you agree? Now read the next one."

Gabriella ran her finger down the page. " 'Call it a neo-Duchampian coup or just another episode of cynical showmanship, but the exhibition 'Ten Untitled Objects,' currently on view at the Balakian Gallery in Chel-sea, is anything but what it appears to be.' " She frowned and skipped ahead. " 'Indeed,' " she went on, " 'the secret was out almost before the show opened. These large fabric works, meant to resemble antique flags of the Soviet Union, are widely thought to be the collaborative effort of two of the gallery's star artists, who, for reasons best known to themselves, have chosen not to lend their names to the exhibition.' " Gabriella looked up in annoyance. "But this is caca, no?"

"Maybe Ron's working a sideline," Turner conceded. "I'm not sure. But I do like it. And the other texts are all just as good. Major writers, blue-chip artists, the works."

"So what will happen next?"

"We'll see. I need to think about the larger scheme of things." He looked at his watch. "In the meantime, shall I take you to lunch?"

"Ah, no, I cannot. I have to meet this person." Gabriella rolled her eyes to suggest entanglements too exasperating for comment. "Tomorrow, though"—she brightened—"you may take me to that new place on La Boétie."

Turner spent the next hour returning phone calls. An inconveniently large part of his job involved currying favor with elderly men and women who owned desirable objects but for one reason or another lacked suitable heirs. Such people tended to be solitary, whether by design or circumstance, and they enjoyed pretending that Turner's attention was social, even personal, in nature. Their pride could be easily hurt if they felt they were being neglected, and they competed unabashedly for his time, yet it was always understood that in some fundamental sense he was their fool. Such were the rules of the game.

He was considering closing up for the afternoon when Odile appeared in the doorway, a little out of breath. She wore dark sunglasses and an orange-and-gray floral-patterned dress cut close at the hips.

"Hello," she said. "Am I interrupting?" Without waiting for an answer, she swept into the cluttered room, taking it in with a series of darting glances.

Turner rose to greet her. "What a surprise. How did you get up here?"

She shrugged. "Was someone supposed to stop me?"

A Benin bronze head that Gabriella had unpacked earlier caught her eye, and he watched as she went over to inspect it. Dark, cruel, and commanding, the African artifact had been set atop its shipping crate, polystyrene pellets strewn before it as though in offering, and Turner thought he saw Odile shudder as she contemplated this tableau.

"Beautiful, isn't it?" he said. "1550 AD, give or take. Excellent condition."

"So it's real, then?" She removed her sunglasses and turned to look at him.

"Very." He whisked the copy of *ARTnews* from the chair Gabriella had vacated. "Please, have a seat."

Instead she went to the window, parted the curtains, and peered down at the courtyard. "I thought we had an understanding."

"So we did. And I'm happy to report that your problem has been taken care of."

"Really? You think so?" She wandered over to the lightbox and switched it on. Turner had been sorting through color transparencies of the unsold flags, and their glow now gave Odile's features a ruddy cast. "Then you overestimate your influence."

"Oh, I'd hate to think that. Was there an incident?"

"Last Friday night someone threw a Molotov cocktail at me and my friends. It was dramatic and quite intimidating. The police came."

"I see. And what did you tell them?"

"Nothing." She sat down on a Shaker bench, next to a pile of old auction catalogs. "But this cannot continue. These people are crazy. I want my life back."

Resting his chin on his fist, he contemplated his visitor. She was agreeable to look at, more so than he'd thought, full at the hips but slim overall, with upturned breasts, a wide-set mouth, and large, cognac-colored eyes. She carried herself well. She projected sullen confidence and a willingness to engage. Yet it seemed to him that there was also something ascetic about her, an unplumbed capacity to do without, to withdraw, to reduce and simplify, to exist among essences or endure their absence. It was like a glimpse of another woman, one quite capable of indifference, even cruelty, and Turner quickened at the recognition.

"Maybe now would be a good time to tell me what these Russians really want from you," he said.

"They want to know where they can find Thierry Colin."

"Thank you. And do you have any idea where he is?"

"No." She folded her arms across her chest.

"No but what?"

"I saw him last at the station in Brest. We'd split up for customs—his suggestion. I took the bags through—my choice. Then he disappeared." She made a face. "He was very hungover."

"So as far as you know he never crossed into Poland."

She assented European style, with a quick intake of breath.

"What could have happened to him, then?" said Turner.

"I don't know. There was some kind of trouble at the station, a big crowd of people trying to get out, military police. Also, he had his wallet stolen right before we left Moscow, so I don't think he had much money."

"Passport?"

"He still had his passport, yes, I'm certain."

"Anything else you want to tell me?"

"No. Well, yes. He'd been talking on the train about whether it's possible to start a new life. He seemed to be speaking theoretically, but also with a kind of irony that I found very annoying. I was meant to find it annoying. He wanted to throw me off track."

Turner nodded sympathetically. "So he maneuvered you into taking charge of the flags and went his own way, probably with something that didn't belong to him. It's not unknown."

"Those guys want him very badly," she said.

"But here's what I wonder, Odile. Why haven't you told the Russians what you just told me? If that's all they want?"

She appeared genuinely taken aback by the question. Turner watched her swallow, open her mouth to speak, then abruptly shut it again. Following her gaze, he saw Gabriella standing in the doorway.

"Excuse me," she said. "I didn't realize you were busy."

"No, it's okay," Turner answered. "Odile, this is my assistant, Gabriella. Gabriella, Odile."

As the two women considered each other, an idea came to him. He supposed it was the opportunity for which he'd been waiting. "I'll tell you what, Gabriella. Why don't you take the rest of the afternoon off? We can deal with the bronze tomorrow."

"Really? Are you sure?"

"Positive."

"All right, if you say so." She looked at him dubiously. "See you in the morning." She said goodbye to Odile and left.

"Look," Turner said, "I understand about the Russians. Guys like that, you don't want to give them anything. All I'm suggesting, Odile, is that next time, in the interest of your peace of mind . . ."

She nodded.

"Besides, as I mentioned, I think you'll find that you've seen the last of them. Sometimes it takes a little while for word to filter down, but the person I talked to is highly regarded. People don't often cross him."

"Thank you," Odile managed to say. She didn't look at all convinced.

"My pleasure." He glanced at his watch. "Now. When was the last time you had your portrait painted?"

"My portrait?"

"Yes. An artist friend is painting my portrait, and I'm due at her studio for a sitting. She's an exceptional woman—in her seventies, but she sees everything—and I'd very much like you to meet her. In fact, I'd consider it a personal favor."

"Oh, but this would be difficult. I . . ."

She would object, pleading prior commitments, making excuses, stalling, but Turner knew she would come along to Céleste's apartment. Such moments had their own logic, a kind of internal necessity. It was as if, he thought, they were meant to be.

UPSTAIRS AT HIS STUDIO, in the screening room, Max was watching *Fireflies* for the fifth time that afternoon. He had bought all seven copies that the megastore had had in stock, two on videocassette, five on DVD, and was playing them at six times the normal speed, one after another, watching for anomalies. It was oppressive and fruitless work that left him feeling distinctly humiliated.

When the phone rang, he paused the film and took the call. It was Eddie Bouvier, who'd spoken with the video distributors of Max's films and been assured that all was as it should be. Sales since the release of *White Room/Black Room* had risen substantially, and there was even talk of rereleasing the four earlier titles if the uptick continued. Max thanked him, bookmarked the DVD he'd been watching, and went downstairs.

"So?" asked Jacques. "Did you find any improvements?" He sat behind the editing console, wearing a backward-turned baseball hat and a T-shirt that had *Mal Vu, Mal Dit*—Badly Seen, Badly Said—printed across the chest.

"Nothing," said Max. "There's nothing to find. I'm crazy to look."

"To look is never crazy. Someone told me that."

"Right." It irritated Max unreasonably to hear his own words tossed back at him. "Listen, stick around, okay? I may need you later."

At the apartment, he washed his face and flushed his eyes with saline droplets. He felt sullied by the afternoon's pursuits, with their overtones of spite and retrospection, and he cast about for how to redeem what was left of the day. Then, remembering Allegra's e-mail, he booted up the computer, launched the telecom software, and, after sitting a few moments blankly before the screen, began to type.

*Dear Allegra*, he wrote. *Thanks for your message, which I really appreciated. You've got your mother's wit and preemptive good sense. Lucky girl.*

*I was sorry to hear about your friend Alison's troubles. You're right, I really did like her: she's smart and seemed to be a real friend to you. I won't embarrass us both by giv-*

*ing you the standard-issue drug lecture at this point. Let's just say that she showed bad judgment in letting that guy stash his pills in her locker. Legally that makes her an accomplice, and juvenile court is no place anyone wants to be. Enough said. I hope things work out for her.*

*About the summer.* Here Max hesitated, choosing his words carefully. *I understand your wanting to be with your friends, especially when you're about to make the move to upper school. You've got big changes coming up and exciting times. But family is important too.* Again he paused. Just by using that word he was laying himself open to the whole arsenal of sighs, sulks, and ironic silences that Allegra deployed to remind him of his perfidy and to chastise herself, a girl so catastrophically wanting, as he knew she sometimes suspected, that she didn't even deserve a father. But Max persisted.

*Your mother and I love you very much, and you will always be our daughter. Nothing can change that, sweetness. So I'm thinking about you, and I'd like to find a plan for us to be together this summer. Maybe you could spend half of it in New York, half of it here. I'll call later and we can talk about it, okay?* He added a paragraph of small news, a word of love from Odile, then signed the note and hit the send button.

CÉLESTE PULLED TWO PORTRAITS of Turner from the storage rack and propped them up against the adjacent wall. The strains of a Shostakovich string quartet wafted in from the front room, and the scent of linseed oil hung in the air like ripe fruit.

Lighting a cigarette, Céleste contemplated her work. "You know, he's not so easy to paint," she told Odile. "The features are strong, and the hands. But one senses right away that this man—"

"I can hear every word you're saying," Turner called from the kitchen, where he was attempting to replace an electrical switch on the water heater.

"—that he isn't comfortable in his skin. He has several methods of hiding this, all of them convincing enough to anyone but himself. The problem becomes, how to capture this richness? Because to be fallible to oneself is a kind of richness, no? It is human."

Odile approached one of the portraits. Turner was depicted standing nude against a whitewashed brick wall, his arms folded across his chest, his brown-black eyes glistening with a mix of bravado and something that Odile didn't rush to identify. "You must know him well," she said.

Céleste gave her a sideways glance. "To me it's like traveling. For the first twenty-four hours in an unfamiliar city, one can see and understand its entirety. Afterward, one may live for many years in that same city before understanding it again." She blew smoke toward the ceiling. "With people it is the same. I painted that one when Turner first arrived in Paris. I'm satisfied with it."

Shifting her attention to the other portrait, Odile saw that it had been done some time after the first. Turner, again nude, was seated beside a green metal café table, against a cream-colored backdrop. He held a glass of pastis in one hand and was unshaven, studiously casual. About the eyes, a smudge of fatigue. He appeared disconsolate.

"That was two years later," said Céleste, "right before he began working for the auction house."

"I'm not sure I would have recognized him," Odile said.

From the kitchen came the sound of metal clattering to the floor. A string of curses followed, then another small crash.

Céleste smoked and studied the portrait. "It is not a success, this painting. Maybe I was distracted by the obvious. I don't know."

"But not at all," said Odile, surprising herself. "Here the obvious is true. You caught him with his guard down. A rare moment."

"Yes?" Céleste kept her eyes on the portrait. "Then you also must know him well."

"No," Odile replied. "We're only acquaintances."

Céleste was returning the paintings to the storage rack when Turner appeared, holding the faulty switch in one hand, a screwdriver in the other. "You know, Céleste, I'm really not the ideal electrician." He paused, as though waiting to be relieved of his chore. "All right," he said at last. "Fine. Is there a hardware shop nearby?"

"Go right out the gate, then right again," Céleste told him.

He looked from one woman to the other, shook his head, and left.

"I tease him because he's spoiled," Céleste explained. "But also charming, and I enjoy being charmed. Don't you?"

"Not so much, no. I don't have the patience for it."

Céleste's deeply lined face expanded in a smile of pure delight. "What a pleasure to meet you, Odile." Her blue eyes glistened. "May I offer you coffee?"

SEATED AT THE KITCHEN TABLE with that afternoon's *Le Monde* spread out before him, Max was startled by the repeated dull thump of someone dragging a plastic bin over the cobblestones below. It was Rachel, come to drop off their garbage. He cranked open a window and invited her up.

"Don't you want some footage of me hauling trash?" she asked when she reached the top of the stairs. "It's, like, so representative."

Because the Seine was not legally part of Paris, refuse generated on the river could not be disposed of within city limits, and clandestine dumping was universal. "Maybe later," Max replied. "What I need now is your company and sweet good nature."

Miming a curtsy, Rachel smiled at him and crossed the room to install herself on the sofa. She wore white canvas sneakers, faded black jeans cut low on her hips, and a red jersey top that stopped well short of her navel. Her jet-black hair was up, carelessly gathered in a clip but parted at the scalp in a zigzag pattern Max hadn't seen before. Her heavy black-framed glasses perched lopsidedly on her nose, slowly sliding down until she was obliged to push them back up again. Even sitting down, she looked taller than her actual six feet.

"How's the *Nachtvlinder*?" Max asked. "Get her cleaned up?"

"Pretty much. One part of the wheelhouse roof is burned through, but we were really lucky. It could've been much worse."

"Definitely. What if we hadn't been there to put it out? There'd be nothing left, right?"

Rachel shuddered. "Let's not visualize."

"Very strange, though," Max said, shaking his head. "I wonder who did it."

"Groot thinks it was someone who wanted our berth," Rachel replied. "All the legal places to dock in Paris are taken, and there's a waiting list that goes on forever. Maybe this person got tired of waiting."

"Maybe. But if somebody really wanted to burn you out, wouldn't he pick a time when you weren't there? The hose, the fire extinguisher, all of us sitting there in plain sight—it must have been obvious, even in the dark, that we could put out the fire before it did any serious damage. Whoever was responsible had to have known that."

"So what are you saying?"

"I'm saying this was meant to intimidate you and your guests, not burn up your boat."

She smiled wanly. "Well, whichever, it didn't work. That's all I care about."

"You're a pragmatist. An outcome-type person."

"That's right," she said. "I'm an American like you, remember?"

They laughed together. It was an unspoken imperative of expatriate life in Paris not to cluster with fellow countrymen. Doing so suggested a lack of moral resources or, worse, of wit, and Max sometimes felt that flouting this rule lent an extra edge to his interest in Rachel. They were each the only American that the other saw with any regularity.

"At least I'm married to a French girl," Max said. "What kind of credibility do you get from Groot? People here think the Dutch are all pornographers and pot smokers."

Rachel laughed. "Poor Groot. But really, to be fair, I've never understood why the French have this reputation for rudeness. They're so nice to me, always offering their help. I sit down in a café, open a menu, and right away somebody's translating for me and telling me not to order the pig's feet."

"You fulfill a national fantasy," he said. "The American ingénue. Jeanie Seberg in *Breathless*."

"Right. I'm so innocent."

"But you're not, of course. What people respond to lies much deeper. It's just that they need an excuse to succumb to their own good intentions."

"Unlike the average California girl," Rachel added, "who needs an excuse not to."

Max went to the kitchen and poured two glasses of mineral water. He could hear the widow from the building immediately behind the mews remonstrating with the couple next door, a jeweler and a contractor who were raising their roof by half a story. The widow claimed that the heightened chimney would send smoke directly into her kitchen window. The couple argued that the prevailing winds blew in the other direction. Hundreds of bitter words, spread out over days, had been expended on the subject.

Returning with the drinks, Max found Rachel polishing her glasses with a lavender tissue. He sat down opposite her and when she finished, said, "I've been trying to think of just how to ask you this. It's a bit awkward, and I don't want to overstep." He looked carefully into her deep blue eyes.

"Go ahead, Max."

"I guess it boils down to this: if Odile were in some kind of trouble—a tight spot that for one reason or another she didn't want me to know about—would you tell me if I asked?"

Rachel didn't blink. "Probably not, no. Not if she didn't want me to."

"Right. That's the only decent answer, isn't it?"

"Sure, a friend's a friend."

"But if the situation got out of hand, and she couldn't deal with it herself?"

Shifting in her seat, Rachel began to look uncomfortable. "Max, I'm sure that if she were in real trouble, she'd tell you, okay?"

"It's been on my mind."

"Just stop worrying. I mean it."

They drank their water and talked of other things. Someone they both knew had recently been arrested for identity theft—credit card and telecom fraud in three time zones. A sous-chef with a wife and two children, he wasn't at all the type, but neither Max or Rachel could think of much to do for him.

"IT IS NOT SO OFTEN that I have a visitor who would appreciate these," Céleste said, "but when you mentioned you were a designer . . ."

Odile nodded. "They're beautiful."

The two stood side by side in Céleste's bedroom with the closet open and several items of antique couture laid out on the bed. A gown of golden silk, pleated in a twist. Another of black lace, embroidered with hundreds of tiny seed pearls. A scoop neck burgundy dress, a midnight-blue suit, a bustier in brocade, a backless dress in emerald taffeta. Odile studied them all, lingering over the details. Here was a treasure trove of design ideas, and even as she admired these clothes, each item custom-made, she saw how to adapt them, simplify them, take them in different directions. She reached out to touch a dress of jade-green silk, wrapped at the front and secured with a dozen hidden fasteners.

"Would you like to try it on?" Céleste asked.

Odile kicked off her shoes, stripped to her underwear, and slipped into the dress. She and Céleste were still struggling with the fasteners when Turner, his duty now discharged, stuck his head into the room.

"Lovely," he said, looking Odile over. Then to Céleste, "Are we going to paint today, because if not . . ."

Céleste stopped what she was doing and went over to inspect Turner, drawing him into the room, circling him as she looked. "You didn't lose the kilo," she concluded.

"There was no kilo."

She shook her head grimly. "Something is not right. I'm going to set that painting aside for awhile and let it breathe." Turning back to Odile, she seemed to assess the situation and, after a moment's thought, announced, "This afternoon, with her permission, I would like to paint Odile."

Odile pushed the closet door shut and regarded herself in the mirror bolted to its front. Not infrequently she felt her true self to be obscured by her appearance—Max understood this well—and she'd been intrigued by the claims Turner had made for Céleste's insight. Meeting the older woman's eyes in the mirror, she said, "Yes, why not. I'll wear the dress."

Céleste set her up on the sofa, helping her to find the most natural pose, and after several tries Odile positioned herself upright in the middle. The green dress was bright against the maroon upholstery, her pale skin luminous.

"It is more relaxed to lean back," Céleste suggested. "Yes, like that. Good."

Turner sat astride a folding chair, watching the choreography unfold. Odile was keenly aware of his gaze but refused to let him spoil the moment. For whatever reason, she found sustenance in Céleste's attention. It seemed to be something she'd been waiting for.

"Now, the dress." Céleste approached. "If one were to undo the front..."

Without hesitation Odile unhooked all the fasteners so it fell open like a dressing gown. Céleste came forward, slipped the fabric off one shoulder, then the other, letting the upper part of the dress slide down to gather in the crooks of Odile's arms. Stepping back to survey the effect, she frowned. "The brassiere and panties. Please, it is better you take them off."

Odile threw Turner a defiant look, then stood and did as she was told. When she sat back down and arranged the dress as before, bodice at her elbows, skirt open to frame her naked hips and thighs, she felt quite at ease.

"Perfect," Céleste proclaimed. "That's it exactly." Retiring to the spot where she'd set up a blank canvas, with Turner beside her in his chair, she produced a stick of charcoal and began to sketch in the forms of what she saw.

For a time the only sound was the muted scratch of charcoal on canvas. The music had stopped. No one spoke.

And although Odile was aware of Céleste's eyes on her, and secondarily of Turner's, she let her own gaze bypass them and focus instead on the expanse of rooftop Paris framed by the windows beyond. Crisp sunlight illuminated chimney pots, dormers, petunias in flower boxes, bedspreads and throw rugs hung out to air. A man in a snap-brim hat drew a tape measure across a balcony ledge and squinted at the hatch marks. A cat pounced.

Odile thought: *It's out of my hands.*

AFTER MAX HAD SEEN RACHEL to the door and said goodbye, he went back to the kitchen and made a pot of coffee. Their conversation had left him in a reflective frame of mind, and as he sat by the upstairs window, waiting for his cup to cool, he looked out over the narrow courtyard and began to brood.

If he was serious about Rachel as a film subject, he would soon have to find the narrative framework to support his scrutinies. How closely it might correspond to actual events was entirely up to him, at least at this point, but that didn't mean, despite what the filmgoing public might believe, that there wasn't a right way and a wrong way to go about it. Choosing what reality to be true to: everybody had to do it sooner or later. But it was recognizing when the moment of choice had arrived that counted.

He was pouring himself another cup of coffee when the phone rang, a single long note indicating the direct line from his studio. He took the call. "You absolutely must see this, Max," Jacques said. "It's just how that girl described it."

"What is?"

"The other ending to *Fireflies*. I've found it."

# CHAPTER 10

IT IS DUSK. The protagonist brings his battered sports car to a screeching halt on West Street, where a half-ruined pier juts nine hundred feet into the Hudson. At the end of the pier a woman stands silhouetted against the dying light, her back to him, her arms folded, her hair lifted in the wind. Tied up alongside her: a vintage motor yacht freshly painted white. In the distance: sirens. The man runs toward the woman at full speed while the camera, which has been pursuing him in a tracking shot, stops partway down the pier to follow the rest of the action from a distance.

The woman turns to face him. They begin to argue, though their words aren't audible on the soundtrack, given over to ambient urban noise: traffic, the sirens, a passing boom box. The argument continues until she finally reaches out and covers the man's mouth with her hand. She says a few measured words, and when she withdraws her hand the two appear to be at peace. He climbs aboard the boat, goes below, and emerges a moment later onto the pier with a large duffel bag, obviously quite heavy, slung over his shoulder. Without looking at him, the woman boards the boat and disappears below. The man heaves the duffel bag into the river, and the splash it makes, along with the watery sounds that follow, replaces everything else on the soundtrack. He follows the woman onto the boat. She is now heard in voice-over, very near to the ear, with only the gurgling river water also audible. "It isn't really love, it's the illusion of love ... It ends badly ... Well, no. Finally, it ends well." The boat starts up and pulls slowly away from the pier, headed for the bay and open sea. "Or"—the camera rises and, from a vantage point high in the air and still rising, observes the boat as it accelerates, the long drawn-out V of its wake phosphorescent in twilight—"it ends badly." Roll credits.

Max ejected the DVD.

In the two days since Jacques discovered the sequence—it was on the last of the five disks, the only one Max himself hadn't inspected—they had both viewed it repeatedly. Neither found any further alterations to the film, whose overall running time had been increased by only a minute and fifty-six seconds. Still, as Marie-Claire had so confidently announced at Studio des Ursulines, the revamped ending did substantially change the meaning of the film.

While the contents of the discarded duffel bag remained ambiguous—the story structure allowed for two possibilities, conceivably three—its existence had been firmly established by Max himself in a lingering shot halfway through the film. He'd shown the bag open, completely unzipped, on the floor of the woman's apartment, while she and the male protagonist walked back and forth across the frame, talking to each other over their shoulders. In post-production he'd considered cutting the scene—for carrying more tone than meaning—but in the end found he liked the effect. So, apparently, had his phantom revisionist.

Between them, Max and Jacques had worked up a hypothetical model for how the add-on footage might have been synthesized. Using wire-frame imaging, micro-slice sound technology, and a high-speed computer, any reasonably proficient video editor could have created it in the studio over a short weekend. Even the aerial shot, which would seem to present the most difficulties, could've been done on the computer, assuming the maker had access to stock images of New York seen from above, images readily available, Max happened to know, on technical DVDs. From a mechanical standpoint, the whole process was almost laughably simple. It was the human element, the who and why, that eluded him and aroused his creative appetites.

"Max? Can I come up?" Odile's newly solicitous tone cheered him. Over the past two days she'd seemed happier, less distracted, more relaxed than he'd seen her in weeks. She had even sketched out a few new design ideas—always a good sign.

"Hurry!" he called down to her. "Duplicity! Copyright infringement! Fraud!"

She arrived, wearing a green sundress that he liked and smiling her slightly snaggled smile. "Theft," she added, and plumped herself down in his lap.

They had been through this cycle of tension and relief countless times, the breath of marriage as they understood it: lengthy tethers, mutual regard, a limit reached, a rush to reconcile. Max brought his nose close to his wife's temple and inhaled her scent.

"So," she said, drawing back to see his face, "do you think we'll find this person, this . . . what to call him? This vandal of your film?"

"Vandal. I like that. No, I don't think we'll find him. The standard procedure in a case like this, what everyone always tells you, is to follow the money. Who benefits from the crime? But here there's no money to follow; I didn't make all that much on *Fireflies* myself. So what's to be gained sixteen years later from tampering with the end?"

"Max." She nuzzled his neck.

"What is it?"

"*Fireflies* is brilliant, just as you made it."

"Thanks, Odile. I'm glad you think so."

"It's not an opinion. It's a fact."

"All the better."

She kissed him pensively—at the collarbone, the neck, behind the ear—then fell still, as if she'd just asked a question.

"Lately I have this sense," said Max, "that everything I've already done keeps changing, while whatever future I have is fixed. A regressive thought, I know, primitive, sub-scientific, ignorant. And yet I have it. What does it mean, I wonder?"

"It means you're trying to avoid thinking about death," she said.

"Death?"

"Yes. You give the past the qualities of the future because when you consider the future you see fixity. Fixity is death."

"Touché." He tucked a hand between her left arm and breast as he held her. "And you? What's your topic? You seem happier lately."

She shrugged. "I told you, I've decided to stop worrying. We've had our share of criminal events—bad luck, maybe, but even bad luck runs out. Now I want to concentrate on work and ordinary pleasure."

"Happiness," he suggested.

"Sure. Why not?" She pressed her forehead to his. "Although, as Bastien likes to say, *Le bonheur n'est jamais gai.*"

" 'Happiness is never cheerful,' yes. How totally French."

"But also true," she said matter-of-factly. Gently disengaging herself, she stood up and walked over to a long worktable set against the east wall.

With a cross-armed gesture she reached down, pulled her dress off over her head, and, boosting herself up onto the edge of the table, sat there naked, swinging her legs, waiting for him.

Max undressed without hurry. When he came to her, she leaned back on her palms and opened her thighs to him. "Anyway," she said, quivering as he kissed the corner of her mouth, her throat, her breast, "to be cheerful is not at all natural."

Later, when Odile had dressed and gone, he brought a chair over to the worktable and examined the packaging of the rogue DVD under a magnifying glass, using a legitimate copy for comparison. He'd never liked the cover design, which featured a color photograph, not his own, of a five-gallon glass jug full of real fireflies, a swirl of them passing up through its narrow mouth into a midnight-blue sky. No actual fireflies figured in his film, and Max had objected strenuously to this misrepresentation. Marketing had been unimpressed by his arguments.

Now, with the real and counterfeit DVD boxes laid out before him, Max noticed that in the latter the cover image had picked up a distinctly greenish tinge; otherwise the front sides of the two were identical. Opening the boxes, Max removed the booklets that accompanied the disks. The same stills from the film, along with a short critical essay, appeared in both editions; he vetted the text line by line and found nothing amiss.

Flipping the boxes over, he inspected the copy on the back. It was oddly punishing work to examine one's own product for signs that it was actually someone else's. Yet he persevered, reading the reviewers' blurbs, the plot summary, the credits, the warnings and advisories, each layer of text printed in smaller type than the one above it, so that finally, even with the magnifying glass, he began to have difficulty making out the words. It occurred to him that he was probably the first person ever to try.

Just as he was about to give up, Max noticed a small asymmetry in the two editions' last line of type. Bringing the desk light closer, squinting through the magnifying glass, he willed his eyes to focus. He tilted the light, trying to eliminate the glare of the plastic jacket. It was the copyright line: the copyright symbol and date followed, in the authentic version, by the name of his production company. In the other version, though, his company wasn't mentioned. In its place appeared the words "La Peau de l'Ours," followed by an address in the twelfth arrondissement.

"La Peau de l'Ours," said Max aloud. The Skin of the Bear. He knew of nothing by that name.

Twenty minutes later, the address in hand, he emerged from the métro at Ledru-Rollin. This part of Bastille, south of rue Faubourg-Saint-

Antoine and north of the river, had yet to be fully gentrified, and the mix of ancient commercial concerns, recently converted loft spaces, and cafés both old and new made the area agreeably unpredictable, block by narrow block. A few light-industrial enterprises—metalworks, spinning mills, printers—still clung to life, but they were obviously clearing out, with artists, designers, and young professionals rushing in. The upper floors of many buildings had plants or curtains in the windows.

Pedestrian traffic was heavy—it was lunch hour—and several times Max had to abandon the sidewalk for the street. There seemed to be an inordinate number of Koreans around, clumped in tour groups and taking photographs. He walked past them. He looked for shop signs, street names, and numbers. A tremendously fat woman waiting at a bus stop farted loudly as he passed, then began humming to herself.

When he found the address given on the DVD box—an eighteenth-century limestone building with the standard six stories—he saw nothing that might conceivably call itself La Peau de l'Ours. The ground floor was mostly taken up by a real-estate agency, with photos of desirable local properties displayed in its vitrines. Also on the ground floor, squeezed in at the north end, were a Judaica bookstore and a tobacconist. Max double-checked the address, then peered through the window of the agency. The place was deserted. At the door a cardboard clock face with metal hands invited him to suppose that the proprietors would return in thirty-five minutes. Spotting a café across the street, he decided to wait.

Taking an outdoor table, Max ordered a draft beer. He was halfway through it when a woman he didn't know—blond, thin, tattooed on one shoulder with a wheel of many spokes—stopped at his table and addressed him in French.

"Are you alone?" she asked.

"Yes."

"Do you want company?"

"No," he answered truthfully.

"Good," she said. "Neither do I." And with that, though several other tables were available, she sank into the seat opposite him. Rummaging through her backpack, paying him no further attention, she appeared at once utterly preoccupied and obscurely resentful. He watched her produce a notebook and fountain pen, which she placed before her on the marble tabletop. When the waiter arrived, she ordered a grenadine. Then, seemingly oblivious to Max's presence, she opened the notebook to where she'd left off and began writing furiously in green-black ink.

Ignoring her, Max kept his eye on the building across the street. He had not until now considered how to approach La Peau de l'Ours, should such a thing actually present itself, but it did occur to him that litigious posturing was probably not the smartest tactic. His curiosity had been piqued, and if he expected to satisfy it to any appreciable degree, a bit of flair would likely be necessary. Maybe, he thought, he should introduce himself as a furrier.

Some minutes later, apparently content with her efforts, his visitor closed her notebook and put down her pen. She looked at Max quizzically, as if noticing him for the first time. Then, with a hint of challenge, she smiled at him.

"Did you get it all down?" he asked, indicating the notebook with a lift of his chin.

"Enough, I hope."

"That's the trick of things, isn't it? Enough. Knowing what to put in, what to leave out. Enough is the secret of a life well lived, don't you agree?"

"Yes, of course. Although one must allow that excess has its advocates too." She gathered her hair in her hands and brought it forward over her shoulder in a twist. "You are looking for an apartment? I saw you at the window."

"I'm not sure what I'm looking for, now that you mention it. Have you ever heard of something called La Peau de l'Ours?"

"Is it a nightclub?"

"I don't think so. I was given that address, supposedly a video distributor or something like that. A film company, maybe."

"I see. So you're a filmmaker?"

"Yes. And you're, what, a graduate student?"

She nodded once. "Slavic studies."

Max thought he saw a ghost of her earlier smile flicker across her features, but an instant later he wondered if he'd imagined it. He held out his hand. "I'm Max."

"Véronique," she said.

But as she uttered her name, Max saw a man unlock the door across the street and, preceded by the woman who accompanied him, disappear inside. He had the impression that they were arguing. "Well," he said, "I see that my bears have arrived." Getting to his feet, he put down enough cash to cover their bill. "But I've very much enjoyed talking to you, Véronique."

She shrugged. "I come here sometimes."

He said goodbye and crossed the street.

The door had been left ajar, so Max, pushing it open, entered with unintended stealth. He found the front office deserted. From somewhere in back came the voices of the couple he'd seen from the café. They weren't quarreling, but speaking in anxious tones, their words sometimes overlapping. He lingered in the front office and pretended to study the splash-lit photographs pinned to the wall.

"I still can't believe it," she was saying. "Of all people."

"Everyone has a dream," he said.

"But what will we say if they come to us? They'll think we knew."

"It doesn't matter. We knew nothing, remember?"

"You think the truth carries any weight in an affair like this? They'll run us out of business at the very least. Dump our bodies in the Seine."

"Don't be stupid."

"Stupid? Who suggested him in the first place? Why are we even involved in this?"

"You said you wanted to expand the business, right? Good. This is how it's done. A favor for a favor. How did I know he was going to disappear?"

"But he's your cousin, Sylvain!"

"Enough. You're giving me a headache."

Realizing that the conversation was coming to an end, Max walked silently back to the front door and pushed it shut with the heel of a hand. "Hello!" he called out pleasantly. "Anyone here?"

The woman emerged first, a strained smile on her face. With her compact body, the clipped precision with which she moved, and her closely shorn brown hair, she had a coiled efficiency that to Max suggested disappointments gamely overcome. He took it as cause for caution. "Good afternon," the woman said in turn. "How may we help you?"

"My wife and I," Max began, "are thinking of moving, and I thought I'd get an idea of what rents are running lately. Here, I mean, in Bastille."

"Very well. And what price range are you looking for?"

"Under twenty thousand. Let's say eighteen thousand francs a month, plus or minus."

She frowned. "Difficult, but perhaps not impossible. Let me see what I have here." From a shelf behind the desk, she pulled down two loose-leaf notebooks, one for the fourth arrondissement, the other for the twelfth. "Have you considered buying?"

But before Max could answer, her male colleague emerged from the back. No taller than the woman but noticeably younger, he regarded Max with an assessing eye and introduced himself as Sylvain Broch. "You have come to the right place."

"I hope so," Max said. "Your agency has been highly recommended to me."

The woman, Madame Leclère, led him to a green leather sofa set diagonally across one corner of the office, a glass-topped coffee table positioned before it on a kilim. There she laid open the first of the notebooks, and for the next twenty minutes they leafed through the current offerings, sometimes stopping while she listed the amenities of those she thought he ought to be interested in. Seated at a nearby desk, Broch worked the phone.

When Max had had enough, he thanked her for her help and got to his feet. Broch had finished with his phone calls. Together they walked him to the door.

"You see," she said, "you ask too much for your price range. It is necessary to be more flexible."

"Thank you, Madame. Maybe I'll try again in a week or so." Max had his hand on the doorknob, but then, as if in afterthought, he turned back toward the two realtors. "This *is* La Peau de l'Ours, isn't it?"

"La Peau de l'Ours?" the woman cried. "No, no, no! You see, Sylvain! What did I tell you?"

"What my colleague means to say," Broch explained, "is that this other establishment you mention has nothing to do with us, nothing at all, other than having once occupied these premises, long before our tenancy." He shrugged sadly. "It is confounding. Sometimes we still get their mail."

"But is it true that La Peau de l'Ours also handles real estate?" Max ventured to ask.

"Unfortunately, we know nothing at all about their business."

"I see," said Max. "Please accept my apologies." He started to turn away. "Goodbye, then."

*"Au revoir!"* they both said immediately.

As he left, he felt their eyes on his back. Véronique had abandoned the café. He walked the length of the block without undue haste, then turned the corner and kept on going.

# CHAPTER 11

SEATED HALF CLAD on Céleste's maroon sofa, Odile by degrees began to say things that she knew bordered on the reckless. Her trip to Moscow, Thierry's disappearance, her Russian stalkers. The fire-bombing of the *Nachtvlinder*. Céleste attended her fully, laying down the first layer of paint in reds, yellows, and off-whites.

"So finally," Odile said, "when I was out of ideas, I asked Turner to put a stop to these Russians and their stupid games. Can he do that, do you think?"

"Probably. He's very well connected." Céleste held the brush up vertically before one eye, checking her subject's proportions. "Also he likes you. Maybe he's a small bit smitten."

Odile was intrigued despite herself. "Really? With me, the vagabond dressmaker?"

"He sees you as a kindred spirit, I think. Are you attracted to him?"

"No. Anyway, he knows I'm married."

"Married! What difference does that make?"

Odile smiled. "You haven't met my husband."

"No, but I've had husbands of my own." Céleste squeezed a curl of alizarin crimson onto the glass plate that served as her palette. "Is yours very jealous?"

"No more than most. But he hates tedium. This is his great advantage."

"Ah," Céleste said, "then everything is possible." Tilting her head, she resumed her inspection. "Now would you please keep your gaze directed out the window? And don't drop your chin. Good."

The light around Odile began to change, going from nickel gray to silver as the morning clouds burned off. She blinked, her eyes grew moist, she slipped into a luminous reverie.

And then it was as if she were viewing the world through a surveillance camera, one that looked down not on Céleste's studio but on the vestibule of what seemed to be a place of entertainment—a small theater, perhaps, or an after-hours nightclub. A crowd of well-dressed people were waiting to be admitted. Red velvet ropes held them in check, and they were speaking atop one another in a Slavic-sounding language; silver flasks were being passed back and forth, and there was intermittent laughter. Then a woman's high heels sounded in a quickened staccato and Odile saw herself, or a likeness of herself, still from the overhead angle, hurry into the vestibule from the street. She was wearing Céleste's jade-green dress and appeared quite out of breath. *Please,* she heard herself tell the burly man behind the velvet rope, *there is a man following me.* Without a word the bouncer unhooked the rope and let her pass. She pushed through the red leather padded door into whatever lay beyond, club or theater, then the scene fractured into zigzag static and at once went black.

Odile's eyes flew open. "I fell asleep," she said, sitting up and taking in her surroundings. "Was I out long?"

"Thirty seconds, not more. Do you feel all right?"

She felt as if she'd just had a full night's rest. "I'm fine," she said. "Shall we continue?"

And so they did, working in silence, until early afternoon. Céleste had prepared a charcuterie plate and salad for lunch, but Odile politely declined, saying she had an appointment. She didn't ask to see the portrait in its current state, nor did Céleste invite her to look. After making a date for the next sitting, one week hence, they embraced and parted company.

Bursting out onto the street, Odile was seized by the sudden human turbulence around her. A man on a motor scooter called out to her as he passed. Two Islamic women in head scarves made a wide detour around a miniskirted girl walking a wet-nosed dog. Where Céleste's street intersected rue Saint-Jacques, students were collecting signatures on behalf of undocumented aliens.

Making a right onto rue Soufflot, skirting the Panthéon, she considered and then dismissed her blackout episode at Céleste's. The portrait sitting had left her energized, confident. Buoyed by this new, nearly accidental friendship, she wondered again at the passivity with which she had lately been waiting on events. Such negligence, so unlike her, suddenly struck her as an invitation to calamity. She crossed the street and turned left. Two blocks east, Thierry Colin's last known place of domicile entered her field of vision.

It was a narrow white-brick apartment building, recently renovated, with a smoked-glass entry and modern intercom. Twice before she'd come here, buzzing his number to no avail, but those attempts now seemed fatally halfhearted, even false. Slowing her pace to a stroll, she approached the entrance, where a woman holding grocery bags stood on the step. Odile watched her punch in the four-digit entry code, then the door clicked, and she disappeared inside. A minute later Odile reentered the numbers, pushed the door open, and stepped into the tiny unlit foyer. She summoned the elevator, a cage barely big enough for two, rode it to the fourth floor, and got out.

This was her plan: to knock long and loud on his door until she was sure no one was home, then open the frosted-glass hallway window that looked out over the courtyard, carefully gauge the distance to Thierry's balcony terrace—a meter at most, she guessed—and squeeze through the two vertical bars of the window guard, jump the distance from sill to terrace, then, using her driver's license as a shim, jimmy the terrace door open and calmly enter his apartment.

Her fist was poised to begin this sequence when she noticed a buzzer set into the jamb at the normal height, and for reasons not immediately available this caused her whole plan to evaporate. Her heart was beating hard. She tried the knob and it spun in its mechanism, engaging nothing. Then, realizing she wasn't the first trespasser here, she pushed, and the door swung soundlessly open.

"Hello?" she called. "Is anybody home?"

She closed the door behind her and turned the deadbolt.

Traveling with Thierry, sharing sleeping quarters with him and noting his fastidiousness, Odile had formed an impression of how he lived in Paris, and she now found that impression largely confirmed. The shelves of books, grouped by language and alphabetized by author; the CDs, mostly classical and jazz; the academic journals, neatly stacked beside the bookcases; the mass-produced Scandinavian-style furniture—all this she felt she could have predicted item for item not twenty-four hours into their journey to Moscow.

But as she grew calmer, her sense of trespass beginning to fade, she became aware of other elements that complicated her view. Laid out on the dining table was a chess set abandoned in mid-match, a couple of empty vodka bottles, and an over-inked Russian newspaper, roughly folded open to the business page. That the Russians had staked out Thierry's home wasn't a surprise, but their apparent quiescence—nothing broken or out of place—left her puzzled and mildly irritated. She'd half expected the kind of ruin that had greeted her and Max.

Moving now without caution, satisfied she was alone, Odile passed into the bedroom and scanned it: the low, neatly made-up bed, its white coverlet partly turned down as if for a guest; the desk and chair; the computer system, piles of weighted-down papers on either side of the keyboard; the closet, with its louvered wooden doors and, opposite it, a half-length oval mirror framed in distressed mahogany.

Advancing toward her reflected image—brow knit, mouth set, eyes moist and unblinking—she experienced a sudden flush of purpose. Thierry's presence was strong here, the faintly rootlike scent of his cologne seeming to hover. Turning from the mirror, she went to his desk and, casually at first, then more systematically, began to go through his papers. Examining bills paid and unpaid, class schedules, faculty memos, newspaper clippings, reading lists, she began to piece together a picture of Thierry as a popular professor whose classes were oversubscribed and whose extrascholastic interests—witness the article he'd clipped on a fainting contagion at an Iranian girls' school—tended toward the esoteric. According to his charge statements, he spent quite a lot of money in brasseries and clubs, not much on travel, less on clothes. His phone bills were moderate. He collected fountain pens.

Odile was in the midst of rifling the bottom drawer of his desk when she noticed a worn leather briefcase set unobtrusively against the baseboards beneath. Finding it locked, she cast about fruitlessly for a key, then took a paper clip from the desk, straightened it out, and, inserting one end into the brass keyhole, worried the satchel open. Inside were a sheaf of printed documents bound in plastic and a smaller, paperbound notebook of the sort used by university students. She turned first to the notebook, which appeared to be a kind of journal, though the entries were undated. The handwriting was Thierry's. After flipping through it back to front, she began reading.

*Night, and once again I am lost in the powder-white sands of insomnia, my thoughts racing senselessly, my heartbeat numbering the minutes of my longing. How I wish I could return to my previous ignorance, to the countless ways in which I misunderstood these intimations that rule me now as might a wicked clown, an emperor clown, a true lord of misrule. When I thought that what I longed for was fortune, I gambled, of course—what else if not gamble? A marvelous moment, that not-quite eternity between the bet and the outcome, when the ball rolls contrary to the wheel, spiraling down toward that larger rotation and the imperatives of physics, of red and black, odd and even, the number chosen and the ones that might have been. A man can live in that interval, and I did, between bet and outcome. The outcome was important, yes, but not because with it one lost or won; the outcome was essential because only then could one place another bet and so enter again into that whole marvelous process of suspension in which the moment, each moment, holds the promise of being unique. So it goes without saying that I lost more than I won and yet played on and on and on until I reached the state of indebtedness in which I now so comically exist, working like an indentured servant for S. An appropriate punishment, since what is it I do for S if not duplicate the duplicate, reiterate the reiterated, repeat and repeat what has already been completed and known and registered, so that the very possibility of singularity is mocked by my efforts and torn pitilessly into self-identical pieces? But what I longed for wasn't fortune, as it turns out. Nor love, nor any of the other things I mistook it for when I was so blessedly ignorant, that is to say young, not so many months ago.*

Odile drew the chair out from the desk and sat down. There was a pack of cigarettes beside the computer keyboard; she lit one up and went on to the next entry.

*Yesterday I finally prevailed on S to upgrade his hardware. In principle it should now be possible for me to turn out twelve units every three minutes, twenty-four hundred on the average night. This is a considerable improvement, though S insists he could dispose of ten times that many daily through the existing network. No doubt he could, but I can only work with what he gives me. Why, I ask myself, doesn't he invest enough in equipment to meet the demand? He must be paying more off the top than I thought. Protection money? Maybe. But it remains true that the less I know about the mechanics of his operation, the better.*

The next several entries consisted of little more than columns of figures set beside short strings of letters. Failing to make sense of them, Odile skipped impatiently ahead.

*Or is it that my very longing for another life prevents me from seeing what is right in front of me, that every moment is a door through which I could pass, leaving behind the daily repetitions and redundancies of this world in which everything of consequence, really everything, is already known? Sometimes I almost think so. Surely this is what I secretly hope for when I send one of my projects out into the streams of com-*

*merce and consciousness, and, however circuitously, into the minds and souls of strangers. What began as an exercise seems more and more an effective tactic with real-world applications, possibly a model for a different future. And so maybe instead of shielding myself from the details of S's operation, I should immerse myself in them and make them my own. Last night, at Bar Flou, S was drinking heavily—in celebration, he said—and I let him ramble on, waiting for my opportunity. It was his usual monologue, more or less: the demands of business, his own "essentially artistic" temperament, the dark but unspecified interests from which he feels "duty-bound" to protect me. Finally, when I saw that he was prepared to go through it all yet again, I decided to—*

A sound of metal on metal caused Odile to look up with a start, and she heard a key working the front-door lock. Jumping to her feet, she stuffed the notebook back into the briefcase, thrust it back under the desk, and stubbed out her cigarette. The tumbler of the deadbolt lock turned over with a heavy clink. Looking around wildly, she went first to the window and then to the closet, where she parted the clothes and wedged herself inside, pulling the louvered door shut behind her.

For some seconds she heard nothing. Then the door closed, a few footsteps sounded, and the tinny chatter of stereo headphones wafted faintly through the apartment. She adjusted the louvers to gain a view of the bedroom. The smell of tweed enveloped her like a musk.

When the girl came into the bedroom and flung her turquoise leather purse down on the bed, walking back and forth reading a letter and then tossing it, too, on the bed, Odile recognized her as Turner's assistant without at first being able to recall her name. She had shoulder-length blond hair and a disapproving mouth, and now stopped before the mirror just as Odile had done minutes before. The stereo fell silent. Gabriella slipped the headphones off her ears and, approaching the mirror, took hold of it with both hands. For a moment she seemed to stare into her own gray-green eyes, then, bobbing her knees slightly, she lifted the mirror off the wall and laid it on the bed. Set into the plaster where the mirror had been was a safe with a combination lock.

Watching Gabriella take up the letter again and return to the safe, Odile became aware of the absurdity of her position. It mortified her to be hiding like the maid in a French bedroom farce, yet to be discovered would be worse still. She stepped farther back into the closet and continued to watch.

Gabriella spun the combination lock several times, then, consulting the letter, turned the knob left, right, left, and pulled down on the latch. It didn't budge. With a sigh, she spun the lock a few times to clear it and tried again. This time the safe swung open. Reaching inside, she withdrew a small, squarish package and a sealed business envelope. She closed the safe, went back to the bed, and slipped the package into her purse. Leaving the envelope on the bed, she gingerly returned the mirror to its place on the wall, stepped back to gauge whether it was straight, went forward to adjust it, and then, apparently satisfied, scooped the envelope up again.

At that moment the phone began to ring. Gabriella stared down at the bedside extension, letting it ring two, three, four times before she lifted the handset from its cradle.

"Hello?"

There followed a brief silence, then a sigh.

"No, Monsieur Colin isn't home at the moment, I'm afraid. With whom am I speaking?" Gabriella's eyes narrowed. "Sir, I'm only the house-keeper . . . Yes . . . That I can't say, but if you'd like to leave a message I'll be sure he . . . Hello? . . . Hello?" Frowning, she lowered the phone, hung up, and sat down on the edge of the bed, looking at nothing. Then, discovering the envelope in her hand, she opened it and scanned its contents.

Immediately she was on her feet again, headed straight for the closet. Odile ducked and burrowed in deeper behind the clothes. Flinging the door open, Gabriella reached in and, not a foot from Odile, grabbed a plas-tic shopping bag off the floor. Then the door swung shut again, and Odile, her knees buckling, sank into a crouch. Through the slats she watched Gabriella extract from the bag a black gift box tied with pink ribbon.

Until this moment Odile had assumed, without really thinking about it, that Gabriella had come here on Turner's behalf, sent to perform some professional errand, however dubious, but now, as she watched her open the box, part the black tissue paper, and remove, with a small gasp of plea-sure, a brassiere and matching panties of dark rose lace, finely cut and worked, she was forced to think again. Laying the lingerie out on the bed, Gabriella quickly undressed, peeled off the underwear she had on, and stuffed it into her turquoise bag. Naked, she possessed a beauty that the harsh set of her mouth otherwise obscured. She was young, her body fresh and unspoiled, and Odile had a momentary vision of her own physical decline, a vertiginous failing of the flesh she knew had already begun. Gabriella wriggled into the panties, put on the bra, and, reaching back to fasten it, gazed haughtily at herself in the mirror. She walked back and forth, her eyes on her reflection. Odile felt a flash of hatred that was fol-lowed immediately by shame at her own pettiness, and, a moment later, by detachment.

When Gabriella went into the bathroom and closed the door and the faucet began to run, Odile emerged without haste from her hiding place. A shaft of sunlight slanted across the turned-down bed and the toilet flushed. Odile slipped through the apartment, out into the hall, and down the stairs.

On the street she thought: *Turner's in serious trouble.*

## CHAPTER 12

THAT WEEK the unseasonably mild and sunny weather broke, and a steady rain settled over Paris. Water gushed from the gargoyle spouts of churches and cathedrals, streamed off mansard roofs and marble statuary, flowed down cobblestone streets and curbside gutters, across esplanades and plazas, down métro station steps and escalators, through every channel and crevice in this city without storm drains to spill at last into the swollen river that ran westward through its heart.

By Thursday afternoon the Seine had risen nearly three meters—up to the shoulders of the Zouave, the statue beneath the Pont de l'Alma by which Parisians reckon their floods—and Max, who had been watching the TV reports and brooding, decided it was time to shoot some video. He and Jacques loaded their gear into the rusted-out Citröen that Max kept for such purposes and drove with belated urgency to the quai de la Tournelle, where, it soon became apparent, a crisis was in progress.

The *Nachtvlinder*'s stern mooring had torn loose, and she now trailed treacherously out into the river's near branch, restrained only by her bow line from being carried off by the seething cocoa-brown torrent, either to crash against her houseboat neighbors or to have her wheelhouse sheared off by the next bridge downstream. The water had risen over the quai and partway up the steps that led to the street. Gathered there were Groot, Rachel, and a handful of their fellow houseboaters, all talking at once, a gray wooden dinghy tossing skittishly in the river at their feet.

"A moment of truth," Jacques said, as he and Max surveyed the scene from the sidewalk above. "Too bad we didn't get here earlier."

"What do you mean, earlier?" Max replied. "I've spent the whole day working out the timing on this. We're here now."

Jacques brightened. "Obviously. So how do we handle it?"

"Let's just get down there. I'll shoot, you take sound. And if Rachel and her boyfriend split up, you stick with her. Keep her talking. We might want to run her in voice-over."

They got their equipment out of the car and hurried down to join their subjects, where the roar of the river made it necessary to shout in order to be heard. Groot was listening to a grizzled Frenchman in oilskins who kept pointing to the *Nachtvlinder* with an accusatory finger that then traced a short arc to the houseboats immediately downstream, which, though riding perilously high, remained secure at their moorings. Groot nodded, then, noticing Max filming, spoke directly into the camera.

"He says that to haul her in by the one line would be very dangerous. The current would drive her into the other boats. Since I am the incompetent one, he says, I should cut the *Nachtvlinder* loose and not endanger innocent people. But of course I cannot do that." He shrugged and turned toward Rachel, who had grabbed his shoulder from behind and was speaking into his ear. Max motioned Jacques to bring the sound boom in as close as possible.

"We have to move soon," she was saying, "or we're going to start losing votes here."

"Yes, Rachel. I'm thinking."

"I know you are, I know. But what I want to say is, Boudu has gone to get his grappling hook. He'll expect us to give it a try."

Groot looked out over the river. "I can't use the hook. The risk of damage is too great."

"No, Groot, listen. Damage to the boat we can repair. It's the damage to community relations that we should worry about. There's no point in saving the boat if we can't live here afterward."

Declining to reply, he instead went to where a pair of oars had been propped against the stone retaining wall, took one in either hand, and walked down the steps to the dinghy. Max tracked him with the camera.

"Wait!" A squat man in his forties with a full mustache and beard hurried after him and, coming abreast, held up an entreating hand. "Don't be foolish! You can do nothing with this boat in such a current. Believe me, you'd be lost before you begin."

Groot placed the oars in the dinghy and turned to face him. "Suppose you're right. What would you suggest I do?"

"You must wait for *la fluviale*," the man said. "They alone have the equipment to save your boat. And eventually you'll have to report to them anyway. This is the law."

Shaking his head, Groot went to where Rachel stood shivering on the steps, her long hair drenched and her thick glasses rain spattered. Jacques, as instructed, hovered nearby with the sound boom.

"In the end," Groot said, "it's up to us alone. Only we can decide what to do. Agreed?"

Rachel swallowed. "Yes."

"Good. I'm going to swim out there with a line that I'll tie to the stern. You can organize the neighbors to haul her about on that line until she's again facing downstream. Then we'll use both the bow and stern lines to bring her in. With two points of control, no damage is possible."

Max zoomed in slowly. The shot composed itself: the finely wrought Dutchman and the tall American taking counsel together.

"But Groot, that current! Do you really think you can make it?"

"Yes, I do. Anyway, I'll swim with the line tied around my waist."

Rachel pursed her lips. "I don't like it."

"No? Well, liking it is optional. Doing it is what matters."

Behind the camera, Max exulted. The shot continued to flow, accommodating all the little hesitations and human flutters that on the screen would translate into something larger, something that might, if all went well, make visible what performance more often than not obscured or, as he was coming to think, quite possibly replaced.

Groot called out to a boy carrying a coil of fluorescent orange rope over his shoulder. He laid the rope down, and Groot began to undress.

"What about the water?" said Rachel nervously. "You'll be poisoned before you even get halfway."

"Don't worry. I won't drink it, I promise."

"Hepatitis, dysentery, conjunctivitis. Polio, if they still have that."

"I'll disinfect afterward." Stripped now to his briefs, Groot secured one end of the rope to an iron ring set into the retaining wall, then went back down the steps, followed closely by Rachel.

Jacques waited for Max to finish the shot, then the two of them took up new positions down by the water's edge.

"What if he drowns?" asked Jacques. "Wouldn't we have a hard time shooting a film around that?"

"On the contrary. If he drowns, the film makes itself." Max held a light meter up and took a reading. "That doesn't necessarily mean we want him to drown, you understand. What we want is to film. About everything else we're essentially neutral. Got it?"

Jacques grinned. "Sure."

"And try to get Rachel to talk. I'll be shooting him, but she's our real subject, okay? Let's do it."

Groot was tying the line around his waist as he spoke to Rachel. "If I get into trouble, I'll wave an arm. Don't do anything unless you see that wave. And don't panic. In situations like this, things often look worse than they are."

"Yeah, right."

Max let the camera linger over their embrace.

"Hurry back," she said.

Groot waded down the steps into the churning water and, once he was waist deep, started swimming upstream at an oblique angle so the current would eventually drag him to the boat. He was, Max thought, an astonishingly strong swimmer.

"Your boyfriend is risking his life to save a boat," Jacques said to Rachel. "Is that wise?"

She looked past the sound boom to where Groot labored through the onrushing waters, his broad back twisting from side to side as he swam. "You're trying to provoke me, aren't you? For your film."

"No, I only mean that you must be worried for him, out there by himself, in such dangerous conditions."

She removed her glasses, wiped them dry, and put them back on, scrutinizing Jacques carefully before turning again to the river. "Groot's physically courageous," she said. "I've always been attracted to guys like that, probably because my father was in the military—the United States Navy, as a matter of fact. So to answer your question, the *Nachtvlinder* is where Groot and I live, she's our home, but she's also a nautical vessel, and there's a really ancient history of how you're supposed to deal with one that's in distress and under your command." She paused. "Excuse me, but isn't this going to seem, like, totally contrived?"

Jacques hastened to reassure her. "We'll fix it in the editing. Just say whatever's on your mind."

Keeping Groot snugly framed in the viewfinder, Max struggled to stay calm, galled that he had no control whatsoever over the present action. Yet the scene itself was riveting, so rich with texture that there was almost too much of it.

"What's on my mind right now," said Rachel, "is his safety, obviously. But I know Groot, and I can tell you that all he's thinking about is the boat. Everything we care about is tied up in her. You just get so connected, it's not really something you can explain." She hugged herself. "A boat's like a living thing."

For the first time Max became aware of the debris being borne along on the current. He panned upriver to take in tree branches, a tire, a plastic bucket, and a battered aluminum canoe, following it all as it flew past.

Groot was more than halfway to the boat, still swimming strongly. His neighbors stood huddled together on the steps.

In an effort to keep Rachel talking, Jacques mentioned their good fortune in not being on board when the *Nachtvlinder* lost her mooring.

She shook her head grimly. "Actually, this is all pretty much my fault," she said. "We should've been on board, but I talked him into taking me skiing in Chamonix for a couple of days, which we definitely couldn't afford, even without the flood. Now we come back to this."

"Any idea what went wrong?" Jacques persisted. "None of your neighbors' boats broke loose."

"We had her rigged with a system of backup cables. I don't know, maybe we should have—"

But at that moment a wooden orange crate, hurtling along on the wild waters, spun into the air and struck Groot in the back of the head. Max zoomed in as he went under, panning left with the current. Two, three seconds passed. When Groot resurfaced, fifteen meters downstream, he was bleeding from the scalp and nose.

"Oh my God!" Rachel grabbed hold of the orange rope that now ran some seventy meters from the ring bolt to Groot's waist. "Help me!"

Stricken, Jacques looked back and forth from her to Max.

"Wait!" Max shouted, holding up a hand as he continued to film. "He's okay!"

The neighbors all began shouting contradictory instructions.

"He said he'd wave," Jacques reminded Rachel. "Didn't he say that?"

The current had driven Groot even with the boat. He struggled to maintain his position, then turned to look at the people gathered on the bank. He seemed to shake his head.

"He's hurt," Rachel said, "and we can't just leave him out there. Help me!"

Jacques again hesitated.

"Okay, I'll do it myself."

But before she could begin hauling him in, Groot turned back toward the boat and resumed swimming. A dozen strokes later, he grabbed hold of the ladder at the aft of the *Nachtvlinder* and, hand over hand, dragged himself on board as the onlookers applauded. Max filmed him on deck, arms upraised against the steel-gray sky. Then, as Groot untied the rope that encircled his waist, Max pulled his focus back steadily until the shot again included Rachel, standing to the left in the foreground with her back to the camera.

She turned around, bedraggled but quite beautiful, and, seeing Max, smiled demurely. "Did you get all that?" she asked.

Some time later, after the *Nachtvlinder* had been hauled safely back to her high-water berth and Groot had been disinfected with a bottle of whiskey and the neighbors had dispersed, Max and Jacques took their equipment back up to street level and stowed it in the Citroën. The rain had tapered off.

"You were right about the timing," said Jacques. "How did you know?"

"I didn't. I just waited as long as I could before going in. Mind-set is half the battle in a project like this, especially when you shoot in real time."

"Well, one thing's for certain, Max. We've really got a film now."

He gazed irritably over the car roof at his assistant. "Which film is that?"

For an instant Jacques seemed at a loss. "But Max, this is exactly what you've been looking for: Rachel in adversity, a woman of the American type, innocent but hardy, all that."

"Sure," he agreed. "All that. But suddenly I have the feeling there's a piece of this I'm not seeing yet. Some overall tendency of events, I don't know. Fear and pity, maybe."

"Fear and pity? No, please. It worries me when you quote Aristotle."

"Ah, you see," said Max, "that's my problem. I don't know how to disengage." Shaking his head, he opened the passenger-side door. "Really, it'll be my undoing."

He had Jacques drive him and the equipment to the studio, where he backed up the day's work and filed it with the rest of the Rachel footage. Then he crossed the courtyard to the apartment and had a hot shower. Odile was with a client in the fifth arrondissement. Max expected her back for supper at nine.

Watching the TV coverage of the flood, a glass of whiskey in his hand, he was stirred anew by the force and drama of the river: its balletic surge, the sheer mass and velocity of its roiling waters, its absolute conformity to physical law. At times he had to remind himself that it was Paris he was seeing and not some improvident biblical city in the grip of a senile God.

Not everyone had fared as well as Groot and Rachel. The international news channel repeatedly ran footage of a classic Dutch *tjalk* ramming into the Pont Mirabeau, where it stuck fast, the remnants of its superstructure accordioned against the bridge's steel under-struts. Moments later an errant telephone pole stove in the hull, and the boat sank with dismaying dispatch. Max watched the sequence several times, fascinated. *A boat's like a living thing,* Rachel had said. He got up and poured himself another whiskey.

Odile arrived at half past nine, flushed and faintly aglow. Her client, an Algerian-born doctor's daughter with an advanced fashion sense, had some weeks back commissioned a wedding dress, encouraging her to experiment, and they'd just been over the first set of drawings. The meeting had gone well.

"You would enjoy her," Odile said, pouring herself a glass of mineral water. "She has a natural grace, Fatima. Mischievous and sexy. Like a djinn."

"But won't you basically have to cover her from head to toe? I'm assuming she's Muslim."

"Muslim, yes, but very modern. No head scarf, no djellaba, none of that." Leafing through the day's mail, she blew a puff of air. "Have you heard any more from Allegra? You called her, right?"

"E-mailed her." Max opened the refrigerator and contemplated its contents. "Why do you ask?"

"No reason. I'm just trying to get a picture of the summer."

From the meat compartment he removed two veal chops wrapped in brown paper. "Probably what will happen is she'll spend a month or so with us—June or July. But it still has to be worked out. With her mother, I mean."

Odile sat down at the kitchen table with that afternoon's *Le Monde*. "Diana will cooperate."

"Yes, but she'll drag it out, exacting her small revenge."

"Ignore her, then. Your concern is Allegra."

Max unwrapped the chops and ran cold water over them. While it had been understood, virtually from the outset of their relationship, that he and Odile would have no children of their own, he sometimes wondered if she was as unconflicted about this as she seemed. The official line, that their respective professional ambitions precluded responsible child rearing, was sound enough, and Odile relished her personal freedom. But occasionally he could feel a shadow pass and would worry that something essential had been sacrificed. A room left dark in the marital mansion.

"Max?" She had laid the newspaper open on the table and was scanning the headlines. "Don't make a chop for me. I think I'll just have salad."

"What? But you adore veal. Aren't you feeling well?"

"No, I'm fine, really. But I—" She looked up.

"Yes?"

She shrugged. "My meat-eating days are finished. I've just decided."

He blinked, awaiting clarification.

"Oh, come on, Max. I just feel like a change of diet, okay? Don't take it personally."

Retrieving the brown paper from the garbage, Max wrapped the second chop back up and put it in the refrigerator. "You're not undergoing a religious conversion, are you?"

"Rest assured," she told him, returning to the newspaper.

Over dinner he recounted the rescue of the *Nachtvlinder*, taking pains not to embellish or overdramatize, seeking in Odile's reaction some clue to the nature of the day's events and the film that had begun to coalesce around them. She listened closely and asked the occasional question, trying to visualize it all. Together they entertained the possibility that a second act of sabotage had taken place, that the firebombers had returned to cut the *Nachtvlinder* loose and send her to ruin. But of course that hadn't happened, and it strained belief that the would-be saboteurs could have failed a second time.

"What I wonder about," Max said, pouring them coffee, "is why Groot's putting so much energy into restoring the engines if he isn't planning to move the boat."

"How do you know he isn't?"

"Various things Rachel's said. Today I heard her tell him there was no point in saving the boat if they alienated the neighbors. Which wasn't an exaggeration, I'm beginning to see. Those houseboaters are tough."

"Okay. But what's your point? Say he moves the boat. So what?"

Max shook his head vexedly. "It's not that alone. I have to consider the big picture. Up till now I've just been shooting Rachel on spec, a kind of extended screen test, really. But with what I got today I can begin to imagine an actual film, one I'd kill to make."

"The one you've been looking for?"

"Maybe, yes. So the problem becomes, how hard do I push it? Do I let it come to me, which is what I've done till now, or do I take a more proactive approach? Because my instinct tells me there's more at play here than I've got a grip on."

She leaned back in her chair and regarded him shrewdly, holding the coffee cup before her lips. "You know what Bastien says."

"No, what?"

"Better a lie that's big enough than a truth too small."

"Well, good for him, the old terrorist. I'll have to remember that the next time Allegra tells me film's just another kind of lie."

"He likes you, you know. Despite what you think."

"Spare me. He'd have me sent to the countryside for reeducation if he could." Max wiped his mouth on his napkin. "To the gulags."

"That's Stalinism. He's a Trotskyite, remember?"

"Whatever. Dustbin of history, either way."

Leaving Odile to do the dishes, he went outside to smoke one of his small black cigars. The sky had cleared, and in the moonless night the stars scintillated with a fiery brilliance that was rare over Paris. He let himself out through the gate of the mews, turned left on rue Léon Maurice Nordmann, and walked a block west to La Maison d'arrêt de la Santé, the neighborhood's most notable though least remarked-upon feature, a top-security nineteenth-century prison whose glowering hulk occupied an entire trapezoidal block adjacent to boulevard Arago. Eighteen-foot stone-aggregate walls surrounded the facility, shielding it utterly from view, and in the warmer months Max had fallen into the habit of making a brisk circuit around it while smoking his postprandial cigar. The atmosphere at such times inclined him toward introspection of a strangely detached sort that he often found therapeutic. Lockdown was at six, and there was rarely anything to be heard from inside the prison after that, but earlier the sidewalks outside would be filled with the relatives of inmates—women and children and young men—calling out to their loved ones inside, who would then respond, their harsh voices requesting justice or cigarettes, damning faithless accomplices and friends, vowing love or revenge or vindication in several languages. These scenes made Max uneasy, so he confined his walks to the later hours. The communion he sought was with silence, the massive penitentiary hum of captive souls.

When he returned to the apartment, Odile was sitting on the sofa in her bathrobe, painting her toenails and watching *Chinatown*. He poured himself a Calvados and sat down beside her. Roman Polanski thrust the point of a switchblade up Jack Nicholson's left nostril and said, "Hold it there, kitty cat." Odile took a sip of Max's drink. "You are a very nosy fellow, kitty cat. You know what happens to nosy fellows?" Scene for scene, Max reflected, *Chinatown* was quite possibly the greatest American film of all time.

Afterward, in bed, he and Odile sought each other out with an avidity that seemed to refer to lately unspoken things. Cupping her buttocks in his hands, he drew his tongue up between her legs in slow, deliberate strokes, sometimes pulling back for a beat or two, waiting her out, until she buried her fingers in his hair, locked her ankles at the small of his back, and, pushing herself hard against him, let loose a long keening cry that made his senses trill. When her spasms trailed off, he entered her and they began again, slowly, ascending together. The night was close about them, dense and many chambered, provisionally infinite.

Max woke much later in a confusion of dream fragments and half-remembered voices. Odile slept with her back to him, clutching a pillow to her chest. He got up to get a glass of water, and, in the living room, cranked open a window. Three doors down, the anarchists were having a party and their guests had spilled out into the courtyard, smoking and conversing in low voices while Brazilian hip-hop emanated from inside. He listened for awhile, reminded of his own youth. He had been rash, dismissive of reason, fearless. It didn't seem all that long ago.

When he returned to bed, Odile stirred. "Is everything okay?" she asked.

"Everything's fine. Go back to sleep."

She came into his arms. "Max?"

"Yes?"

"Did I dream it or did you say . . . did you say this is a film you'd kill to make?"

"No, I did say that."

"Good." She sighed and wriggled closer. "That's what I thought."

And though her breathing soon evened out, Max's thoughts ran on, attaching to nothing in particular but giving him no peace, and he lay awake beside her, awash in nameless feeling, until nearly daybreak.

## CHAPTER 13

TURNER'S SQUASH CLUB was on the Left Bank, in an unassuming building on rue de Pontoise, and he played twice a week when he could. From a strictly business point of view, the Ritz might have offered more suitable contacts, but it was expensive and sufficiently *ancien régime* to put him off his game. Worse, it had no Asian members. All the best players Turner knew were Asian.

He had booked a court for five thirty. When he arrived Sylvain Broch was already warming up, smashing the ball against the wall with a vengeance. Turner hadn't seen Broch since he had suggested Thierry Colin for the Moscow trip, but now, with the development of the flags well under way, he was curious to hear what the man might want to tell him about his missing cousin.

"I thought maybe you'd gone back to the States," Broch said when they shook hands. "Is everything okay?"

"Very okay, my friend."

"So it's a woman. I knew it."

Turner laughed. "No, not a woman. Not really. I'll tell you later."

"You will, because I'll insist."

They volleyed until they were both warmed up. Broch spun the racquet, Turner won first serve, and they began.

Although technically they were well matched, Turner had discovered that the younger man harbored a small, subconscious fear of being hit—by the ball, by the racquet—that tended to hamper his game. Sometimes he was able to use this fear as a spur to more aggressive play, working willfully ahead of it, but more often it shaved just a fraction of a second off his moves, and he'd spend the whole match trying to catch up. Turner had never been able to determine if Broch was aware of this weakness, but over the course of their acquaintance he'd lost more often than he'd won.

They played hard for about an hour. Turner lost the first game and was about to lose the next when he gave in to temptation and began slamming the ball off the front wall so it came straight back at Broch, who then had to fight it off blindly or step aside and wait for it to rebound off the rear wall. Soon Turner had him on the run, and before long Broch was spending as much energy avoiding the ball as he was chasing it.

"Enough, you bastard," he said at last, bent over at midcourt, panting for breath. "I don't know what's wrong with me tonight."

"You're a little out of shape, that's all." Turner laid a hand on his shoulder. "Been working late?"

"Fuck off. Drinks are yours this time."

They showered, dressed, and repaired to Bar Flou, small, chic, but studiedly informal, where the patrons were regulars, the drink was champagne, and dinner was never ordered before ten. The walls were painted a deep brothel red, making it seem even smaller, and behind the minuscule bar a single Corinthian column rose to meet the stamped-tin ceiling to bizarre effect. Turner rather liked the place, and it wasn't expensive.

The tables around them quickly filled with people settling in for the evening. Most knew one another at least by sight, and the small rituals of self-display—a sweater brandished and draped over bare shoulders, a cigarette proffered and lit, an earring adjusted—lent the proceedings a collective intimacy. Conversations eddied and overlapped.

When their champagne arrived, they clinked glasses.

Turner looked at him. "You asked earlier if I'd met a woman and I told you not really, but in point of fact I have. You know her, I think. Her name is Odile Mével."

Broch frowned and shook his head. "What does she look like?"

"Pretty, auburn hair that's almost red, marvelous breasts. Early thirties, I'd say. You'd remember."

Broch opened his palms. "Who is she?"

"I'm still finding that out myself, but she was the woman I hired along with your cousin, you remember, to run that Moscow errand?"

"Oh, yes." Bored. "But I never met her."

"No? I thought maybe Thierry might've mentioned her to you."

Broch finished his champagne and signaled the waiter for another. "It's possible. I don't remember."

"But have you talked to him lately?"

"Lately? No. He has a full teaching schedule, and examinations are coming up. Anyway, he's just my cousin. I don't pay much attention to his social life."

Turner nodded. At a corner table two women kissed lavishly while the man who'd brought them cut and recut a deck of cards, speaking all the while to a couple at the adjacent table. They listened intently, watching his hands.

"The reason I ask," Turner said, "is that Thierry never showed up to collect his fee for the Russian trip. I mean, I realize that thirty thousand francs isn't what it used to be, but somehow I thought he'd want to be paid. Any idea what happened to him?"

The waiter whisked away Broch's empty champagne glass and put a full one in its place. Broch drank it down and handed the glass back to the waiter, who put a third one before him and swept off with the empties. "Is he dead?" Broch asked, avoiding Turner's eye.

"I don't know. Should he be?"

A moment of thoughtful silence ensued, which an instant later made both men laugh.

"He can be a pain in the ass," Broch said. "This is certain. But he's reliable in his way. He did what you asked him to, didn't he?"

"Absolutely."

"So." Broch dismissed the subject with a shrug. "I wouldn't have recommended him otherwise."

They sipped their champagne.

There were three aspects of Broch that Turner considered worth knowing, and with all three the trick was to know nothing more. First, he was afraid of squash balls traveling at high velocity. Second, his real-estate dealings quite probably constituted the lesser part of his financial interests, the rest of which Turner assumed were, to one degree or another, illicit. This he had gathered from a number of hints Broch had let drop from time to time and, more tellingly, from the intuitive grasp he seemed to have of the workings of the art market, which, while not necessarily illicit, nevertheless responded agreeably to selectively applied bits of intelligence. This aspect of Broch presented some difficulties, since not only was Turner curious to know what he was up to, but Broch himself seemed to want to tell him, an eventuality to be avoided at all costs because with knowledge came liability. Third, and most problematic, Broch felt his true talents were being squandered. What exactly these talents might be remained unclear. Turner had the impression that he considered them to be imaginative or possibly artistic in nature, though again there could be no advantage in knowing more about them. What mattered was that they had no suitable outlet, which, at least in principle, made him a likely recruit for any number of adventures in self-vindication. *Here be monsters,* Turner thought. He disliked getting involved in people's hopes for themselves.

"So," Broch said, "tell me about this woman. You are in love with her, yes?"

"Certainly not," Turner replied primly, glancing reflexively around the room to see if anyone had heard. "Besides, I have no time for women these days. An accidental tumble, maybe. An actual woman with needs and grievances, no thank you."

"Are you fucking her?"

"It hasn't even crossed my mind."

Broch nodded gravely. "Tell me about her. You'll feel better."

"I don't want to feel better. I'm fine." Turner finished his champagne and caught the waiter's eye. "How about you? Break any hearts lately?"

"You know my situation."

"Yes, but—"

"The same. Unchanged."

His situation, as Turner understood it, was curiously strenuous. He was not only sleeping with his partner in the real-estate business, a recent widow, but also had undertaken a second liaison with a much younger woman, a music student from Strasbourg who liked to show up unannounced and be taken to the city's most fashionable restaurants and nightclubs, preferably with a gram or two of cocaine to give the experience scale. That Broch was headed for a train wreck could not be doubted, but what impelled him in that direction—audacity or sorrow or simple fecklessness—remained opaque to Turner, who was happy enough to leave it at that.

"In any case," Broch was saying, "I'd like your advice about something. My great-aunt died this winter and left me a small inheritance. This is awkward, you see, because, okay, she was a bit eccentric, and . . ." He stopped, exasperated.

The waiter set two fresh glasses of champagne in front of them and hurried off.

"What I mean is—"

"To your health."

"To yours. What I mean is this inheritance . . ." Again Broch stopped. He inspected his wine closely, then drank all of it.

"It's okay," said Turner. "I think what you're telling me, and correct me if I'm wrong, is that this is a small *cash* inheritance, right?"

"Exactly." Broch sighed with relief. "In U.S. dollars, to be precise. And I want to invest this sum in, I don't know, something that doesn't require much paperwork, an art object perhaps, if something suitable could be found. Of course, knowing this is your specialty, I'm more than curious to hear your thoughts."

Turner nodded and, leaning forward, said in a mock-conspiratorial whisper, "How much?"

"Fifty thousand," Broch said a bit unhappily.

Turner eased back in his chair. "Let me think."

As far as he knew, Broch had never asked what exactly his cousin had been dispatched to Moscow to retrieve, but now that the goods had been secured on French and American soil it didn't much matter anyway. Ten of the flags had been sold through Balakian's gallery at thirty-five thousand dollars each; of those, three would soon be donated to major New York museums at Turner's suggestion, the purchase price to be recouped by the donors in tax write-offs confirming, for the record, the objects' value. While he hadn't planned on selling prior to auction any of the flags still in his possession, chance had brought him opportunity. Still, there were risks.

At the corner table, the man fanned cards out before the couple he was addressing and invited them to choose one. The two women he'd brought were feeding each other escargot from tiny forks, oblivious.

"You understand," said Turner, "that if it's a quick turnaround that you're looking for, art is not your friend."

"Yes, yes," Broch said, "I know. My main concern is to find a solid long-term investment that doesn't require much paperwork. Purely for the sake of convenience."

"And your inheritance—it's fully accessible when?"

"Anytime. Immediately."

"Good." Turner assumed the brisk, professional manner with which his clients were most comfortable. "Come by my office tomorrow afternoon and I'll show you something I think will meet your needs. I hate to part with it, but, considering your position . . ."

"Thank you."

"In return I ask only that you keep the sale quiet. The price you men-tioned will amount to a discount that others acquiring comparable objects have not been offered, so naturally there's a need for discretion. I can't have my clients made unhappy."

"Of course not. I understand."

Turner's spirits soared. The world was with him. He watched two expensively dressed men enter the bar and take a look around before leav-ing. It seemed to him that the shorter one had nudged the other in the ribs and they'd both glanced at his table, but the next moment he was sure he had imagined it.

"So," he said, "now that we've solved your dilemma, are you going to tell me what's really going on with your cousin? I mean, what's his problem, exactly?"

Broch appeared to suffer another bout of ennui. "Oh, it's nothing. He owes some money, that's all. I thought the trip to Moscow would help him to pay it off sooner, of course. He'll be back."

The card shark at the corner table said, "Queen of spades," and the man who'd drawn the card held it up to his girlfriend to confirm its identity. "I can't believe it!" she exclaimed fetchingly.

"To whom does he owe this money?" Turner asked. "You?"

A dolorous sigh. "Yes, me. Who else?" He seemed to be on the point of elaborating when, from the depths of his pants pocket, his cell phone began to ring. He considered the situation, then apologized to Turner, extracted the device, and answered. "Yes, hello?"

Turner watched his features expand in a rictus of professional bon-homie. "Not at all! I was planning to call you myself . . . Yes . . . Yes, that's true . . . No, I understand, but . . . Yes, and let me assure you that every-thing . . ." He listened, a mask of bewilderment descending over his face. "Of course." Avoiding eye contact, he shrugged and held out the phone. Turner took it.

"To trust is good," said the voice on the other end. "Not to trust is better. Traditional Russian expression."

"Nikolai! What a pleasure to hear your voice." In fact Kukushkin's voice, which he hadn't heard since their conversation in Balakian's gallery, pro-voked a whole range of feelings, but pleasure wasn't one of them. "Where are you?"

"Is not important. Maybe later I come to Paris. You are well?"

"I'm fine. And you? Business is good, I hope?"

"Currently is transition period. We have decided to downsize, as they say in U.S. Certain positions to be eliminated in very near future."

"Well, I'm sure it's for the best," Turner said, "given today's climate."

"This is precisely true, yes." Kukushkin sighed. "Now, Turner. I must suggest you seek alternative company at earliest convenience."

"Excuse me?"

"The man with whom you are sitting is about to receive disappointing news, to be delivered in person. Is most essential that you not be with him."

"I see."

"Good. Because the messengers have strict instructions to leave no extraneous elements behind, okay? You have my drift?"

"So it's imminent."

"No. In motion."

"Aha. Okay, then. I'll certainly do that, Kolya. Thanks for calling." He pressed the end button and looked up.

"What is it?" Broch's liquid brown eyes searched his. "What did he say?"

Turner gave him back the phone. "He wants me to bid on something for him at auction next week. I can't really talk about it."

Broch put up a hand. "Not my business, I understand."

Looking at his watch, Turner forced himself to stay calm. Nothing definitive would happen inside the bar, he reasoned, but the space was tightly enclosed and had only one exit and entrance. "Listen, Sylvain, I hate to cut this short, but I just realized I've got to stop by the office to pick something up. Do you mind if we get the check?" Already he was signaling the waiter, making writing gestures at him across the crowded room.

"I didn't know you knew Nikolai," Broch said, sounding a little hurt.

"Yes, well, that's Paris, isn't it. You bump into everyone sooner or later." He brought out his wallet and inspected its contents. It would be desirable to pay in cash.

"And I wonder, how did he know you were with me?"

"No idea. You must've mentioned it to him."

"Me?" Broch seemed obscurely troubled by the notion. "Why would I do that?"

Up front a party of people in their twenties had arrived, perhaps eight or ten of them, streaming in through the door even as the manager tried to shoo them out again. They backed up beside the bar, scanning the room for a free table, exclaiming to one another about the crowd. Cell phones sprouted.

"Thank you, sir," the waiter said, delivering the check.

Turner put down several bills and stood up, the blood suddenly rushing from his head. His vision granulated and grew dark. When it cleared again, he was gripping the back of his chair and the man with the cards was switching places with the one who'd drawn the queen of spades. The girl-friend clapped her hands and laughed delightedly, while the other two women looked on with new interest.

"Ready?" said Broch, and the two of them edged their way toward the front.

Accustomed though he was to people and their needs, Turner found it difficult to make sense of what was about to happen. Evidently Broch was working for Kukushkin in some capacity, his performance had been found unsatisfactory, and now there would be a reckoning, probably violent. Whether he himself had wandered into this skein of circumstance acciden-tally, as it seemed, or as part of somebody else's design, Turner was at a loss to know. He wanted to believe that it didn't matter, but of course it mat-tered quite a lot.

The young people had now reversed course and were flowing back out onto the sidewalk, trying to agree on a destination, and Turner and Broch trailed behind them. "But the DJ at Colors is a thousand times hotter than whoever's at Le Charbon these days," one of the girls insisted petulantly.

The night was clear. Cars prowled the streets. Pedestrian traffic had thinned.

Turner was taking his leave, shaking Broch's hand and thanking him for the game, when the men he'd seen earlier rounded the corner and stopped, stepping into shadow even before he could look away.

At the curb, a woman was getting out of a taxi.

"Listen," Turner said. "Come by the office tomorrow and we'll take care of business, okay?"

"Great. I appreciate it, Turner. Really." Broch sounded genuinely grateful.

The young people, having come to a decision, crossed the street together and passed under a pair of chestnut trees at the bus stop, then were gone. Turner sprinted for the taxi. He gave the driver his home address and, as they pulled away, looked back at Broch, who'd set off for the métro.

Broch had taken no more than five steps when suddenly he was jerked violently back as if someone had seized him by the belt from behind. In the next instant his chest exploded. He convulsed again, then twice more before collapsing—eight shots in all, Turner thought. The two men walked briskly across the street. Abruptly Turner looked away, willing himself forward, out of this moment and back into a world made credible by destinations and streetlights and appointments it was perhaps still possible to keep.

# CHAPTER 14

"LA PEAU DE L'OURS?" repeated Odile, tearing open a croissant. "But that's so interesting. Why didn't you tell me sooner?"

Max frowned and peered vexedly into his morning bowl of café au lait. "I don't know. First there was the flood, and then I guess I had other things on my mind. Don't tell me you've heard of it before?"

"But of course I have." She took a bite of croissant, ignoring the raspberry jam Max had set out for her, jam being another thing she had decided to renounce. "Didn't Jacques explain it to you?"

"My assistant," said Max, "believes me to be a man of attainment. He respects me and avoids humiliating me more than absolutely necessary. Which is why it falls to you, my love, to deliver me from ignorance, if you're not too busy."

Raising an index finger, she took a long swallow of coffee. "La Peau de l'Ours," she said, setting down the bowl and touching her napkin to her lips, "refers to a fable by La Fontaine that every French child learns at a very young age and then probably never thinks about again. It begins: 'Two comrades, pressed for cash, / to their neighbor the furrier sold / the skin of a bear who was still alive, / but whom they soon would kill, / according at least to them.'"

"Pithy," said Max. "A parable about speculation, perhaps?"

"Exactly. Because this is what happens. A price is agreed upon, and the two boys say they will deliver the skin to the furrier within two days. They set out, but before they can find the bear, the bear finds them. Realizing suddenly that they've given no thought to the bear's part in their contract, they panic. The deal's off, every man for himself. One guy climbs a tree, the other pretends to be dead. The bear sniffs at the one playing dead, then goes back about his business and disappears into the forest. Climbing down out of the tree, the boy embraces his friend—now they're just happy to be alive, obviously—and then asks what the bear said to him. And his friend says, 'He told me that one must never / sell the skin of a bear / that one has yet to bring to ground.' Good, no?"

Max thought about it. "But what's it doing on the copyright line of my DVD? My vandalized DVD, to use your word."

"Ah, that's another matter completely." Odile finished her coffee. "But very likely you'll soon find out, don't you think?"

"I will?"

"Well, I don't know. Have Eddie sort it out." She looked at her watch. "Shit. I'm late. We can talk about it later, okay?"

Taking the number 6 métro from Glacière, transferring to the 4 at Denfert-Rochereau, Odile replayed the breakfast conversation in her head. The La Fontaine fable lent itself to so many real-life situations that she'd felt compelled to make light of it before Max could extrapolate. One might, for example, be tempted to read it as a comment on filmmaking in general, where standard accounting practice dictated that those involved were forever selling something that had yet to be sighted, let alone subdued. Other, darker enactments of the tale also suggested themselves. Odile refused them all. She had promised herself a productive day.

She got off at Strasbourg-St. Denis, in a quarter known as Le Sentier, where the night shift of prostitutes had for the most part punched out, and the garment trade, which for well over a century had claimed the daylight hours, was in full swing. Pakistani porters pushed clothing racks through the narrow streets at bracing speeds; trucks waited to be unloaded; sewing machines attended by Chinese, Cambodians, Indians, and Turks whined in courtyards and glass-roofed passageways; managers and salesgirls stood in doorways recently vacated by hookers of many nations. Odile knew the district well—it was like the souk of Paris—and she took pleasure in cultivating its more prominent players.

The man she'd come to see, a corpulent Tunisian Jew named Monsieur Ibrahim, owned several local business concerns but operated officially out of a small storefront in the Passage du Caire, another bit of Orientalist fantasia originally inspired by Napoleon's Egyptian adventures of 1798. She found him at his usual post, loudly berating his son for accepting delivery of an inferior shipment of Indian cotton. In the cubbyhole where the son normally worked, *Titanic* was playing on a small video monitor. Gargantuan seas washed over the beleaguered ocean liner, and as Odile waited politely for Monsieur Ibrahim to finish, she found herself identifying with it. She supposed everybody did. It was a Hollywood film.

"Ah, Madame! Excuse me!" this man exclaimed when he finally noticed her.

They embraced, and the son slunk past them out of the shop.

"It has been too long! You and Monsieur are both well, I hope." He led her to a seat beside a mosaic-topped table and poured them each a glass of mint tea sweetened with honey. "I love my son, but he is an imbecile. Perhaps this is my own fault. I don't know."

"But he's still young!" said Odile. "He'll be fine. You'll see."

Monsieur Ibrahim shook his head unhappily. "He wants to be a singer in nightclubs, an entertainer. From his mother he gets this idea. I can do nothing." He drank his tea. "How may I assist you this morning?"

Odile described the wedding dress she was designing and asked to see samples of white taffeta in various weights. Restored to his usual good humor by this request, the Tunisian excused himself and, after a brief interval, returned with several fabric swatches. He and Odile discussed the merits of each, then she chose the next-to-lightest of the samples and bought six meters of it, charging it to her account. Having until recently been in arrears to Monsieur Ibrahim, she started to apologize for not paying cash, but he cut her off.

"Let me show you something." From his son's workspace he retrieved a lockbox, which he set down on the table between them and opened up. Inside were stacks of crisp new five-hundred-franc notes in paper-banded packets. "That's sixty thousand francs, right there. Take one."

She plucked a bill from the stash and held it up to the light.

"It looks good, does it not? You see the watermark, the quality of the paper and ink, the sharpness of the printing?"

"Yes. It looks fine to me."

Monsieur Ibrahim took another five-hundred-franc bill from his wallet and handed it to her. As she compared the two notes, he produced a pen-sized ultraviolet light and shone it on both bills. The one from his wallet fluoresced brightly at the lower left-hand corner, while the other went dull purple. "Those in the box are all counterfeit. Le Sentier is flooded with them. I myself took in almost ninety thousand in fakes before I realized it."

She gave him back the bills. "But where are they coming from?"

"The police won't say. But I have talked with other wholesalers here, and though nobody is certain, we think the source is Eastern European— Warsaw, some place like that." He shrugged. "Whoever it is, they are very skilled."

Odile watched him put the box away. "Maybe it's no longer necessary to be skilled," she said. Outside, a rack full of astrakhan coats wheeled by. "Now that everything's going digital, I mean."

She made arrangements to pick up the fabric later that afternoon, then emerged onto the Place du Caire, where pharaonic heads in stone gazed out languidly from the facade of the square's principal building. She remembered the Egyptian heads Turner had shown her when she'd delivered the flags to his apartment. Two of the heads were genuine, he said, three fake. She felt quite certain that if she saw them again she would know which were which.

Errands and small appointments occupied her for the rest of the morning. At one o'clock she had an omelette and a salad in a café near the Centre Pompidou. Then, on impulse, she called Rachel on her cell, and they agreed to meet at the Jardin du Luxembourg, by the Medici Fountain. They hadn't seen each other in four days.

"I have so much to tell you," Rachel said as they embraced.

Odile had commandeered two chairs at the statuary end of the fountain, in the shade of the giant sycamores that flanked it. "Me too," she said, though she wasn't entirely sure what she meant by that.

Rachel's big news was that she thought she'd located a pair of vintage London taxicabs of the sort that could provide parts for the *Nachtvlinder*. She ran across them while surfing the Internet at a cybercafé in Oberkämpf, but because she had yet to hear back from the owner and indeed had no idea where he or his taxis might actually be found, she'd held off informing Groot of her discovery. "I mean, for all I know, they could be in Australia," she said. "Plus I hate to think how much the guy probably wants for them. It's not as if we're in the car collector's income bracket, after all. Still, it would be so great to get those parts."

"Maybe you can get them copied," Odile suggested. "Wouldn't that be cheaper?"

"In theory, maybe. But finding someone to do the work isn't easy. Once the machinery goes out of production, you're pretty much at the mercy of the spare-parts market." She took a packet of sunflower seeds from her knapsack and poured some into Odile's cupped hand. "One way or another, though, we'll get her fixed up. That much I know." She began shelling the seeds and eating them, dropping the husks in a bandanna she'd laid open in her lap. "How are things with Max?"

"Not bad. Better, I think. He's in his *auteur* mode."

"That's good, isn't it?"

"Definitely. I finally saw the footage he shot of you and Groot during the flood, by the way."

"You did? Is it like totally dramatic?"

"Yes, it is. The two of you come across very well—understated, connected, fateful. You're yourselves plus something extra. It's what happens when Max gets serious behind a camera."

"Really? Is he serious about making a whole film?"

"He wants to, yes. Does that bother you?"

"No, I guess not. But it's not a straight documentary, is it?"

Odile shrugged and dropped some husks into Rachel's bandanna. "I don't know. Probably he hasn't made up his mind yet. Anyway, you don't have to do anything you don't want to. Just tell him no."

"Right. I bet you do that all the time."

"But of course I do." Odile frowned. "Well, once in awhile. Sometimes. To keep him guessing."

They had a giggle together. Sunlight dappled the grass around them, and the water in the fountain's elongated pool shimmered a deep bosky green.

"There's something else I've been wanting to tell you," Rachel said, "but you have to promise not to repeat it, even to Max. Okay?"

"I won't say a word, I promise."

She studied the ground at her feet, took a deep breath, and said, "Groot proposed to me."

"Oh Rachel, that's—" But seeing her eyes brim, Odile cut short her congratulations. "When?" she said instead.

"The night the boat got loose, after all the excitement. We sat up late celebrating the rescue, and then, out of nowhere, more or less, he asked me to marry him."

"And what did you say?"

"I . . ." Rachel took off her glasses. "I told him I needed time to think about it. I don't know why I was so surprised, but I was. Somehow marriage just hadn't entered my mind. He was hurt, of course, but what could I do?"

"You did the right thing, Rachel. Groot wouldn't want you to answer impulsively. I'm sure he understands."

"I mean, I know I'm twenty-five, and it's normal to think about where we go from here. But marriage! That just sounds so . . . drastic." She lifted one corner of the bandanna to clean her glasses, forgetting about the sunflower husks, which fell to the grass without her noticing. "Truthfully, I can't see past this summer. Fixing up the boat, living day to day. That's what I want. Am I being totally infantile?"

"Not at all. Just tell him."

Rachel held her glasses up to the sylvan light, sighed, then resumed polishing them. "I think it's too late for that. Whatever I decide, I don't think there's any going back to the way it was before he asked me." She blinked back tears. "I mean, is there?"

Odile reached out and caressed her friend's cheek. "No, probably not. But you can still have your summer."

"I'm selfish and pathetic, I know."

"Listen. Groot is the soul of patience. He'll understand." She drew back to look at Rachel. "And of course there's the boat, which is the perfect distraction. You said it yourself."

Rachel nodded dutifully. "You're right. There's always the boat."

They talked for awhile about Groot's plans for the overhaul, and Odile, recalling Max's worry that the boat might escape his lens prematurely, was counseling caution when a small voice interrupted her.

"Excuse me, Madame."

Odile turned to find herself addressed by a blond-headed little girl, maybe five years old, in a floral-printed pinafore and red Mary Janes.

"Hello, little one. What do you have there?"

The child thrust forward a folded slip of paper. "It's for you."

"Well, thank you. What a surprise! Is it a present?"

"No, Madame. That man over there sent me." She pointed across the fountain's basin and, emitting a shriek of delight, ran off.

Several people were seated on the opposite side of the fountain, and at first Odile recognized none of them. She opened the folded paper and inside, handwritten in English, the message read: *Circumstances have changed. My apologies for earlier misunderstanding. May I speak with you and your friend?* Looking up, she saw a man refold the newspaper he'd been reading. He wore wraparound sunglasses, black leather pants, a linen shirt striped silver and navy blue, and a black linen jacket. Smiling at her, he requested her indulgence with a stylized cringe.

"Oh my God, Rachel. It's that guy. One of the Russians who, you know, threatened me."

"Where?" The man nodded at Rachel. "Oh." She touched the clip in her hair and carefully refastened it. "What do we do?"

"He wants to talk to us."

"I'll get the police."

"No." Odile stayed her with a hand on her knee. "I think . . . I think it's okay."

"What, are you kidding?"

"There are people around. Let's find out what he wants." She lifted her chin to the man.

He got up from his chair, walked around the fountain, and, standing somewhat formally before the two women, held his hand out to Odile. "I am Sergei Dmitrovich."

Ignoring the proffered hand, Odile said, "This is Rachel, whose boat you tried to burn down."

"I am very sorry," he said, turning to Rachel. "Was terrible mistake. Procedural error."

Rachel gave him her hand. "Charming," she said as she scrutinized him.

The man looked quickly around, spotted an empty chair, and brought it over to where they were sitting. "Now is ideal time to talk. I think maybe we all will benefit."

"Where's your bad-smelling friend?" asked Odile.

"Ah," said the man, "your complaint is noted. And I am most pleased to tell you that he is undergoing aromatherapy as we speak."

"The other guy," Odile informed Rachel, "was the muscle."

"So this guy's the brains?" Rachel asked her. "I'm waiting to be impressed."

Dmitrovich tilted his head and smiled. "I understand you may think badly of me. Sometimes my manners are not what they should be, but you see I work under imperfect conditions, very often with pressing time constraints as well." He produced a pack of cigarettes, offered it to Odile and Rachel in turn, then lit one for himself. "So it is in this present case, involving Thierry Colin."

"You say circumstances have changed," Odile reminded him. "How?"

"The criminal Thierry Colin remains at large," said the man, "so my office has decided to take you into our confidence. For the greater good, as we say."

"Us?" exclaimed Odile, touching a hand to her chest. "But how flattering! How very nice!"

The Russian drew deeply on his cigarette and considered the two women without favor. "These are the details," he said, taking a small leather notebook from his breast pocket. "First. As previously mentioned, the Frenchman Thierry Colin has violated international statutes regarding the export of national patrimony. While it is known that you, Madame Mével, participated in this illegal activity, no action against you is contemplated at this time."

"Ah," said Odile, "so suddenly you are police again."

"Second," continued Dmitrovich, consulting his notebook. "Thierry Colin's trip to Moscow had as its primary object not acquisition of aforementioned objects of national patrimony but instead illegal transport into France of Belarussian nationals for purposes of prostitution and conscripted labor." Here he paused to look evenly from Odile to Rachel and back again. "Most unsavory objective, do you agree?"

"What proof is there?" asked Odile.

"You were in Brest station. I leave you to judge if citizens of Belarus enjoy lifestyle so impeccable they cannot be persuaded to leave by cheap promise. Third. The fugitive Thierry Colin is compulsive gambler with many debts in Paris and elsewhere which he has attempted to pay off through above-mentioned trafficking in illegal immigrant labor. Other activities are suspected. Most interesting at present is identity of his representative in Paris, who continues to carry out his instructions. This is you, perhaps?" he asked Odile.

"No."

"Okay. Already we know it is not you. Fourth!" Sergei Dmitrovich took a long drag on his cigarette. "Fourth. We have informations that Thierry Colin will contact you, Madame Mével, in very near future regarding his uncollected fee of thirty thousand francs for illegal import of Russian patrimony as previously discussed. Question, please: have you heard from this man since your return from Moscow several weeks ago?"

"No, I haven't."

The Russian nodded and put away his notebook. "My request is simple: I ask only that you inform me when Thierry Colin contacts you. Most likely he will call you by phone, so please, you will say you must call him back. You will reach me at this number"—he handed her a business card—"and my office will handle the matter from there. This is agreeable?"

"Well, I don't know," said Odile, looking at the card. "First you say one thing, then you say another." She turned to Rachel. "This whole affair is getting very confusing, don't you think?"

"Really," Rachel agreed.

Dmitrovich took a last pull on his cigarette, then flicked it into the fountain. "So," he said to Rachel. "How is this film? You like being the movie star?"

"I'm no star," she said, blushing. "It's Max's film. He shoots what he wants, but I don't even act. Not that it's any of your business."

He nodded thoughtfully. "It must be expensive, shooting film."

"What are you suggesting?" Odile asked him.

"Nothing." The Russian displayed his palms. "I am just a fan curious about how movie business works. He is good filmmaker, Max?"

"The best," answered Rachel. "He's got tons of awards, and plenty of people would give their eyeteeth just to work with him. He takes risks, real risks, because he's an artist, not some Hollywood hack."

"And you like this type, Rachel? Guy who takes risks?"

"Yes, as a matter of fact I do." Her eyes flashed darkly, and she seemed on the point of saying more when Odile intervened.

"Excuse me, Monsieur Dmitrovich. My friend and I are very busy, so unless you have something to add—"

He smiled and got to his feet. "Please, you will think about what I said. Trafficking in illegal peoples is most egregious crime, crude but very lucrative. You have no reason to protect Thierry Colin. If you help us, I personally guarantee you a small honorarium for your trouble, okay? We will be in touch." He looked at each woman for a moment as though to fix their features in his mind, then headed off.

"What on earth was *that*?" said Rachel when he was out of sight, the fountain before them gurgling on.

"That," said Odile, "was desperation."

In her mind's eye she saw Brest station. All was as it had been—the dimness, the silence, the crowd, the ruin—but now she imagined she also saw Thierry Colin passing through the unruly crowd and distributing squares of pink paper with numbers on them. She saw those who received a number stop their shoving, inspect their slips of paper, drop away from those still trying to buy a ticket, then leave the station by a service gate.

"Desperation for sure," Rachel said. "But smuggling people out of Belarus? Does that kind of thing actually go on?"

"I don't know. I guess it's possible. It's true that Thierry had gambling debts; I read that in his notebook." Odile recalled hiding in Thierry's closet, a memory she found troubling. "I probably should've never gotten involved in this," she said after a moment.

"Don't think like that," said Rachel. "It's stupid."

## CHAPTER 15

MAX, Jacques, and Eddie Bouvier sat watching Rachel on the video monitor in the screening room. The screen showed her organizing her neighbors at the crest of the flood, splitting them into two teams to haul the *Nachtvlinder* back to safety, one by the bow line and the other by the line Groot had moments before swum out with and made fast to her stern. Rachel exuded cool authority and a low-key charisma that the camera captured very well. Those she pressed into service seemed to drink her in with their eyes as she addressed them. It wasn't hard to imagine them going into battle for her, primed to do or die.

Glancing furtively at Eddie, Max saw that none of this was lost on him. He watched the sequence raptly, his lips slightly parted, one fist tucked under his chin. His attention appeared to be complete, and Max felt a surge of certainty that what his camera framed, others would recognize.

He let the sequence run to the end, when the boat was again secure and Groot back on the steps with Rachel, then he flipped on the lights. Eddie turned to him and nodded briskly. "Really good, Max. Dramatic but subtle. Real."

"Yeah?" He had shown most of the raw footage he'd shot of Rachel so far. "Glad you like it, Eddie."

Jacques got up to turn off the video monitor and roll it back to its dormant position against one wall. "Everything you just saw was shot with available light," he volunteered. "Not to mention available budget."

"Very persuasive." Eddie leaned back in his chair, arms folded, and seemed to address the ceiling. "Especially the interior scenes. They have a kind of elegiac quality that on film might be too much. But on video..."

"How about the girl?" Max asked him. "Rachel. Or am I completely deluded?"

"No, no, not at all. She's everything you said. Absolutely. But, when one is working in a *vérité* mode, or some version of it, so much depends on events over which one has no control." He rocked back on his chair's rear legs. "It's one thing to have a script and not use it, another thing entirely to discard all pretense. Here I'm speaking solely as your business manager, you understand. You may find investors reluctant to commit themselves until you have a finished film. But that you knew already."

Max began to pace. "People and their money. It could make you weep."

"Save your tears," said Eddie. "Give me a copy of the key scenes, edited to seduce, and I'll see what I can do."

"Fine. But keep those zombies away from me. Final cut is my decision alone, right?"

"Naturally." Eddie spread his arms in a personification of reason. "You do your work, Max, and I'll do mine. As always."

"Sorry, Eddie. I'm a little jazzed."

He and Jacques spent the rest of the morning choosing scenes for the prospectus package Eddie had proposed. And while the footage he'd already shot was rich with implication, suggesting several narrative lines even as it gave natural precedence to Rachel and to the boat's renovation, Max couldn't help feeling he had overlooked some crucial element or tendency—in the woman, or the setting, or the forces that shaped them— that, when finally laid bare, would upend his understandings and reduce all his labors to insignificance. It was a foolish notion, distinctly counterproductive, but he found it difficult to dismiss. Maybe, he thought, he was trying too hard.

At one o'clock he sent Jacques home and closed up the studio. He lunched alone and paid some bills, then, with most of the afternoon still ahead of him, took the métro to the Centre Pompidou, where an exhibition of Brassaï photographs had opened the night before. Viewing them, he hoped, might somehow allow him to see Paris afresh. It seemed important that he shift perspective.

The show was unusually crowded for a weekday afternoon—tourists, mainly—and the galleries dimly lit so as not to damage the vintage prints. He moved patiently from one section of the exhibition to the next, waiting his turn to stand before each picture, which he would then examine until he had his fill, heedless of those shuffling by behind him according to the dictates of the instructional headphones they'd rented. And the images were ravishing: nighttime scenes from the 1930s, dark tableaux of bordellos and bridges, lovers and lowlife, addicts, apache dancers, and architectural monuments, all of them suffused with the night vigor peculiar to Paris, where dawn could seem an afterthought and daylight more like a distraction than the main event.

He was examining a scene depicting two *clochards* barely visible in the darkness beneath a bridge over the Seine when he heard himself addressed from behind by a voice he recognized without at first being able to identify, a woman's voice speaking softly in French.

"You're alone?" the voice asked.

"Yes," he answered without turning around.

"Would you like some company?"

It was Véronique, the graduate student he'd encountered at the café across from the estate agent's. "Maybe so," he said.

"Good, me too."

They laughed. She was prettier than he remembered, her thick blond hair gathered in a French braid down her back, and she wore a darkly floral perfume redolent of gardenia. Together they moved on to the next photograph.

"It is a cliché to love Brassaï," Véronique said, "but I don't care. He captured most of what's best about Paris—both the romance and the heartlessness. He makes you see how they can be the same thing."

The print before them depicted a prostitute standing on a deserted corner in shadowy profile; a light source outside the frame picked out the back of her head and shoulders. Across the street a shop sign read FROMAGE.

"You see?" Véronique said. "It should be a bad joke that she stands under a sign advertising cheese, but no, not at all. Instead, the effect is of tenderness without illusion. The world is what it is, neither more nor less. Extraordinary, don't you find?"

In fact the photograph, with its closely valued blacks and silver-white highlights, aroused in Max both envy and a flicker of despair. "Yes, it's good. Great, even." They lingered over the picture. "And the lighting's sublime."

She looked at him curiously. "Yes, you're a filmmaker. I remember."

"Lit from the side like that," he said, "the scene's indelible. The camera rests in darkness, complicit with the night. Likewise the viewer. Hitchcock does the same thing in some of his films."

"I love it," she said simply, returning her gaze to the photograph.

And as they progressed through the show, adapting to each other's pace and exchanging comments on what they saw, Max began to form an impression of someone quite unlike the graduate students he was used to. Secure in her intelligence, at home in the physical world and its representations, Véronique seemed free of the need to prove herself or establish her bona fides, intellectual or otherwise. Her observations about the photographs were astute, but casually offered. She displayed none of the exacerbated sense of time, the gotten-up anxiety, that others thought demonstrated their commitment to a purpose. Yet the air of unfocused aggression he noticed at their first meeting remained latent in her gestures and in how she carried herself; it wasn't hard to imagine her flying into a rage, and Max wondered whether she herself knew why she'd sought him out.

After leaving the museum, they crossed the plaza to the Café Beaubourg for coffee. She insisted on sitting upstairs, away from the sidewalk traffic, and when they were installed side by side on a banquette overlooking the staircase, she said, "So you're a filmmaker. Have I seen your films?"

"Probably not," he answered.

She nodded. "I almost never go to the movies. The important thing is, are you a *successful* filmmaker?"

"That depends on what you mean. My films get made, distributed, and seen. Some of them win awards. None of them has made anybody rich."

"And do you want to be rich?"

"I want to make more films, and for that money's required. Otherwise I'm indifferent."

"You're lucky," she said. "Me, I want to be filthy rich, rich to the point of nausea and beyond. It's a burden, this desire—completely at odds with what I've set myself up to do." She ferreted a cigarette from her backpack, and he lit it for her. "Yet there it is. Undeniable, you know?"

"And what is it you've set yourself up to do?" he said.

"My field is Slavic studies—Russian history, literature, art—so in effect I've set myself up to teach. But I'll never do that. Maybe business or international relations, something in the real world, such as it is." She exhaled smoke through her nostrils. "Do I shock you?"

"Me? Hardly. Not that I know what you mean by the real world."

She gave him an odd little smile, started to say something, then visibly reconsidered.

The waiter brought them their espressos.

"I'm not an expert," said Max, "but I'd think that Russia would be a pretty good place to get rich these days. For someone who's not going to teach."

"There are opportunities," Véronique allowed, "but one has to have the right contacts. Where the rules are uncertain, personal influence is the only reliable index of worth. Access, that's the game. Anyway, I didn't say I wanted to make money myself. Not at all. What I want is for someone else to make it for me."

"I see," said Max. "So you have a business plan."

She laughed. "And you're American, yes?"

"By birth, citizenship, and sensibility. But I live here now." Raising the espresso cup to his lips, he saw her register his wedding ring. "My wife is French," he added.

"And you love her, this wife of yours?"

"I do, yes."

"Good." Véronique leaned slightly away as she withdrew one arm and then the other from her little cardigan sweater. Underneath she had on a lavender tank top, and on her near shoulder was that tattoo, a finely etched wheel of many spokes. "Then we have no misunderstandings, right?"

Max considered his answer. "Okay."

"Tell me," she said, "did you find what you were looking for the other day?"

"In a word, no. But of course I didn't really know what it was I was looking for."

"La Peau de l'Ours," she replied helpfully. "Something by that name."

"Yes, but the people in the office said they knew nothing about it. They were very emphatic." Not entirely to his surprise, Max became aware of Véronique's bare shoulder pressed in seeming negligence against his. He decided to elaborate. "I've been having problems with pirated videos of my films. The one that came to my attention was issued under that label, La Peau de l'Ours, at that address. But it seems that both the name and the address were false, at least according to what I was told."

"Really?" Her gray-blue eyes scanned his. "That must be so frustrating."

"It's nice of you to take an interest in my situation," he said. "What's yours?"

"Mine?" She expelled a puff of breath. "But I've already told you—"

Still looking at her, he discreetly increased the pressure where their shoulders touched.

"All right," she said. "I was watching too, waiting for someone I had reason to believe might show up there. When you arrived, I thought you might be him, but of course you weren't." She shrugged.

"So this guy you were after, you'd never seen him before?"

"No. I was acting on behalf of a friend."

"I see. Not the friend in your business plan, by any chance?"

She smiled, acknowledging the connection even as she invited him to share her amusement at his having made it. "I told you my desires are burdensome."

"Yes, well, whose aren't." He drew away somewhat peevishly.

"The problem," she said, "is that my friend's too much of a gentleman to tell me about his business decisions. This makes it hard for me to help him. So sometimes I have to strike out on my own."

"To protect your interests. Sure, I understand."

She stubbed out her cigarette in the ashtray. "Have you been back to the agency?"

"No, what for?"

"I just thought maybe you had."

Max considered her. "Do you want to tell me who you're looking for?"

"Better not. But you'd know him if you happened to run into him. You'd realize right away." She took a card from her backpack and wrote a phone number on it in green-black ink. "This is the best place to reach me."

He glanced at the card and put it in his pocket. "You know," he said, "I'm always reading about the Russian mafia, how they've infiltrated this business or that, using legitimate operations to launder black-market profits, manipulating currency rates, bribing officials, killing competitors, all that. But I never really thought they had much of a presence in Paris."

"They don't. Not really." Her eyes shone with what he at first took for glee but a second later couldn't interpret at all. "Anyway," she said, "what does it matter? One must cultivate one's own garden, no?"

"Absolutely," he said. "One must."

When they parted, outside on the plaza, Véronique pressed her body fleetingly to his before cheek-kissing him goodbye. *"Ciao,"* she said. "Call me whenever."

Max watched her go. Her perfume clung to him, making him feel vulnerable and distinctly absurd. Now he'd have to change clothes at the studio before going home. He couldn't recall the last time he'd been so expertly handled.

On rue Charles V he stopped at a bookstore and killed half an hour there by reading the first and last pages of whatever volumes caught his fancy. It was what he did whenever he found himself needing to clear his thoughts. At four thirty, somewhat refreshed, he decided to revisit the realtors.

There was a police van outside when he arrived and two officers loading it with cardboard boxes filled with manila file folders. Madame Leclère stood by the door of the agency, fuming. "Idiots!" she said. "Flunkies!"

Max watched from across the street, looking up and down the block and pretending to check his watch as though inconvenienced by someone late for an appointment. A third officer emerged from the office and attempted to engage Madame Leclère in conversation. She turned on him. "This is an outrage. I'm a French citizen. What has any of this to do with the crime committed against my partner?" Catching sight of Max, she seemed suddenly to call him to witness. "The crime of murder!" she cried.

Max hastened to look away.

"Why am I being punished? And my business? Can't you see what they've done to me?" She began to weep. The police officer took her arm and spoke into her ear, but she shook him off. "Please! I'm not a child."

Max decided to walk around the block.

When he returned, minutes later, the police were gone and the door was locked. He hesitated, then rang the buzzer. Madame Leclère appeared, dabbing at her eyes with a handkerchief, and through the glass she tried to shoo him away, but he held his ground. After staring hard at him, she let him in.

"Madame," he began, "I saw what happened just now, with the police. If you plan to file a complaint, I would be more than willing to—"

"Who are you?" she demanded.

"I came by before, about an apartment in Bastille."

She sighed. "Ah, yes. Well . . ." She stepped aside to let him in. After locking the door again, she turned and walked past the deserted front desk to the back room. He followed.

"Please." She gestured toward a green leather sofa.

Sitting, Max saw that she didn't remember him.

A bottle of peppermint schnapps stood open on the desk where she now lingered, and from the bottom drawer she produced a teacup. "An aperitif?" she asked.

Max shook his head.

She filled the teacup from the bottle, closed her eyes, and drank the contents down in two quick swallows, and then, with a shudder, sank into the club chair opposite him. "I must still be in shock," she said.

"What happened?" Max asked.

"What happened? Well, they murdered him, shot him down in the streets like a dog and left him there, that's what."

After a brief interval Max said, "They?"

"He took risks, of course. That was Sylvain. But I never thought he'd get into serious trouble. I thought he was mostly trying to impress me." She got up and poured herself another half cup of schnapps. "Excuse me, but my husband died barely a year ago, in a car accident. Now this." She made a face and downed the drink. "Do you have any idea how I feel?"

"I'm sorry," Max said, watching her return to her chair.

"And on top of everything else, the police. They've got it all wrong. You saw, they took my files! What morons!"

Max shifted in his seat. "Who do the police think killed your partner?"

"Professionals is the word they used. That was their brilliant hypothesis, based on their painstaking evidence—namely, that he was shot eight times in the chest on a busy street." She shook her head wearily. "This is not me. I'm not saying this."

"Believe me, I know the feeling." Max leaned forward. "These people your partner was in trouble with, might they be . . ." He cast about for a suitable term. "Could they be Russians?"

She stared at him. "What makes you think that?"

"It's just a guess. You said professionals."

"No, really. I want to hear." She straightened in her chair. "What makes you think that my partner was killed by the Russians?"

Max tried to recall the logic that had led him to this supposition, but in fact there didn't seem to be any, only impressions that had accumulated over the last several weeks, half-formed thoughts belatedly given shape by Véronique's insinuations or his own reading of them. *They'll dump our bodies in the Seine*, Madame Leclère had told Broch during Max's first visit here. It had happened before. "I don't know," he said at last. "I shouldn't have said it."

Madame Leclère appeared to contract slightly. "Did I tell you I had to identify the body?" She shivered. "It was bad, Monsieur. Very bad."

"Yes, I can imagine."

"They should've shot me also. That would have been more respectful." She looked fiercely around the room. "Ah, but they're bastards," she added, and, burying her face in her hands, began bitterly to weep.

For nearly a minute Max stayed where he was. At the back of the room, past the open file cabinets that the police had emptied, a doorway framed a wrought-iron staircase leading to the upper floors.

Max got up, went over to her, and laid a hand gently on her back. "Please. Is there anything I can do, Madame?"

Still bent over in her chair, she shook her head.

"A glass of water, maybe?" he persisted.

But before she could respond, the front buzzer sounded—a sustained note followed, after a pause, by a staccato flurry of shorter ones.

"Let me get it," Max told her. She sniffed but made no move to stop him.

Waiting at the entrance was a round-faced, swarthy man dressed in a khaki jumpsuit. He glared at Max through the glass. The key was still in the lock; Max turned it and opened the door.

"Monsieur Sylvain Broch?" the man asked, reading from a clipboard he held cradled in one arm.

"No, I'm sorry. Monsieur Broch isn't available."

"He has a delivery of twelve cartons. You will have to sign for them."

Looking past him, Max saw a dark brown panel truck parked outside. A man got out of the cab, went around to the back of the vehicle, threw open its rear door, and began unloading boxes.

"Wait a moment," said Max. But just as he turned to call for Madame Leclère she arrived at his side, her equilibrium seemingly restored.

"Excuse me, Monsieur," she said to the first man, "but we're not expecting a delivery. You must have the wrong address."

The man rolled his eyes in a paroxysm of self-control. "Twice we tried delivering this shipment to the designated address," he said. "At neither time was there anyone to receive it. I am therefore obliged to deliver to the billing address, which is here. So if one of you will just sign the manifest, we can be done with this before our grandchildren bury us."

Madame Leclère grimaced and took the clipboard from him.

Reading over her shoulder, Max saw that the shipper was a computer-supply wholesaler and that the boxes were to be delivered to an address in the tenth arrondissement. The purchaser was indeed listed as Sylvain Broch. A red stamp across the bill declared the shipment paid for.

"But what do these boxes contain?" asked Madame Leclère.

"That is not my concern, Madame," said the deliveryman, handing her a pen.

The man unloading the cartons approached with the first six stacked on a hand truck. Madame Leclère stopped him, then turned to Max. "Would you mind?"

Accepting a box cutter from the driver, Max slit the top carton. Inside, wrapped individually in cellophane, were forty packages containing fifty blank DVDs each—two thousand a carton, twenty-four thousand all told.

He handed one of the packages to Madame Leclère. She read the label and shook her head in bafflement.

"What are these?" she asked.

He told her.

She sighed and, signing for the cartons, said, "This is a complete mistake."

# CHAPTER 16

WHEN THREE DAYS PASSED without a visit from the police or any mention in the media of Sylvain Broch's murder, Turner began to brood. It was one thing to have someone killed—and Kukushkin had doubtless done it before—but to erase the act as well as the man required very deep resources indeed. Worse, he found himself unable to discount the possibility that the men he saw kill Broch were the same two Odile had complained of—a troubling notion, since it meant Kukushkin had been making sport of him in New York, at Balakian's gallery, when offering to find out who they were. Whatever the truth, Turner understood that he could no longer pretend to be uninvolved.

He picked up the phone and punched in Odile's number. The line was still ringing when Gabriella swept in with the day's obituary clippings, which she deposited in his inbox, and two plastic shopping bags stuffed with small objects wrapped in newspaper. When Odile's voice invited him to leave a message, he hung up. "Are those what I think they are?" he asked.

His assistant smiled with demure satisfaction. "I told you I could do it."

For months he'd been trying to win the confidence of an elderly woman in Auteuil, the former mistress of a highly placed Vichy official who had bequeathed her his *netsuke* figures, mid-nineteenth century and earlier, the finest collection Turner had ever come across. When his best efforts at wresting them from her had proved unavailing, he sent Gabriella in as backup. Playing to the old harridan's fears as well as her vanity, she succeeded, and the woman had now agreed to put the ivory carvings up for auction. The house commissions would be substantial.

"My superb Gabriella," he said, embracing her, "you've outdone yourself."

She blushed. "The key was her son. When she told me he votes Socialist, I helped her see that if she left the collection to him, he would certainly sell it and give the money to the illegals and Arabs, or at least their advocates. I was afraid she'd have a stroke before I got out of there with the consignment."

Turner shook his head in sad wonderment. "We risk our lives for art, and no one cares."

"But of course people care! Besides, someone has to do it." A hint of caution passed across her features. "What do you mean, our lives?"

"Figure of speech," he said.

"Oh, I almost forgot. Look what she gave me." Reaching into her purse, she produced a slim volume elegantly bound in blue calfskin and stamped in gold with Cyrillic characters. "Pushkin, first edition."

He leafed through the book, a prose work in six chapters and a conclusion, no more than fifty pages in all. "But can you read Russian?"

"Not a word. She told me the story, though, or at least part of it. I'm going to get a French translation. Isn't it beautiful?"

Indeed the book was a treasure, and handling it Turner experienced a moment of avarice. "She just gave it to you?"

"I was very surprised. We'd been talking about gambling—she goes every summer to Biarritz to play roulette—and she was impressed that I knew the French laws about where you can or can't play, which, by the way, I bet you don't know."

Turner did not.

"Gambling is legal only in towns that have natural hot springs. In any case, the title of this book"—she took it back from him and opened it to the title page—"translates as *The Queen of Spades*, and it's about a guy who's obsessed with finding a system for winning at faro. I think it ends badly. There's a ghost involved."

In his mind Turner saw the ruddy interior of Bar Flou. He saw the man fan out the deck of cards before the couple, saw the younger man draw out the queen of spades and hold it up for his girlfriend to see. She exclaimed. He saw the two men switch places while the girlfriend clapped her hands in delight and the other women looked on. "Why the queen of spades?" he asked. "Does it have some special meaning?"

"I don't know," replied Gabriella. "I'll tell you when I find a translation."

After she'd retired to the basement storage rooms to begin cataloging the *netsuke*, Turner set an auction date for the flags, on the second Thursday in June—as late in the season as he dared push it. International buyers would by then already have begun touring the summer art festivals and could reasonably be expected to make a stop in Paris, while French buyers, if any, would not yet have left. The flags would be exhibited a full week prior to the sale, and the catalog, lavishly illustrated and annotated, would go out three weeks before that. Turner had nearly finished writing the copy.

He took lunch alone at a nearby bistro, and as he lingered over coffee his thoughts returned to Odile. He hadn't seen her since the afternoon at Céleste's studio, but that image—her sitting nearly naked for the portrait, the green dress open like a robe, her features defiant, even imperious—remained vivid to him still. It was like a taunt, and he recalled how casually he'd brushed aside her worries about the men who were harassing her, with what certainty he'd told her the problem had been taken care of. Now he was certain of nothing.

Through Céleste, Turner had been able to fill in many of the blanks. He knew about her filmmaker husband, their money problems, her American friend Rachel, the houseboat. He knew Odile had lived in New York at about the same time as he had and that she'd met her husband there. He knew about her father, the charismatic geographer and Trotskyite. He even knew she'd recently given up eating meat. All this he had learned, yet far from laying his questions to rest this new knowledge seemed only to underscore the incompleteness of his understanding, not just of Odile but of the events now unfolding around him, events in which she might or might not be playing a part. *I'm half obsessed with her,* he thought. And though he waited for other, less drastic formulations to offer themselves, though he knew better than to personalize what was at bottom no more than a set of circumstances, the notion remained uncontradicted in his mind and he was forced to wonder what it might portend. He sat a second longer with the thought, then roused himself and signaled the waiter for his check.

BILLIE HOLIDAY WAS SINGING "All of Me." Amber sunlight bathed the sofa on which Odile sat half dressed, and the air smelled of oil paint, turpentine, and cigarette smoke.

"So he has only the one daughter?" asked Céleste, pausing to squeeze another measure of cadmium red onto her palette plate.

"Yes. And Allegra's very well brought up for an American kid— respectful, well spoken, not at all spoiled. But at the same time she's thirteen years old and the child of divorce; one cannot expect her to be unaffected."

"No, of course not. In which case one must ask whom she blames the most: you, him, her mother, or herself?"

"Herself, certainly. But she takes it out on Max, which in itself wouldn't be so bad if he just didn't respond so helplessly. It's painful to watch, you know? For a serious man to learn doubt and guilt at the exact moment when real success has come to him . . . Ah, but life is cruel and stupid. Why complain?"

"One complains because one is human," said Céleste. "Now turn your head a bit to the right. Not so far. Good." She drew thoughtfully on her cigarette and contemplated Odile. "Yes, I'm beginning to see how this painting must go. Only now do I see what I'm up against."

"Really?"

"You have the face of a maenad in repose. I look at you and think, here is someone who may be capable of anything. Murder, even. And yet there's also a kind of control."

"You flatter me," Odile said with a small laugh.

"Not at all. I simply tell you what I see." She resumed painting, her brow furrowed, her eyes darting from Odile to the canvas and back again. "Keep looking out the window. Good. This will be difficult, perhaps impossible, but I must try. There's an opening, at least that. You'll work with me?"

"Yes."

"It will take longer than I thought. But just maybe . . ."

Two buildings away, near the middle of Odile's rooftop vista, a woman appeared bare-breasted at a window, flung it open, and dropped an armload of clothes to the tar-paper surface of the roof just below. Immediately after, a man in his undershorts climbed out, landing likewise on the tar paper, while above him the woman slammed the window closed again and shut the curtains so violently that they shimmied back and forth for a few seconds. The man began to dress, taking his time. When he was done, he straightened his jacket, lit a cigarette, and sauntered out of sight past the chimney.

"Have you seen Turner lately?" Odile asked.

"Yes, yes. He comes by often. Sometimes I think I must have married him in another life. But I do enjoy him, you know. So charming for an American."

"Maybe. Yet I get the impression that in his personal affairs he isn't so happy. Does he have anyone?"

"There are girls. Nothing serious."

"And I suppose he prefers it like that?"

"I don't think he likes it or dislikes it. This is simply how life has turned out for him at the moment." She stepped back from the canvas and scrutinized it briefly before changing brushes and addressing it anew. "When he lived in New York, though, things were different."

"Really? You mean he was in love? It's hard to imagine."

"I don't know much about her, except that she was also involved in the art business. 'Brilliant eye' was how he once described her to me. They were together two, maybe three years, I think. She died in a car accident."

"Is that why he moved to Paris, then? To make a fresh start?"

For some seconds Céleste painted in silence. "It was definitely an incentive," she said.

Letting her eyes go fractionally out of focus, Odile sorted through the mental images she had of Turner, searching for one that might match the man Céleste had just summoned up for her, a man in love, a man driven by grief to change his life. But no such image presented itself, and her curiosity about him segued, for lack of concrete information, into a kind of waking dream in which he repeatedly displayed his passport to her, explaining himself in a voice that only occasionally penetrated her understanding. He seemed to be asking a favor.

She sat for Céleste until the afternoon light began to fade and color gave way to shades of silver and gray. A delicious melancholy settled over the studio. Shedding the green dress, Odile danced a few improvised steps across the floor to shake the numbness from her limbs, then retrieved her street clothes from the bedroom and put them on. Céleste was examining the canvas in the dying light.

"Progress?" asked Odile, who by now knew better than to ask to see the painting.

"Yes, progress of a kind. But it's strange. I've found the maenad and lost the other thing."

"What other thing?"

"I don't know." Céleste shrugged. "But never mind. We're sure to do better next time." She offered Odile her cheek. "Until then, sweet."

They embraced, then Odile hurried down the stairs, through the courtyard, and out into the street. The spring temperatures and lengthening twilight had brought the local student population out in force, and as she passed the Place de la Sorbonne, the mingled sounds of laughter, giddy conversation, and a lone street violinist sent a shiver of unexpected feeling up her spine. Her own days at university, which she hardly ever thought about, had been a blur of violent discovery and relief.

She took the bus from Val-de-Grâce, sitting in the rear beside a nattily dressed blind man who from time to time would ask her what street was next. When he got off, two skinheads in motorcycle jackets boarded the bus and immediately set about harassing anyone with whom they could make eye contact. Odile signaled for the driver to stop, then went to the front and demanded that he eject them. When he equivocated, she marched back down the aisle and, using arm motions completely new to her, shooed them out the back door herself. Her heart was still pounding three stops later when, at Arago, she again pressed the red stop button and stepped out into the gathering darkness.

At the corner market, a modest but immaculate establishment run by a wizened Chinese couple, Odile picked up the ingredients for an asparagus risotto she planned to make for dinner. Paying with a crisp hundred-franc note, she watched with interest as the shopkeeper's wife ran it under a small ultraviolet light newly installed by the register. The bill fluoresced. Odile thanked the couple and, waving off their apologies, left with her change and purchases.

There were no lights on in Max's studio when she arrived at the gate of the mews. She punched in the entry code, walked the length of the court-yard to their apartment, also dark, and, setting the groceries down outside, fumbled through her purse for the keys. When at last she had hold of them, just as she was about to unlock the door, she sensed someone approaching from behind. Whirling to face him, she made a swipe at the intruder with her keys, but he caught her wrist and held it.

"It's me," Turner said.

She saw that it was. "Let me go."

He did. "We have to talk," he said.

"Don't ever do that to me again," she said, opening the door and switching on the lights.

"Sorry." He followed her in.

She closed the door behind him. "Are you crazy?" she demanded.

"That could be it," he said.

They stared at each other.

Turning away, she saw her dressmaker's dummy, layered in muslin pattern pieces, in the center of the studio. She snatched a cotton sheet from her worktable and threw it on top. "We'd better go upstairs," she said, gathering up the groceries.

In the kitchen she put away her purchases, then took a bottle of pomegranate juice from the refrigerator and poured them each a glass.

"Where's your husband?" Turner asked.

"Max? Finishing up work. He'll be here any minute." She set two small bowls on a platter, filled one with ripe olives, the other with almonds, and took the whole unnecessary ensemble into the living room. Turner followed with their glasses.

"If this is trouble," said Odile, taking her drink from him and settling at one end of the sofa, "I don't want it."

He put his own glass down on the coffee table and sat down beside her. "Not trouble, exactly. A situation."

Contemplating him—a large-eyed, hungry-looking man in an olive cotton suit, his shirt striped black and tan, his raw-boned hands clasped between his knees—Odile was not comforted. "I'm listening," she said.

"Three nights ago the man who recommended Thierry Colin to me— his cousin, in fact—was shot dead in the street. I was there when it happened. The guys who did it, I think they might be the same two who've been bothering you and your houseboat friend."

Odile sniffed. "You mean those Russian idiots?"

"Right. Them." A muscle in his jaw began to twitch. "The unfortunate thing is, they work for someone I know, a Russian banker with connections."

"I remember," said Odile. "The guy people don't like to cross."

"Well, he warned me about the shooting right before it happened, but he also made certain it happened where I could see it and draw the appropriate conclusions."

"Which were what?"

"I think it's safe to say that he's not very happy with Thierry Colin." Turner took a sip of his juice and grimaced. "Are you sure you don't know where he is?"

"Of course I'm sure. I told you. He just disappeared."

"Right." Turner massaged the twitching facial muscle with his thumb. "Do you have any tranquilizers, something like that?"

She shook her head. "I can give you whiskey."

"Would you mind?" He handed her his glass. "It's been a stressful week."

In the kitchen she tossed his juice down the drain and poured four fingers of scotch into a fresh glass. For whatever reason—his evident anxiety, their overlapping predicaments, a rogue maternal impulse—she felt marginally more sympathetic toward him. When she returned with the whiskey, she found him standing just inside the bedroom door, peering at the discreetly framed and matted Giacometti drawing that hung there.

"It looks genuine," he said, accepting the glass.

She turned on the picture light. "It is. You're the one who keeps fakes, remember?"

The drawing was of an upright female nude, gaunt and haunted-eyed, rendered in a storm of pencil strokes from which she seemed only partly to emerge. In places the density of line was built up almost to blackness—along the inside of the thighs, across the abdomen, under the breasts—while elsewhere it thinned to a faint, negligent scribble. The effect was uncanny, as if the figure were shimmering into being of its own accord. Odile had always found it bewitching and troubling in equal measure.

"Do you like it?" she asked.

"Yes, it's good. Very good."

They looked awhile longer, then went back to the living room. Odile settled into the corner of the sofa with her legs tucked under her.

Turner eased down next to her. "Understand my position," he said. "Whatever Thierry Colin did to upset my banker friend, people are being held accountable. It would be a pity if you or I were needlessly misjudged."

She studied him curiously. "So what do you propose to do about it?"

"I thought we might start by pooling our information. Did Thierry say anything to you about being in debt?"

"We were on a debtor's errand," she replied. "That was a given."

"Yes. But maybe he let something slip about, I don't know, how he liked to spend his money. Does he have a girlfriend, for example?"

"He didn't mention anyone," she said carefully. She was wearing a necklace of many finely wrought silver chains bunched together, a gift from Max, and as her fingers toyed with it now she thought of Gabriella parading up and down before the mirror in Thierry's apartment, wearing the dark rose underwear that was also a gift, and she was again as dismayed as she had been then. "Not that he would have," she added.

"You mean he came on to you?"

"He tried, the first night on the train. But I quickly put a stop to that."

Turner nodded. "What about drugs?"

"No. I would've noticed."

"What else?"

She hesitated. "I think he had gambling debts."

Turner put down his glass in surprise. "Gambling? Really?"

"We didn't talk about it. But he kept this notebook, journal, whatever. I got a look at it, just a few pages. He was trying to work off what he owed." Hearing herself speak these words, she grew alarmed. Her mind raced, and she imagined a swift cascade of events in which her presence in Thierry's apartment had somehow become known to Gabriella after all, with consequences to match. "But all that was before Moscow," she added quickly. "I'm surprised you didn't know."

Turner shook his head in annoyance. "And you?" he asked after a moment. "What do you think happened to him?"

"I have no idea. But I can tell you what one of those Russian half-wits told me. He said that Thierry smuggled a group of Belarussians into the country for prostitution and forced labor."

"I don't believe it," Turner said. "Do you?"

"Stranger things have happened."

Turner reached for his glass again and drank the last of the whiskey. When he looked at her, his lips were parted in an odd half smile.

"What is it?" she asked.

"Nothing."

"No, really."

He set his glass down. "How's it going with Céleste?"

"Very well. We're becoming friends, I think. But she must have told you that." He had moved closer to her, and she could feel his warm whiskey-breath against her face.

"More or less," he said. "So I guess by now you know the story of my life."

"Your *life?*" Odile snorted in exasperation. "Look, Turner. You said you'd make this problem—this very tedious and stupid Thierry Colin problem—go away. Fine. But still I'm being harassed, and now you tell me someone has been killed. Excuse my naïveté, but isn't it time to turn this whole infuriating mess over to, for example, the police?"

He sighed. "I'm afraid not. You see, my banker friend ..." Waving a hand vaguely in the air, he seemed to suggest complications too numerous or disagreeable to articulate. "No, now the only thing is for us to find Colin ourselves."

"What?"

"You and I together. Us."

Odile looked away. She'd left the light on over the kitchen counter, its soft yellow incandescence spilling over the wooden cutting board and the asparagus she'd placed there, so that from where she sat, with darkness intervening and the twin pools of light cast by the sofa-side lamps making everything near her visible and ordinary; the small kitchen tableau glowed like a distant stage. The sight transfixed her, filling her with a strange expectancy to which she could attach no object.

"I doubt it's worth anything," she said, "but one of those Russian thugs told me Thierry would soon be contacting me about his fee for the Moscow trip. Why me and not you, I don't know, but I have a number I'm supposed to call when he does."

"They gave you a number?" Turner's dark eyes appeared to dilate, and for the first time Odile understood the extent of his fear. It enveloped him with a dreadful magnetism that embarrassed her.

"Those guys are such buffoons," she told him. "Most of what they say, they make it up on the spot. Or they have to write it down to keep it straight. Thierry has no reason to contact me."

"But if he does," said Turner, "would you call me first?"

She couldn't help staring at him. "Yes. All right."

He started to say more, but then, as if belatedly acknowledging a fact long known to both of them, he brought his hands up under her breasts and, leaning into her, pressed his lips to her neck, breathing into her hair until she shivered.

To her chagrin, she discovered herself less than surprised. "Don't you have enough problems?" she asked, laughing at him softly.

He drew back in surprise. "I guess not," he answered a moment later, then brought his mouth to hers.

There was an instant when she might have struck him—she fully intended to—but somehow it passed, and she let him kiss her, waiting for him to realize his mistake. He tasted of whiskey and desire and something else that she couldn't identify, something metallic that she felt against the back of her throat. When she realized it was fear, the force of the recognition sent a confused thrill through her. Time jumped—she saw herself standing in darkness before her father's cellar steps—and then jumped again. She had begun to respond to his kiss: grudgingly, less grudgingly.

His hands at her breasts lifted them and seemed to take their weight away. Her nipples grew taut between his fingers. When he started to undo the buttons of her blouse, she broke the kiss and, without actually deciding anything, arched her back to make it easier for him.

She wondered at her recklessness.

Looking down at him as he lowered his mouth to her nipple, she found it all infinitely strange. There was something she wanted to say, something hard that might do justice to the precipice toward which they were rushing, but she had yet to discover the right words when a sound from downstairs brought her up short.

A key in the lock. The front door opening.

*"Enough!"* she hissed, thrusting a forearm between them. Immediately she was on her feet, buttoning her blouse, straightening her hair, gathering up their glasses, switching on the overhead lights.

"Odile?" The front door swung shut.

"Hi, Max," she called down the stairs.

Turner stood uncertainly, awaiting instructions. She glared at him and pointed to the sofa. After a moment's incomprehension, he saw the impressions their bodies had made on the down-stuffed cushions and flipped them over.

"You won't believe the day I've had," said Max, starting up the staircase.

Odile glanced at her reflection in the mirror beside the landing. Her upper lip was abraded where she'd been kissed, and she rubbed the spot with a saliva-moistened finger. "Me too," she called, dabbing at her hair. Then she turned on her heel and stepped into view just as he reached the top of the stairs. "There you are," she said, smiling at him.

They kissed.

Max set a grocery bag he was carrying on the kitchen floor. "I hope you haven't already—"

Turner cleared his throat, and Max looked around in surprise.

"Oh, I'm sorry." Odile hastened to interpose herself between them. "Max, this is Turner, from the auction house. He's here to appraise the Giacometti for us. Turner, my husband, Max Colby."

They shook hands warily.

"It's a beautiful drawing," Turner said.

"Yes, it is, isn't it." Max turned in bafflement to Odile. "Are we selling it?"

"No, no. I just thought we ought to get an idea of what it's worth. For insurance purposes."

"You really should keep it insured at value," Turner offered. "To be on the safe side, I mean."

Max looked quizzically from this stranger to Odile and back again. "Okay. Would you like something to drink?"

"Thank you, no," Turner answered.

"He just needs to see the papers," Odile added quickly. "Provenance and certificate of authenticity. We were waiting for you."

"No problem," Max said. "Just give me two seconds to wash my hands."

While he was in the bathroom, Odile took the Giacometti from the wall and laid it on the kitchen table. Turner started to say something, but she hushed him at once, refusing to meet his eye. He took a photographer's loupe from his pants pocket and began examining the drawing.

"You know," he said when Max returned with the papers, "something like sixty percent of the Giacomettis on the market today are forgeries. I've seen dozens, lots of them with very convincing provenances."

"Is that right," said Max.

Odile stood slightly apart from them, her arms folded across her chest, her mood contentious.

"But this one's good," Turner went on. He straightened up and handed Max the loupe. "See how even the pencil line is? The dark areas are built up by superimposition. Most forgers can't help increasing the pressure a little when they have to darken the image. That's because they want to draw like Giacometti without thinking like him. They're focused on product, not process. It's a dead giveaway."

"Right." Max hunched over the drawing, peering at it through the loupe. "I read somewhere that he never finished anything, just abandoned it." Max passed the loupe to Odile. "And that he liked to work in fading light, right up to the point of darkness and beyond. True?"

"Quite true."

Both men watched her examine the drawing. When she looked up and saw them staring at her, she flushed. "So, are we about finished here?" she asked, handing the loupe to Turner.

There remained the business of the papers, which Turner examined closely. The drawing had been a wedding gift from Max's mother, who'd bought it on a trip to Paris the year before he was born, and she had been assiduous in acquiring the necessary documentation. When Turner was satisfied that everything was in order, he took a business card from his pocket, wrote a figure on it, and gave it to Max, who glanced at it before passing it to Odile.

"That's my best estimate, if you were to sell it now," Turner told them. "I'll have my assistant write up a formal appraisal and send it to you by the end of the week."

He had priced the drawing at 350,000 francs.

"Thank you for your time," Odile said, giving him her hand.

"Not at all." He managed a strained smile. "I hope you don't sell it, but if you decide to, please call me."

Once he'd left, Odile hung the drawing on the bedroom wall, then went into the kitchen to start dinner. Max paced in the living room.

"That's quite a price," he said, "considering my mother paid a hundred and fifty bucks for it straight out of the gallery."

"I don't want us to sell it." Odile put the asparagus in a colander and ran cold water over it. "I just thought we should have an idea what it's worth."

"What about that guy?" Max said. "Turner. You think he's legitimate?"

"I called the auction house, and that's who they sent me," she said with a shrug. "Why, don't you like him?"

He now came up behind her at the sink. "I hadn't really thought of it in those terms. But he seems to like you well enough."

She laughed, shut off the faucet, and, drying her hands on a dish towel, turned to face her husband. "That's all right," she said, letting her eyes grow wide and still. "I don't like him much either."

## CHAPTER 17

HE KEPT THREE PHOTOGRAPHS of Allegra on his dresser. In one she was the radiant child, three years old in a red party dress, standing on a sunstruck bench in Central Park, her face thrust forward in transports of hilarity. The second showed her four years later, at the Caribbean resort where Max and Diana had made their last attempt to salvage their marriage. Here she was standing beside a fountain in the open-air lobby, her right arm extended to accommodate a parakeet that was balanced on her forefinger, her eyes turned uncertainly toward the camera; she'd lost her baby fat, and her hair had darkened to honey blond. The third photograph had been taken a year ago at her mother's apartment. Here Allegra was seated somewhat formally on the sofa, her hair pulled back in a ponytail, a book in her lap. She looked into the camera defiantly, a half smile on her face, and though she was a pretty child, her eyes, it seemed to Max, had become calculating. From one picture to the next, her physical resemblance to him increased so markedly that it sometimes took his breath away. Not infrequently he wondered if she'd ever forgive him for it.

That weekend, with Odile in Vertou for Sebastien's sixty-ninth birthday, Max decided it was time to settle the question of Allegra's summer plans once and for all. He waited until he knew she was at her Saturday-afternoon riding lesson—horses had lately become her presiding obsession—and then called Diana at home. To his surprise, his ex-wife shared his view about Paris.

"It would do her good to get away," she told him. "The kids she hangs with now have got a bit of a jump on her developmentally, and I think she feels the pressure. You know—to be more mature, quote unquote."

"Mature?" Max repeated warily. "You mean in the physical sense?"

"No, Max, not in the *physical* sense—surely you've noticed that much." Diana sighed. "It's this false sophistication kids have at that age, a kind of contempt for what they were the day before yesterday. Allegra's just not that cynical yet, bless her."

"They have a saying here," Max ventured, "that the two worst times in a woman's life are when she's thirteen and when her daughter's thirteen."

"Thanks for that," said Diana in a tone he couldn't interpret.

"Anyway," he added, "we're agreed that I'll take her for June, right? Eddie's daughter Dominique will be here, so she'll have a friend. Plus I'm shooting locally, as far as work goes. Allegra and I, we'll have a mutual growth experience."

A brief silence ensued. "Okay, Max," Diana said quietly. "I'll leave you to tell her about it yourself." Then, before he could respond, she hung up. It was a little after nine o'clock.

Having made no plans for the evening, he spent the better part of an hour cleaning out the tiny garret room upstairs which served as the guest quarters. It would be necessary, he decided, to put a full-length mirror on the back of the door and get her a telephone. Allegra would certainly bring her own books and laptop, and he could decide later whether to leave the film-still decor intact or replace it with something less personally freighted. A room too eagerly prepared, he recalled from his own adolescence, could be even more off-putting than one not prepared at all.

At ten o'clock, with at least two hours remaining before he could reach Allegra across the six time zones that separated him from New York, Max changed clothes, stopped by the studio to pick up a still camera, and headed for the quai de la Tournelle to look in on Rachel and Groot.

He found them seated on the *Nachtvlinder*'s quarterdeck with Katje, the Dutch photographer. She and Groot were sharing a hash-boosted cigarette while Rachel spliced two lengths of rope. They all three hastened to their feet at his approach.

"You're just what this group needs," said Rachel, flinging her arms around him in greeting. "Isn't he, Groot?"

Groot smiled and shook his hand. "Rachel thinks I've become stodgy in my old age," he explained.

"She didn't say old," Katje corrected him. After kissing Max hello, she took his camera from him, snapped two pictures of Rachel in rapid succession, and gave it back. "She did say stodgy, though," she added, laughing.

Groot disappeared belowdecks and returned a moment later with a bottle of Armagnac, which he poured out equally among four glasses. All drank.

"Tell him about the engines," Rachel said.

"*Ja*, the engines." Groot lit another reworked cigarette and passed it to Max, who hesitated—he still intended to call Allegra—before drawing on it thoughtfully. "We have found on the Internet," Groot continued, "two duplicates of the *Nachtvlinder*'s engines, still in their original taxis. The owner was asking ninety thousand francs each, which of course we cannot pay, but yesterday we find that in fact the owner has died, and his widow is willing to consider other offers. So maybe we will be lucky, who knows? I will go next week to look at them."

"They're in Reims," Rachel added, "so it might actually be doable." She took the cigarette from Max and, to his surprise, inhaled deeply from it before passing it to Katje. She seemed to be running a little ahead of herself.

"Are you going too?" he asked her.

"I don't know yet," she said, smiling brightly. "Maybe."

Since the flood, Max had been shooting Rachel and Groot together whenever possible in an effort to accustom the Dutchman to the camera. He wasn't the natural subject that she was, but he had a flair for the dry aside that sorted well with her physical expressiveness, and more than once, replaying the results in his studio, Max thought he discerned a darker undercurrent in their exchanges. Then he would look again and decide he'd imagined it. Such a sublime instrument, the camera: it revealed everything except the secret of its indifference. Maybe he, too, would have to go to Reims.

"So now that everyone's in a better mood," said Katje, flipping the cigarette butt over the side, "are we going to do anything fun?"

Rachel was already on her feet. "Let's go, guys," she said, extending a hand to Max and Groot. "Redeem yourselves."

They drove in Katje's minivan to a nightclub in the tenth, a renovated theater whose lavender-and-black interior was sparsely lit by ice-white sconces of frosted glass and miniature spotlights playing over the half-filled dance floor. On a dais at the far end, enclosed in Plexiglas, a DJ in dreadlocks commanded two turntables, a laptop, a mixing board, and a headset microphone. Running the length of an adjacent wall was a cherrywood bar.

Max ordered champagne all around, and, when it came, the four of them clinked glasses and drank. He was gratifyingly high.

"Dance with me," said Rachel, taking his glass from him.

Max handed his camera to Groot and let himself be led onto the hardwood floor.

Rachel was a wonderfully fluid dancer, responsive to Max's lead without ever seeming to wait for it, and again and again her eyes flashed at his in unfeigned delight. The DJ cross-faded a jumped-up reggae vamp into a party mix of "How Insensitive," bringing up the bass and speaking a few unhurried exhortations through the fuzz-boxed microphone. Rachel spun in and out of Max's arms like a skater, lending him a grace not normally his own. They kept it up for a good thirty minutes.

Later, having handed her off to Groot, Max sat at the bar chatting with Katje and a startlingly beautiful Ivorian transvestite of her acquaintance. Yvette, as the man styled himself, had two different lives, two different plans. In one he was a film critic of some repute, who knew Max's work and was writing a screenplay. In the other he was an African queen, hoping to open a beauty school on rue de la Goutte d'Or. At one point, Katje seemed to suggest that Yvette and she were lovers. Max thought it unlikely.

He tried shooting some photographs of Groot and Rachel dancing, but by then the club was packed and he had trouble getting a clear line of sight. Thwarted, he ordered another glass of champagne. At a little after two, his patience exhausted, he excused himself and went outside to call Allegra on his cell.

A line of would-be revelers waited on the sidewalk, trying to engage the doorman's attention. Max crossed the street and sat down on a bus-stop bench facing the club. Protocol dictated that he try Diana's number first, but he got the answering machine and left no message. After a moment's deliberation, he punched in Allegra's cell-phone number. It rang three times before, amid loud music and voices, someone not his daughter answered.

"House of Babes," the girl said. "How may we serve you tonight?"

Peals of teenage laughter sounded in the background.

"Allegra, is that you?"

"Um." A stricken silence replaced the laughter. "Just a minute." There was a crash as the phone dropped to the floor. "Shit." Someone turned down the music. "Allie! I think it's your dad." More urgent whispering. The phone changed hands.

"Hello?" Allegra said.

"Sounds like you girls are having a party."

"Oh. Hi, Dad. Yeah. I'm at Camilla's with some friends. We're having a sleepover." Her voice was studiedly casual.

"That's great. Are Camilla's parents there?"

"They're downstairs watching a movie." She hesitated. "Do you want to talk to them?"

In fact, as Allegra knew full well, Max didn't want to talk to them, whether they were home or not. "That's okay," he said, "but I do need a word with you, if you've got a moment."

"All right," she said, affecting a tone of utter bafflement. He heard her leave the room and close the door behind her. "What's up?"

Across the street a small altercation had broken out in front of the club: two men in their twenties scuffling over a woman. The doorman looked stolidly away, his arms crossed.

"Your mother and I," Max began, "think the best thing would be for you to spend June here in Paris. You'll still have July and August with your friends, but we'll get a chance to visit first, you and me. How does that sound?"

"Okay, I guess."

"Dominique will be here. She's really looking forward to seeing you. And Odile, too. We'll have a great time."

There was a sullen silence. Outside the club the woman at the center of the dispute now pummeled the doorman with her fists, demanding that he stop the fight, which, in keeping with local custom, consisted almost exclusively of verbal insult and fierce physical posturing. Max had yet to see either man land a clean blow.

"Dad?"

"What is it, sweetheart?"

"Like, I don't want to be rude or anything, but it's just totally obvious that Mom wants me out of the way this summer so she can be with Willard."

"Willard? Who's Willard?"

"Her new boyfriend. That's where she is tonight—you know, on a *date*. You called the apartment first, right?"

Max sighed at his daughter's stratagems. "Nobody wants you out of the way, Allegra. And your mother deserves to have a life, just like anybody else." As he watched, the doorman sidestepped the woman, grabbed the two men by their collars, and banged their heads together, sending them reeling off in opposite directions to light applause from the crowd. "So I'll book you a ticket for, let's say, the Friday after school lets out."

"Whatever," she said, as though suddenly bored by her own obstinacy. "Hey, will I still have my own room?"

But before he could answer, the line was again hijacked by screechy teenage laughter. "Woah, Allie! You are *so* dark shadows tonight!" And another voice: "Yeah, can we get a little *light* on the subject, please?" Gales of giggles, music.

"You *guys*! I'm on the phone." Then another door slammed shut, and it was quiet again.

"Allegra," said Max after a moment, "do I need to worry about you?"

"No, Dad. Really. Everything's cool."

"All right. So I'll see you in, what, three weeks."

"Okay. Bye. Love you, Dad."

"I love you too, Allegra." He hit the end button and leaned back on the bench. After a moment, he took a small black cigar from his jacket pocket and lit it. Long-distance conversation with his daughter often left him feeling stupid and regretful—as he felt now—but sometimes there was another element to his response, one that trumped everything else. Probably all fathers felt it. All fathers of daughters. He stood and began pacing back and forth as he smoked, trying to work out what it was.

"Max!" cried a voice from across the street. "Oh, Maximilian!"

He looked up to see Katje beckoning to him from the rolled-down driver's-side window of her minivan, Rachel, Groot, and Yvette already aboard, waving giddily. Max tossed away his cigar, crossed the street, and, getting in up front with Katje, was suddenly excruciatingly awake.

"You think you can escape," said Rachel, passing him another cigarette, "but you can't."

"Of course I can," he replied. After taking a long drag, he handed the cigarette back over his shoulder. "Why can't I?"

"In the theater of the real," the Ivorian assured him, "nearly everything is possible."

Groot laughed softly to himself.

"I know exactly what you're thinking," Rachel told him. "Exactly."

Then Katje put the van in gear, turned on the radio, and in an instant Paris was passing by like a dream—sparsely trafficked, elegantly lit, alive with night thirst.

Their ostensible goal was an after-hours club whose name and address Katje insisted she'd remember in just a second, though she was quick to add that she'd never been there and couldn't recall who had told her about it. Max soon determined, however, that arrival wasn't the point, driving was the point, and as the conversation grew more and more disjointed, and the van kept approaching the same intersections from different quadrants before lurching off again to a renewed chorus of encouragement from the backseat, he belatedly began to realize what had him so on edge.

"Stop!" he told Katje.

"Here?" she demanded, pulling over. "Why?"

"I just need to walk for awhile. Clear my head." He leaned back over the seat to kiss Rachel goodnight and shake hands with Groot and Yvette. "Thanks, everybody. It's been great."

"But how will you get home?" Rachel asked. "The métro's closed, and taxis—" She looked up and down the empty street.

"Don't worry about me. I'll be fine." He got out with his camera, said goodnight again, and, as the van lurched off down rue du Faubourg du Temple, took stock of his surroundings. It was nearly three o'clock, with everything closed or pretending to be, and he believed himself to be within five blocks of the address he'd seen on the manifest for Sylvain Broch's shipment of blank DVDs.

He walked for twenty minutes, checking street names and questioning whether he had remembered the address correctly. When he finally turned the corner onto what he thought was the right block, he saw, at its far end, a man loading boxes into a dark green panel truck. Max got there just as he pulled the rear door shut and slapped it twice with the flat of his hand, sending the vehicle careering off into the night. With all the self-control he could muster, Max greeted the man, slipped him a fifty-franc note, and asked what was in the boxes.

The man shrugged. Merchandise, he didn't really know.

But where was it being taken, then?

After appearing to check the sky for adverse weather conditions, the man told him that quite possibly the boxes were bound for Saint-Ouen, at the north end of Paris, where, though naturally he himself could not say, it was conceivable that their contents would be sold later that morning at the flea market—or perhaps not, as the case may be. Then, bidding Max an abrupt goodnight, the man unlocked a bicycle leaning against a nearby wall, mounted it, and pedaled off.

Max turned to inspect the building from which he judged the man to have emerged. The ground floor was occupied by a cell-phone franchise, and neither it nor the three darkened stories above showed any sign of life. But also set into the limestone facade was a knobless metal door painted red. Max was about to knock when he reconsidered, gave it a tentative push, and slipped inside, the door closing behind him.

A man lay on his back in the middle of the floor, playing slow, dissonant chords on an electric guitar strapped across his hips. Overhead, ultraviolet lights provided the only illumination, while at the room's peripheries, in darkness, a drummer kept complex, skittish time—cymbals and snare— and a bassist provided a lush arpeggio.

As his eyes adjusted to the gloom, Max made out a half-dozen circular tables with two or three customers at each, a waitress leaned up against a wall smoking, a man passed out on a corner banquette. Closer to him he saw a small bar, a skinny bartender, some stools.

Max sat at the bar and put a fifty down in front of him.

After awhile, the bartender brought him a clear iceless drink in a plain glass, took the fifty, and came back with the change.

Max leaned across the bar and asked, "Is this La Peau de l'Ours?"

The man stared at him, uncomprehending.

"Okay, not important. But how about Sylvain Broch? He rents a space here, yes?"

"That depends."

"It's all right. I'm a friend of his."

The bartender looked hard at Max, then lifted his chin to indicate the freight elevator in back. "Third floor."

Crossing the room, Max peered down at the recumbent guitarist, who appeared to be in a trance, his eyes rolled back in their sockets, but with his band behind him and his small audience fixed in place, he seemed quite ready to go on for hours. Max took care not to disturb him.

The elevator opened, at the third floor, onto a shallow space created by a steel-mesh screen blocking access to the main area. Max felt around for a light switch. A ring-shaped fluorescent tube sizzled on overhead, and he saw that the pass door was secured not with a lock but with a twisted coat hanger, which he undid without difficulty. A string brushed his face; he pulled it.

He found himself in a medium-sized loft of whitewashed brick and wooden floors, its street-side windows painted black. Along one wall was a folding cafeteria-style table, set up, very much as he had envisioned, with a computer and a linked series of DVD burners, twelve in all. On the floor beside this array was a carton half filled with blank DVDs and another with black plastic boxes for the completed product. Farther on, against the adjoining wall, another table held two color printers and a stack of stick-on labels. It was all there—all the instruments of intellectual piracy—except, of course, the intellect and the pirates.

He sat down in front of the computer and switched it on. When the boot sequence ended with a password prompt, he got up and began a more methodical inspection of the place, working counterclockwise around it. He'd almost completed his circuit when he noticed a loop of wire protruding from the drywall on the north end. He pulled the loop, a door opened, and he switched on another light.

Inside was what seemed a personal refuge for whoever worked the computer, with a neatly made-up cot, its white coverlet turned down as if for a guest; a bookshelf stocked with commercial DVDs and academic journals; a board resting on cinder blocks to form a narrow desk; a jar of several fountain pens; a binocular microscope next to some loose DVDs; and, pushpinned to the drywall above the desk, a laser-jet photo of a building seen from above in black and white.

He went first for the shelved DVDs, which were arranged alphabetically, so that *Fireflies,* the genuine version, was flanked by *Fanny and Alexander* and *Fort Apache*—company he was hardly inclined to disavow, whatever the circumstances. After scanning the shelves for his other films—all, he thought, more successful than his first—he turned with small enthusiasm to the microscope. The DVDs beside it bore a pale amber coating on their data side, an almost transparent veneer he decided must be some sort of quality-control indicator. Tilting one of the disks back and forth in the light, he felt a sudden wave of fatigue that forced him to sit down on the cot behind him and, a moment later, to stretch out on it at full length, disk still in hand. He closed his eyes.

Then he was in a race of some kind, a polycathlon in which he moved through pine forest on cross-country skis, wearing night-vision scopes, with a high-powered rifle slung over one shoulder. Other contestants, intermittently visible through the trees, loped along parallel trails, and he shot at them, downing two and winging another before the slope grew precipitous and he had to jettison the rifle to stabilize himself for the downhill run, crouching over his skis like a racer, the poles tucked under his arms. When he hit the jump, the wind ripped the night scopes from his eyes and he flew or fell, pure velocity, into dark unbounded space.

He awoke in a state of confusion. At first he thought he'd been incarcerated in a jail cell or hospital room, but the DVD in his hand reminded him what had brought him here. Pocketing the disk, he glanced at the shelf of academic journals—back issues of *Revue de la Chimie Organique et Biomoléculaire,* not his subject—and was about to leave the little room when his eye fell on the laser-jet photo over the desk.

The building depicted, a massive fortress with barred windows and thick stone walls, was unfamiliar to him, but given its trapezoidal shape, and the stone aggregate walls ringing it, he knew that it must be La Santé prison, around which he had walked countless times, after innumerable dinners, two blocks from home. Inspecting the photo more closely, he noticed that one of the prison windows had been circled in red.

He went back out to the loft space, found his camera, and systematically set about photographing everything—the computer and DVD burners, the printers and stick-on labels, the shelves of movies and journals, the cot, the microscope, the prison photo—all the while imagining legal proceedings in which such documentation would prove useful. Eddie Bouvier would know how to handle it.

Emerging from the freight elevator at the ground floor, he found that the music was over and the audience had left. At the bar, beneath a hanging lamp, the waitress he'd seen before was reading sports scores aloud from a newspaper while the guitarist, now becalmed behind dark sunglasses, listened attentively. Max said goodbye and stepped outside into the dirty dawn.

# CHAPTER 18

"EVERY DAY," said Turner from behind his desk, "people die, divorce, go bankrupt, or become incompetent in the eyes of the law." He let his glance drift up to the dust-dimmed chandelier overhead. "Naturally, on such occasions, property changes hands. Our job is simply to see that this process unfolds in a timely and reasonable fashion, with due regard for the legal position of our clients, who in this case happen to be ourselves." He returned his gaze to Gabriella, seated before him. "What part of this do you not understand?"

"You know quite well that it's a risk," she said. In her lap she held the galley proofs of the catalog copy Turner had written for the flags. "Why create a false provenance for objects that no one expects to be documented in the first place? It draws unnecessary attention."

"My dear Gabriella. Did I or did I not ask you to acquaint yourself with Russian patrimony law?"

"Certainly, but as I also told you, those statutes have never been enforced in France. And even if they were, it wouldn't happen over a roomful of Soviet flags. Some fifteenth-century icons, perhaps; but not those things."

"Well," Turner said after a pause, "let's just say I think we need an extra layer of deniability in this instance, given the likely media coverage. Okay?"

She said nothing, but as she turned away he saw her jaw tremble and clench.

"Gabriella, what's the matter?" He came around the desk and she rose reflexively to meet him, sending the galleys cascading to the floor. He enfolded her awkwardly in his arms.

"It's nothing," she said. "I'm stupid."

"What can I do?"

"Nothing. It's not about the flags. You know I have exactly zero interest in what the law thinks of me or you or anyone else."

"Ah, Gabriella. You are a treasure beyond price."

She gave a small sniff. "Not *completely* beyond price," she reminded him.

"No, of course not. I didn't mean that literally."

She stooped to gather up the galleys and walked across the office to set them on the bench facing Turner's desk. "By the way," she said, "I wrote up the appraisal letter for that Giacometti drawing you looked at last week, but it didn't go out until Friday. You forgot to give me the dimensions. I had to call the client."

Turner's stomach pitched. "Really? How was that?"

"No problem. She was quite nice, in fact. Odile Mével, yes?"

"That's right."

Gabriella took a step toward him, her arms folded across her chest, her eyes flashing. "Wasn't she the courier you hired to pick up the flags in Moscow?"

"She was. Her and that other guy." To his chagrin, Turner found himself loath to pronounce the name of Thierry Colin. "Why do you ask?"

"I hope you're being careful," she said.

"Gabriella, please. Tell me what's wrong."

She shook her head.

"Are you pregnant?" he asked before he could stop himself. He had no idea why he said it. As far as he knew, she didn't even have a serious boyfriend.

"Pregnant?" She laughed a little, but looked, Turner thought, rather sad. "No, believe me," she said, "pregnant would be the easy version of what I am." Glancing unhappily at her watch, she excused herself and left the room.

That afternoon Turner had lunch with Horst Wieselhoff, the Swiss collector he'd met through Balakian. Wieselhoff had just come from Düsseldorf, where he acquired two massive oil paintings on canvas—twelve by eighteen feet each, with steel and lead elements attached. He'd brought along color transparencies for his friend's inspection. "What are those rusty jagged things sticking out?" Turner asked, holding one of the transparencies up to the light. "They look like——"

"Bear traps," Wieselhoff said with satisfaction. "Forty of them on that one alone. Each painting weighs almost three quarters of a ton. They are companion pieces on the theme of Lilith, and, I have been assured, the last major works the artist intends to sell to a private collector. Future efforts will go only to museums. What do you think?"

"I think you must have paid some heavy coin," Turner said. "What, two million each?"

The Swiss smiled. "More."

Much as Turner admired the paintings—and they were frighteningly successful, the best he'd ever seen by this artist—he didn't covet them. Thus unencumbered, he performed a rough mental review of the man's probable assets, the contents of his collection, and the likelihood that this newest purchase had left him overextended. But he had always found Wieselhoff hard to read, impenetrably Swiss, so he handed back the transparencies and said, "You bought them for love, which would make them cheap at twice the price."

"Exactly so," Wieselhoff said.

"Congratulations, Horst. A coup."

Their lunch arrived—sliced duck for him, turbot for his guest—and while they ate, exchanging inconsequential news and gossip, Turner's mind circled back, as it had repeatedly over the last few days, to Odile. Everything that had happened between them at her apartment—the kiss she'd warmed to by degrees, the unconsidered way she'd arched her back to hasten his fingers at the buttons of her blouse, the cool logic with which she'd explained his presence to her husband and, having done so, her obvious impatience as she awaited the scene's pedestrian conclusion—all this remained perfectly vivid to him, as though it were a joke he was constantly obliged to tell himself, a joke of which he was the butt. He was without illusion and saw himself as she must see him, yet he couldn't help sensing that, whatever their professed intentions, they each possessed something the other required. The desire to be known by her, known and not despised, encouraged him to imagine a world more forgiving than the one he believed himself to inhabit. Surely he wasn't alone in his wishes; perhaps, he thought, everyone had them.

"I saw our friend Kukushkin last week," said Wieselhoff. "He sends his greetings."

"And I send him mine," Turner answered. "What was he doing in Düsseldorf?"

"Banking business, something to do with currency exchange." The Swiss poured himself more wine. "I don't inquire too closely, you know."

"Kolya is a man of many talents," Turner agreed. "Did you show him the paintings?"

"Of course. In fact he came with me to the artist's studio. Very cultivated, Kolya. Not like the so-called New Russians one meets everywhere these days, with their designer labels and vulgar habits. True, he is an entrepreneur, but that doesn't prevent him from seeing more than most men. Can one accurately describe him as a visionary? I wouldn't too soon say no."

"Who calls him a visionary?" asked Turner.

The Swiss shrugged, as though deferring to an absent third party. "We talked quite a lot about you, by the way. I didn't realize you two were so close."

"Oh," Turner said. "Yes, Kolya and I go back a ways." He cut the last slice of duck in two. "What was on his mind?"

Wieselhoff hesitated, then laid down his knife and fork. "If I may speak frankly?"

"Please."

"He worries for your safety. He didn't go into detail, but rumor has reached him that someone claiming connection to you is involved in a cross-border crime, possibly kidnapping." Wieselhoff raised a placatory hand. "Understand: Kolya knows you could never be involved in such a thing—as do I, of course, as do I. But still he worries."

Turner nodded affably. "Sure, I see. And who am I supposed to have kidnapped?"

"Not you. No one thinks that."

Turner waited.

"It could be one person," Wieselhoff allowed, choosing his words carefully. "It could be possibly a truckful. This is the rumor."

"Aha." Recalling what the Russians had told Odile about people being smuggled out of Belarus, Turner grew momentarily despondent, though he did his best to conceal it. "Really, Horst, I'm just no good at these things. Did Kolya say what I should do?"

"No, no. He only wanted to be sure you knew, so you could take precautions."

"Okay, then. Thanks for the heads-up." But Turner harbored no illusions about Kukushkin's message, its purpose was plain, and though he was quick to steer the conversation to other topics as the waiter cleared the dishes and brought coffee, though he listened attentively to Wieselhoff's plans to exhibit his recent acquisitions at a well-regarded *Kunsthalle* in Basel later that month, he knew that if he really proposed to save himself—let alone Odile, who as yet had small interest in his help, or anyone else's, if he read her correctly—he would have to do some very inventive market positioning indeed, starting at once.

"Horst," he said, "you asked to be informed if more of those Soviet May Day flags turned up. I have a small group coming to auction—this will be the last of them—but I'm prepared to let you have one now at the same price Balakian's buyers paid, with a single proviso."

The collector brightened. "Tell me."

"If I sell the flag to you, I'd like you to show it with the rest of your new acquisitions in Basel, giving it equal prominence. This would be mutually beneficial, as I'm sure you can appreciate."

Wieselhoff's eyes grew moist with emotion. "When can I see them?" he said.

Turner called for the check.

Back at the auction house, he allowed Wieselhoff to choose his favorite of four medium-sized flags, and in return Wieselhoff wrote him a personal check for 210,000 francs. Then, after Gabriella had rolled the flag into a cylinder, wrapped it twice in butcher paper, and tied it up with twine, Turner sent this satisfied customer out into the afternoon with his purchase—even though Turner knew that no collector, however fortunate, however Swiss, could truthfully be described as satisfied.

"What do you bet he'll be back for the auction?" he asked Gabriella.

But she just shook her head and busied herself with other things.

Turner spent the rest of the afternoon consolidating his gains. He drafted a press release announcing the flags' impending sale, placed a few discreet calls to his best media contacts, letting them know what to expect, and wrote a private memo on the subject to the director of the auction house. The thing was coming together. He'd taken risks, yes, but with a steady hand and a willingness to improvise he would soon see a handsome return on his investment—as much as five million francs, after the house commission. And yet Wieselhoff's message from Kukushkin—or what Turner understood the message to be—weighed unpleasantly on his mind. It occurred to him that a prudent man in his position might do well to acquire the means to defend himself. A small handgun, for instance. He'd never use it, of course, but using it was not the issue. Morale was the issue.

He waited until Gabriella had departed for the day before calling the brothers Battini, the Corsican pair he'd sent to ransack Odile's apartment, and to Marco, the elder and marginally less excitable of the two, he described his needs. After some back and forth in which Marco tried to persuade him to place his safety in the hands of contract professionals, experienced individuals such as himself and his brother Pasquale, he finally agreed to meet Turner at Parc des Buttes Chaumont in two hours' time, near the top of the steps inside the park's west entrance.

At six o'clock Turner left the auction house, withdrew four thousand francs from a cash machine on rue la Boétie, and walked east on boulevard Haussmann. Passing the Opéra, he picked up rue Lafayette and continued east at a businesslike clip, periodically switching from one side of the street to the other in an attempt to discover if he was being followed. As far as he could tell, he wasn't.

Arriving early at Buttes Chaumont, he decided to take a short turn around the grounds, a former quarry and garbage dump that Baron Haussmann had transformed into a hilltop arcadia complete with an artificial grotto, a lake, and a classical pavilion. There were a fair number of people about—the park stayed open until eleven—and Turner found their presence reassuring and worrisome in equal measure. He crossed the Pont des Suicidés, ninety feet above the lake, and found an empty bench near the appointed spot. Sacré-Coeur glowed white in the distance. Overhead, storm clouds gathered.

Marco Battini arrived some twenty minutes late, carrying a black nylon gym bag and a rolled-up newspaper. As the sky continued to darken, people left the park in a steady stream, filing past the bench Turner had chosen, and Battini indicated with a toss of his head that they should seek a more secluded spot. When they were sheltered under two large gingko trees, he unzipped the gym bag and extracted an object wrapped in red cloth. "Go ahead," he said, offering him the bundle. "See if you like it."

Turner gingerly unwrapped the object, careful not to touch it directly. He knew little about handguns—the only other he'd actually seen was the revolver pressed to his temple some years ago by the unhappy buyer in TriBeCa—but he was relieved to see that this one looked nothing like that.

"Nine-millimeter semiautomatic German-make," Battini informed him. "Top of the line." He took the gun and released the magazine catch to show that it was loaded. "Fifteen rounds, sixteen if you keep one chambered." He pushed the clip neatly home. "Never jams. Cost to you: thirty-five hundred."

"Is it clean?" Turner asked.

"Clean and sterile." Battini turned the gun over slowly to demonstrate that its exterior serial numbers had been obliterated. "Same on the inside. Want to try it out?"

"Here?"

Battini laughed. "Suit yourself. But this weapon's going to make you very happy, I guarantee it." He handed the gun to Turner, then reached again into the gym bag and brought out a small cardboard box. "And because we've done business before, I'll throw in some extra ammo." He shoved the box at him impatiently. "So that's thirty-five hundred cash. You brought it, right?"

Turner laid the gun and ammunition on the bench beside him and produced the money, which Battini flip-counted before stuffing it into his jacket pocket. "Good," he said.

Both men rose, and as they shook hands Turner thought he saw a glint of genuine curiosity in the Corsican's eyes. Other people's troubles, he supposed.

"Use it in good health, Monsieur," said Battini, not unkindly. Then, seizing the gym bag and newspaper, he padded off down the darkening path.

Turner hadn't anticipated the problem of transporting the weapon—somehow he'd imagined it would come in its own carrying case—but after fumbling with it for a few panicky seconds he jammed it into the waistband of his trousers, in back where his jacket would cover it. Then he picked up the box of cartridges and, feeling curiously lightheaded, set out for the park's east gate. The sky had grown very dark, and there were glimmers of lightning.

Once on the street, he flagged down a taxi, which delivered him to his building in Bastille just as the heavens opened. In the short dash to the entrance he was drenched. He punched in the access code, rode the elevator to his floor, and let himself into his apartment.

Leaving the gun and cartridges on the kitchen table, he changed into dry clothes, then poured a glass of scotch and took it into the living room. Forked lightning sundered the skies, sending tremendous thunderclaps through the ozone-charged air and rattling the apartment windows until he feared they'd shatter. He left the lights off and pulled up a chair to watch.

Years ago, hiking with friends in the White Mountains, he'd seen someone nearly electrocuted in a lightning storm. Having been caught more or less in the open, on a meadow plateau between two rocky rises, the man had sought shelter in a slight depression in the ground, thinking to present less of a target there. But he'd been mistaken. The current already running through the ground used his body to bridge the depression, and for two or three seconds he was encased in a crackling blue suit of light that was as terrible as anything Turner ever expected to see. The man had survived, but barely. The story had no moral, and Turner disliked being reminded of it.

By eight o'clock the center of the storm had passed. He prepared a supper of leftover fusilli putanesca and salad, washed down with a half bottle of chianti. Afterward he examined the gun closely, removing the clip and inspecting the firing mechanism until he understood it, then stowed both gun and cartridges in the bottom drawer of his dresser, with his socks, where he hoped never to see them again. So much for self-defense, he thought.

Still restless, he tried reading—he'd recently taken up Montaigne's essays, as much for companionship as for mental stimulation—but the very naturalness of the prose seemed to rebuke him at every pass, and he couldn't stay with it. Instead he poured himself another drink and began walking around his apartment like a stranger, inspecting his possessions for clues to what it was he was always looking for, as if knowing might help. The fragmentary Greek *kouros*, the African stool, the Japanese screen, the Egyptian heads. He was drawn to them because they were beautiful, though that did not, he couldn't help but note, make them indispensable. Far from it. They were beautiful, and that was all.

He paused before an eighteenth-century Venetian mirror he'd acquired two years ago in a trade. It was narrow—the glass just five inches wide by thirteen high—and ornately framed in carved wood painted pink and gold. Beneath it hung a matching pendant, flush to the wall and shaped like half a pedestal, on which three votive-style candles stood clustered. He lit them and saw his face illuminated from below like a face by Caravaggio, melodramatic, violent, blood-smart. It spooked him but did not instruct. Maybe, he thought, he wasn't in a learning frame of mind.

He went into the bedroom and turned on the television. The public-affairs channel was running a documentary about a guerrilla insurgency in Myanmar, a hundred and fifty men led by two nine-year-old twin boys their followers regarded as divinities. The boys were radical ascetics, wore fatigues many sizes too big for them, and smoked cigars with the lit ends in their mouths. Finding them hardly less taxing than Montaigne, if for opposite reasons, Turner was about to change channels when he heard, from the front of the apartment, a faint disturbance. He muted the TV to listen, but could make out nothing further until three knocks sounded, somewhat tentatively, at his twice-locked front door.

He was on his feet before he knew it. Whoever wanted in knew the downstairs entry code and ought by rights to be a friend. But he was expecting no one, and his situation didn't lend itself to spontaneous drop-ins.

"Just a moment, please!" he called.

Barefoot, he went to his dresser, opened the bottom drawer, took out the gun, and, giving it a wary once-over, racked the slide. *So*, he thought. *So so so so.*

His visitor knocked again, this time with more resolve.

"Coming!" he called, and walked to the front hallway, where he stopped to listen. "Who is it?" he asked. "Who's there?"

There was a silence, followed by what could only be full-body blows to the door, someone throwing himself repeatedly against it in a rage of impatience. For a moment Turner considered shooting right through the door, never mind the consequences, but something persuaded him not to, and instead he undid the locks and cautiously opened it.

Odile stood framed there for an instant, then walked coolly past him into the apartment. "Hello," she said.

She was soaking wet, her hair plastered to her cheeks and forehead, her blouse translucent, the hem of her skirt dripping water onto the floor. Turner could make no sense of what he saw until he remembered the rain. He closed the door still holding the gun, but it had been pointed at the floor the whole time. Odile ignored it completely.

"I thought you were someone else," he explained feebly. And then: "Where's your umbrella?"

She spoke abruptly, not bothering to hide her irritation. "Don't ask stupid questions." Putting her purse down on the floor, she scooped her hair away from her face with both hands, sending water droplets flying. "What time is it?"

He checked his watch. "Ten-ten."

"We'd better hurry, then. I have to get back." She stepped out of her heels and, leaving them where they were, walked down the hall as if she'd passed down it many times before.

"Back?" he repeated. Each word he spoke left him feeling stupider than the last.

"To my husband," she said over her shoulder.

Mute, wreathed in unknowing, he followed slowly after her. By the time he reached the bedroom, her clothes lay in a small damp pile on the rug.

"Give me that," she said, pointing at the gun. He gave it to her, and she tossed it across the room into the laundry basket. Then she lay down on his bed, drew the fingers of one hand up between her legs, and said, "So finish it, Turner. Finish what you started."

He undressed, wordless, and went to her.

# CHAPTER 19

THAT WEEK Groot went as planned to Reims to inspect the defunct taxis Rachel had found on the Internet. After an hour of polite conversation with the owner's widow, he was invited to acquire both vehicles for the sum of forty-two thousand francs, provided he remove them from her property by day's end. Rachel persuaded her parents to wire her the money, then met Groot in Reims, where they loaded their purchases onto a flatbed truck he had rented for the return trip. At a junkyard just outside of town, they stopped to extract the engines and discard the remains. Then, three tons lighter, they drove straight through to Paris.

Max and Jacques met them in Bastille, at the Bassin de l'Arsenal. There the engines were to be transferred by winch to a small barge that would ferry them out of the marina and down the Seine a short distance to the *Nachtvlinder*. Worried he might miss the scene, Max had arrived almost two hours early, but waiting had only increased his anxiety. The sheer quantity of human detail seemed to conspire against him at every turn and put his work unconscionably at risk. Now he and Jacques, with the camera on a tripod between them, stood midway down the park side of the marina. They were watching Groot back the rental truck up to the loading dock while Rachel engaged the winch operator, flirting with him in pidgin French. The late-afternoon light gave everything a burnished look.

Max said, "I think it's time we go on the offensive here."

Jacques squinted at him, then returned his gaze to the scene spread out before them. "If it can be done, you may be sure we'll find a way."

"Better get the other camera, then. I'll shoot this part from here, but once the engines are loaded I want you to go with Rachel to the *Nachtvlinder* so we can cover the delivery from that angle. I'll stick with Groot on the barge. Something tells me he might be ready to share his thoughts with us on camera."

"What about her?" Jacques asked.

"It's hard to tell. On the one hand, she says she's happy they got the engines. On the other . . ." Max peered briefly through the camera's viewfinder. "I don't know. Just try to get her talking. See if she'll tell you her plans."

Jacques left. The barge arrived at the mouth of the narrow waterway. As Max watched it edge toward the loading dock, he began preparing himself for the role he would shortly have to play in the proceedings if he really proposed to coax a film from this de facto cast. Actors, nonactors—he should've known that in the end it made no difference. The problem was the same. People wanted you to provoke them into becoming who they really were.

He shot the transfer in two takes. In the first, he kept the whole scene in the frame. Rachel climbed onto the truck bed, trussed one engine in a sleeve of chains, and stood back while the winch operator lifted his load, swiveled it out over the barge, and lowered it into Groot's guiding arms. For the second take, Max stayed focused on Rachel, who secured the second engine as she had the first, gave a thumbs-up, and watched the cargo rise into the air. Max zoomed in until her face filled the frame. She followed the movement of the engine with her eyes—an arc of anxiety that ended, finally, with a tired smile. Then she took off her glasses and, though Max knew she was too nearsighted to see him at this distance, looked straight into the camera for a baleful second before turning away.

He waited until he saw Jacques appear at Rachel's side with the second camera, then joined them.

"Max!" said Rachel. "I had no idea you were here. Did you film that?"

Ignoring her, he stepped onto the barge, camera and tripod in hand.

"Max?" she repeated uncertainly.

"Don't worry about him," Jacques advised, taking her by the elbow. "He's really busy right now, but I'm still with you. We're going to the *Nachtvlinder,* right?" Assuring her that everything would be fine, he shepherded her back toward the truck.

"Congratulations, Groot. You got them after all." Max vigorously pumped the Dutchman's plump hand. "You must be very happy."

"It was a stroke of luck, for certain," Groot agreed. He was wearing a blue-and-white-striped fisherman's jersey and a gray, flat-brimmed felt hat that made him look like a Netherlandish shaman.

Max's mood improved a little. "I thought I'd ride along with you, if that's okay," he said. "Maybe get you to say a few words for the camera."

"Yes, why not." Groot smiled modestly. "Just let me coordinate with our captain over there"—he pointed to the barge's pilot, who was loudly cursing everyone present —"and I'll get back to you."

The two diesel engines lay side by side on the deck, bleeding oil into a thin, rainbow-hued slick that seemed to be swirling in on itself. Max set up the camera and filmed the engines at repose for fifty seconds. Later he would find the right audio to run behind the image, preferably a bit of pithy dialogue between Rachel and Groot, something oblique but not entirely inapposite. Not that anything, in his films, ever really was.

Stalking the deck of the little barge, he began to construct the impending shot in his mind. They'd pass through a lock at the south end of the marina to get to the Seine and then drop some seven feet to reach river level. Anything facing west would start out bathed in golden light and move gradually into shadow as the barge entered the iron-gated lock and descended, before emerging into light again once on the river. Visually, the shot explained itself, but getting something useful out of Groot was another matter entirely. It would take ingenuity and, Max suspected, force.

He picked out a spot on the port side of the barge and set up his camera as the pilot prepared to cast off. Max was about to reclaim Groot and bring him to his mark when his cell phone began to vibrate. It was Odile.

"I'm working," he told her. "They got the engines. So I'm shooting."

"Good. That's great. Will you be home for dinner?"

Max caught Groot's eye and beckoned urgently to him. "I don't know. Maybe. Can't promise."

The barge started to move away from the dock.

"I see. Okay. And are you going to let me know later or do I just guess?"

Her tone of voice, disproportionately angry, brought Max up short. Dinner hour was not something either of them worried much about. "I'll try, all right?" Then, before he lost his temper, he ended the call and pocketed the phone. "Groot, I want you over here, by the railing. Closer. Good. Not facing me, though. Look toward the river. That's perfect."

Through the viewfinder, Groot appeared to belong to another era, his features timeless beneath the flat-brimmed hat, the declining light imbuing him with a kind of elemental grace, part Vermeer, part Dutch comedy.

"What will we talk about?" he asked Max.

"I want to try a few things. But you can start by telling us about the engines, how you plan to use them, that kind of stuff. Don't be afraid to look at me if it feels right, but mainly we want to see you looking forward—you know, to the river, the future, whatever. Okay? Here we go. Three, two, one, rolling."

Max filmed, Groot talked. In the background, the hulls of the various pleasure craft tied up there slipped by, lending the shot an agreeable intermittence. The words Groot spoke barely registered on Max; he was too absorbed to notice more than their overall tenor and pace. He was waiting for the lull, the break, the moment when the face turned soft. Whatever would give him a way in.

"...so it's like finding an organ donor," Groot went on. "Both engines run surprisingly well. They're probably the last two in the country. Maybe the world. So, now we'll match up the best parts from all four to make two ideal engines, and, well, that's it. We'll have done it." He glanced at the camera and looked back out toward the river. "Restored her to life. A kind of miracle."

Max kept filming. "And Rachel's parents? What's their role in this?"

"They gave her the money to buy the engines, yes. Wired it to her."

"And she gave the money to you. Do you think Rachel told them what it was for?"

Groot hesitated. "I don't actually know what she told them."

Max waited and filmed. The barge was halfway to the lock. "Does Rachel love you?"

Nodding minutely to himself, as if he'd expected this question, Groot said, "Rachel loves me, yes."

"And do you two ever talk about getting married?"

A faint smile flickered over the Dutchman's features. He took a pack of cigarettes from the pushed-up sleeve of his jersey, shook one out, and lit it. After a couple of drags he said, "I proposed to her, yes. Just recently. She was ... taken by surprise. You can say it? Taken by surprise? She said, well, that she needed time to think about it."

Plane trees flanked the lock, and the shadows of the leaves of their outermost branches now began to run softly over Groot and dim the boats docked behind him. "I agreed to this, of course. A woman making up her mind: it is normal, ordinary, but at the same time ... worth waiting for. True, she is much younger than me, but this has never been a problem between us. We live our lives, day to day, and that's how it is. Neither of us likes a drama, but we know how to be happy. It's ... not so hard."

The barge slipped into the lock, and his face passed into deeper shadow. Behind him, the view of the marina was replaced by the timber, sodden and marvelously dark, that the lock was made of. Its iron gates ground slowly shut.

"But now, you know, now I begin to feel that I broke the spell. By asking her to marry me I made her think about the future—where she'll be, what she'll be doing, who she'll be with—and just by asking the question I put a limit on the present. You might say I wrote its death warrant."

The water level in the closed lock began to drop and the barge with it.

"But isn't it possible," Max said, "even likely, that she'll say yes? Then the present goes on as before, into the future, right?"

With the barge inside the lock, Groot no longer had a view forward, so he looked up at the light overhead. "No, I would say not. It's strange, I know, but already things that were easy before have become ... elusive. We breathe, but now we are aware of our breathing. It's like that."

"Do you think Rachel will accept your proposal?"

Groot looked around uneasily. Behind him, the lock walls that till moments ago had been underwater were now revealed to be completely covered with blue-black mussels.

"I think she will stay with me until the *Nachtvlinder* is rebuilt," Groot said. "She wants to see that through. But love is brutal. I accept this. What is difficult—" He broke off, distracted, and, shielding his eyes with a forearm, turned toward the timber wall behind him.

The mussels, in their thousands, were spraying Groot and everything around him with a fine mist of water that the light refracted into a rainbow fog.

SEATED AT THE VANITY she kept downstairs in her studio, Odile examined herself in the mirror. She'd lost weight since renouncing meat, and it seemed to her that the change was most noticeable in the planes of her face, whose high cheekbones had taken on a new prominence, not at all displeasing. Dipping a bit of sponge into the bowl of water before her, she began wiping her features down roughly, stripping away the dead skin and bringing fresh color to her cheeks. *That's when it really started,* she thought. *When I refused the veal chop.* And, a moment later, *I am so predictable.*

The night of the storm, she'd returned from Turner's apartment to find Max upstairs, strenuously absorbed in painting the garret guest room a pale brick red. Her first instinct was that he had somehow sensed where she'd been and had sought to stifle that awareness in mindless accusatory labor, but a few minutes of conversation convinced her otherwise and she went back downstairs to bath and bed. By the time he joined her, she was dead asleep.

Setting aside the sponge and bowl of water, she brushed her hair out hard, stroke after stroke. She had been wrong to press Max about his dinner plans. She'd done it out of guilt, appealing to their domestic selves in an effort to protect them both from the consequences of her actions—actions past, present, and, most especially, future—but all she'd done was make herself tiresome. She felt no remorse at having slept with Turner. Maybe later she would be sorry, but for now she believed in what she was doing, even if she couldn't explain it. A life was to live. Anything else could take a number and wait.

She had just finished plaiting her hair when there came a sharp triple knock at the door. Wheeling around in her chair, she saw four youths at the window, desperately signaling for help. When she opened the door they came tumbling in, and she pressed the door shut behind them.

"What's wrong?" she demanded.

Her visitors—three boys and a girl in their late teens—had thrown themselves to the floor, just beneath the window. "The cops," the girl hissed, and immediately clapped a hand over her mouth.

Before Odile could inquire further, a policeman did in fact appear at the window. She cranked it open. "Hello, Officer."

"I'm sorry to bother you, Madame." The man grimaced to suggest the distasteful necessity of his errand. "But I would like very much to talk with your neighbors in number eight, if at all possible. However, they don't seem to be home. Perhaps you know them?"

"But of course. The anarchists." Odile smiled at the officer. "My husband and I, though, we haven't seen them for weeks. I think they went to Maastricht for the trade conference." She frowned in citizenly concern. "Is there trouble?"

"That I cannot say. At present they are wanted only for questioning." He sharpened his gaze and looked her sternly in the eye. "Tell me, Madame, have they ever mentioned La Santé prison to you? Maybe asked you to sign a petition, join a demonstration, something of that nature?"

"La Santé? No, never. Why?"

The policeman shrugged. "Certain sources . . ." But already his interest seemed to wane. "There's no cause for alarm, I assure you. However, should your neighbors return—" He handed her a card.

"Of course, Officer." She let her eyes linger on his until he blushed, then bid him goodbye.

When the sound of his footsteps had died away, the fugitives stood up, shaken and uncharacteristically silent.

"So things are heating up, I see." Odile knew all four by sight, but she could never keep their names straight.

"Yes, they are," said the oldest-looking one. "Things are heating up because that is our single purpose, always and everywhere to engage the oppressor." He stroked his wispy blond mustache thoughtfully. "But the cop, he was just bluffing about La Santé. A stab in the dark, right, Chantal?" He turned to the girl, who regarded him with fathomless contempt.

"We must thank Madame for her help," she said evenly.

"Absolutely," said the boy, returning his attention to Odile. "We are in your debt. Thank you."

"Not at all," she told them. "Activism runs in my family." She opened the door. "So until the next time . . ."

When they were gone, she went over to her worktable and studied the drawings for the wedding dress she'd designed for her client Fatima. Despite the girl's liberal views, or maybe because of them, Odile had taken her inspiration from the burka and other Islamic garments of concealment: she wanted to emphasize the drama of exposure by framing it within an expanse of fabric that veiled and draped and trailed behind in a tantalizing train. Now she realized her design wasn't radical enough. She made some new sketches that heightened the tension, then she stripped the muslin pattern pieces from her dressmaker's dummy, tossed them into her scrap bag, and went upstairs.

Without really having a plan, she opened a wardrobe that held the clothes she'd designed solely for herself. Sorting peevishly through them, she shoved garment after garment aside until she found something she could stand to look at—a deep blue microfiber shirt-dress that fit her like a skin. She got out of her jeans and put it on. She was considering the question of footwear when the phone rang: Eddie Bouvier, with news for Max.

"He's down by the *Nachtvlinder*, shooting," she told him. "Where are you?"

"On Richard Lenoir, headed north."

"Ah, you're driving! Perfect. Come pick me up and we'll surprise him."

Eddie hesitated. "Are you sure that's a good idea? While he's working?"

"Look at the light," she said. It was barely seven o'clock, and, with two and a half hours till sundown, the air over Paris glowed a heatless but prodigal gold. "He won't even notice we're there."

"Okay," Eddie said, downshifting audibly. "Five minutes."

AFTER JACQUES FILMED the transfer of the engines from the barge to the deck of the *Nachtvlinder,* Max sent him to buy a case of rum and several liters of orange juice. Now, with the twin diesels secured topside, Groot and Rachel had invited their houseboat neighbors aboard to view the new hardware, other friends were arriving by the minute, and what had begun as an ad hoc celebration was rapidly turning into a drunken revel. Ray Charles's voice issued from belowdecks at high volume.

"Okay, now I get it about the rum," Jacques said. "But what if things spill over into incoherence?"

"We keep filming," Max said firmly. "That's what we're here for."

"And Rachel?"

"What about her?"

"She's noticed you're avoiding her. She thinks she's done something to disappoint you. As material, I mean."

"Really? She said that?"

"Pretty much, yes."

"Excellent. Keep her guessing. And, in the meantime, get as much anecdotal footage as you can. Anything anybody does or says that we might use for local color, shoot it. I'll let you know when I'm ready to go in on her, okay? Oh, and Jacques?"

"Yes?"

"Don't worry about coherence. It's usually just a matter of how you frame the shot."

Jacques smiled and headed with his camera toward the stern of the boat.

Two girls Max had never seen before were dancing to the music, swaying indolently in place and lifting their arms over their heads, eyes closed in wordless transport. Each time the four-word chorus came around, they roused themselves to sing along in fetchingly accented English—*Lez, go, get, stoned*—before retreating once more into the reverie of movement. Max filmed them at it, then shifted his attention to a group of men who'd gathered around the engines.

He recognized some of them from the day of the flood. Open bottles passed from hand to hand, and the mood was philosophical.

"No one makes such engines anymore, not even the Germans." The speaker was known locally as Boudu, in ironic reference to the Renoir film. "In fact, I wouldn't mind having them myself."

"Fat chance," said another. "But if you're serious, you'd better start by finding a rich American girlfriend of your own. Without her, two of us together couldn't afford these engines."

"Don't be idiotic," said a third man. "She has no money. Besides, since the flood, he is one of us." He raised his bottle. "To the *Nachtvlinder*! May we all have second lives."

Max panned slowly right. Just forward of the companionway, two men in their twenties stood facing each other, absorbed in a rite of mutual discovery. First one of them would take a long pull on the bottle they were sharing, square his shoulders, shout a single insult at the other, and slap him full in the face, causing them both to dissolve in laughter. When they recovered, the bottle would change hands, and it would be the other one's turn. Another insult, another slap, more laughter. The exchange played surprisingly well on camera, its logic serenely unassailable.

Katje and Yvette, the Ivorian transvestite, cruised slowly by in the middle distance, arm in arm, apparently oblivious to the exertions around them.

"We're sailing to Sicily!" someone shouted. "We're sailing to Sicily! We're sailing to Sicily! We're sail—" But before Max could locate this enthusiast, she was cut off mid-word and heard from no more. He looked up from the camera. For some time he had been aware of Odile and Eddie Bouvier standing discreetly behind him, scrupulous not to enter camera range.

"Why's everyone so drunk?" Odile asked him.

"Don't know," Max said. "I think it's the light." He peered vexedly at the sky, which had begun to go pink around the edges. "Hi, Eddie. What's up?"

"The police closed down that DVD operation this morning. No arrests, unfortunately. But they got the equipment. I thought you'd like to know."

"Thanks, I appreciate it." Max held up a light meter and took a reading. "There's more."

"Oh, yeah?" Returning the device to his pocket, he watched three children run across the deck holding pinwheels before them, a glossy black dachshund in close pursuit. "Listen," he said, "why don't you two go get yourselves a drink, and I'll catch up with you in a bit. There's a scene I'm waiting to shoot, but it needs to ripen up a little first, okay? I'm still prepping the principals." He looked at his wife and business manager directly for the first time since their arrival. "Thanks. It won't take long."

Odile kissed him lightly and, taking Eddie's arm, led him off. Max reflected on his good fortune in having married a woman so innately determined to rise to the occasion, whatever it might be. Her pride was a thing of beauty, a little dangerous, as large as life. It helped him see the world. And for that he was prepared to go quite far indeed.

A woman sitting on her boyfriend's shoulders whooped and handed Max a bottle. He passed it on without drinking. Someone staggered into him and fell to the deck. When Max realized the man wouldn't be getting up, he stepped over him and began weaving through the throng to the stern.

The first thing to catch his eye was Jacques's anxious face. Following his gaze, Max saw Rachel and Groot, standing off to one side clutching the railing unsteadily, engaged in what appeared to be a private discussion. He hurried over as unobtrusively as possible, set up his camera, and started to film. They seemed not to notice. The light decayed.

"But what possible difference could it make?" Rachel said, flipping her French-style braid back over her shoulder. "I mean, really?"

"I want to know," Groot said. "That's the difference." He was drunker than she, stolid in his insistence, ready to wait her out. His hat shaded his forehead to the eyebrows.

"I told them I needed it," she said. "They're my parents. They sent it. What's the big deal?"

"That's exactly my point. There is no big deal. So why won't you tell me?"

"Because look at you!"

He laughed unpleasantly and reached for the bottle at his feet.

"You're not in your right mind," she said. "You're drunk and you're angry."

"Just tell me what you told them it was for. I want to know."

She folded her arms over her chest and shook her head.

"You see," he said, "you deny my existence."

She snorted with exasperation. "Maybe we would've been better off without the engines. Is that what you're saying? That it's more polite not to get what you want? More *gezellig*?"

"You deny my existence," he said, "and you twist my words." As Groot raised the bottle to his lips, Rachel looked away in disgust and, for a fraction of a second, blundered into eye contact with the camera. Her face registered surprise, but along with surprise Max thought he saw a tiny flash of pride, followed by a runic smile, shrewd and half complicit. She recovered at once.

"We needed forty-two thousand francs," she told Groot. "You didn't have it, and I didn't either, so I asked my parents. There's no shame in that."

"We'll pay it back." He wagged the bottle at her like an accusing finger. "Tell them we'll pay it back."

"But we won't pay it back. We can't. How could we?"

"There's always a way. We're not derelicts."

"God, you're a drag when you're like this." She took the bottle from him and took three long swallows. When he reached out to reclaim it, she laughed at him and dropped it neatly overboard into the Seine.

He shrugged and looked away.

"Wait a minute," she said. "I get it. How could I not have seen?" Her eyes narrowed on him. "It scares you to think you might be in debt to me, doesn't it? That's what this is about."

"You don't know what you're saying."

"I sure do. This has nothing to do with my parents. It's your ego, isn't it? Come on, admit it. You'd rather not get what you want than get it through me, right? Your California girl."

"This is madness. This is shit."

"Your little fantasy of self-sufficiency. That's what really matters to you, isn't it? And anything that—"

"Don't be stupid."

"Anything that threatens it is crazy, right? *Or* stupid. Because the one unshakable rule is that Groot can do it all himself. I mean, God forbid you should accept anybody's help. Then the whole myth of your independence or whatever the fuck it is goes right out the window."

"*Ja,*" he told her. "I am a man who walks alone in my clogs." He shoved his hands into his pockets. "Garbage. Ignorance. Shit."

"Think so? Then why do you want to sabotage the very thing we've been working toward all this time? What are you afraid of?"

"Me? It's you who are afraid."

"So sensitive. Your big, scary male ego—so vulnerable."

"These are only insults. Why embarrass yourself?"

" 'Don't hurt me! Don't hurt me!' " she said in a high-pitched voice meant to be his.

"Bitch. You childish, spoiled, American—"

They argued in circles, letting pettiness and spite become the point of the exercise, its deeper meaning, its only meaning. Max filmed. The light decayed. Either one of them might do anything now.

# CHAPTER 20

ODILE WOKE UP with a hangover and an imperfect memory of the night before. Max had already left, and she seemed to recall him saying that he was meeting Eddie Bouvier for breakfast. Or was it lunch? She sighed and got out of bed.

In the kitchen, over café au lait, she tried to reconstruct her evening aboard the *Nachtvlinder*. She remembered Rachel and Groot quarreling, she remembered Max filming, she remembered Eddie leaving early to pick up his daughter. Bits of conversation came back to her, faces and gestures. She recalled talking to a woman who was wearing a knockoff of one of her designs—an off-the-shoulder dress that had once appeared in *Vogue*—and that she'd impulsively poured her drink down the woman's front, pretending it was an accident. Other moments resurfaced, other encounters, yet the sense persisted in her that something significant was missing from her inventory of events—a person, an image, a turn of phrase, she didn't know. Alcohol now repelled her as much as meat. She wanted nothing more to do with it.

Downstairs in her studio she spent the better part of the morning working up a revised set of drawings for Fatima's wedding dress. While the earlier design had invoked the burka's billowing excess, this one called for a tightly wrapped sheath, closely fitted fabric inset with mesh hexagons of the sort that, in the traditional burka, allowed the wearer her only means of seeing out. Here they served the opposite function, allowing the observer, at strategically placed intervals, to see in. It was a daring solution, bold but not blatant, and Odile was eager to see it realized. She faxed the drawings to her client, along with a note asking her to call, then went out to do some errands.

When she returned, the phone was ringing. She raced upstairs and snatched the handset from its cradle, but the caller had hung up.

She put away her purchases, looked through the mail, made a pot of camomile tea. Thinking of the previous day's visit from the police, she went to the window, but everything in the quiet little courtyard appeared to be in order. Across the cobblestone walk, on the green metal table that belonged in common to the inhabitants of the mews, someone had left a jarful of marigolds and a well-thumbed deck of playing cards. A three, seven, and ace lay face up in a row.

The phone rang a second time. She answered.

"I realize, Odile," the caller said, "that you may not be completely happy to hear from me."

She sat. "Thierry."

"And for what it's worth, I want to apologize for my admittedly hasty departure in Brest. That wasn't part of the plan, but, you see, people weren't where they were supposed to be and, well, I had to improvise a little. Anyway, I knew you'd be safe, because everything about the flags had already been taken care of. I made a point of telling you that, you may recall."

"What plan?" Odile managed to say. "I thought you and I had the same plan." His voice was very clear in her ear.

"And we did, assuredly. Only, there was another aspect to my part in it, a side project, one could say, that you weren't involved in. Nobody thinks otherwise. Nobody at all. Understand?"

She bit her lip. In the background she heard birds. "Where are you?" she asked.

"Not where I'd like to be, I'll tell you that. But it'll do for the moment."

Odile glanced at the answering machine plugged into an outlet beside the phone. She hesitated, then pressed record. "Okay. So what do you want from me, Thierry?"

"Very simply, I need my fee for the Moscow run, the thirty thousand that, it must be said, I earned just as you did. The fact is that I hadn't expected this . . . hiatus in which I find myself. Naturally, there are expenses."

"But why call me?" she asked. "Turner's the one with the money."

"Yes, Turner." Thierry laughed softly. "Tell me, do you like him?"

She left a small silence, then said, "He's okay."

"See? How can you doubt that I have your best interests at heart? I knew you two would get along."

A chill passed through her, but she refused the bait. "You haven't answered my question, Thierry."

"No?" He struck a match, and she imagined him lighting the cigarette. "All right." He exhaled at length. "I have the feeling it might be awkward for Turner to deal with me directly at the moment. For purely circumstantial reasons, but nonetheless. So if you'd be willing to act as intermediary—"

"Then no one need be inconvenienced. Is that what you mean?"

"Yes, exactly."

"I guess you really have been out of town." Standing, taking the phone with her, she began to pace. "And supposing I were to do you this favor, how would I get the money to you?"

"We can arrange a place for you to drop it off. In Paris, of course, somewhere mutually convenient."

"Ah, but Thierry, this is so vague." She walked to the window. "I'll have to think about it. Give me your number and I'll call you back."

"Odile, please."

"What, you don't have a number?"

"It's not that. But as to where I'll be later . . . My schedule—"

"It's very complicated, I'm sure." She pinched off two yellowing leaves from the potted geraniums on the windowsill. "By the way, Thierry. Have you spoken to your cousin lately, the one who recommended you for the Moscow trip?"

A short silence ensued, broken only by the complex warbling of the birds on Thierry's end.

"Don't worry," Odile said. "I know you haven't. Because, for better or worse, he's dead."

"That's not funny."

"No, not at all. I never joke about things it's too late to change."

"Are you saying he was murdered?"

"So it would seem."

There was another pause. Then, in the patient tone of someone determined to misconstrue, he said, "My cousin sometimes lacked judgment in his selection of business associates. Real estate offers many opportunities to make stupid decisions of this sort, needless to say. Most likely a deal went bad, an investor took revenge. People don't realize how cutthroat the real-estate industry is."

"Really? Is that how you read it?"

"Yes," he said, "it is. Now, about the thirty thousand. Will you help me, Odile?"

"I don't know. I'll have to ask Turner for it, obviously."

"When?"

"Tonight, maybe."

"Do it, please. I'm depending on you, okay?"

"But Thierry—"

"Don't worry about that," he said. "You'll hear from me." And before she could protest, he hung up.

She went to the answering machine, pressed stop, followed by eject, and removed the cassette. Sorting through her purse, she found the card Sergei Dmitrovich had given her at the Jardin du Luxembourg. She considered the phone number written there, then returned the card to her purse, threw in the cassette as well, and left the apartment, already late for her weekly portrait sitting with Céleste.

"A PITY I COULDN'T STAY last night," Eddie Bouvier said from behind his desk. "Did you get everything you needed?"

"I got a lot." Max was seated on a cream-colored leather sofa in Eddie's office, a modest but carefully appointed suite of rooms off the Champs-Élysées. "I got lucky, maybe."

"A man makes his luck, Max. You know what you want. Most don't."

Max's eye drifted to a row of head shots, signed and framed, that ran along the wall behind Eddie's desk. One of them was of Isabelle H., whose comely and expensive features, so recently under contract to Max, occasioned him a moment of senseless gloom. "So tell me what you found out about our bootleggers. No arrests, you said."

"Correct. I gave the police the address of the loft you mentioned—or, rather, the loft you broke into and illegally searched, as they reminded me not too politely—and it turns out that the place was indeed leased to the guy you mentioned, the real-estate agent."

"Broch," Max prompted. "Sylvain Broch."

"Exactly. A man the police were already interested in because—I'm going to assume you didn't know this—he'd been shot dead a few days earlier. So they raided the premises, confiscated equipment consistent with

DVD piracy, seized the answering machine, and did whatever else they do. Their conclusion, which I strongly urge you to embrace, is that Broch was killed for dabbling in the notoriously profitable bootleg-video trade, said to be controlled by organized crime, foreign malefactors, and your great-aunt's dog—all right? Nobody cares. What matters is that the police believe that the piracy explains the murder, so instead of having two open investigations it's a single closed case, end of story."

Max shook his head, vexed. "I don't buy it. Why the reworked ending on *Fireflies*? And what about La Peau de l'Ours? Surely we ought to be looking into that."

Sighing, Eddie reached for the pitcher on his desk and poured himself a glass of water. "You're a filmmaker, Max. Don't put your health at risk."

"My health?" Max stared at him. "You've never mentioned my health before, Eddie."

"You don't want to pursue this," Eddie said. "Because in my considered opinion nothing good will come of it."

"I need to know what you know," Max said. "It's as simple as that."

Eddie grimaced and set his glass down without drinking. "In that case I'd better bring in the legal department." He picked up the phone. "Lisette, I've got Max Colby here. Would you pull the file on La Peau de l'Ours, please?"

Lisette was a short, fine-boned woman in her forties whose air of bustling efficiency seemed to carry with it the certain knowledge that any victory over disorder was by definition provisional. When she appeared in the doorway, file folder in hand, Max hastened to his feet to greet her. She raised an eyebrow and offered him a measured smile.

"Max," said Eddie, gesturing for her to sit down, "would like to hear what we have on La Peau de l'Ours. Also any commentary you might care to add, speculative or otherwise. Entirely off the record, of course."

She chose a straight-backed chair that placed her midway between the two men and a bit to the side. "Unfortunately," she began, "this information is not so easily obtained. La Peau de l'Ours appears to be a shell corporation comprising several separate interests, all of them seemingly legitimate but perhaps with illicit sides as well. For instance." She removed a document from the folder. "There exists a postproduction film facility called La Peau de l'Ours, apparently quite aboveboard, if curiously hard to track down. And yet, as you are aware, this was also the name of the counterfeit-DVD factory that the police shut down yesterday. So maybe the postproduction studio was really the pirate operation. We don't know."

Eddie raised a hand. "Max. Consider this carefully. Do you really need to hear more?"

Max waited.

Eddie dropped his hand, and Lisette continued.

"So, one corporation, several enterprises." She consulted a second document. "The other branches of La Peau that we were able to turn up represent themselves variously as a travel agency, an investment firm, a resort casino, a string of restaurants, and a medical group. What any of these businesses might have to do with the others, or, for that matter, whether they actually provide the services they ostensibly offer, we cannot say. All we know for certain is that they are wholly owned subsidiaries of La Peau de l'Ours and are incorporated under that name in the Republic of Malta."

"Malta?" repeated Max. "Why there?"

"It's a convenient tax haven," Lisette informed him, "with banking laws that favor privacy."

"You see?" said Eddie. "These matters have nothing to do with you, Max. Forget about them. Make movies."

Ignoring him, Max appealed to Lisette. "What about addresses? The bootleg factory was easy enough to find. What about the other companies?"

"If they are real," she allowed, "they could perhaps be located. In principle. But at the moment, we have only a post office box in Valletta. Regrettably, even the name of the person renting this box is beyond our reach."

Max slumped back on the sofa in defeat.

"Thank you, Lisette," Eddie told her. "Your research is impeccable, as always."

She flushed becomingly, took up her papers, and hurried off. After a short silence, Eddie produced a leather cigar case and offered it to Max, who declined.

"You know," Eddie said, removing a Cohiba from the case, "I've been in this business a long time now, and the people I deal with, lots of them, they have histories that are maybe not so savory, okay? And yet we find ways to work together. We find a comfort level." He paused to fire up the cigar, turning it slowly in his lighter's butane flame. "What I want to tell you, as your friend, is that the operation you've just heard described could not be more radioactive if it were based in Chernobyl. All the signs are there. And if you call attention to yourself, if you irritate these people, whoever they are, in any way, I promise you'll be very, very sorry." He exhaled a long stream of blue smoke and watched it waft gently toward the ceiling. "Am I getting through to you, Max?"

"Oh, definitely," Max said, hauling himself upright. "Loud and clear."

"Good. Because I look forward to representing you and your films for many years to come." Eddie leaned back in his chair and settled an indulgent eye on his client. "Now, let me tell you what I've got in the pipeline for you."

When Max left the office, twenty minutes later, he headed moodily down rue François 1ᵉʳ, oblivious to pedestrian traffic. That there would now be money for his film suddenly seemed all but certain; he was free to concentrate on the work before him and give it shape as he saw fit. Yet it still troubled him that while he accepted Eddie's assessment of La Peau de l'Ours and also believed that yesterday's police raid had put an end to the bootlegging of *Fireflies,* he couldn't help wondering why the counterfeiters had taken the trouble to alter its ending. Such an intimate violation, so mindful of details—he found it hard to shrug off.

Cutting through the Tuileries, he saw a little boy let go of a red balloon. His mother reached distractedly for the string of the balloon as it rose, but it slipped through her fingers. Then she made a small, calibrated jump—no more than a foot—caught the string, and returned the balloon to her son. Max quickened his pace.

Back at the studio, he located the DVD he'd pocketed that night at the bootleg factory, the pale amber wash on its data side glinting as it had then. He put the disk in the screening-room player, but the monitor showed only static interrupted at irregular intervals by a succession of black bars. He examined the disk under a magnifying glass, to no avail. Finally, remembering the little room at the back of the bootleggers' loft, the microscope and the shelves of scientific journals inside, he took the DVD downstairs.

"What we need," he told his assistant, "is a biomolecular chemist."

Jacques accepted the disk and looked it over suspiciously. "But why?"

"Just find one, will you? Have him tell you what this is."

Getting to his feet, doubt clouding his thin features, Jacques held the disk away from him as though it might constitute an affront to hygiene. "And what do *we* think it is?"

"We don't have the least idea," Max said, opening the door that gave onto the cobblestone courtyard.

THE WORK WENT BADLY almost from the moment Odile took up her pose on the sofa, or at least that was how she interpreted the grim silence that settled over Céleste as she painted. Holding her long, thin brush at nearly arm's length, she would touch it first to a dish of turpentine, then to one of the smears of oil paint on her palette plate, and finally to the canvas, using short, smooth strokes to render what she saw. She never swiped the brush more than five or six times without her eyes darting back to Odile. Every so often she'd step away from the canvas and stare ferociously at it for a minute or more before shaking her head and resuming work. Odile had yet to be granted so much as a glimpse of the painting, in any of its states, and now was beginning to doubt she ever would be.

"I know what you're thinking," Céleste said suddenly. "But if I let you see it now, it would change how you show yourself to me, and that's out of the question since you change enough as it is."

"I do?"

"Yes. Today, for instance, you look completely different from all the other times. That's why I'm having such trouble." She gave a small rueful laugh. "But don't worry. I'll get it right eventually, and then you can see it, I promise."

Odile glanced down at herself: her bare breasts and thighs framed by the green silk dress, her pale lacquered fingernails and toenails, her knees. "But I can't have changed completely since last week. It's impossible."

"I agree," said Céleste, "yet you have, so I must adjust my painting. That's how it is."

For the next hour, with Céleste too absorbed for conversation, Odile felt adrift in a welter of conflicting impulses. She hadn't planned to tell Céleste about her evening with Turner, not least because she assumed he himself already had. Even now, wanting to say something after all, she forced herself to refrain, certain that Céleste would attribute her change in appearance, if there really was one, to Turner's influence alone. It was all quite adolescent and embarrassing, truly absurd, and she was relieved when, at three o'clock, Céleste declared an end to the session. Odile dressed, agreed on a day to return, embraced her friend, and left.

Once on the streets, she walked without direction until arriving by default on boulevard Saint-Michel, outside a movie theater advertising a John Huston festival. She had two hours to kill before the rendezvous she'd hastily arranged with Turner by phone the day before, and consulting the screening schedule she saw that *The Maltese Falcon*, undubbed, had just begun. She bought a ticket, took a third-row center seat in the darkened theater, and delivered herself gratefully into the keeping of Bogart, Astor, Lorre, and Greenstreet.

A hundred minutes later she emerged refreshed. The world depicted in the film, for all its duplicity, innuendo, and fruitless striving, resembled the real world only in part. Why she should draw strength from this utterly ordinary observation, available to virtually anyone on earth for the price of a movie ticket, was beyond her, but as she started east on boulevard Saint-Germain she felt its power in every step she took.

Crossing the Pont de Sully, she stopped to peer down at the *Nachtvlinder*. Tarps now covered the newly acquired engines, but otherwise there was nothing to suggest recent activity, and she continued north.

At Turner's apartment, she let herself in with the key he'd given her. He was not yet back from work. She washed her face, put on fresh lipstick and a little perfume. Finding Berg's *Lulu* already loaded in the CD player, she turned it on at low volume and made a pot of tea, then leafed impatiently through an American art magazine.

When Turner arrived a few minutes later, she felt sharply glad to see him but reluctant to show it. "I should have told you," she said, remaining seated, moving the teacup away from her mouth, "that I'm always very punctual."

"If only I'd known," he said with a straight face. Taking the cup from her hand, he drew her to her feet.

"What are you doing?" she said teasingly as he led her down the hall to the bedroom.

In bed, making love, she felt him apply himself, attentive to her every move, deferent to her pleasure. She tried to make light of it, laughing a little at his assiduous pursuit, but before long there was no room left for playfulness or pretense and she cleaved to him, ankles locked at the base of his buttocks, arms wrapped tight around him. In her mind's eye she saw a clock being wound, a nylon duffel getting unzipped, rope playing out from a dockside coil. A long, bright moment became a sound that lasted. Not until her cry died away did she realize that she had uttered it.

They lay together for awhile, listening only to their breath.

Had she come to the apartment knowing exactly how she intended to handle Thierry's call, by either refusing his request outright or agreeing to it in some form that might or might not include her contacting the Russians, then she would've informed Turner of the situation—and her decision—at once, before going to bed with him, in hopes of learning something more about the man with whom she dealt. As it was, she'd postponed telling him—and deciding—in hopes of learning something more about herself. Either way, she thought, it was a brutal business.

When she'd had enough of self-discovery, she got up and, for economy's sake, retrieved the tape cassette from her purse and played it for Turner on his own answering machine. She watched him register Thierry's voice, saw the shine come to his eyes and the absent-looking smile settle over his features. Her mood shifted. The taped phone message came to an end. There was no need to replay it. She waited.

"Okay," he said, "but what about the first part of the call, before you started recording?"

"Right." She spoke carefully, aware that if she wasn't clear now then they might both suffer later. "First, he apologized for disappearing in Brest. He said that people weren't where they were supposed to be, that he'd had to improvise. He mentioned a side project he had going that I didn't know about but wasn't implicated in. Nobody thought I was. He emphasized that."

"Any idea what he meant?"

"None. There's that people-trafficking business, but who knows how real that is."

Turner repositioned the pillows behind him until he was nearly sitting upright. "It might be just one person," he said unhappily, "or, who knows, maybe a truckful."

"What?"

He told her of his lunch with Wieselhoff and the message he'd relayed from Kukushkin. He also mentioned the Russian's helpfulness in getting the flags through Belarussian customs.

"But I don't understand," Odile said. "If you know this man, why can't you deal with him directly and settle the whole thing once and for all, regardless of what it is?"

Turner sighed. "Direct," he said, "is not Kolya's way."

"It seems to me that having someone killed is quite direct."

"Yes, but there's more to it than that," said Turner. "He wants me to figure out on my own what the problem is and then act accordingly. It's as if he sees himself as my mentor, which maybe he is. But unfortunately this lesson's lost on me. I don't know what he wants."

Hung on the wall opposite the bed were three etchings of what appeared to be antique prison interiors—Odile wondered if they could be Piranesis—and as she let her eye travel the eerie bridges, passages, and cell blocks they detailed, places that owed more to the imagination than to the pragmatics of penology, she felt the weight of indecision lift and her mind grow clear. "All right," she said. "I'll do it."

Turner looked at her as if he feared he'd misunderstood.

"Just give me the thirty thousand, and I'll meet Thierry and hand him over to the Russians." She got out of bed and began to dress. "Quickly, okay? I've got to go."

The relief that passed across Turner's face shamed her for a moment, but she regained her calm when he left the bedroom to get the money. It was as Thierry had said. She wanted to believe a new life was possible, even if not for her.

# CHAPTER 21

MAX SURVEYED THE CAFÉ for undesirable patrons, found none, and chose a table under the green canvas awning that extended partway over the sidewalk. He set a manila file folder he'd been carrying down on the table, then moved it beneath his chair. When the waiter arrived, he ordered a café-calva and dashed across the street for a copy of *Le Monde*. He returned to find Véronique settled in at his table with a mineral water, very much as if she'd been waiting there all along. She was wearing sunglasses and a sleeveless blue dress that left her shoulder tattoo exposed, the wheel of many spokes.

"You're prompt," he said, sitting down beside her.

She shrugged. "Your call came at the right time. I've been working day and night on a translation I never should've agreed to in the first place. Maybe you'll be amusing. If not, too bad, I go back to work."

Max looked her over thoughtfully, downed his coffee, and signaled the waiter for another. "I have to ask you," he said. "At our last meeting you more or less told me to pay a second visit to that real-estate office, which I did. Did you already know what had happened to Sylvain Broch?"

She showed him the flushed, half-coy smile with which she acknowledged her lapses and indiscretions. "I had an idea. But at that point I didn't know for certain, no."

"Still, you guessed he was dead, so you could probably guess who did it, right?"

She shook her head. "This isn't the sort of thing I like to know. But if he was running a bootleg-video factory—which is what you told me, no?—then he would've had any number of enemies. It's a very competitive business, I'd imagine."

From her backpack she took a cigarette, and as he lit it she held his out-thrust hand as if to steady it. The scent of her gardenia-drenched perfume brought back jumbled memories of their last encounter, when he'd been blindsided by her youth and perfect lack of compunction. It would be necessary, this time, to take a more considered approach.

"Speaking of business," he said, "how's your partner, the one in your plan? Has he gotten any more communicative? He made it hard for you to help him, you said."

Her laugh was engagingly musical, agreeable to hear. "No, none of that has changed. It's his nature, you know. A man conducts his business but takes care not to trouble others with the details. Very proper and masculine, but in this case personally frustrating to me, as I think you can appreciate."

"And what about that guy you were looking for? Still missing?"

"Alas." She looked at him hard, no longer troubling to hide her impatience.

"Sorry to hear it," said Max. "But maybe you'll be interested in this Peau de l'Ours circus, which, in my small way, I'm still researching." Reaching under his chair, he retrieved the folder and took out the amber-washed DVD, which Jacques had returned to him the day before. "Ever seen one of these?" he asked, handing it to her.

She frowned over it noncommittally, but when she turned it data side up he saw her blanch for an instant. "Sure," she said coolly, giving it back. "It's a video disk. Why, is it counterfeit?"

"I did find it at that factory Broch operated in the tenth," he admitted, "but it's not one of the counterfeits." He held it up for her further consideration. "See that amber coating?" He removed a photocopied document from the file and passed it to her. "It took my assistant most of yesterday to track down the author of this paper and me most of last night to understand what the guy was talking about. But now I have the gist, I think."

Véronique examined the document warily. " 'Molecular Screening and the Digital Video Disk,' " she read aloud from the title page, then leafed through the paper without enthusiasm. "I have not the slightest idea what this 'molecular screening' means. Is it lucrative, I hope?"

Max laughed. "You are one focused woman," he told her. "I won't be surprised when your business plan kicks in."

She granted him a luminous smile that, though fleeting, left a pleasant afterglow in its wake. When the waiter arrived with Max's café-calva, Véronique relinquished her water and ordered a beer.

"What this paper describes," said Max, "is a cheap and efficient method for using ordinary DVDs to profile a person's entire genetic makeup, sequencing the DNA from a single sample—a drop of blood, an oral swab, whatever—and storing the results on disk. I'm told the technology has been around for awhile, but only recently perfected. Any of this sound familiar?"

She shook her head, but looked, Max thought, rather unhappy.

"Well, for instance." He flashed the disk at her once more. "The sample here belongs to a blond European female, probably not you, given your eye color, which I remember as gray-blue." He waited for her to lift her sunglasses, but she didn't. "I found several of these disks at the loft Broch was renting, so I think it's fair to assume that movie piracy wasn't his only extracurricular interest." He put both disk and document back in the folder, stowing it again under his chair. "Oh, and La Peau de l'Ours is incorporated in Malta as, among other things, a medical group. So maybe there really is a lucrative side to all this—not in the testing procedure, naturally, since that's hardly a secret, but in whatever was being tested for, which could be anything."

Véronique stubbed out her cigarette. "And you are telling me this why, exactly?"

"Because last time we talked you seemed interested. Also, you told me you were watching Broch's office in case this guy you're looking for, whoever he is, eventually showed up there, which leads me to wonder if he wasn't working for Broch in, well, one capacity or another." He shrugged. "But for me it's academic now. I got the police to close down the bootleg operation, so my problems with La Peau de l'Ours are over. The rest is really none of my business."

For some seconds Véronique stared at him through her dark glasses, absorbed in difficult mental calculations of a sort that didn't seem entirely abstract. Then she pulled a cell phone from her backpack, excused herself, and, walking to a spot some twenty yards away, almost into the street, punched in a number.

Watching her—and as soon as she got a connection she began pacing up and down, gesticulating with her free hand, talking nonstop in a voice lost in the traffic's heedless snarl—he experienced a moment of clarity that amounted to an insight. Its purport was that the visible world, to which he'd devoted most of his waking life, exercised its power over the human imagination precisely because it had no meaning. What it had instead was detail, infinitely exfoliating, capable of lending itself to every human interpretation without losing any substance at all. A kind of magic, almost. A plenitude.

He kept his eye on Véronique as she abruptly snapped her cell phone shut, returned to the table, and sat down beside him. Still fuming, she sipped her beer in silence. "Is there anything you want to tell me?" Max asked.

Turning to him, she took off her sunglasses.

He was encouraged to see he'd been right about her eyes.

"This man I'm looking for," she said, "he has something of mine, something personal."

"You'll find him," Max said.

"I intend to," she replied, putting her shades back on. "Now." With her head tilted to one side, she considered him. "Tell me about your wife. You love her, I remember that. What else?"

"What do you want to know?"

She drank the rest of her beer and set the glass down on the table. Despite the other patrons and the heavy sidewalk traffic and the seething, anarchic swarm of vehicles circling the Bastille monument, it was as if the two of them were alone together, tête-à-tête in a place of suspended fortune.

"Tell me everything," she said.


THROUGHOUT THE MORNING, in countless small ways, Odile found herself inexplicably at odds with the physical world. She forgot to put water in the espresso maker and returned from taking out the garbage to find the apartment acrid with the smell of burnt metal. A crystal vase she was washing slipped through her fingers and shattered in the sink. Downstairs, when she switched on her studio lights, they flared out with a small pop, and when she turned on her desk lamp it, too, burned out. She cut herself sharpening her fabric shears.

When by noon she still hadn't heard from Thierry, she felt a glimmer of doubt. Maybe it would be unwise to involve herself further in Thierry's plans, instead letting him and the Russians settle their differences without her. Her motives seemed to shift with each passing minute, yet she told herself that the prospect of having the whole affair over and done with remained argument enough for seeing it through.

Going to the living-room bookcase, she reached behind Max's collected

Chekhov and extracted the envelope Turner had given her the day before. She counted the contents—thirty thousand francs exactly—then sealed the envelope with tape and put it in her purse. Having thus committed herself, she took a set of linens from the hall closet and made up the bed in the guest room. Allegra's imminent arrival had begun to occupy a small but definite place in her thoughts. It was hard to know exactly what to prepare for, since she hadn't seen the girl in almost two years, but she doubted the visit would be entirely tranquil.

Then she emptied out the guest-room closet, vacuumed the tiny room, took down the curtains, and washed its single window. From her studio she brought up a small maple rocking chair, setting it in one corner, and a radio for the nightstand. She was contemplating additional improvements when the phone rang, and she hurried downstairs.

"Did you get it?" Thierry asked.

"It's with me now."

"Odile, you have no idea what a help this is. Thank you."

She listened for birds but heard nothing.

"I want to make it easy for you," he said. "There's a news kiosk next to the taxi stand at Place de la Bastille. Put the money in an envelope with my name on it and leave it with the lady behind the counter, Madame Genève. She'll see that I get it." He paused. "Hello?"

"Yes, I'm here."

"Can you do that?"

"When?"

"This afternoon. I need it today."

She said nothing.

"What is it? What's wrong?"

"I'm thinking," she said. Thinking that she didn't have to go to the newsstand at all. That she could call the Russians, tell them where to look for Thierry, return the money to Turner, and avoid all knowledge of what happened next. Yet she wavered. Maybe she'd have to be there anyway, just to be certain.

"My dear Odile, listen to me. There's nothing to worry about, okay? I admit I was shocked to hear what happened to my cousin, but this has nothing to do with that, I promise you." He sighed. "The fact is, I have a small debt to pay off. Nothing alarming, but there's interest on it and I want to avoid defaulting."

"A gambling debt?"

He paused. "So you know." Another pause. "How interesting you know that. Yes, a gambling debt."

"Actually, Thierry, I'd feel much more comfortable doing this if you told me what you were really up to. That side project of yours, for instance—it worries me. Can't you give me some idea what it involves?"

"No," he said immediately. Then, recovering: "Not on the phone. Just trust me for the moment. Can't you do that?"

She left another silence. "I suppose so, if it's that important."

"Good. When can you get there?"

"I'm leaving now," she said, and hung up before he could respond.

She went to the kitchen, hooked up the water purifier she'd bought the day before, and drank two glasses of filtered water in succession, having been thirsty without realizing it. In this thirst simultaneously discovered and quenched, she caught a glimpse of her present self, the one that Céleste had described, rightly or not, as capable of anything. *I feel like screaming,* she thought. Then, taking her purse from its spot by the landing, she descended the stairs and left the apartment.

The day was bright and mild, the warmest so far of the season. Correction officers with machine pistols had blocked off both ends of rue de la Santé while a bus carrying newly arrived detainees lurched into the prison, provoking jeers of welcome from those already interned. A lone black dog trotted down the sidewalk ahead of her. Otherwise Odile encountered only elderly people and young mothers with strollers as she walked the short distance to the Glacière métro stop.

On the train, which started out aboveground but soon plunged back into darkness, she sat behind two middle-aged women who talked endlessly about a trip they were taking to Biarritz for the summer music festival, gushing over the musicians they'd see. Their self-congratulatory tone grated unreasonably on Odile, and she was relieved when she had to change trains at Place d'Italie. Once seated in the connecting train, she took the envelope from her purse and wrote Thierry Colin's name across it in block letters. It suddenly seemed important that she fulfill as much of her promise to him as possible, even though she was going to betray him and the money would almost certainly end up in the hands of the Russians.

At Bastille she emerged from the station onto rue de la Roquette, where she paused to take in her surroundings, shading her eyes against the sun. The traffic circling the monument, the cafés packed with afternoon idlers and tourists, the steps of the Opéra Bastille on which other idlers basked, the pickpockets and scam artists circulating in pairs among the pedestrians that thronged the sidewalks: all this Odile had seen innumerable times, yet in the space of half a second it was as if a veil had been lifted to reveal a scene completely new to her, one in which every particular was strange and without precedent. She knew where she was, but each thing she saw was the first of its kind: the first bicyclist, the first wine carafe, the first woman to tie a sweater around her waist by the arms. The air shimmered. The first pigeon, the first waiter, the first menu to be snapped shut. The first book. She blinked. From where she stood she could see five news kiosks, and she went for the one by the taxi stand.

"Excuse me," she told the gray-haired woman behind the counter. "I'm looking for Madame Genève."

"Yes, that's me."

Odile took the envelope from her purse. "I was told I could leave this for Monsieur Thierry Colin. Do you know him?"

"Certainly, Madame." The woman accepted the envelope and put it in a cigar box on the shelf behind her. "I'll be sure to give it to him," she said, nodding once, her eyes already on the next customer.

Odile thanked her and quickly walked to a spot beside the taxi stand, outside the woman's line of sight but with a partial view of the kiosk. There she deliberated, pacing up and down, sorting through scenarios, wanting to be certain of what she was about to do, until at last she realized that her deliberations were beside the point, and she took out her cell phone and keyed in the number Dmitrovich had given her.

He answered on the first ring—not by saying hello but by unleashing a torrent of Russian that seemed to be the continuation of another call, one that her own had inexplicably interrupted or replaced. She listened in confusion for several seconds, wondering whom he thought he was addressing, before she could summon the force to interrupt. "Enough! Do you think I'm your Natasha?"

A brief silence ensued. Then, in English: "Madame Mével. What a welcome surprise. We were beginning to grow just a tiny bit discouraged."

"He called me," said Odile. "The guy in question."

"Excellent. And he is where, please?"

"That I don't know. But I can tell you where he soon will be, provided—"
"Yes?"

"Provided you don't try to contact me or my friends again. No more surprise visits, no threats, no calls, nothing. All that's finished, understand?" A traffic light changed, a phalanx of pedestrians advanced.

"You may be certain of it," said Dmitrovich.

"I should hope so." She resumed pacing. "He was calling about his fee for the Moscow trip, as you predicted. I got the money, he called again, we made arrangements for him to pick it up. He'll be here any minute, so you'll have to hurry. Come to—" A patch of bright color caught her eye: a turquoise handbag, a sun-pinked shoulder. *Of course,* thought Odile. *How could I not have known?* The handbag was opened, the envelope went in, the bag's owner stepped away from the kiosk: Gabriella, grimly efficient in a sand-colored dress and matching pumps.

"I'll have to call you back," Odile said, pressing the end button before he could protest.

Gabriella checked her watch and without a backward glance set out across the traffic island toward the streets radiating from the square to the south and east. After a prudent interval, keeping her distance, Odile followed.

Gabriella crossed at rue de Lyon, walked past the Opéra and the people scattered across its steps, then headed up rue de la Roquette. A series of small obstacles in Odile's path—a flock of nuns, a boy on a bicycle, some workmen carrying a sheet of plate glass—caused her to fall farther and farther behind. When she lost sight of Gabriella altogether, she stepped into the street itself and began to run.

She arrived at the next intersection just in time to see Gabriella, half a block ahead of her, pass through the entrance of the Théâtre Bastille, a well-regarded two-stage venue on the east side of the street. Retreating to the sidewalk, she forced herself to slow down. Whatever awaited her inside, she would need to keep her wits about her if she really meant to complete her errand. For a moment she couldn't even concentrate on what that might entail.

The lobby of the theater was attended by a bored young man seated behind a table on which he'd laid out a game of solitaire. He hardly glanced at her before pointing to a descending staircase. "Downstairs," he said, dealing himself another card.

The staircase lights were out, and a familiar dread—of darkness, of basements, of bottomless descent—passed over Odile as she moved down to the lower level. The foyer there, too, was dark. Spotting a set of doors, she pushed through them into an intimate space with a stage at the bottom and perhaps fifty rows of seats rising steeply up to where Odile now found herself. A man stood in darkness at the extreme left of the stage, speaking into a microphone while a slide show of what looked like underground caverns and tunnels was projected onto a screen behind him. The audience was sparse, seated here and there singly and in small clusters, but it was too dark for Odile to see if Thierry or Gabriella was among them. She took a seat in the last row, waiting for her eyes to adjust.

"What you must understand," said the man at the microphone, "is that the subterranean Paris you see here bears very little relation to the official version, the one visited by tourists and familiar to most of us from photographs of the Catacombs. The neatly stacked skulls, femurs, and tibias that one encounters on the guided tour, while justly celebrated, are far from typical." The slide changed. "Here is a more characteristic ossuary, where the bones, as you can see, are piled randomly together—some thirty generations of Parisians originally buried in the Cimetière des Innocents, then moved into the underground quarries in 1785."

She continued to scan the audience. The slide changed.

"But forget about bones. In the eleven years that I've been exploring subterranean Paris, I have charted hundreds of kilometers of passageways on several distinct levels, and I can attest without exaggeration to the existence underground of an alternative Paris, one by no means populated exclusively by the dead. This man, for example, whom I call the catacyclist."

None of the people seated below Odile resembled Thierry or Gabriella, at least from behind, and she tried to retrace in her mind the layout of the building. Maybe the man in the lobby had misdirected her.

"However," said the speaker, "the vast majority of underground passages are too low or too narrow to negotiate by bicycle; indeed, quite frequently one must be prepared to crawl. Here you see my friend doing just that, as he follows me into what was once a command post for the Resistance."

Odile felt a soft rush of air as the door behind her opened and closed.

"Note the mural, a later addition."

As discreetly as she could, she looked over her shoulder. There was no one.

"Let me take this moment to remind you," the speaker went on, "that it is a crime to enter these tunnels, and you will be severely fined if caught. In recent years concerns that terrorists might use underground locations to mount an attack have led to the closure of many points of entry, though more remain open than is generally supposed." The slide changed. "Here is a little-known entry in the thirteenth arrondissement, accessible only through a partly collapsed wine cellar dating to the eighteenth century."

Odile was debating whether to check the bathrooms when she saw a female form in silhouette begin to edge into a row of seats midway down the incline to the stage. Almost at the same moment the slide changed again, replaced not by a new image but by a brilliant rectangle of white light, a vacancy in the slide tray, that illuminated Gabriella as she sidled past a pair of spectators to take a seat beside a man sitting alone. He had a shaven head and wire-rimmed glasses, but when he looked up at Gabriella, Odile saw that it was Thierry. Then the next slide came on, and the audience was swathed once more in darkness.

"There exist as many reasons for entering our city's underground labyrinth as there are people who do so. This man, whom I have met on more than one occasion, comes to practice his fire-breather's art in a place utterly devoid of light. As you can see, the effect is quite spectacular."

For several minutes Odile stayed where she was, half listening to the speaker as she waited for some small understanding to come to her, some idea of Thierry's recent activities or their purpose, some sliver of explanation that might satisfy her curiosity. But nothing came. Both Thierry and Gabriella seemed fully absorbed in the lecture. Odile waited a little longer, then got up and left the theater.

She called Dmitrovich from the street. In a bookshop opposite the theater she browsed the new releases until she saw the Russians' black sedan pull up outside and both men get out. They entered the theater briskly, straightening their jackets as they went.

She didn't linger for the rest. On her way home she called Turner.

# CHAPTER 22

"YOU'RE SURE?" Turner stood with the telephone to his ear, watching the man from parcel post stack cardboard boxes against one wall. Gabriella, who normally would've overseen the delivery, had asked for the afternoon off. "I mean, did you actually hand him over yourself?"

"No," said Odile. "But I waited until I had him cornered—in a theater in Bastille, sitting in the dark—before I called the Russians. Believe me, they got him. I just saw them go in."

"Good, so it's settled." Without putting down the phone, Turner took the clipboard handed him by the delivery man and signed for the boxes. "And what about you—are you okay?" She had never called him at the office before.

"You mean do I feel guilty? Why? Do you?"

He spoke carefully. "It wasn't our business, Odile. You did the right thing."

"But they'll kill him."

"You don't know that." Taking a mat knife from his desk, Turner slit open one of the boxes and removed two copies of a glossy paperbound volume. One he gave to Ronald Balakian, who had been hovering nearby in an attitude of polite abeyance; the other he set on his desk. "Anyway, we had no choice, given the situation."

"Tell me," said Odile, "is your assistant there?"

"Gabriella? No, I gave her the afternoon off. Why?"

To this she didn't respond.

"Look," he said. "I can't really talk right now, so why don't we save it till we see each other. We are on for tonight, aren't we?"

"I don't know yet. It's complicated. I'll have to call you."

Turner hesitated. "Everything's going to be all right," he heard himself say.

"I'll call," she repeated, and hung up.

Balakian had taken a seat on the Shaker bench and was paging slowly through the auction catalog. He'd flown in from New York to attend the opening that evening of an exhibition at the Centre Pompidou, a mid-career survey devoted to one of his artists. "Trouble?" he said, without looking up.

"No, no. Just a friend who's feeling a little emotional right now." Turner sat down at his desk and picked up his own copy of the catalog. "So what do you think, Ron? Am I going to sell some flags?"

"It's a very professional job," Balakian said, still looking. "Of course I'd expect no less from you."

In fact Turner was well pleased with the catalog, and these copies were from the second printing. Each of the flags was reproduced in lavish color across a right-hand page, with the facing page of text giving the corresponding particulars. Very often, in Turner's experience, two or three well-chosen sentences of description could make the difference between an adequate sale and an extraordinary one. People wanted to be romanced, and he tried to oblige.

Balakian closed the catalog and said, "I see you're low-balling the estimates pretty aggressively."

"And why not, since it works." Turner leaned back in his chair. "Certain price expectations get set up—I decided on a hundred and twenty to two hundred thousand for the least-interesting flag—and once those numbers are exceeded there's no way of judging what a reasonable price might be. People get excited, they bid high. Considering the groundwork I've done here—with your help, needless to say—I expect a hammer price closer to three hundred thousand each."

"And you'll probably get it." Balakian cocked a steely eyebrow. "Myself, though, I prefer a retail environment. Fewer variables."

"More control."

"That too," Balakian agreed.

They had a laugh together.

Later, after Balakian had left, Turner reviewed the list of people to whom the catalog had already been sent, cross-checking it against the larger database maintained by the auction house. Publicity remained a concern, but once the rest of the catalogs went out he'd call in a few last favors from his media contacts. Then only the pre-sale exhibition and the auction itself would be left to attend to. Money would be made, the thing would be complete.

Yet satisfaction eluded him. Whatever pleasure he might have taken in the success of this venture—hearing of the flags, recognizing their worth, and, by force of will and imagination alone, turning that worth to profit—now seemed fleeting and insubstantial, an artifact of a self already half shed. Recalling the night Odile had walked in on him, he winced. It had been years since he'd allowed his personal well-being to come so frankly under the influence of someone else. He doubted very much whether any good could come of it. Still, he would have to try.

When his thoughts grew calm again, he called Céleste.

MAX ARRIVED half an hour late at the quai de la Tournelle to find that Jacques, whom he'd sent ahead with the equipment, had been pressed into service as a proxy mechanic, helping Rachel dismantle the second of the engines. The other had already been cannibalized and taken down to the engine room.

"That's quite a cologne you're wearing," Rachel said as she and Max embraced. "What is it, hibiscus?"

Max stepped back and scanned the boat without favor. "Where's Groot? He's not here?"

"Sorry, he left for Rotterdam this morning."

"Rotterdam? But we had an agreement! I can't shoot this scene without him."

"I know, and he asked me to give you his apologies." She wiped her hands on a rag and passed it to Jacques, who accepted it gratefully. "His mother's sick."

"Really?" Max had never heard Groot mention his mother. He handed Jacques the manila folder he was carrying. "Is it serious?"

"I don't know." Rachel gave a small, nervous laugh. "I mean, he says it's his mother, but he's still pretty fixated on the money my parents wired us for the engines. I never should've teased him about it because now he really wants to pay it back. Wants to a whole lot. So maybe he went to raise the money somehow, or maybe just needed a break from his killer-bitch girl-friend. Or maybe his mother *is* sick."

Max glanced at Jacques, who commenced setting up the camera and sound equipment. "Okay," he said to Rachel, "we'll just have to make the best of it." She was wearing jeans and a red leotard top that contrasted nicely with her jet-black hair, a strand of which strayed across her cheek. "Can you walk us through the mechanics of what you're doing here with the engine?"

"No problem."

"We'll keep it kind of free-form, if that's all right. Don't worry too much about staying on topic, just follow your thoughts. Jacques, you shoot it. I'll take sound."

"Check."

When Rachel was again positioned over the engine, removing the fuel pump, Max cued Jacques and they began. She explained what she was doing, pointed out which parts would probably replace their opposite numbers in the *Nachtvlinder*'s original engines, and managed to convey a genuine enthusiasm for the mysteries of the diesel-combustion cycle. It was peculiar, Max thought, the hushed zealotry with which she and Groot spoke about the boat, almost as if it embodied a cause of some kind, a spiritual principle larger than themselves, to which they felt privileged to sacrifice their time and resources.

When he sensed that Rachel was nearing the end of her technical commentary, he intervened. "You've said before, Rachel, that a boat is like a living thing. Could you expand on that a little for us?"

"Sure." She pushed aside the errant strand of hair, leaving a smear of engine grease across her cheek. "Every boat has her own character, a combination of traits that makes her unique. How she handles, what she's capable of, what she was designed to do, all that. Plus, from the moment she's launched, she accumulates a history that shapes her just like experience shapes a person. In the case of the *Nachtvlinder,* that's more than a hundred years. We've seen logs that show her sailing throughout the former Dutch colonies, from the Antilles—Curaçao, Aruba, Saint Martin—to the East Indies—Java, New Guinea, Sumatra, Borneo, the Moluccas, and the rest. She's been around the world, for sure. And that kind of history leaves its mark."

Max threw a quick look at Jacques to make certain he was getting all this. "So am I right that your and Groot's attachment to the *Nachtvlinder* is personal, even intimate?"

"Oh yes. Definitely. She's our baby."

Leaving a small silence, Max allowed the sense of this last remark to settle. Then he said, "Where's Groot today?"

Rachel looked momentarily confused. "Groot went to Rotterdam." She hesitated. "We had a quarrel."

"What about?"

"Money, supposedly." She seemed to think about it. "But we wouldn't really fight over money. That's just an excuse."

"Yes? So what's the real issue?"

"Well, us—him and me. Do we go on or not." She folded her arms and shook her head in a wry approximation of perplexity. "And actually the *Nachtvlinder*'s at the center of all that, because she's like a standard of some kind, an example of endurance and good faith, nothing false about her." She laughed. "I realize how frivolous that might sound to people who don't know boats, but believe me, it's real enough to us."

"So I gather," said Max. He adjusted the sound level. "But Groot did ask you to marry him, and now you two seem to be at odds—if not over money, then over whatever it stands for, right? Power, freedom, family—you tell me."

Rachel's features seemed to thicken and her mood to falter. "Getting the engines was a surprise," she said. "We thought it would take all summer to rebuild the old ones. Now we'll be done much sooner."

"Does that mean you have to make up your mind sooner, too? About marrying him?"

"No. Why should it?" Behind her glasses Rachel's eyes flashed with something quite like anger. Jacques zoomed in slowly.

"Hey, no reason." Max hastened to return the conversation to its previous footing. "So what happens after you finish with the engines?"

"We'll put her in dry dock, get her caulked, filled, and painted, clean her props. There are bound to be some surprises—planks that need replacing, that kind of thing." She turned her face into the wind, giving Jacques and the camera her profile. "Sorry, Max," she said after a moment. "Maybe we should—"

But she did not complete her thought. From the quai came a briskly cadenced sound. All three turned to look. Six black-uniformed police, trotting two abreast in tight formation, were headed across the packed-sand quai to the *Nachtvlinder.*

"Oh, my God." Rachel fell back a step, her hand over her mouth.

"Stay cool, guys." Max handed the sound boom to Jacques and took over the camera. "We're all on the same side."

"Better watch it," Jacques said under his breath. "They're CRS."

"Riot police? But doesn't French law let me photograph anyone I want to in public, cops included?"

"Yes, but—"

Already Max was filming the police as they barreled up the gangway, their boots sounding in unison, their service pistols holstered but conspicuous at their hips. They didn't slow their pace boarding the boat and were almost on top of Max and the others before their commanding officer raised a hand and brought them to a halt. He took in the scene—Max behind the camera, Jacques with the sound boom, Rachel hovering over the partly eviscerated engine—then he said, *"À qui appartient ce vaisseau?"*

Rachel came forward uncertainly. *"Excusez-moi?"*

"I said, who owns this vessel?"

Seeing another policeman move toward him, Max stepped out from behind the camera with both hands raised in a pantomime of surrender. He'd left the camera running on its tripod.

"Oh, you speak English!" said Rachel gratefully. "Well, the actual owner is away right now, but he and I live here together. And these two guys, they're just, you know, filming."

The officer appeared unmoved. "Identity cards, please."

When all three had produced photo IDs, he addressed himself again to Rachel. "Who else is on board at the present time?"

"No one, Officer. Just us."

"I have orders to search this boat, Madame. It will go better for everyone if you do not create problems." He smiled mirthlessly. "Do you understand?"

"Yes, of course."

The officer lifted his chin to his men, and they set off at a military pace—one to either side of the wheelhouse, three down the companionway. Max was again behind the camera, recording these maneuvers as best he could without giving up his prime spot on the foredeck. Jacques had propped the sound boom among the legs of an overturned deck chair so that the mike dangled directly, but without his physical intercession, over Rachel and the commanding officer. Past experience with the CRS had inclined him toward caution.

From below came the clamor of invasive search—stowage lockers flung open and shut again, furniture pushed aside, batons sounding the bulkheads for hidden compartments. Each of these noises registered on Rachel's face, which the officer observed with clinical interest. Finally she said, "Please, sir, I'd like to cooperate, but I don't know what you're looking for."

He nodded as though listening to some familiar music doubtfully rendered, then, half begrudgingly, reached into his jacket and produced a photograph for Rachel's inspection. "Do you know this man?" he asked.

To get a shot of the photo, Max had to remove the camera from its tripod. He came around behind Rachel and the officer, filming over their shoulders as they considered the black-and-white image.

"No, I've never seen him before."

"Are you certain?"

The man in the photo was a nondescript, balding Caucasian of middle age, wearing a white lab coat and heavy black-framed glasses, standing in a high-tech industrial interior of some kind and cradling a clipboard, his lips pursed to suggest the confidence and resolve befitting a man of reason. The photo reminded Max of something from a year-end stockholders' report, a visual aid usually run alongside optimistic earnings forecasts and three-dimensionally rendered pie charts.

"Positive," said Rachel. "Why? What's he done?"

"That remains to be determined," the officer replied with a sniff. Already his men were coming back empty-handed from their search. Turning to speak to them, he saw Max filming. "Sir, if you don't put that camera away I'll arrest you for obstruction."

Max backed off a couple of steps and continued shooting. The officer glared at him, then looked away. "Mathieu!" he said to one of his men. "Did you turn up anything?"

The man stood at attention. "No, sir! Nothing!"

Shifting his attention to Rachel, the officer smiled unpleasantly. "This is the same *Nachtvlinder* that was firebombed a few weeks ago, is it not?"

"Yes, but what does that have to do with—"

"Let me ask the questions," he replied. Taking a radio phone from his belt, he called headquarters. "The situation," he said after identifying himself, "is that there is no situation. We've tossed the boat from stem to stern. Nothing. No doctor, no illegal aliens."

To keep both Rachel and the officer in the frame, Max had to move several steps to the left.

"What do you suggest?" the officer said.

Behind Max, heading upstream, a *bateau-mouche* churned by, roiling the holly-green waters. The officer put his radio back and started toward Max, and at almost the same moment someone seized Max's camera and yanked it away. He whirled round in outrage, ready to defend his rights, only to see that Jacques now held the camera, and, from the look on his face, that Max had made a mistake. He turned back just in time to receive the full force of the officer's fist in his solar plexus.

It had been many years since Max had taken such a punch. He crumpled at once to the deck, gasping for air.

"You don't listen, sir," the officer said. "For your sake, I hope you learn to." He nodded curtly to Rachel, then led his men across the deck and down the gangway in the same martial manner in which they'd arrived, the sound of their bootsteps quickly fading on the quai.

Rachel and Jacques helped Max into a deck chair. He was thinking about the night he'd met Odile and been obliged to fight the man pursuing her. It seemed like only yesterday.

"You went too far," Rachel told him.

"No," Max began, "I think . . . I think it was . . ."

"Don't talk," Jacques said. "Breathe."


ODILE RETURNED HOME in a state of mounting unease. She tried working on the wedding dress—Fatima had called the day before to pronounce herself delighted with the new design—but couldn't concentrate and was forced to set it aside. Anyway, she reasoned, to proceed was pointless until she got her client to agree to a fresh fitting.

Upstairs, she brewed a cup of rosehip tea and stood sipping it in the bedroom, studying the Giacometti drawing. The half-emergent woman it depicted, formed of welter and waste, seemed to demonstrate some irrefutable fact of life, a truth that Odile recognized yet couldn't name, and for quite some time she remained transfixed. Then, abruptly, she grew frightened. The afternoon's events had left her feeling flayed, vulnerable, raw.

She hurried back to the kitchen and, at five thirty, called Turner, who asked her to go with him to an opening at the Centre Pompidou, an idea so preposterous that she almost hung up. After she made her feelings clear and he'd sufficiently apologized, they agreed to meet at his apartment instead.

She dressed carefully, aware of wanting to please him: black lace brassiere and panties, a plum-colored dress of her own design, black lizard-skin heels, drop earrings, no perfume. Contemplating the effect in the mirror, she recalled there were several kinds of guilt that sometimes, properly handled, could cancel one another out for an hour or two. She left Max a note saying that she was with a client.

At Turner's apartment, before she could even get the key into the lock, he flung the door open. She stared at him.

"Aren't you coming in?" His eyes, so dark the pupils were hardly distinguishable, shone as he took stock of her.

She hurried past him. "I just needed to see you," she said as he closed the door.

"Same here," he replied. "You've been on my mind all day."

Turning to see if he spoke ironically, she was instead surprised by how genuine he seemed. "Really? All day?" She laughed, teasing him a little.

"Yes, really." Then he said, spacing out the words as if to clarify, "I think about you night and day."

The laughter died in her throat, replaced by a citric sting that made her eyes water. She swallowed, wanting to speak, but it was too late for that.

In bed she let need supersede judgment and held nothing back, not even trying to excuse herself. When she felt him about to come, she slipped out from beneath him, pushed him back on the mattress and vaulted on top. With her hands planted side by side on his chest, she chased him down, matching thrust to thrust, unstinting, until her vision darkened, he said her name, and a blood tide lifted her up and away. She loosed a long, low cry that ended, as she fell forward onto him, in a sob.

They lay together afterward, drained, still, and blank. She clung to the blankness, working it down into a thin sleep in which she could rest, a moment of nullity, no more than that. She woke with a start.

"He looked different."

"Who?" said Turner, stirring.

"Thierry. His head was shaved. And he was wearing glasses."

Turner shifted her gently off him onto one side, then drew her back into his arms. "You know," he said, "I could've sworn that for a moment there, just a moment, you were really with me. Am I wrong?"

She left a small silence. "No."

"Well, I'm glad to hear that. Because I don't want to be childish about this, but I do have feelings for you." Saying it seemed to sober him. "Yes, I do. And I don't see much point in pretending otherwise."

Wriggling closer, she willed him to be quiet.

"Do you?" he persisted.

In the five years of her marriage to Max, Odile had never till now been unfaithful to him. She shivered. "There's always reason to pretend," she said.

"Maybe so, but in your case I can't." He seemed to be arguing a point of order. "Anyway, you're here. That must count for something."

"It is what it is," she told him.

"But I'm not the only one who cares," Turner insisted. "Or do I flatter myself?"

"No," she surprised herself by saying. "I do care for you. Of course I do. But feelings solve nothing. Surely you know that."

"Well, at least I got you to admit it," he said after awhile. "That's something."

Softly she disengaged from him, got out of bed, and began dressing. Aware of his watchful eyes on her, she suddenly felt certain that he understood her better than he let on, maybe better than he realized. The thought wasn't altogether unwelcome—as he'd said, being there must count for something—but she felt compelled to resist it nonetheless. Reaching behind her back, she fastened her brassiere. "Things are about to get busy for me at home," she told him. "My husband's daughter is coming to visit from New York."

"For how long?"

"A month." She picked her dress up off the floor. "It's been in the works for awhile."

"I see. And are you close to her?"

"Yes and no. I mean, she's thirteen. Who can tell?" She pulled the dress on over her head, shook it into place, then sat down on the edge of the mattress, presenting her back to him. He zipped her up, and she was on her feet again, scooping her hair clip and earrings off the dresser, collecting her shoes. "Anyway, there'll be a lot to do. You know—family things."

Turner got out of bed, took a bathrobe from the closet, and put it on. "So when will I see you?"

"I'm not sure." She stood before the mirror, dabbing at her hair. "It'll be hard."

He came up behind her and put his arms around her waist. "But you'll find a way."

"I'll try," she told him.

He saw her to the door, and she took the elevator down.

On the street, walking to the métro, she let bits and pieces of the day replay themselves in her mind—the envelope of money, the turquoise handbag, Thierry and Gabriella in the theater, the slide show of tunnels and catacombs, the Russians in their jackets, the car they'd left unattended—until her sense of the day's events composed itself into a kind of refrain that, as she considered it, grew alarming.

There had been a calamity. She had lent herself to a calamity.

## CHAPTER 23

MAX WATCHED HIS DAUGHTER enter passport control. Her figure had filled out incredibly in the three months since he'd seen her in New York, she was wearing a chartreuse minidress he suspected she'd changed into on the plane, and the official overseeing her transit onto French soil appeared to be flirting with her, delaying her passage with droll commentary and artfully timed glances. She emerged from his attentions looking puzzled but pleased, her passport held gingerly before her.

"Breaking hearts already, are you?" said Max. In his arms she froze as she had for the last year or more, mortified by his love. He forced himself not to take it personally. "How was your flight?" he asked, releasing her.

"Okay, I guess. I slept through most of it." A quick frightened smile crossed her face. "Hey, what time is it here anyway?"

They retrieved her luggage—an oversized nylon duffel bag stuffed improbably full—then took it through customs and caught the RER into town.

At the mews, Odile greeted Allegra with a hug, which, Max couldn't help but note, his daughter returned with all the natural warmth that had deserted her in his own embrace.

"Oh how lovely! Look at you, sweet—so grown up! I'm very happy to see you again!"

"Thanks," said Allegra, the blood rushing to her face. "It's good to see you, too."

"And such a stylish dress! Maybe while you're here we can design something special together. I'm always looking for someone with a good fashion sense to wear my clothes. That's the only kind of advertising I believe in, you know?" Odile glanced surreptitiously at her watch—but she wasn't wearing her watch, Max noticed, her wrist was bare, and she now rubbed it distractedly with her other hand.

"Unfortunately, Allegra, right now I must go to work. A client who's getting married, her wedding dress, some last-minute changes . . ." She made an upward spiraling gesture with the hand that had briefly covered her wrist. "So I'll see you later, okay?"

Allegra nodded vigorously, they kissed cheeks, and Odile left Max to help his daughter settle in. She seemed marginally relieved that it was again just the two of them.

"How's your French these days?" he asked, as together they climbed the stairs to the garret room.

"I don't know yet."

"You'll be fine." He set her duffel bag down at the foot of her bed. "Now here's your house key," he said, holding it out to her. "That opens the downstairs door, which locks automatically when you go out, don't forget. You remember the gate code, right?"

"Yes." She was taking in the room in a series of small glances, each of which seemed to leave her a little more at ease. Her last visit had been just two Christmases ago, but it now felt to Max unfathomably distant.

"A few house rules. You're thirteen, and I think that's old enough for you to go out by yourself. But when you do, I want you to tell either me or Odile where you're going and when you'll be back. Can you do that?"

"Yes, *Dad*." She rolled her eyes, but he saw that she was pleased.

"Good. I'm counting on you." He opened the drawer in the bedside table and extracted the cell phone he'd bought for her. "Now this little item is essential to our arrangement, okay? I want you to keep it charged up and switched on whenever you go out. You'll find it already programmed with numbers for me, Odile, and your friend Dominique, who, by the way, expects to hear from you sometime this afternoon. You've got a hundred and eighty prepaid minutes there, more than enough to get you launched. Okay?"

"Cool, Dad! Thanks." She inspected the phone happily.

"What else? Oh, I invited Dominique and her father to dinner tonight, so you'll see her then. Be sure to ask Odile if you can help with the cooking; I think she has something special planned." Max found himself staring at his daughter's hair, selected strands of which shone blonder than the rest. "How are you for cash?"

"Mom gave me two hundred in traveler's checks."

"Okay. Hang on to that." He took out his wallet. "Here's three hundred francs, which is your weekly allowance while you're here. Things are expensive in Paris, and I won't bail you out, so pay attention where it goes."

"*Jawohl!*" she said, saluting.

"Don't be cute." He struggled unsuccessfully to hide his amusement. "Are you hungry?"

"Not really. They gave us something on the plane." She plopped down on the bed, then held the cell phone up at him. A flash went off, she bent over the LED screen to examine the image. "Dad! You look so serious!"

"And a good thing, too," he told her. "Listen, why don't you unpack, relax, take a bath if you want, then come down to the studio later. I've got a few work things to take care of."

"All right," she said, with an exaggerated frown. Shrugging. "If you like." Going on to herself in French as he descended the stairs.

In the courtyard he interrupted the anarchists preparing to launch what appeared to be an improvised weather balloon, a beach ball–sized sack of aluminized fabric with a wire-frame gondola suspended beneath. Directing their efforts was the pale blond girl he'd seen some weeks ago with the clipboard. He raised a clenched fist to her in passing, and she smiled at him before returning to the task at hand.

"Jacques?" he called as he let himself into the studio.

That morning, in an afterthought so belated it made him cringe, Max had sent his assistant to Saint-Ouen to scour the flea market for DVD titles issued by La Peau de l'Ours. He had the idea that if he could discover what changes had been made to the other counterfeited movies—and surely *Fireflies* hadn't been specially singled out for revision—then something useful might be learned, if not about the violator of his film, then about himself, the kind of man he was and the kind of films he might yet make. But Jacques hadn't returned, and alone in the studio, Max put the idea out of his mind.

Upstairs, he watched the footage of Rachel he'd shot aboard the *Nachtvlinder* the day of the police raid. The light off the water gave her a shimmering immediacy that played well against her musings about the boat and its hundred-year history. Juxtaposed, the two elements carried a hint of foreboding. Max rejoiced.

Film: he would never be done with it.

But as the police entered the picture, boarding and searching the boat, as their commanding officer requested identification from everyone present and began to interrogate Rachel, an unwelcome thought occurred to him. Recalling how bitterly Madame Leclère had complained of her own experience with the police, in particular their confiscation of her files, he found he couldn't entirely dismiss the possibility that a connection existed—something in the files that had led the police to the *Nachtvlinder*—though nothing he could point to supported such a notion.

More troubling still—and here he froze the frame—was the photo of the man in the white lab coat. A doctor, according to what the officer had said, presumably meaning research scientist rather than medical doctor. The very fact of this man, an apparent fugitive, fit so unexpectedly with what Max had learned of La Peau de l'Ours, at least in its medical aspects, that he had to remind himself that there was no reason at all to suppose that the two were related. He was just free-associating. A hazard of the profession.

Suddenly annoyed, he switched off the video monitor, plucked a cigar from the box on his worktable, fired it up, and opened the window that looked out on the courtyard.

The anarchists and their science project were nowhere in evidence. Instead, standing on the cobblestones just beneath the window, two sleekly dressed men, somewhat foreign in aspect, gazed up at him in an attitude of pained expectancy. They seemed to be waiting for a word from him, an announcement, perhaps, or a small speech. Amused, he gazed back.

*"Bonjour,"* he said.

They nodded in acknowledgment of his greeting and continued to look. Then the heavier of the two men said something to the other, something Max couldn't make out, and without further consultation they left, as if they'd come to the mews for no other purpose than to exchange stares with him.

He expelled a stream of blue smoke into the courtyard, then tossed the cigar irritably after it. He couldn't concentrate worth a damn today.


"I CAN'T STAY LONG," said Odile. "I just thought that, you know, since I was in the neighborhood . . ."

"Your timing is perfect." Céleste wheeled her painting cart out from behind its screen and parked it beside the portrait-in-progress. "The light is better than last time, a little more golden, and painting you I need all the help I can get. We will work for one hour maximum. If that's all right with you."

"Yes, that's fine." Odile removed her clothes, draped herself as before in the green silk dress, and took up position at the center of the sofa, her pose by now second nature.

Céleste came forward to adjust the fabric, then drew back again. For several seconds her cornflower-blue eyes drank Odile in before she chose a brush from the six or seven she held bunched in her left hand and dipped it in turpentine. "Now," she observed to herself, "we begin again."

For some time she painted in silence, her attention washing over her subject like an astringent bath. The sudden need to be seen in this way, clearly and without sentiment, had brought Odile directly here from Fatima's fitting, which had turned out to be more a hand-holding exercise for the jittery bride. Now it was Odile who required reassurance. She sat as still as she could, her bare skin tingling.

After several minutes Céleste said, "I think we're getting somewhere."

"Really? What makes you say that?"

"The maenad has returned. I lost her for awhile, but now she's back."

"Back? You mean in me or in the painting?"

"Both," Céleste said simply. "Please don't turn your head."

"But do I still look like someone who—someone capable of anything?"

Céleste continued to paint, offering her no answer, until the silence itself became the answer and the question evaporated, as if it had never been asked.

Gazing out at the now-familiar rooftop vista, Odile saw, on a tiny terrace two buildings away and a story below, a woman berating a small boy. He was hugging a medium-sized black dog and crying. The woman, her hands on her hips, continued to harangue him, then picked up a garden hose, handed it to him, and retreated into the apartment.

"I'm sure you know by now about me and Turner," Odile said. She sighed. "He's different from what I expected. Less cynical, maybe, though I don't know about that."

"You've discovered his optimistic streak," suggested Céleste.

"Is that what it is?" Odile watched the boy stroke the dog and speak to it as though in consolation. "I wonder. Everything you told me about him that first day, the day he brought me here to meet you, is true, of course. That he's comfortable in his skin, that he's fallible to himself, unexpectedly human, all that. Yet for an optimist, if that's what he is, he has some very worrisome friends."

Céleste swore softly to herself.

"What's wrong?" said Odile.

"Nothing. I've got ahold of you at last, the person who keeps escaping me." She looked fiercely from the canvas to Odile and back again, painting. "What friends?"

"Do you know someone named Kukushkin—a banker, I think?"

"Turner has so many business associates."

"But surely not that many who can have a man killed."

Céleste didn't answer immediately. The boy on the terrace began to hose down the dog, who cowered miserably beneath the jet of water, pressing himself against the masonry wall as though he might somehow evade notice there. Odile looked away.

"The thing you must understand about Turner," said Céleste, "is that he always lands on his feet. He doesn't plan it, but he survives. It's one of his gifts."

Odile said no more. The certainty with which Céleste had spoken encouraged her to examine things from a more rigorous perspective, one in which she saw that her time with Turner had already come to an end. She'd indulged herself, that went without saying, but her curiosity about him had been genuine, her interest that of a fellow traveler not afraid to detour. Feelings had been had, possibly an insight or two. But that was all over now.

Later, just before they quit for the day, Céleste said, "I know what you're thinking."

"You do?" Despite herself, Odile let a hand stray to her hair.

"I ask only that you not cut it until I'm done with you."

Odile stared at her and promised she wouldn't.


DESCENDING THE STAIRS with a platter of sliced lamb, Allegra first began to giggle, then lost her composure completely as she ferried the food out to the green metal table in the courtyard. Behind her, looking furiously amused, Dominique followed with the *haricots verts.* Rachel and Eddie Bouvier were already seated, and Chinese lanterns flickered in the overhanging chestnut tree.

"The girls are stoned," Max said, looking down on the scene from the living-room window.

"Don't be absurd. They're just enjoying themselves on a perfect June night." Odile handed him a bowl of split spring potatoes.

"Think so?"

"Yes. And would you take the other bottle of wine down too, please?"

At the table, when they were all seated and served and the meal had begun, Eddie said, "Today I did something I promised myself never to do. Yet I can't say I regret it. In fact I am quite content."

"Tell us," said Rachel, spooning garlic sauce over her lamb.

"Your regret is merely latent," Odile added. "As your friends, we will help you find it."

Dominique nudged Allegra under the table and soundlessly mouthed something that sent them both into fresh bouts of hilarity. Max pretended to ignore them.

"As you know," said Eddie, "my brother Gaspard lives in Strasbourg, where he teaches music at the conservatory. For two years now he's been in love with one of his students, a very pretty girl, lavishly gifted as a violinist, but also stupefyingly selfish and equipped as well with a truly incredible appetite for cocaine, which, needless to say, he often has to finance. In short, a complete horror. In her favor I can add only that I once heard her play Biber's *Mystery Sonatas* with such clarity that—"

A small crash ensued as Odile, who had been taking a second helping of the ratatouille she'd prepared for Allegra and herself, knocked over her water glass, which fell to the cobblestones and shattered. Blushing, she apologized and bent down to pick up the pieces.

"But Odile!" said Eddie, glancing at her plate. "This delicious lamb— why do you not permit yourself to enjoy it?"

"She's a vegetarian," Allegra said delicately, leaning back in her chair as if to demonstrate that she, too, had forgone the lamb.

"Or maybe a Buddhist," Max added. "We're not sure."

"Go on, Eddie," said Odile.

"So, this is the love of my brother's life, at least in his opinion. But there's more to this story, because the whole time he's been seeing her she has also been seeing another man, someone in Paris who knew nothing of Gaspard." Eddie paused for a sip of wine, nodded his approval in Max's direction, and continued. "I know this not only because she missed no opportunity to tell my brother about this other man but also because I twice ran into her with him, quite by accident, here in Paris."

"Let me guess," Rachel said. "The man she sees here is married."

"Not married, but in essence you are correct. There was already a woman in his life, a small-business owner of some kind who had recently lost her husband in a car accident. In all likelihood this woman, even today, has no inkling whatsoever of this girl from Strasbourg."

Allegra turned to Rachel. "How did you know that, Rachel?"

"Car accident?" Max repeated.

"Feminine intuition," Rachel said.

"At any rate," said Eddie, "this whole precarious state of affairs came to a sudden halt a short time ago when the other man, the Parisian, died unexpectedly, I don't know how. Realizing, no doubt, that it was time to secure her future, the girl right away gave my brother to understand that, were he to propose to her now, she might look upon his offer with an open mind, or at least not humiliate him completely. Naturally, against my advice, he proposed to her."

"And naturally," said Odile, "she turned him down."

"I'm afraid not." Eddie cut himself a bite of lamb and chewed thoughtfully, then, at precisely the same moment, Dominique's and Allegra's cell phones rang in chiming synchrony. Stricken, the girls hastened to silence the devices, though they didn't actually answer them. "And yet Gaspard is my brother," Eddie went on, impaling a potato on his fork. "I cannot be indifferent to his happiness."

"So you intervened," Rachel suggested. "You saved him from himself, right? And from her, too, I bet."

Dominique again nudged Allegra under the table, but this time her eyes were wide and serious. "Tell them what you did, Papa."

"I hired a detective," said Eddie, "someone to follow this girl, research her, assemble the facts." He looked at each of the adults in turn, as though to forestall their disapproval or merriment. "True, my brother's besotted with her, but even he would reconsider if something serious came to light. And if nothing does, then what harm? She can still play Biber like no one else."

"Wow, that's *so* prudent," said Rachel, although anyone could see she was thoroughly shocked. "You two must be very close."

"Or competitive," said Dominique under her breath.

"How did you choose your detective?" Odile asked quickly, hostess first, but also curious.

"I hardly need tell you," Eddie said, "that the film profession, from time to time, brings one into contact with an element that can only be described as criminal in nature. So it is anything but a mystery that I know a few detectives." He raised an eyebrow in belated feint toward irony. "Nonetheless, since we're speaking here without benefit of lawyers, entirely among ourselves, at dinner, I must ask your discretion in this small personal matter."

"Cool!" said Allegra.

"You don't think that—" Max looked at Eddie in anguished surmise. "I mean, it would be a gigantic coincidence, but—"

"What are you saying?" said Eddie. "For once I don't follow."

"Never mind. Forget it, I'm hallucinating."

"This is your brain," Allegra said to Dominique, holding up a fist. Abruptly, she splayed her fingers and wiggled them wildly. "This is your brain on drugs." A portentous pause. "The choice is yours."

The girls slumped against each other in helpless laughter.

"Max, perhaps our guests would like some more lamb," said Odile. "And I'm almost certain I put another bottle of mineral water in the fridge."

Max got up, shaking his head, and went inside.

"The point is," Rachel said, "I mean, isn't the point really that marriage is a doomed but noble gesture, quaint and powerful like, I don't know, 'The Charge of the Light Brigade'? You throw your fate to the winds, right? Because you have no choice."

" 'Into the valley of Death rode the six hundred,' " Eddie recited pensively. "Yes, in effect." He poured Rachel more wine. "Not bad at all, that."

"Don't let him fool you," Odile said. "He's been married three times, yet not once has he died, at least to our knowledge."

"All I'm saying," Rachel offered, "is that I don't think this detective will have much effect on your brother, one way or the other." She drank deeply of her wine. "But what do I know? I've also been proposed to quite recently, I myself."

Eddie raised an eyebrow. "And you answered how, if I may ask?"

"I declined to answer on such short notice. I gave the answer of no answer." Her eye fell on the girls, who were regarding her with renewed interest bordering on awe. "How about you two? Boyfriends?"

They shook their heads.

Rachel smiled. "That's also the answer of no answer. Don't think I can't remember how that goes."

"But if you really love the guy," Allegra said.

"Oh, I do really love him, I certainly do. It's just that—well, love, you know, sometimes it can end up creating more problems than it solves. Right, Odile?"

"Frequently," Odile agreed. "Often."

"But we'll see. Because he's coming back tomorrow. From the old and aptly named town of Rotterdam." Rachel finished her wine.

"How's his mother?" Odile asked.

"She's better," Rachel said. "She was sick, and now she's better."

"But certainly this is good news," said Eddie.

"Oh, for sure." Rachel stared at her glass as he refilled it once more. "But then again, Dutch mothers—that's a whole subject unto itself."

The sound of a motorcycle turning onto rue Leon Maurice Nordmann created a brief lull in the conversation. When the engine cut out and the gate to the mews swung open a moment later, only Odile and Allegra were still paying attention. Jacques, wearing a crash helmet and a small beat-up leather backpack, dismounted, leaned the bike up against the wall, and let himself into Max's studio. He didn't appear to notice anyone at the other end of the courtyard.

"He's really kind of cute for an older guy," Allegra observed.

"There's more lamb," Max announced, emerging from the apartment with a platter in one hand, a bowl in the other, "and, for those of you who object to eating flesh, or even if you don't, there's salad." Once everyone was served, he said, "Odile, you got a phone call just now. Male voice, nobody I know, youngish. But he wouldn't leave a message."

"Strange." She glanced down to check her watch before she remembered she was without it. "French?"

"Definitely. A little high-strung, maybe."

Eddie laughed and bit his lip. "It's only that we have so much to be high-strung about," he added apologetically.

"He'll call back if it's important," said Odile.

Max thought she seemed relieved that her caller was French, but an instant later he could no longer be sure. Like her father, she had scant patience for the phone.

Midway down the mews, the anarchists' door opened. A young man stuck his head out and peered peevishly skyward, surveyed the heavens, then ducked back inside, closing the door behind him. His observations had been carried out against a backdrop of strange music emanating from the apartment, something dusky-voiced that seemed to promise eventualities both sweet and spiteful.

"British, I think," said Eddie.

"East London," Dominique confirmed. "Leytonstone and that whole scene." They were speaking of the music.

"Dad?" said Allegra, laying her fork across her empty plate.

"Yes, my sweet."

"How come you didn't, like, *tell* me there was a high-security nineteenth-century *prison* practically next door to where you *live?*"

"Actually," he said, "I did. Last time you were here."

"Really? I think I would've remembered that."

"Well, maybe your sense of social concern hadn't fully blossomed yet." He smiled at her unthinkingly; she had been eleven at the time. "Why, do you want a tour?"

"A *tour?*"

"I just meant that—" A glance at Odile, whose lips had composed themselves into a lopsided smile, confirmed the delicacy of his position. He made at once for firmer ground. "People do go to prison," he told Allegra, "and prisons have to exist somewhere. That one exists here. That's all I meant."

"Right." Allegra sighed, her worst suspicions evidently confirmed. "I mean, did you even *know,* Dad, that almost three-quarters of that prison's inmates aren't even French *citizens?* Or that most of them have been convicted of no crime at all; they're just waiting to be charged with something, anything, sometimes for years? And that the *suicide* rate—"

"She's quite right, of course," said Eddie, hurriedly dabbing his mouth with his napkin. "An appalling scandal for which no excuse can suffice." He threw a quick glance at Max, who nodded minutely in response. "But," Eddie added, now addressing Allegra, "La Santé, among French prisons, is a special case."

"Tell us," said Dominique with a note of mischief in her voice. She raised her water glass to her lips, and Max saw again the bluebird tattooed between the thumb and forefinger of her left hand.

"Right, like special in what way?" Allegra said.

Max made no move to interfere.

"First," said Eddie, "it is the rule in Paris and environs that detainees are assigned to a particular prison alphabetically by name. La Santé receives, with certain exceptions, those whose last names begin with the letters T through Z, which means, in practice, that it receives all illegal immigrants, since these individuals are always, by convention, given the last name of X by the state. Okay?"

"But they actually do have names," Allegra said, her chin jutting militantly.

"Obviously, but since these men are without documents there's no way of knowing if they are who they say they are, so officially they are X. Not a perfect solution, of course, but that's why La Santé's population has so many noncitizens."

"Curiouser and curiouser," Rachel observed to her glass.

"What else makes La Santé different?" Dominique asked.

Eddie began to look a bit uncomfortable. "Of course it *is* a prison, so naturally the men inside it can only be unhappy, one must expect this."

"But?" Odile prompted, fixing Eddie with a level gaze.

He took a swallow of wine and pressed on. "Although it isn't widely known, there exists at La Santé a program, very sophisticated and well regarded, that tries to match willing inmates with some of the world's finest medical researchers. Participation is strictly voluntary, of course, but this program allows inmates access to experimental treatments that would otherwise be completely beyond their reach. In many cases, lives are saved. Sometimes, when, in due course, a successful technique is introduced to the world at large, many thousands of lives are saved. Anyway," he concluded, "this is why I say that La Santé, despite its undoubted shortcomings, must be considered a special case."

By way of response there was a shocked silence.

"So really these inmates are, like, human *guinea pigs?*" Allegra said.

"No, no, not at all. As I explained, they are volunteers."

"That's so disgusting. I mean, how can a prisoner be a volunteer *anything?*" She turned to Dominique. "I wonder if Chantal and the black team know about this."

"Chantal?" said Max, who felt that there were just a few too many things going on right now for him to process. "Black team?"

"Girls," Odile said firmly, "would you help me clear the table for dessert?"

Allegra and Dominique hastened to their feet, and Rachel along with them.

"Not you," Odile told her, laughing gently.

She sat back down.

When Odile and the girls had gone inside with the plates, leaving Rachel alone with Max and Eddie, who yet again was filling her glass, the three of them became aware almost simultaneously of a soft battering sound just above their heads, a kind of drubbing, at once senseless and urgent. They looked up.

Around each of the Chinese lanterns in the overhanging tree, perhaps a dozen moths fluttered, hurling themselves repeatedly against the illuminated rice-paper globes, drawn beyond all resistance by the candle flames that burned within. For the better part of a minute, everyone watched, neither able nor willing to look away.

" 'Theirs not to reason why,' " Rachel said.

# CHAPTER 24

TURNER GLANCED one last time at his watch. The press conference, which he'd called for eleven that morning, was already twenty minutes late getting started—the most he dared push it. He stepped up to the podium and tapped the microphone twice with his forefinger.

Crowded into the auction house's second-floor galleries, along with the freshly installed Soviet flags, were perhaps two dozen members of the working press, including three video crews—a gratifyingly strong turnout for a Monday in June. When he had his audience's attention, Turner introduced himself, then told them what he thought they needed to know about the flags. He explained their origin in the May Day competitions among Soviet factories. He mentioned dates and places, collectives and historical figures, but he devoted most of his comments to the banners' status as art objects. They were slated for auction that Thursday evening.

After speaking for about thirty minutes, he took questions for another twenty. Interest seemed to be running high, and the curiosity was both informed and sympathetic. Only once was he invited to comment on the political ironies of selling communist artifacts in a venue so aggressively market oriented, but he'd rehearsed his answer, which was that history had prepared it for him, and this provoked general amusement. Finally, an Italian journalist, elegantly shod and dressed, surprised him completely by remarking upon the similarities between the flags and Warhol's portrait paintings of the 1970s and '80s. Did he, she wondered, expect comparable prices? He politely declined to speculate, and the event came to an end.

Climbing the stairs to the third floor, Turner encountered the director, a fastidious horse-faced man who sometimes pretended to disapprove of Turner's freewheeling methods. Today, though, he congratulated him on the press conference with a collegiality that struck Turner as a bit smug. Maybe, he thought, he'd been too hasty in declaring the ironies of the Cold War defunct.

Finding his office empty, he shut the door, checked his phone for messages—there were none—and, reminded now of what he was unhappy about, sank without relish into his desk chair.

In the three years Gabriella had worked for him, she never before had failed to show up on time. Her truancy this morning, at first only irritating, now began to set off in him a series of faint alarms whose nature, though distantly familiar, he hoped very much not to discover.

Thinking back, he seemed to recall that on Friday, when asking him for the afternoon off, she'd hinted at a family crisis. Though he'd never really believed in this crisis, her request required no excuse, and he'd sent her off without a second thought. Still, supposing there actually had been an emergency, and that it had persisted over the weekend, surely she would've called him this morning to say so. And that, he realized, was what troubled him: not the absence, but the not calling in.

He went to her desk, located in a small alcove outside his office, and stood leafing through her phone log for nearly a minute, even though he knew he wouldn't find anything there. Then, assuming a pleasantly quizzical expression for the benefit of whoever might happen by, he sat down and began to go systematically through her desk drawers.

Amid all the expected office supplies and personal effluvia, only two things struck him as possibly noteworthy, though neither one lent itself to easy interpretation. The first was a computer printout of a document titled "Traité Mondial de Coopération de Breveté"—Worldwide Patent Cooperation Treaty—a numbingly technical agreement that he couldn't imagine Gabriella ever having the patience or occasion to read. After a moment's thought, he dismissed its presence as almost certainly circumstantial. The other artifact to catch his eye, though, was more troubling.

Finely printed on a multiply folded sheet of onionskin paper were the particulars of a Swiss medication, itself nowhere in evidence, whose purpose was specified in French, English, German, and Spanish as "maximal ovulation induction." At first Turner could make no more sense of this document than of the patent treaty—surely if Gabriella were attempting in vitro fertilization, he'd know about it—but then he recalled his own strange question to her some weeks back, the day he had sold a flag to Wieselhoff and later bought the gun. "Are you pregnant?" he asked her, for no reason that he knew. And then her still stranger reply, delivered, it had seemed to him, with an unintended shading of sadness: "No, believe me. Pregnant would be the easy version of what I am."

He sat awhile longer at her desk, sensing the convergence there of forces that might well have engaged him at his best, driving him to new prodigies of invention and craft, had he only been party to them and their possibilities from the outset, had he only been—and the word struck him with the comic force of a Zen blow to the brow—*younger.* He couldn't help but laugh out loud at this insight. Every day he knew less than the day before. Perhaps, despite everything, he was getting somewhere.

He had just finished putting Gabriella's desk back in order when a call came in on her line, the receptionist downstairs letting him know that the car service he'd requested had arrived. Before he could protest that he'd ordered no such thing, she corrected herself. The car had been sent by a Monsieur Kukushkin, who very much hoped Turner might join him for a celebratory lunch, if he was free. Turner, greatly relieved to know that he'd been restored to the Russian's good graces, replied that he was indeed free and would be down directly.


THAT SAME MORNING, at a boat chandlery forty miles downstream from Paris in Conflans-Sainte-Honorine, Max stood crouched over his camera, filming the *Nachtvlinder*'s perilous ascent to dry dock. Visually, the scene was captivating to an almost biblical degree: a thirty-ton, century-old boat being hauled from the Seine onto a wheeled chassis that ran on railroad tracks into an enormous hangar, where it would be worked on nonstop for two days, to emerge, at last, in all its former glory, ready to return under its own power to the quai de la Tournelle. Meanwhile, like figures in a Breughel painting, Groot and the staff swarmed variously across the camera's field of view, facilitating the boat's transfer while seeming also to serve other purposes known only to themselves. Finally, there was the light: diagonal shafts of silver that emerged from charcoal-gray cloud cover with marvelous rectilinear clarity, like a mathematical proof of the ineffable. All this Max recorded gratefully. It would play very well on a big screen and moved the narrative along with a dispatch that no amount of planning could have improved upon. Yet his mind was already half elsewhere.

When, at length, the *Nachtvlinder* was safely ensconced in dry dock, he joined Jacques, who'd arrived at the site separately and had been taking sound throughout, to stroll the arc-lighted hangar with Groot and the ship chandler, a leather-faced Breton in a soiled blue captain's hat. Max shot some close-up footage of the *Nachtvlinder*'s river-fouled hull and props, which hadn't been out of the water in years, prevailing on Groot to provide a bit of commentary to go with it. Then he loudly thanked everyone present and pulled his assistant discreetly aside. "Well?" he demanded.

"I can't swear to it," Jacques said, "but this is what I think happened, in some version." He cast a furtive glance about him. "It turns out that there were actually two different lines of bootleg DVDs coming out of the loft rented by this guy Sylvain Broch. One of them was, so to speak, legitimately illegitimate: in other words, duplicate disks of well-known movies being pirated for profit. Fine. Maybe we don't like it, but we understand. It's normal."

"Was this operation Russian owned?" Max asked.

"Naturally, no one would say. But it's possible." Jacques paused to light a cigarette, and Max, looking reflexively around, blundered into eye contact with Groot, who veered toward them.

"We're going out for lunch," he said, "while the shop calculates what I must pay them for the job. I don't think it will be too bad, now that I've seen what has to be done. You are coming, yes?"

"Definitely," Max said. "We'll catch up."

They watched him go.

"Rachel has retired to her tent in righteous wrath," Max told Jacques.

"Really? Why? What tent?"

"I'll explain later. You were saying, two lines of bootlegs."

"Right. The regular ones and then these Peau de l'Ours numbers." He took a long drag on his cigarette. "Of those I found only the seven titles I left for you last night at the studio. Nice classic films, don't you think? *Fanny and Alexander, Blue Velvet, The Marriage of Maria Braun, La Dolce Vita,* you saw what they were."

*"Knife in the Water."*

"Exactly. So maybe, you know, this part of the operation is more specialized—the films a little artier, less popular, not obvious moneymakers, but successful enough critically that they'll sell steadily over time. And they have a certain prestige." He paused, staring at the end of his cigarette. "I don't know if you've had time to look at them."

"My daughter's here. I've been busy."

"Okay. In short, then, all the Peau de l'Ours titles have had their endings altered to about the same extent as the faux version of *Fireflies*—not grossly, just enough that you'd have to rethink the film, if you know it." He seemed to consider the matter. "It's interesting. There is a finesse behind the changes, a certain élan—a definite sensibility."

"Sensibility," repeated Max. "So they were all done by the same person?"

Jacques flared his lips moodily and then looked him in the eye, as though to put the question beyond doubt. "Yes," he said, "the same person. This is what I think."

"Sylvain Broch?"

"It's possible. But, all things taken into account, I would say probably not." He dropped his cigarette on the floor and ground it out with his boot heel. "Broch was in it for the money, in my view. This other thing, it has more the feeling of a gesture, you know? Something one might do in protest, maybe. To make a point."

Max squinted up at the overhead lights. They were too bright for his present state of mind and reminded him unpleasantly of antiquated movie sets. "What point?" he demanded. "To whom?"

Jacques shrugged. "Maybe," he suggested, "it doesn't matter."

"It matters to me."

"Well, you'll have to see the changes for yourself, and this is only my opinion, yes? But I think this guy wanted to show that anything, no matter how perfect, can always turn out differently and still be convincing. What looks inescapable can be replaced with something else that looks just as inescapable, just as foreordained. Essentially, another way, another life, another outcome is always possible. Something like that."

Max looked angrily around the hangar. "Isn't that kind of metaphysical for a petty criminal?"

Jacques watched curiously until Max's eyes again met his own, then stirred himself to answer. "Maybe," he said after a moment.

They held each other's gaze awhile longer before Max capitulated. "You're right. Whoever this guy is, he's not petty." He squinted at the boat, elegantly stranded beneath the lights. "But neither is he a director. Which is what you, I'm beginning to think, might very well end up becoming, by the way. And despite my best efforts."

Jacques gave a short laugh.

Max said no more, and they gathered up their equipment and set off for lunch.

"THIS IS JUST PURE SPECULATION, right? I mean, where's your evidence?" Odile stood with the phone pressed to her ear, watching Allegra bop back and forth across the living-room floor, damp hair swinging, personal stereo in hand. She was wearing high-performance headphones, a lavender top, no bra, and a zebra-print miniskirt. Rachel was on the line.

"I just *know*," Rachel said. "Where else would Groot get that kind of money?"

"Maybe his mother gave it to him." Lowering her voice and turning her back guiltily to Allegra, Odile added, "Besides, you're not exactly the poster child for a drug-free Europe yourself. Or am I missing something?"

"Personal use is one thing," Rachel declared, "dealing is another."

"We're speaking of hashish, yes?"

"Well, I assume so. But actually I don't even know that. Shit!"

Cupping a hand around the mouthpiece, Odile said, "Hashish is legal in the Netherlands, remember?"

"I'm losing my mind. Actually going bonkers."

"Look," Odile said, "where are you? Come for lunch." She turned around to see Allegra mouthing something at her and pointing repeatedly out the window. Odile nodded, trying to understand her. "You've got to calm down," she told Rachel. "It's just not that big a deal."

"But it is! I mean, I was so pissed off I wouldn't even go see the *Nachtvlinder* into dry dock with him. I bet Max is really happy about that. He's filming today, you know."

"Don't worry about Max."

"My point is, Groot and I had an agreement not to get involved in this kind of thing. Ever. And he broke it."

"What kind of thing?"

"Dealing dope! So how can I trust him now? And he wants me to marry him? No way. Absolutely out of the question."

"Rachel, stop talking. You've lost perspective. Come here now."

A titanic sigh. "I can't," she said. "I'll call you later."

Hanging up, Odile glanced reflexively at her wrist, but her watch was on Turner's bedside table, where she'd left it on Friday—an infuriating lapse that suggested an ambivalence she was fairly sure she did not feel. Already Max had noticed the watch's absence. Preempting his questions, she mentioned in passing that she'd taken it to the jeweler's to be cleaned. Nevertheless it would have to be reclaimed soon, probably in person, and then she'd have to explain herself to Turner, something she had hoped very much to avoid. She was weighing the merits of calling him now, before he fully understood that his assistant wouldn't ever be coming to work again, when suddenly she realized she was alone in the apartment.

"Allegra?" she called, then went to the foot of the garret stairs. "Where are you, sweetheart?"

Sun falling through the garret skylight made a box of light midway up the stairs and Odile stared into it, trying to reconstruct what Allegra had silently mouthed to her while she was talking with Rachel. Then she remembered the cell phone. She got her own from her purse and punched in Allegra's number, but the phone just rang on and on, as it sometimes did when the other person was out of range—in the métro, usually. Odile pressed end and began pacing. *Something bad is going to happen,* she thought. And even though she knew it was a childish notion, a superstitious attempt at warding off the unknown, she couldn't get the idea out of her head. She went into the kitchen and made a pot of peppermint tea. The mail came. She leafed through a magazine. Every ten minutes or so she tried Allegra's cell again.

Finally she went to the living-room window and cranked it open for a breath of air. Midway down the courtyard Chantal and two of her comrades were crouched over bedsheets, writing slogans across them in red and black spray paint. She hurried downstairs.

"Are you coming to the demonstration?" Chantal said, straightening up.

"What demonstration?"

Together they looked at the banner she'd just completed. "WE ARE *ALL* ILLEGAL ALIENS!" it read.

"Tomorrow at three," Chantal said. "Place de la République."

"If I can," Odile said, waving away the aerosol fumes. "But right now I'm looking for my stepdaughter, an American girl, thirteen, blond, I'm sure you've seen her. She tried to tell me where she was going, but I was on the phone and—"

"Oh, sure! Allegra!" Chantal's eyes lit up. "She's a treasure, you know— someone with a natural sense of justice. Fierce." She put her paint can down. "Come with me."

Odile had never been inside the anarchists' quarters and wasn't prepared for the row of glowing computer monitors that ran unattended along one wall of the ground-level studio, which, like theirs, retained its original dirt floor. Overhead, sagging bundles of color-coded electrical cable supplied power. The walls bore inspirational graffiti in several hands and, by the stairs, a grid of maybe sixty small snapshots, indecipherable from where she stood. At the back of the space, four teenagers, all of them wearing knee-high rubber boots, together lowered a large circular tabletop onto its flared support. When they had the thing in place and the latches fastened, Chantal called out to them, "Where's Allegra? Her stepmother's here. Our neighbor and comrade."

One of the four came forward, greeted Odile, and shook her hand. She recognized the wispy-mustached boy as one of those she'd let take refuge in her studio the day the policeman had come. "She's upstairs with Josée and Anne," he said, "drying her feet."

"We had a plumbing mishap," Chantal explained apologetically. "Let me get her."

Left alone with the boy, whose name was Fabien, Odile asked him about the computers.

"All recycled," he said, "castoffs. Now we use them to attack the forces they once served."

"Really? What forces are those?"

"Banks, multinational corporations, instruments of state."

"La Santé prison?"

"Who knows? Even La Santé." He smiled. "Of course, that would require them to install a computer system first. One shouldn't hold one's breath."

Odile was about to inquire further when Allegra appeared, descending the stairs at a pace meant to communicate decorous puzzlement. "I told you where I was going," she said sullenly when she reached the bottom.

"I know. But I thought you'd like to come with me to Monsieur Ibrahim's."

"Monsieur Ibrahim?"

"To pick out fabric for your dress," said Odile.

Chantal arrived at the head of the stairs. "We'll look for you tomorrow," she called down. "Three o'clock, don't forget!"

"We'll try," Odile said, taking Allegra by the hand. *"Ciao!"*

Once they were outside, Allegra snatched her hand away. "I'm not a child. You shouldn't embarrass me in front of my friends."

"Friends already! Well, I wouldn't have had to if you'd answered your phone."

"It didn't ring!"

Deciding not to debate this, Odile steered her out of the mews into the street. "Look," she said, "they mean well, Chantal and her group, and I agree with a lot of what they say. But the police are investigating them. It would be a very serious matter if you got caught up in their trouble, okay?"

"You think I'm stupid."

"Not at all. The opposite, in fact."

"Besides, what do you care? You're just *babysitting* me while my father makes his idiotic *movie*." She began to cry. "I shouldn't even *be* here."

"Darling." Odile put her arm around the girl's shoulders. "Your father loves you. You know that. He can't always choose his shooting schedule." Allegra's tears continued unabated. "We've both been looking forward to your visit so much."

They walked together to the bus stop. Allegra's canvas-topped shoes were sodden, presumably from the plumbing problem Chantal had mentioned, but Odile didn't want to know about it and didn't ask.

Later, on the bus, when she'd stopped crying, Allegra said, "Are we really going to design a dress together? One just for me?"

And later still, at Monsieur Ibrahim's, sorting through fabric samples beneath the Tunisian's indulgent eye, she looked at Odile and said, "My friends are *not* going to believe this."


THE ONE CALLED SERGEI approached him, took his chin in one hand, and peered clinically into his eyes. "Ah, so you are with us again."

Turner's head hurt. He was seated in a straight-backed wooden chair with his wrists handcuffed behind him, and except for his undershorts he was naked. "Us?" he said.

Sergei and the other one, Volodya, laughed at him. He was extremely confused. "Where am I?" There were newspapers spread everywhere and an empty syringe by his feet. Industrial hooks, chains, and winches hung from the ceiling timbers, but there were also domestic furnishings: an upholstered easy chair, a table, a chessboard, lamps with shades, a daybed. "What happened to . . . Where's Nikolai?"

"Mister Kukushkin is unable after all to join you for lunch. I tell you this at least—how many times, Volodya?"

"Four minimum. It becomes tedious."

"But fortunately we are easily entertained," Sergei told Turner. "So, where is she?"

He felt very hot, and the things around him seemed to pulsate. Inside them, other things were trying to get out. "Where is who?"

Shaking his head, Sergei turned his back to Turner and walked a short distance away. Simultaneously Volodya stepped forward. He wore a row of heavy gold rings on his left hand and, after studying Turner for a second, slapped him across the face, right and left in quick succession. Both blows hurt, but the second seemed to lift him partway out of his chair onto a plateau of blinding white pain entirely new to him. He spat blood.

"What, please, is the name of your assistant?" Sergei asked.

"Gabriella," Turner managed to say. "Gabriella Moreau."

"Excellent. And you saw her last when, exactly?"

"Last Friday, at the auction house. She asked for the afternoon off."

"Did you give it to her?"

"Yes."

"And where did she go, please?"

"I have no idea."

"Really, Turner, this is most hard to believe." He looked at his companion, who seemed about to intervene again. "Volodya," he said, "why you don't put on some music, something with maybe a little feeling, okay?"

Volodya snarled a few words in Russian but went over to the stereo deck in back.

In a quiet voice Sergei said, "Confidentially, he is psychopath. You notice the smell?"

Turner said nothing. He had noticed the smell.

"I require him to wear cologne, but, you know, with hormone imbalance like his . . ." He shrugged. It seemed to Turner that Sergei's lupine features were only temporarily human and that at any moment—any *second*—he might actually turn into the wolf he resembled. The phrase "Don't sell me no wolf tickets" streaked across Turner's mind. It was an expression from his childhood.

"So," said the Russian, clapping his hands together in a brisk return to business. "How long your assistant Mademoiselle Moreau has been consort of Thierry Colin?"

"Consort?" Turner's heartbeat took off on him, just up and away.

"Mistress, girlfriend, fuck." Sergei appeared angry. "What is wrong, please, with *consort*?"

"Nothing. I just didn't—" And then he grew truly frightened. "Oh, no, that's not right! Not at all! I would have known."

"Too bad for you, this *is* right." The Russian began to pace. "And they are together now, yes?"

"No! Impossible!" In his panic, Turner was trying to stand up while still handcuffed to the chair. It was made of oak and quite heavy. "They don't even know each other!"

From the back of this strange space came the lush orchestral opening of an updated 1920s pop ballad. It stopped abruptly, and Volodya cursed.

Turner was struggling to throw his weight forward onto his feet when a wonderful thought occurred to him. "Besides!" he told Sergei. "Thierry Colin was already delivered! To you! At that theater!" Emboldened by the beauty of his logic, he actually managed to stand, bent over beneath the chair's weight, and walk a few steps toward Sergei. "On Friday, remember?"

The Russian turned and contemplated him without expression. "There was fuckup." After seeming to think about it, he took a running step and kicked him full in the groin. Turner screamed, fell over sideways with the chair, and began retching onto the newspapers. "Now is good time to share," Sergei suggested.

"But I don't know where they are! I thought you had them! Had *him!* Colin!"

Sergei nodded unhappily. "Volodya!"

Turner's thoughts began to coast, and he fainted.

When he came to, the chair, and he in it, had been hauled upright again. Music issued from large speakers—Sinéad O'Connor singing "You Do Something to Me"—and Volodya was affixing one of the ceiling hooks to the back of the chair.

"You are reader, Turner?" Sergei had pulled the easy chair into the center of the room and sat facing Turner, holding in his lap a slim book lavishly bound in leather. There was a glass of water on the floor beside him. "Pushkin, maybe?"

"Pushkin." Turner was trying desperately to see over his shoulder. The hook, though blunt, was large, poking him in the back.

"This very beautiful edition of Pushkin, original Russian, we find in your assistant's apartment," Sergei continued. "*The Queen of Spades.* You are familiar?"

"No. I mean, yes, I knew she had it. A client gave it to her. But neither of us reads Russian." Volodya, the hook in place, had again escaped Turner's line of sight.

"Pity." Sergei opened the book and at the same moment seemed to fall rapidly away, diminishing to barely half his previous size. To his intense dismay, Turner found himself suspended, still manacled to the chair, several feet off the floor. "Is famous book. Tchaikovsky made opera. You want to hear?"

The forward tilt of the chair, hanging nearly motionless from the ceiling, caused the handcuffs to dig hard into Turner's wrists. "Anything!" he cried. "Please. Just let me down!" Volodya could be heard in back, rattling through hardware and cursing.

"Plot summary only," said Sergei, "since you are non-Russian speaker." He leafed through the book, then looked up pleasantly at Turner as if happy to have his company. After a moment of comradely inspection, he returned to the text. "Okay. Ordinary guy, works hard, saves money, is good citizen like you. Then one day he hears about certain countess—ugly old whore with shitty temper, but also most desirable gift. She can predict, in game of faro, three consecutive cards dealer will lay down. Or so local gossip says." He paused. "Tell me, you know that Thierry Colin is compulsive gambler?"

"No," replied Turner. He yawned convulsively.

"So this bastard decides to find out countess's secret. Charms her granddaughter, gets into house, hides in bedroom, and waits for this old bitch to get home from ball. She comes back, he shows himself. Too bad for him, she dies of fright without telling him secret. Nice touch, no?"

Turner wracked his brains for something he could say that would make this whole scene go away. Possibly it wasn't real.

"Guy feels guilty, goes to countess funeral, despite deceiving granddaughter before, et cetera. But when praying over corpse, he is shocked: countess winks at him. Scared shitless, right? Yet that night he has dream in which countess tells him three cards to play: three, seven, ace. Just like that, one a night, then never again."

Volodya reappeared carrying a red metal cylinder. The music was very loud.

"First night, guy bets on three and wins. Second night, he bets on seven and wins. Third night, puts all his winnings down on ace."

There was a whoosh as Volodya got the nozzle at the end of the metal cylinder to ignite. A propane torch. Turner began to struggle wildly in his chair.

"Okay," said Sergei, tossing the book to the floor, "story time over. Where we can find your assistant and Thierry Colin?"

Volodya tested the heat of the torch, holding one calloused hand a couple of feet from its jutting blue flame.

"I swear I don't know! I didn't even know they were together. Gabriella didn't show up for work today, didn't call in. I have no idea what to think."

"What of Odile Mével?"

"Odile? She told me she saw you go into the theater where Thierry Colin was. She tracked him down for you! We thought you got him."

Stepping forward, Volodya grabbed one of Turner's flailing ankles, brought the torch slowly up under the sole of his foot, and held it there. Turner screamed. When Volodya let go of the ankle, he turned to Sergei and shrugged. "Could be he is a *little* ticklish, I think."

From what seemed to Turner like another world, Sinéad O'Connor sang on, her voice a miracle of insinuation. *"Do do that voodoo that you do so well."*

"You must understand, Turner," said Sergei, "we no longer have time to fuck around. Serious people are missing things. Your assistant and Thierry Colin are both involved, maybe Odile Mével, maybe even you. We need to know what it is you know. Right now. Or you will not enjoy rest of afternoon, I promise."

Turner's foot hurt him very much. "But you know everything already! Everything!"

Wearily Sergei lifted a finger to Volodya, who came forward again with the blowtorch. At the sight of him, Turner struggled so violently in the chair that Volodya was forced to steady it with one hand while he brought the blowtorch up under the seat, directly beneath his testicles. The seat was sturdy oak and maybe two inches thick, but it began to smoke immediately.

"How long has Gabriella Moreau worked for you?" asked Sergei.

"Three years."

"And she is often absent like today?"

"No, never!"

Sergei got to his feet and approached Turner, arms folded across his chest. "To your knowledge, please, she was acquainted with Thierry Colin before you hired him as courier?"

"No! I didn't know she knew him *now*. I told you that." The heat from the blowtorch was rapidly coming up through the chair seat. "Please."

"What are habits of this girl?"

"Habits?"

"Drugs, sex clubs, expensive clothes? Or is good clean French girl who goes to visit mother on Sunday?"

"I don't know! Both! Oh, God! Shit!" A column of intense heat was rising through the chair now, smoke curling up on either side of him, and he struggled to shift his body away from the advancing burn. The handcuffs cut into his wrists. He began to cry from fear.

"You are trying to save this girl's ass, Turner?"

"No! I couldn't!"

"Exactly. You couldn't. But you could maybe make it your most urgent business to find her, yes? Between now and Thursday, maybe before auction?"

"Yes! Yes!" he shrieked as a searing burst of pain rose from his groin to inhabit every particle of his being. Tears streamed down his cheeks. "Please!"

Sergei appeared embarrassed. He put up a hand to Volodya, who lowered the blowtorch. Turner's undershorts were on fire and he was screaming at a pitch that even the music couldn't cover. Sergei took the glass of water from beside the easy chair, poured it over Turner's crotch, and said, in a voice not devoid of sympathy, "You bring it on yourself, you know."

Volodya lowered the chair to the floor. He unlocked the handcuffs, and Turner rolled away from the still-smoking chair. The two Russians began to talk, then argue, their voices inaudible over the music. Seeing a stack of cardboard boxes to his right, Turner dragged himself in that direction, thinking he could hide behind them and avoid further provoking his hosts. He was halfway there when, abruptly, consciousness deserted him.

# CHAPTER 25

"NO, I don't *mean* that," said Allegra. She and Max were walking south along the Canal Saint-Martin under marbled skies. It was Tuesday.

"This guy Willard that Mom's been seeing, I just get the feeling she's serious about him."

"So what's wrong with that? Don't you like him?"

"He's a Martian. He wears sandals with white socks. Plus he's a proctologist: how gross is that?"

Max thought about it. "Medium."

"She's going to marry him, I know it. And then what happens to me? I'm supposed to, like, *obey* this alien? I'm not even related to him. Anyway, it's pretty obvious, whatever she tells herself, that Mom's just fucking him because of his money."

"Hey! Watch the language."

"Which? 'Fucking' or 'money'?" She laughed bitterly. "Everything Mom does, you know, she still does because of you. If you hadn't put every dime you had into your dumb movies, right now we'd probably all be—"

Max stopped and enfolded her in his arms, as he had at the airport, but this time she gave in to his ministrations, pressing her face to his shirtfront and weeping silently. He held her close, wracked with unparsable love. "I'm so sorry, sweetheart. It's unfair, I know."

She looked up at him, her anger now displaced by grief and perplexity. "Then why—"

"There are some things a person just has to do. In my case, it's make movies. I can't help it."

She sighed and drew back to wipe away her tears. "I know, I know. You're a fucking artist."

"Please don't use that word."

She looked him squarely in the eye and, unable to resist, repeated slowly, "Fucking, fucking, fucking."

"No, not that word. The other one."

"Artist?"

"Right. I don't ever want to hear it again."

They had a feeble laugh together and resumed walking.

Since the *Nachtvlinder* had entered dry dock, Max had in fact found his artistry decidedly superfluous. Groot was sleeping aboard the boat, both to guard its contents and to make sure no work was done on it without his approval. Rachel—in protest of what she continued to regard as his ill-gotten gains, though he'd admitted to nothing—was staying on the sofa in Max and Odile's living room, having long, rambling talks with Allegra and weighing the future. None of it made for compelling cinema. But he'd come up with something—tomorrow, or the day after at the latest.

At rue des Récollets they turned west and headed for a patisserie that he recalled Allegra favoring on her last visit. There was a line out the door but they waited, talking now of lesser things: why the French shake hands with everyone, whether anarchy was really a tenable belief system, if Rachel would end up marrying Groot or not. Again and again, he found himself marveling that this well-spoken, inquisitive girl was his daughter, and each time he was pierced once more by sorrow at the time lost to them since he'd moved to Paris—four of her thirteen years. Love was pitiless. It kept track. He knew this as well as a man could know a thing, but of course this knowledge did him no good.

When they reached the glass cases at the front of the line, he let Allegra pick out a sackful of pastries—far more than they could possibly consume—and they left the store and started for the nearby Jardin Villemin to sample their purchases. It was not to be.

Around the corner, a tour bus had sideswiped a couple on a motorcycle, the man and woman now lying motionless in a bright red pool of their mingled blood, their limbs extended at unpleasant angles. Police cars had blocked off the street, their roof lights spinning silently, and ambulances were backed up beside the victims as medics labored with no particular urgency to get them onto stretchers. Both were dead. Parked halfway onto the sidewalk was the tour bus, fifty Japanese tourists fogging the windows in bewilderment. A red and yellow kite fluttered lazily above the park, silent witness to the carnage.

Max immediately took hold of his daughter's arm and tried to steer her away.

"No, wait," she said, resisting. "I saw all this before."

"What do you mean?"

"This whole scene happened once before, exactly like this. That bald medic, the big kidney-shaped pool of blood, the Japanese tourists and their breath, that kite. It was totally and completely the same. You were with me. We were going to the park to eat pastry. I had to go to the bathroom but didn't want to ask. Then a little boy with a soap-bubble wand ran by. A trail of bubbles."

"Sweetheart, you're in shock. Let's find you a bathroom, then we'll go home and relax."

She allowed herself to be led away. "There's a word for it when you have this kind of memory, isn't there?"

"Déjà vu."

"Déjà vu," she repeated to herself.

"Don't worry, it's just a feeling," he explained. "A misfire of the mind, more or less. It'll go away in a minute."

"But I don't want it to go away," she informed him.

He didn't know what to say to this.

They walked. A little boy with a plastic wand ran by trailing soap bubbles.


EVEN BEFORE ODILE took up her pose on Céleste's sofa she sensed that today would be their last sitting. This she gathered not from the painting itself, which she still hadn't been permitted to see, but by Céleste's uncharacteristic irritability, a certain abruptness of her movements as she set to work and the infrequency with which she actually looked at her, concentrating instead on the brushwork, occasionally rubbing the surface down with a turpentine-soaked rag. It was as if Odile herself were already irrelevant, replaced now by her likeness.

Twenty minutes later, looking suddenly fatigued, Céleste put down her brushes. "Voilà. It's done." She lit a cigarette. "You can get dressed."

"But don't I get to see it? After all this time?"

"Of course, my dear. Let's just permit it to settle for a minute. In the meantime one will have a glass of champagne to celebrate, yes?" She seemed to recover some of her vigor. "There's a bottle in the fridge."

Céleste set out plain glass flutes on the dining table. When Odile had changed back into her street clothes, she fetched the bottle, popped the cork, and poured them each a portion. "To the things that last," she said, raising her glass.

Céleste was pleased. "To the things that last!" she repeated. They clinked their glasses and drank.

A blue-tinted glass vase on the table held three sprays of white clematis.

"When I was a little girl," said Céleste, "I had a horror of being photographed. I believed that each time someone took my picture, a layer of my self was shaved away and lost, trapped in the photograph, to which anything could happen. I didn't want to dwindle, you see. I wanted to last."

Laughing as she spoke, Odile said, "And now you're a portraitist, taking all the layers and leaving nothing! A kind of revenge, isn't it?"

"Maybe." Céleste smiled and sipped her champagne. "You can judge for yourself in a moment."

"There's something I need to tell you," said Odile, setting her glass aside. "In confidence, if you don't mind."

"Of course. This is about Turner?"

"As a matter of fact it is. How did you know?"

"He's been calling here, desperate to talk to you. He says you've been avoiding him."

"That's not entirely true. My stepdaughter is visiting, as he knows, so I've been busy. And my cell phone's broken." This last wasn't even remotely true—she'd turned it off on Saturday, before the dinner party—but somehow the lie seemed essential to the truth of what she wished to communicate. "Anyway," she went on, "I've decided to end things with him. I just haven't found the right moment to tell him yet."

Céleste raised an eyebrow. "Ah, he'll be disappointed."

"Maybe at first, but it really is for the best. Even if I weren't married, I'm the wrong woman for him. He needs someone less ordinary, someone who can scheme right along with him and laugh about it afterward. Quite frankly, I'm too conventional for a man like him."

"That's not what he thinks."

"No? But he's a closet romantic, someone with—what did you call it before?—an optimistic streak. I suppose his profession requires it."

"And you? You have no optimistic streak?"

"Not in this world."

"Ah, so the maenad is a mystic. That's hardly ordinary."

Odile laughed and ran a hand through her hair. "I didn't mean that I *believe* in other worlds. I just meant that in this one I'm no optimist."

Shaking her head, Céleste said, "Poor Turner. He's going to suffer more than he imagines. But then again, who of us doesn't? Life makes no promises." She drained her glass. "So. You are ready now?" Without waiting for an answer, she got to her feet and moved the canvas, its painted side still to the window, fully into sunlight. Odile followed, coming around the easel to stand beside her and contemplate the results.

A shiver rippled through her.

In the weeks she'd been sitting for the portrait, Odile had formed a mental image concocted of what she'd seen of Céleste's other paintings—high colored, mildly expressionistic in style—and of what she imagined herself to look like, half draped in the green dress. But her imagination had failed her.

What had seemed like expressionism in the two portraits she had seen of Turner served here more as a corrective to her own self-image, both physical and otherwise. Flesh no longer as young as she routinely imagined it, hands and feet beginning to grow venous, skin that bore only traces—though at least that—of its former translucency. Yet none of this disturbed her. On the contrary, it was as if she were seeing herself for the first time in years. And then there was the face.

In effect, Céleste had solved the problem of the disappearing maenad by giving the painted image two faces. In one, Odile's head was bowed and turned to the side in near profile, creating an impression of modesty lightly borne. Then, as in a photograph in which the subject moves at the moment of exposure, leaving a wavy trail behind, she was shown lifting her head upright and turning to face the viewer, at whom she stared with just the suggestion of avidity. Her features extended in a painted smear from the first position to the second, where they resolved into something very like the maenad Céleste had claimed to see in her. A creature capable of anything, as she'd said—murder, even, though naturally that was an exaggeration, a portraitist's stratagem.

Odile's eyes filled. She looked at the painting for some time. "It's marvelous," she said at last. "Better than I can tell you."

"I'm satisfied with it," Céleste allowed.

"Turner was right," Odile added after a moment. "You really do see everything."

In the distance, faintly, police sirens sounded. The demonstration, thought Odile.

"Call him," Céleste said.

THEY ARRANGED to meet outdoors, at the Promenade Plantée, an elevated railroad bed that had been converted into a strip park running southeast out of Bastille, three stories above street level. He had explained nothing to Odile over the phone, not wanting to alarm her, afraid of what she might say, mistrustful of both the line's security and himself. He arrived fifteen minutes early to stake out a bench under the lindens at the park's north end. His burnt foot hurt him, but rather than use a cane he'd taken a double dose of painkillers. Trivial vanities: he was known for them.

She arrived late, appearing before him with her arms folded over her chest, her whole being luminous with ill-concealed misgiving. He got up, and they kissed.

"Give me your wrist," he said, mock sternly.

Odile stared at him, frowning as she inspected the lurid bruise across his right cheekbone. She seemed about to say something, then thought better of it and thrust one bare wrist forward. He slipped her watch around it.

"Thanks," she said. "I'm glad you understand."

"I miss you, though," he replied. "More than I should."

They sat down on the bench. She looked at him, then lightly traced the bruise on his cheek with a forefinger. "So tell me. Whose door did you bump into?"

"Right. Well, you see, I did finally meet your Russian friends, and they are—how to put this?—quite *actively* disappointed with whatever happened at that theater the other day."

"Disappointed? But I thought they wanted Thierry Colin. I told them exactly where to find him. He was *there*."

"Maybe so, but he got away. And that's not all. You remember my assistant, Gabriella? According to these guys, she's his *consort*, I guess meaning lover, but also aide-de-camp, partner in crime, whatever. Is that possible?"

"I don't know. He never mentioned her."

"But did you see her at the theater?"

Odile hesitated. Turner reached out and lifted her chin until their eyes met and she said, "Yes, Gabriella was at the theater. She came in late and sat with him, right before I left. I didn't think to tell you because, I don't know, I just assumed the whole thing was over the moment I called the Russians. They were very prompt, very businesslike."

He let go of her chin. "And now very pissed off."

"I'm so sorry," she said, looking away. "Did they . . . Well, they obviously gave you a hard time."

He shrugged. "You know how they operate."

A flock of pigeons rose suddenly from the grass promenade and wheeled off north toward the Opéra.

"But that was yesterday," he said. "And now is what we have to worry about. These guys are holding us responsible for Colin and Gabriella's escape. If we don't find them by Thursday we're basically, you know, fucked."

"They said that?"

"They didn't have to."

She shook her head. "This is insane," she said, "totally senseless."

"I couldn't agree more. But there it is." He took her left hand between both of his and, lowering his voice, spoke with as much control as he could muster. "Look. You were with Thierry Colin for, what, five days? He must've said something, done something, that—"

"No, Turner. Don't you think I've been over it in my mind?" Gently she withdrew her hand. "Besides, you know how it is when you're traveling with someone like that, essentially a stranger. You take turns talking but listen with half an ear, just to pass the time. It's normal."

"Yes, normal." Turner sighed. "How are things at home? Everything okay?"

"More or less. Why? Shouldn't they be?"

"I only meant that with your stepdaughter visiting . . ."

Odile blew a puff of air from her cheeks in mock vexation. "And not only her! Rachel's quarreling with her boyfriend, so she's staying with us too. But for the most part everything's under control. Or as much as it ever is."

"Rachel. Your friend whose houseboat was—"

"Exactly. Anyway, she needs a place to think. She's contemplating marriage."

"I see. And what do you advise?"

"That she has the right to remain silent. That everything she says can and will be used against her in a court of law. That roses are red and violets are blue. All that."

Turner laughed despite himself. "I keep forgetting that you lived in America."

"I keep forgetting that *you* did," replied Odile. She seemed to be relaxing a little. "Why did you leave?"

"But surely Céleste told you."

"Something about a girl, wasn't it?"

Besieged suddenly by a storm of recollection—the girl, her exotic laughter, the Cycladic figure, the unhappy customer with his gun, the sister calling from the morgue, the waiting that had turned into guilt and then into a plan, the dream of beauty ruined, the departure that resembled flight, his arrival in Paris and the life that had ensued—Turner found he lacked both the will and the ability to explain. "No, not a girl. My reasons for coming here were professional. France was changing its auction laws. I saw an opportunity."

She smiled at him quizzically, then looked out over the park. "Listen, my friend. There's something I have to tell you."

He raised a hand to stop her. "No. Not yet."

"But it will only be worse later."

"At least it will be later. That's a plus, in my opinion."

She laughed and for a moment slipped her hand between his arm and torso. "Are you so sure you know what I was going to say?"

"Oh yes, my sweet." He caressed her cheek, but she frowned and abruptly pulled away, turning an ear to the breeze.

In the near distance, approaching the Place de la Bastille, a crowd not visible from where they sat could be heard beating tambourines, clapping hands, and chanting something as yet unintelligible. She looked sharply at Turner. "It's the protest," she said. "The illegal aliens and their supporters."

"Is that today?" He closed his eyes and turned his face to the heavens. What he most needed to do was to stop time. If that proved impossible, he would very shortly have to come up with a suitable alternative—that much he understood. "I thought they were at République."

"They started there and marched," she said. "Now they're here."

"Yes, well, that's the complaint against them, isn't it? 'They were there, and now they're here.' Stupid, I agree, but that's what pisses people off. About the illegals, I mean." Odile said nothing, but he sensed her thoughts racing and opened his eyes. "What is it?"

"Didn't you tell me that your Russian banker friend—I've forgotten his name..."

"Kukushkin," said Turner, suddenly uncertain whether he'd told her the man's name before or not.

"Kukushkin. Didn't he pass a message to you, through that Swiss guy, the art collector, that there were rumors about you being involved in, what— transborder kidnapping? One person or maybe a truckful is what you said."

"Yes, but I've never done anything like that."

"Good. I'll believe you, since why not? But consider this: the police raided my friend's houseboat a few days ago. As it happened, my husband was there filming, on location. So there's a record of this incident. And what the police said they were looking for was illegal immigrants—one or more, I don't know—as well as someone they referred to as 'the doctor.' They had a photo of him. They also asked if this was the same boat that had been fire-bombed recently, which of course it was, courtesy of those Russian buf-foons. So for the police, I think, this wasn't just a stab in the dark. Do you agree?"

Turner was already on his feet, staring at her warily. "Doctor," he said. "What kind of doctor?"

"How would I know? I saw a video image of his photo. He was a balding man in a white lab coat, black-framed glasses, that's it. None of us had ever seen him before. Not that we would've remembered."

From the square came the chant of massed voices damning immigration law and the hypocrisies of those enforcing it. The crowd sounded large but orderly. Whatever police presence there was remained mute.

"What about Thierry Colin? Did he make any mention of, say, fertility treatment or something of the sort? In vitro, ex vitro, whatever?"

"No, nothing like that," Odile stared at him. "Why? What are you talking about?"

"I'm not sure, but I think Gabriella, who does seem to have disappeared, was in some kind of therapeutic program or other. Anyway, she was taking a fertility drug."

A brace of laughing teenage girls strode by three abreast, arms linked, eyes flashing, their futures not as distant as they imagined.

"I didn't get the impression," said Odile, "that Thierry had babies on his mind."

"Men usually don't, not until absolutely necessary."

"With fertility treatment they do."

"Right. Point taken."

But now, from being someone wanting to solve the mystery of his assis-tant's disappearance, of her involvement with Thierry, a person he'd hired casually, almost without thought, to perform an errand, Turner became a man in refusal, someone wanting above all not to hear the message that he knew this woman sitting on the bench before him as he paced was intent on delivering sooner or later, a message that was unfair and wrong because it was premature, but for which he had no dissuasive argument because his response, too, would be premature—reckless, certainly self-defeating. To his despair, he understood—or admitted to himself at last—that he loved Odile and that his judgment was no longer something he could trust.

"Let's walk," he said.

They took the steps down to the street.

At the Place de la Bastille, the demonstrators had now all arrived, close to three thousand of them, by Turner's estimate, and were encircled by police vans, each fronted by two officers in token of those who remained at the ready within. But the crowd appeared peaceful and the observing officers already a little bored. A screech of electronic feedback shredded the air as a sound system was turned on, then brought to level. Turner and Odile took up a position at the southeast corner, halfway up the steps of the Opéra, to get a better view. A clutch of children ran by, throwing ice cubes at each other from their soft-drink cups.

Odile stared after them. "I've remembered something," she said.

"Tell me."

At the podium, an Algerian man with a neatly trimmed beard stepped up to the microphone. "Friends! Comrades! Parisians!" he began.

"Ah, but I'm sure it's nothing," Odile said. "Forget it."

"I don't think we have that luxury," Turner replied.

She frowned and looked out over the crowd. "When we left Paris that first day, Thierry had an insulated bag with him. He was very protective of this bag, he held on to it the entire time, not putting it down until we were on the train, and even then he kept it clamped between his ankles. I teased him about it, calling it his purse, until finally he unzipped it to show me what was inside. It was a—how do you call it?—a thermos bottle, you know, but bigger. I said, 'Ah, so you cannot live without your American coffee?' He laughed and said no, it wasn't to keep things hot, it was a refrigeration unit. 'I am bringing caviar to Russia,' he said, which he thought was very funny. 'Excess is my métier,' he said. Naturally, at the mention of himself, my attention wandered."

"But?"

"When we got to Brest—"

The public-address system emitted another squeal, and the bearded speaker said, "We who live at the city gates of Paris, we who are not even granted the dignity of jobs—"

"When one gets to Brest," Odile went on, "there's a wait while the wheelbases on the train carriages are changed to fit the wider-gauge Russian tracks. Thierry excused himself, saying he wanted to stretch his legs. But when he came back, he no longer had the insulated bag with him. I didn't notice it was gone until much later. That's it."

For some time, neither spoke.

A television crew arrived, shot a brief stand-up segment with the crowd as backdrop, and left. A man at the edge of the crowd shouted obscenities at the speaker but was quickly hustled off by the police. Two dogs on leashes barked and snapped at each other until their owners succeeded in dragging them apart.

Turner put his arm around Odile. "Come home with me," he said.

"But you know I'm here to end things between us."

"Yes, but it's too soon."

"There has to be a last time," she said. "It's better to have already had it."

"But we haven't already had it."

"I love my husband."

"What's that got to do with anything? Come home with me."

Odile sighed. "You're going to be hurt," she said.

"Ah, but I'm ahead of you there. I'm hurt already."

She struggled not to smile. "Or my husband's going to get hurt. Or maybe even me, and I detest pain."

"We're all adults. We can work around a little pain."

"Really? How do we do that?"

"I'll show you later. Just come back with me."

She seemed to waver. "But it's already late."

"Four o'clock's not late. This time you can keep your watch on, if it'll make you feel better."

"I'm not expecting to feel better," she said, laughing as she spoke.

Turner's spirits soared. "Don't think about it, then, just do it."

She bit her lip. "But—"

"Come," he said, leading her by the hand.

She went.

Somebody threw a smoke bomb into the crowd.

MAX AND ALLEGRA ARRIVED HOME to a confounding sight. The overhead lightbulb just inside the entrance was half full of water, dripping copiously but still radiant. More water had spilled down the staircase and now lay pooled on the beaten dirt floor of Odile's studio. Max told Allegra not to move, then, skirting the spillage, went directly to the fuse box and switched off the apartment's electricity.

"Shit!" came Rachel's voice from the floor above.

Max picked a flashlight off its hook by the door and, taking Allegra by the hand, climbed the stairs.

"I'm an idiot," Rachel said when she saw him, then threw her arms around him. "Please don't hate me."

"Water does seem to be your element," Max said. "But nobody hates you."

Allegra smirked and retreated to her aerie.

Rachel explained that she'd been drawing a bath when the phone rang— a call she'd been waiting for from her mother. They talked for almost twenty minutes before Rachel remembered the tub and raced to turn it off, but it had long since overflowed. By now, though, barefoot, with her jeans rolled halfway up her calves, she'd mopped up most of the water, and Max helped her with the rest. It wasn't the kind of apartment that was easily damaged by accidents or incidental neglect.

"Dad!" Allegra came rushing down from her room. "I'm going to meet Dominique, okay?"

Max looked over her entirely new outfit: lace-up leather boots, tight black pants, and a low-cut, fluorescent green cotton top. "Where are you two going?"

"Just to her house. I'll be back by seven thirty, I promise."

"All right. Be careful."

She promised she would, flashed a brilliant smile, and, waving goodbye to Rachel, hurried downstairs and out the door.

"She's a wild thing, isn't she," Rachel said, a little wistfully.

"Don't know," Max replied after a moment. "Can't tell. Maybe not."


LATER, when the apartment was dry and the electricity back on, Rachel announced she was going out to buy groceries. Though they didn't really need anything, Max let her go and before long went to the newsstand for the next day's *Le Monde*, then returned home to read it.

On the arts page was a story about Thursday's scheduled auction of the Soviet flags. Turner was quoted twice. Uncertain that he'd remembered the name correctly, Max took the Giacometti drawing down from the wall and examined the business card taped to the back, Turner's estimate of the work's value written on it. As he stared at the words engraved on the face of the card, a number of things that he'd lately been thinking about fell into place.

He left the paper—folded open to the flags story—on the kitchen table and went to his studio to work for a couple of hours. When he came back, Odile, Rachel, and Allegra had all reappeared, the paper was gone, and dinner was being prepared amid an atmosphere of general conviviality that included many bathtub jokes.

At eight they all sat down to a vegetable couscous and two bottles of

Sancerre that Max had been saving for the proper occasion. The meal went on for a long time with much hilarity, as if no one wanted to face the nocturnal solitudes to come.

Afterward, when Rachel was duly installed on her sofa and Allegra asleep upstairs, Max joined Odile in bed. She was wearing a white cotton nightgown that he rarely saw and reading a French translation of *The Lime Works*.

"I see those Soviet flags you brought back from Moscow are coming up for auction on Thursday," he said. "Feel like going? Just for fun?"

She marked her place in the book with a length of black velvet hair ribbon and turned toward him. "No, not really. Do you?"

They looked at each other in silence.

"I might," Max said.

Odile looked a little longer, then reached behind her and turned out the lamp.

## CHAPTER 26

THE *NACHTVLINDER*, cleaned, caulked, and freshly painted, was to be released from dry dock that afternoon, Wednesday, at three o'clock. Max had sent Jacques ahead to Conflans-Sainte-Honorine to interview Groot on camera and record anything of interest that might develop before his own arrival at the boat chandlery. Rachel was driving to the site in Max's ancient Citroën while he filmed her from the suicide seat, encouraging her to reflect on recent events. In the back Allegra leafed through a fashion magazine she'd borrowed the day before from Dominique. From time to time, she sighed theatrically.

"I know I keep saying this," Rachel said, "but I think it all has to do with the *Nachtvlinder* and this actual *duty* Groot and I feel to restore her—not bring her back to life, of course, because she never died in that sense, but to reinvigorate her, make her seaworthy again. I like that word, 'seaworthy.' It gives me hope for the world. Well, not for the world, exactly, but at least it gives me gratitude for the possibilities that still exist, even in the worst of times.

"So, to return to—what to call it?—the melodrama of me: I've decided not to worry any more about where Groot's money came from. I just bought a cashier's check with it and mailed it to my parents. That's it. The end."

Without looking up from her magazine, Allegra turned a page and said, "In other words, you're saying that you're going to marry him and live happily ever after and the whole et cetera?"

Max kept his camera on Rachel. Seconds passed. "Well," she said finally, downshifting as they turned into the boatyard.

The chandlery at Conflans-Sainte-Honorine was the successor to one that had closed years before, and the methods it now employed allowed it to do in two days what once might have taken a month. When Max, Rachel, and Allegra arrived, Jacques was filming the Breton chandler as he detailed for Groot the restorations that had been lavished on the *Nachtvlinder:* weather-damaged planks replaced, every seam recaulked, the props refurbished, teak oil lovingly rubbed into the deck, woven jute fenders dangling from the sides, brasswork brought to a shine, the hull sandblasted clean and repainted a blinding white with an encircling blue boot stripe. A hundred years old, the vessel looked immaculate.

"She's a good one," the man said grudgingly. "Back then they knew how to make them. No fiberglass, no aluminum, none of that shit. With wood, everything lives, everything responds. Pay attention and it can do the impossible."

Groot caressed the boat with his palm. "*Ja.* This is good; very, very good. Thank you so much."

When Groot followed him to a battered oak desk and, without sitting down, began counting out in cash the payment they'd agreed upon, Max set up his tripod and vidcam facing the port side of the boat. He trained it on the spot where he thought it most likely that Rachel, Groot, and the *Nachtvlinder* would next intersect, amidships more or less, and walked casually away, signaling Jacques to take over when the time came. Then he went outside. Standing just beyond the door of the hangar, frowning at the sky and clutching a zippered Bible, was a priest in clerical collar and coat, clearly unhappy to be there but resigned to his mission, whatever it was.

Max went immediately back into the hangar.

The scene between Groot and the chandler was winding up. When it was done, Max whispered to Jacques, "Get Groot and Rachel in front of the camera where I left it. Let them walk in and out of the frame occasionally, which they will do, no instruction needed. Go for minimum self-consciousness. Usable sound would be a plus, but not essential. We'll probably run some other audio over the shot anyway."

"Risky," Jacques replied, thinking about it. "Definitely counterintuitive. But yes, it might just pop."

"I'll take your camera and set up right outside," Max continued. "Remember to let them move in and out of the frame naturally, even if you lose the sound. But keep the sound on them once they leave the hangar—

self-consciousness no longer a factor, okay? When the boat comes out, I'll stick around while you find your new spot, then I'll go down to the water to pick up the medium-shot visuals."

"Check."

"And don't forget the priest. There's a priest out there."

"A priest?"

"Right. Keep him in the mix. Let's hear what he has to say."

Jacques shrugged. "Don't they all say the same thing?"

"Nevertheless."

Jacques nodded, trying to work out Max's thinking. He was by nature a serious young man, his turn of mind unconventional. Max had lately decided to grant him more leeway at work, curious to see what might emerge.

"Okay, then," Max said. "No shortage of variables, right? So let's do it." He took the backup camera and hurried for the door, Allegra hastening after him.

"Daddy!"

"What is it, sweet? I'm working right now."

"I *know*. I just wanted to ask you." She was holding her cell phone in a stage-one adolescent death grip. "Can I go to this party with Dominique tomorrow night? Monsieur Bouvier thinks it's okay."

"Where is it, when is it, and who'll be there?"

"Um, like, I'm not totally sure? But I'll find out."

"Then get your data together and we'll talk again, all right?"

"Cool."

"And watch out for this boat thing. It could be dangerous, I don't know. Stay away from the rails."

"Check," she said, in imitation of Jacques. Laughing merrily, she withdrew to make the necessary calls.

Frowning at the sky, Max set up his camera.

Since coming to the conclusion that his wife was having an affair with this art impresario, a man Max had scarcely thought about before, he found himself prey to a host of conflicting notions. Maybe she'd betrayed him a dozen times, with a dozen men, or perhaps Turner was her first. It was love, it was sex, it was boredom, it was revenge. He was supposed to find out about it, or he wasn't. He was meant to suffer, or he wasn't. Maybe there was a side to her character he didn't know, or maybe her character had changed. But amid all this circular thinking, useless and demeaning, Max knew one thing to be unquestionably true: Odile did nothing without purpose. She had a message for him, and however painful it might be, he wanted to fully understand it. A man could do nothing less. Then, quite often, he had to do much more.

"Excuse me, sir."

Max looked up from his camera to find the priest addressing him. God's servant looked uneasy. "Yes, Father."

"I am not acquainted with these people, this Rachel and Groot, but I have been asked to bless their boat before it is launched. Of course I shall do so; it is my duty. But I wonder if you could tell me: have they married within the Church?"

"Of course, Father. Why else would they have called you?"

"It wasn't they who called me. But no matter. This is an ancient nautical tradition. I am happy to be of service, and of course such is God's will." He withdrew a few steps toward the river, looking, if anything, even more disconsolate. Max discreetly filmed him for nearly a minute as he gazed out over the Seine and paced back and forth. There was always room in Max's films for priests, if only for a few seconds. Their black-and-white raiment made everything surrounding them snap to, visually speaking, and inspired in much of his audience a vague sense of guilt or revulsion, if only subliminal, that served his purposes. Still, there was no point in overdoing it. He stopped shooting and checked his watch.

Moments later, mounted as before upon the wheeled railroad chassis and attended by half a dozen men, the *Nachtvlinder* emerged from the hangar onto the short expanse of flat ground outside. Close behind it, holding hands and staring at the boat like proud parents, were Rachel and Groot, seemingly reconciled, or at least united in the glow of their now resplendent boat. Max zoomed in slowly on their faces, until Rachel noticed and turned to whisper something into Groot's ear. Jacques stood at some distance behind them, holding the sound boom low over their heads. *Good*, thought Max.

The priest cleared his throat, and it immediately became apparent that no one present had expected him. Still, he was a priest, and when he called them to prayer, they all reflexively bowed their heads. That was all he required.

"Hear us, O Lord, from Heaven Thy dwelling place," he intoned. "Thou, Who dost rule the raging of the sea, when loud the storm and furious is the gale . . ." The prayer was mercifully short, another six or eight verses at most, and when amens had been said, he sprinkled holy water over the bow of the *Nachtvlinder*, blessed it, and hurried off as precipitously as he had arrived.

"Now," the chandler announced, slapping the side of the *Nachtvlinder*, "let's see if she floats."

Max took his camera and tripod down the incline to the riverbank.

Not much later, as the *Nachtvlinder* slowly descended the tracks toward him, it came to Max that nothing about the boat was so radiantly beautiful, so infused with hope, as its knife-edged prow, designed to part the waters of the world so that men might pursue dreams of which they were only half aware. *She's been around the world, for sure,* Rachel had said of the boat, the day of the police raid. Max cursed himself for not having shot the *Nachtvlinder* head-on while she was still in dry dock, but there was no time now for second thoughts. The boat was nearly upon him.

The railway track ran down into the river, where the descending vessel would be lifted off the chassis and onto the surface by her own buoyancy. Still, a thirty-ton boat doesn't return lightly to her element, and Max was glad to be no closer to the *Nachtvlinder* than he was when she reentered the Seine, throwing up jagged curls of green-tea-colored water on either side, pitching fore and aft like a yearling horse at play. The vidcam got it all.

When Groot had her tied up to a pair of bollards embedded in the bank, the chandler threw a ladder over the side, and everyone but Jacques, who'd agreed to film the boat's departure and drive the Citroën to the quai de la Tournelle, climbed on board to cluster respectfully on deck. There was enchantment to the moment, an alien magic that Max hadn't anticipated, but he reminded himself to record precisely what was there and decide later what really shone the most. Groot and Rachel embraced and kissed. Allegra spoke excitedly into her cell phone, using, it seemed to Max, some sort of post-linguistic teenage speed-talk. Boldly colored ensigns fluttered crisply in the breeze. And finally, tantalizingly out of sight, were the rebuilt engines, as yet neither tested nor mentioned, though they weighed heavily on the minds of all present.

Three days before, bringing the boat downstream, Groot had chosen not to engage the untested engines until the ship chandler could look them over. Instead he'd hired a tugboat to prod and nudge the vessel into its place of rest. For the journey back, however, there would be no tugboat. There would be a reckoning.

Once aboard, Groot immediately assumed formal command, stationing Rachel and Allegra on the bridge while he went below to the engine room. Max had planned from the first to stay close by Rachel at the helm, to record her response as, for better or worse, the vessel got under way or failed to, taking her and her boyfriend's hopes with it. The scent of diesel hung heavy in the air about them, an uncertain omen. Rachel stared at the control-console gauges: oil pressure, water temperature, fuel. She looked scared and beautiful, Allegra bored and thirteen. Max kept them both in the frame, as closely fitted together as the optics of the lens would allow.

"Now!" Rachel shouted suddenly, her eyes still fixed like a fighter pilot's on the gauges.

There followed the infuriating pause that precedes all diesel combustion, then the starboard engine came to life with a low, stuttering rumble that settled into a roar. An agonizing second later, the port engine did the same. Rachel hopped up and down with joy. Allegra hugged her, hopping too, both soon doing a comic dance of happiness unhinged.

Groot appeared, grinning, at the top of the companionway, his face streaked black with grease. "You see," he said in English. "For the stubborn and the stupid, everything is possible." He said it again in Dutch. "This is the secret motto of my people," he added, laughing. "You can say that— motto?" He gave the chandlery crew a thumbs-up and received theirs in return. They almost seemed to approve of his success.

Relieving Rachel of her post, Groot engaged the port-engine clutch and then the starboard. Slowly at first, but gaining momentum, the boat edged into the river's upstream lane, headed again for Paris. Before long, the *Nachtvlinder* had attained a bracing seven knots, an impressive speed when running against a strong current. Rachel laughed and wept and laughed again, her hair streaming out behind her with such abandon that Max was reminded of mortal things, things he didn't care to name, but that he nonetheless found strangely moving, especially as framed by the camera. All that was merely nautical seemed to fall away before this silencing sight, so real and yet so much like beauty.

"Really, really ultra," Allegra cried, obviously suffering no such inhibitions.

And then, as if in response to her words, Max was suddenly pierced to the heart by a baffling sliver of fear, fear as cold as a steel lancet. It staggered him, almost literally casting him to the deck. Embarrassed, he made gestures of exaggerated landlubberliness and repositioned himself behind the camera, itself serenely stable on its tripod. *Nerves,* he told himself. But he knew it wasn't nerves, that it was something he'd never felt before. So, for want of other options, he filmed. Filming without flinching was what he understood. It was what he did best. And before very long at all he was himself again, seeing the sort of things he saw, filming the sort of things he filmed, his sudden moment of foreboding—if that's what it was—now dispersed and forgotten.

Barge traffic, which had been diminishing year by year on the Seine, seemed unaccountably heavy that afternoon, and the *Nachtvlinder*, which commercial boatsmen contemptuously categorized as a "yacht," was over and over again forced to yield to vast, freight-laden barges whose pilots honked deafening horns at them and shouted imprecations, reminding them that "*yachts* go last." It didn't matter, though; nothing could spoil the crew's collective good mood as the boat churned upstream to Paris.

At Andrésy, not far out of Conflans, Groot threaded them through the crowded lock, navigating between the two rows of barges tied up on either side, where they waited for the gate at the upstream end to open and the water to spill in so they could continue their journey. Groot's was a risky maneuver—normally he should have taken his place behind the last barge, on one side or the other—but he was feeling cocky, and besides, Max thought, it made for good film. The female half of the crew—Rachel at starboard, Allegra at port—stood by with tires suspended on ropes to cushion against any accidental contact with the barges' steel hulls as Groot, defying protocol, took them farther and farther forward. Finally, he chose to tie up to a barge near the front. Turning the wheel over to Rachel, he tossed first one line, then another, over the barge's bollards. Her captain scowled at this heedlessness, but allowed his deckhands to secure the ropes. Shortly after, the gate opened, the lines were cast off, and they were under way again, ahead of most of the pack.

"I shouldn't have done that," Groot confided to Allegra. "I could easily have wrecked our boat."

"What, you mean you did it just for the rush?"

Groot smiled. "That's right. For the rush."

The rest of the passage was smooth going. While Allegra napped in the aft hammock, Max leaned over the side, unable to resist filming the water. It had such variety of color and shimmer, as if it were itself a film or, perhaps, a sly commentary on the light that made film and everything else possible. Then, to his astonishment, an enormous fish—a carp, he thought—leapt from the water, thrashing furiously in the air before splashing back in again, just a few feet away. A sign, had he believed in such things. Anyway, he'd gotten it on camera.

He took a break, keeping Groot company at the helm.

The weeping willows and greenery lining the banks soon were replaced by an ugly sprawl of concrete yards, abandoned industrial parks, ad-hoc dumping grounds, and high-rise buildings with cheap office space. Then, quite suddenly, they were in Paris, passing under the first of the city's bridges. Rachel and Allegra emerged from the companionway with a pair of binoculars.

"They're superpowerful," Rachel was saying, "so you have to hold them very steady. But they're especially good just before twilight, like now."

The girls joined Groot and Max on the bridge, and, fitting her eyes to the instrument, Allegra began a slow survey of her surrounds. "Wow!" she said. "Unreal!"

No one spoke. They passed under the bridges in the appointed order: Grenelle, Bir-Hakeim, Iéna, Passarelle Debilly. When they reached the westernmost tip of Île de la Cité, Allegra inhaled sharply. "Dad?"

"What is it?"

"I can see Odile! She's waiting for us on the quai! Right by the berth!"

"I guess she missed us," said Max. "What else?"

"Her hair. She's cut it very short. And she . . . I'm not sure. Here. You'd better look." She handed him the binoculars and walked off, not waiting for a verdict.

It took Max some time to refocus the glasses and find her, but when he did he saw at once what Allegra meant. Odile had been crying—her eyes were rimmed with red—and she was attempting to light a cigarette: two things she almost never did and would certainly never admit to. As he watched, she gave up on the cigarette and, defeated by the river breeze, threw it pettishly to the ground. Max lowered the binoculars.

It was time to film.

## CHAPTER 27

THAT NIGHT, despite a double dose of sedatives washed down with brandy, Odile lay in bed sleepless, her mind churning. Again and again she looked at Max stretched out beside her in apparent peace and wondered if she shouldn't tell him everything. No doubt he had guessed at her affair with Turner by now, but that—and perhaps he'd sensed this too—was hardly everything. Turner had said that if they didn't produce Gabriella and Thierry for the Russians by Thursday, they'd be fucked. And Thursday it now was. She hoped with an urgency verging on prayer that Max had given up his idea of attending the auction that evening; probably he hadn't been serious about it in the first place, but certainly nothing would induce her to accompany him now. Toward dawn, she fell into a thin sleep that gave her no peace.

Max had a backers' meeting in Tours that day and left early in the car. Allegra set out shortly after, claiming that she was going to the Centre Pompidou to see the Brassaï show. When Odile was finally alone, she made sure her cell phone was off and set to work on Fatima's wedding dress. A tightly cross-wrapped sheath of white taffeta with linen-mesh eyeholes distributed liberally across the bodice and hips, it was coming along, better than she'd envisioned it.

Shortly past two o'clock there arose outside a curiously wavering banshee wail. Although she'd never heard it before—in La Santé's century and a half of existence only two escapes had occurred—she knew at once that it must be the prison alarm. Not much later, she heard the dull, relentless thudding of a helicopter and she went outside to take a look.

At first there was nothing to see, the prison's crises as shut off from the world as its inmates. The helicopter made a slow, banking circuit of the area, looking for escapees, she supposed, then moved into position over the central courtyard. From there, the copilot leaned out the open side of the chopper and, rather haphazardly, it seemed to Odile, dropped three tear-gas canisters in succession. Curious to see what this was meant to accomplish since the inmates were now surely under lockdown—unless they had taken over the prison completely, a virtual impossibility—Odile walked the length of the Arago side of the facility and turned left onto rue Messier just in time to see a stream of prison personnel, nonsecurity staff by the looks of them, emerge from the main entrance with handkerchiefs held over their faces. She couldn't help but laugh—another triumph for French bureaucracy—and briefly wished Max was there to share her amusement. But then she saw something that stopped her cold.

Exiting the prison with the others, looking extremely annoyed, was a balding middle-aged man in a white lab coat and black slacks. In one hand he held a pair of black-framed eyeglasses, while with the other he rubbed his eyes and nose. Odile at once recognized him as the doctor whose picture the police had shown to Rachel—and, inadvertently, to Max's camera—aboard the *Nachtvlinder*. She backed farther down the street, out of his sight, such as it was at the moment, and produced her cell phone, intending to call Turner. Before she could punch his number in, however, she saw he'd left eight messages that morning. She closed the phone without listening to them.

The man walked back and forth at some distance from the others, still rubbing his eyes and muttering to himself. Since he obviously wasn't a prisoner, Odile, recalling what Eddie had said at last week's dinner party, concluded that he was working in La Santé's medical research program, the one involving prison volunteers. Why the police should be after him was a matter she was still considering when, not twenty feet ahead of her, a taxi pulled up and Thierry Colin got out, shoving money into the driver's hand. He then made straight for the doctor, who appeared greatly relieved to see him. They embraced three times, in the Russian manner, and began conversing rapidly in French.

*This is it!* Odile thought. *This is it.*

Without a moment's hesitation, she transported herself to the spot where the two men stood talking and, offering no apology, broke immediately into their exchange. "Hello, gentlemen. Thierry, I've been looking for you everywhere, and I'm hardly the only one. We have to talk. Immediately."

Thierry stared at her, trying to decide what she knew, and Odile began to realize, under his gaze, just how much she actually might. He excused himself to his friend, walked a short distance with Odile, turned to her, and, with his arms folded across his chest, awaited her words. His recently shaved head and rimless spectacles made him seem to sparkle slightly, like a candy Easter chick.

"The police are after your doctor friend," she began. "The Russians are after you and Gabriella both. Two days ago Turner was tortured by two Russian thugs who hoped he'd give you up, as he might have, had he known where you were. And then, of course, there's the doctor over there, who I'm willing to bet is a Belarussian citizen." She took a deep breath. "Should I go on?"

"No, that will do. Tell me what it is you want."

"The bear and not the shit."

Thierry looked bemused. "You ask a lot."

She shrugged. "Yes, but as one no longer uninvolved in your side project, I'm obliged, you see, to make rash requests."

Together they turned to look at the doctor, who'd shed his lab coat, unbuttoned his shirt, and was furiously scratching his chest, sides, and neck.

"The gas," said Odile. "It's a new compound, I'm told."

"Well, he doesn't seem to like it much, does he?"

She thought for a moment. "Listen, Thierry. I live just two blocks away. Why don't the three of us go there. Your friend can take a bath, and you and I can have a few words in private, a few rather *necessary* words, yes?"

He peered at her through his crystalline glasses, as though she represented something new to his experience, then consulted his watch. "I'll tell him," he said.

After a brief conversation, Thierry brought him over to Odile. "Odile Mével, Doctor Aleksandr Tregobov. Sasha, my friend and colleague Odile represents the same interests we do and would like to help us. We'll go to her place, just around the corner. You can wash up."

Looking vastly relieved, Tregobov shook her hand. "I am most grateful," he said in heavily accented French. "Thank you."

"It's my pleasure, what little I can do."

Walking to the apartment, Tregobov explained what had happened at the prison. "Despite its reputation for filthiness and brutality, La Santé seems to me a very permissive facility, at least compared to institutions in my country." He was sweating profusely and still seemed somewhat dazed. "For instance, when the inmates are allowed to walk for exercise, they can mingle as they wish instead of being forced to walk two by two, arms behind their backs, as in most prisons. In any case, today, after the exercise period, three men were said to be missing. Then a head count was taken, and no one seemed to be missing after all. After that, the gas. No one knows why. A kind of farce, you know, but very disruptive. I must get out of there."

"You're working in the research program?" asked Odile.

"Yes, but only because—"

"We'll talk about it later," Thierry interrupted.

Odile punched in the code at the mews' front gate. As they passed the anarchists' door, she cast a surreptitious glance at the adjacent window, but no one seemed to be home and the computer screens were dark. Going on, she led Thierry and his friend into the apartment.

Then, once Tregobov had been provided with towel, washcloth, and dressing gown, his clothes had been thrown into the washing machine, he'd retired to the bathroom, and the bathtub faucet had begun to run, Odile brought Thierry into the living room, where he occupied the same spot on the sofa that Turner had half a lifetime ago. She remained standing.

"So," she said, "you know a man named Kukushkin, a banker of sorts who perhaps has other talents as well?"

Thierry looked glum.

"That's all right, I know you know him." She began to pace, anger rising slowly in her like a taint of the blood. "Your cousin worked for Kukushkin," she said. "You were working nights for Broch, paying off a gambling debt, if I'm not mistaken, maybe—is it possible?—by turning out counterfeit DVDs. Then the flag business presented itself—Turner's pet project—and Broch recommended you as a reliable courier. Good, so off we go to Moscow, you and I. When you don't return with me and the flags, Kukushkin has Broch killed for steering you in his direction, for vouching for your reliability."

"Odile, Odile. Listen to me."

"Yet even this—how to call it?—surrogate vengeance, this murder, fails to satisfy Kukushkin, since he certainly doesn't call off his goons, who continue to threaten me and Turner in ways ever less attractive, because he thinks we know where you and Gabriella, once it comes to light that she's your girlfriend, can be found. And why is that, you might ask. Forgive my frankness, but neither of you seems to me particularly indispensable to the world at large, let alone to someone like Kukushkin. So what is it you have that he wants?" She stood over him. "Is it this doctor, whom no one but the police has asked about? Or is it something else? These silences, you see, they bother me very much. I want them filled. I want them explained once and for all." She bent over at the waist and thrust her face forward until it was inches from his own. "So start talking."

Thierry recoiled slightly but otherwise didn't move.

In the bathroom, water continued to plunge into water.

It suddenly occurred to Odile that she'd be perfectly justified in making a quiet call from the other room and keeping her guests entertained until the Russians, stolid and stupid and tireless, arrived in their black sedan to take them away. But first she needed to hear what Thierry had to tell her. She wanted to be certain, even though she knew that certainty was the invention of a troubled mind. She wanted no regrets.

"Well," Thierry said, settling back in the sofa, "I'll explain what I can. But you must realize that the more you know, the more compromised you are and the more jeopardy you're in."

"Jeopardy! After the last few weeks, I'll take my chances."

"As you wish." He sighed at her recklessness but went ahead. "When Turner was arranging for our passage through customs in Brest—on the way back, that is, with the flags—he called Kukushkin, whom he knows from various other contexts. The thing was done. Now, as it happens, Kukushkin had plans to go into business with our Dr. Tregobov, who is very brilliant, probably number one in his field, but also, as you pointed out, a Belarussian. This is most unfortunate because—"

"What field?" Odile interjected.

"Molecular biology. Anyway it's most unfortunate because Belarus, as you know, is the last communist country in Europe and everything worth having, not to mention everything that isn't, belongs in perpetuity to the state. In this case the property at issue is intellectual: Dr. Tregobov has made a groundbreaking discovery. Anywhere else in the world, the process he's developed would not only guarantee him a Nobel Prize but also make him a very rich man. In Belarus it cost him his passport. The government supported his research, yes, but essentially by imprisoning him in his laboratory. They wanted to keep his discoveries—and the profits they're bound to generate when the patents are approved—in state hands."

Odile had resumed pacing. "So Kukushkin proposed to get him out of Belarus and go into partnership with him. Very enterprising. But what's your role? You don't play at their level."

"Maybe I don't, maybe I do. We'll see. But when Kukushkin heard from Turner that I was going to Moscow via Brest, he called Sylvain to ask if I was dependable. He needed someone to drop something off in Brest for Dr. Tregobov and then, if everything went well, take him to Paris on the return trip. I got the job."

"And you screwed it up. Is that it?"

"No!" Thierry struggled to sit upright on the sofa's down cushions. "Of course not! I told you: some adjustments had to be made in Brest, so I stayed behind and made them."

"Why are the *French* police looking for Tregobov?"

"Because when the Belarussian government realized that he'd escaped the country, they put out a terrorist bulletin on him throughout the EU. Mad scientist, bioweapons, I don't know. These days, obviously, people would rather err on the side of caution. So you get police. Too bad, in my view, but that's how it is."

Odile tapped her knuckles against her own forehead in frustration, then, as calmly as she could, walked over to him and in a quiet voice said, "You're telling me nothing. Why should the Russians be so desperate to find you? I think it's because you abducted Tregobov yourself. For your own purposes."

"If that were the case, don't you think he'd look a little unhappier about it?"

"Maybe he doesn't know all the facts, either. Or maybe you lied to him. How could I know?"

"None of us knows all the facts, Odile. That was a twentieth-century delusion, and I, for one, am glad to be rid of it."

"What about Gabriella? Where is she?"

"Hiding. She's fine."

There was a silence during which they both realized the bath faucet had been turned off some time ago. The tub gurgled as it drained. Odile excused herself and went downstairs to put the doctor's clothes in the dryer.

Though it was obvious that Thierry wasn't telling her everything, she found she believed what he had chosen to reveal. Maybe the problem was her questions; she kept getting sidetracked, as each new supposition replaced the previous one without ever resolving into the certainty at which she still, no doubt foolishly, hoped to arrive.

Upstairs, Thierry had stuck his head out the window and was looking west up the courtyard. Sensing her presence, he drew back inside. "Who are those guys?"

When she looked, she saw three men in their thirties wearing ill-fitting, mismatched clothes and conferring closely, midway down the courtyard.

"No idea," she said. "Probably friends of the anarchist group we've got living here."

Thierry walked back over to the sofa but didn't sit down. "Well, I'll tell you this much, because it's necessary. Dr. Tregobov believes I'm still working for Kukushkin, who I've told him is in Siberia inspecting some oil fields—totally unreachable, but most definitely with us in spirit. I'm his representative, as far as the good doctor's concerned. So are you, for that matter, since that's what I more or less told him just now."

"So you did snatch him!"

"No. I'm merely guiding him to safe haven on Kukushkin's instructions, just as before. The only thing that's changed is that Kukushkin's *temporarily* out of the loop. I'd explain it to him, though right now I don't think he'd be inclined to understand. But eventually he will."

In her pique, she turned her back on him and walked several steps toward the kitchen before forcing herself to stop. "Two questions."

"Ask."

"One. Why haven't the three of you left Paris?"

"We're trying to. But as you can imagine, with the police looking for him and the Russians for me and Gabriella, this isn't so simple. Airports and train stations are out of the question, and rental cars too easy to track. But we're giving the matter our fullest attention. Thanks for your concern."

She turned to face him and was once again struck by his luminescent quality, almost as if he were emitting little points of light. "Two. What was in the package you dropped off at Brest? The 'refrigeration unit,' you called it."

"I did say that, didn't I?" Thierry laughed. "In point of fact that was just a prop, a precautionary diversion, should one be necessary. What I dropped off was a brand-new Belgian-issue EU passport for Dr. Tregobov. In retrospect, that's probably where things got off track."

His eyes went out of focus, and Odile had the impression he was about to say more—one lie so often requiring another for amplitude—when the bathroom door opened and the doctor stepped out, looking thoroughly refreshed in the borrowed dressing gown.

"Madame Mével," he said with a slight bow in her direction. "My most sincere thanks. You have no idea how necessary that was."

She smiled at him and went to get his clothes from the dryer.

The actual necessities, she had begun to realize, were only now declaring themselves.

# CHAPTER 28

LEAVING TOURS THAT AFTERNOON, pushing the Citroën as hard as he could, Max knew himself to be a man in rebellion.

His meeting had been a success. He'd screened a selection of recent footage for his investors, omitting the police-raid sequence, which would only have confused them, and in return had received praise and the assurance of further funding. Yet the entire experience felt like a personal affront, an interruption of his efforts, a humiliation, a joke. He knew he was being petty, but didn't care. And then there was this.

Although he'd never thought he was making a documentary and doubted very much that anyone could think so once the film was done, some of his backers' comments made it obvious that's what they'd expected and thought they were admiring. Maybe it was because he was improvising and using nonactors, maybe it was the film's reliance on natural light, or possibly nothing more than the recent box-office success, unforeseen and to Max inexplicable, of a spate of low-budget documentaries in the U.S. In the end, the reasons didn't matter. Eddie had secured him the right of final cut, so if the investors were unhappy with the film he eventually gave them, too bad. In the meantime he'd have Eddie run interference, and there would be no more days like this.

Flooring the Citroën, he managed to pass a truck he'd been stuck behind for several minutes. It was loaded down with artichokes and, in the rearview mirror, presented a somewhat comic sight as it periodically shed some of its cargo to the wind. Max glanced at his fuel gauge; the needle hovered just a hair above empty.

He refueled at a gas station outside Orléans, washed his face in the men's room, and bought a bottle of mineral water, which he drank half down at a draw. Somebody had left that day's *Libération* on the bench beside the soft-drink machine. Leafing impatiently through it, he looked for a mention of the auction but found nothing. He finished the mineral water, started the car, and lurched back onto the highway, scattering gravel in his wake.

About six kilometers out of Orléans, a police car fell in behind him. Max waited anxiously to be pulled over, but they drove on for another fifteen kilometers before the car passed him, the passenger-side officer looking Max over curiously. Then, an instant later, they shot down the road at full speed, quickly disappearing.

Shaken, Max rolled the window partway down and lit a cigar. When in rebellion, he thought, it was inadvisable to attract the attention of the local constabulary, whose priorities rarely coincided with one's own. Nevertheless, the encounter had sobered him sufficiently that, for the first time all day, he found himself able to take stock of his situation with some detachment, mentally separating one thing from another, as he should have done some time ago. Of course, he'd been preoccupied.

He now took it as a given that Odile and Turner were having an affair. Though the evidence was thin, he felt the certitude of her betrayal in the marrow of his bones. Any doubts he might've harbored had vanished the moment he laid eyes on her the day before, through Groot's binoculars: her struggle with the cigarette, the first he'd seen her with in years; her puffy, tear-stung eyes; her obvious impatience; and, most of all, her newly shorn hair, lightly feathered and glossed. She'd worn it like that the night she'd accosted him in SoHo seven years ago. Never since had she cut it so close, though the severity became her still, bringing out her cheekbones and the fullness of her lips, emphasizing her youth. As she would know.

He liked to think he was above jealousy, but probably most men flattered themselves on this score. Certainly he was competitive enough. If the two traits came to the same thing, as he often suspected, he would soon find out.

For awhile he scanned the fields of new wheat and corn that stretched out on either side of the highway, rippling in the breeze like the surface of a windblown lake. He felt unpleasantly exposed and was wishing for the forest he'd left behind not forty minutes ago when his cell rang. He set the cigar in the ashtray and pulled the phone from his pants pocket.

"Dad?"

"Yes, my little monster."

"About that party tonight, remember? Everything's cool. It's at Lili's parents' apartment in the sixteenth, and the kids are all from Dominique's *rallye*—which I guess is like her group of officially approved friends, who'll probably all be ministers of *state* or *CEOs* or something when they're adults, but right now they're just regular kids, you know? Lili's parents will be there, and Dominique too, so you don't need to worry. I'll give you the parents' number as soon as I can find it; it's here somewhere. Anyway, the party's from seven thirty to eleven, and I'd really like to go. Can I?"

"All right. But I want you to call me at nine thirty and give me an update, okay?"

"Great! Love you, Dad." Then, not waiting for a response, she punched off.

He put the cell phone away, his thoughts momentarily hazed over by love and worry. In the ashtray, his cigar had gone out. He relit it.

The mood of rebellion hadn't left him. For as long as he could remember he'd been aware of the unfairness of the world, and, for almost as long, he'd seen that it could be no other way. Perhaps, he often thought, it *should* be no other way.

Yet now—as he felt his women hurtling off, Allegra toward adulthood, Odile toward another man—an overwhelming exasperation took hold of him. It was like a cry of disbelief, of outrage, that what happened to so many should happen to him.

Just when he felt the need for some recognition of the difficulties involved in what he did for a living, of the optimism and endurance it required, he discovered himself increasingly isolated from those whose appreciation he most needed—his wife, his daughter, maybe even himself. The core of his body pulsed against his rib cage as if about to explode. This anger, murderous and frightening, was of a sort he hadn't felt since childhood, when he was ignorant of its very nature. He forced himself to breathe deeply and regularly until the feeling subsided.

Outrage, disbelief, anger. And beneath all three, an intimation of something else that made him prefer them to it. He pushed it from his thoughts.

The business with Odile would have to be faced—not just soon, but tonight. And much as he might have wished to just confront her and let things unfold naturally in the form of confession or, less likely, denial, he knew that this was not the right approach. A man lied by fabricating false truths, a woman by omitting real ones. This tactical difference not only made women superior liars but also required the serious man to work against his own inclinations if he hoped to determine where matters actually stood.

How strange, thought Max, that he knew this in his films yet so often forgot it in life. He looked out again at the fields on either side of him, admiring their stringent vitality, their orderliness. For how many centuries, he wondered, had they been cultivated, and by how many men. How little was forgotten here.

When he arrived home, shortly after four o'clock, the apartment was deserted. Odile had left a note saying that Rachel and Groot had invited them to dinner aboard the *Nachtvlinder* that evening and she hoped very much he wanted to go. They could discuss it when she got back from Fatima's fitting, around seven, but she really needed to see him tonight. He realized he had expected something of the sort.

Not to be outdone, Allegra had also left a note, this one informing him in purple ink that she had gone with Dominique and Lili to the Turkish baths, where Thursdays were reserved for women, and she'd be back to change for the party, if there was time. No matter what, she promised (underlined) to be home by eleven thirty. Love, A.

Shaking his head, Max went to the liquor cabinet and poured himself a couple of fingers of scotch. He sat by the phone for awhile, thoughtfully sipping his drink, then looked up the number for the auction house and dialed it. A woman answered, and he asked whether it was too late to reserve a bidder's seat for tonight's sale. Not at all, she replied, and after he gave her his name and address, she gave him his bidder's number.

"It starts at eight o'clock sharp, sir," she cautioned him, "but you should get here at least half an hour early."

He said he would, then thanked her and hung up. After pouring himself another scotch, he took it to the window.

Odile's trip to Moscow, the subsequent trashing of their apartment, the firebombing of the *Nachtvlinder*, the altered version of *Fireflies*, La Peau de l'Ours, Turner and the Giacometti, Broch's murder and the confiscation of Madame Leclère's files, the amber-coated DVDs, Véronique, the CRS raid on the *Nachtvlinder*, his wife's affair—all these glittered in his mind's eye like shards of broken mirror, each reflecting one or two of the others but refusing to come together into a whole. If there'd ever been a whole. If it had ever been a mirror.

He took a bath and a nap, then got dressed for the auction.

## CHAPTER 29

TURNER SPENT THE BETTER PART of the afternoon overseeing the transfer of the flags from the exhibition galleries on the second floor to the auction hall on the fourth. Most of the banners, sandwiched now in glass, were too large to fit on the display carousel normally used at sales, so he had it replaced by a large gilt-wood easel that was quite grand, even czarist, in effect. The idea was for the porters to bring each lot in from stage left, place it on the easel for the duration of the sale—about two and a half minutes, if things went well—and whisk it off stage right, newly priced and purchased. After consulting briefly with the auctioneer, showing him which flags might be worth an extra push, he went home to prepare for the event.

Although technically there was no reason for him to attend the auction at all, since he was serving as an unnamed seller rather than a house representative, he thought it desirable to keep an eye on the action. Even at a small sale like this one, bidding irregularities were far from unknown. He wanted no surprises.

At home, shaving, it occurred to him that absolutely anyone with an interest in his whereabouts would know where to find him that night. He stared at his face in the mirror, making a mental list of people who might interfere with his well-being or his project's. Then he went into the bedroom, retrieved the nine-millimeter pistol from the bottom of the laundry basket, where Odile had tossed it, and put it on the bed.

It was a precaution only, he told himself. A small but advisable prudence.

With electrician's tape and two belts buckled together, he rigged a shoulder holster that positioned the weapon inconspicuously against his left side, under his arm. He buttoned his shirt over it, tucked the shirttails into his suit trousers, put on his tie and jacket, and considered himself in the mirror. Armed, he felt no better than before but no worse, either. At six thirty he left the apartment.

His nascent optimism, which he went to some pains to conceal, even from himself, soon began to animate his every step. His blistered foot had healed nicely. He no longer brooded over Odile's failure to return the messages he'd left that morning. Naturally, with her husband's daughter visiting, the opportunities for calling would be scarce, as she'd said. Besides, had she not come home with him just the other afternoon, home to bed, despite trying to think of every reason not to? In his experience, this was a good sign.

As for Gabriella and Thierry, it was a pity they'd provoked the Russians, whom he himself heartily loathed, though he wasn't quite ready to close the books on Kukushkin, for whom he reserved a grain of admiration. Thierry had somehow crossed Kukushkin, Gabriella had tried to help Thierry, so the two would have to save themselves. Gabriella was an extraordinarily resourceful young woman. He wished them well.

Arriving at the auction house, he found Horst Wieselhoff, catalog tucked under his arm, waiting on the inconspicuously secured ground floor with the clear intention of intercepting him.

"Horst. Glad you could make it."

"As am I," said the Swiss, his eyes shining. He looked quickly around the room and lowered his voice. "Unfortunately, everyone else is here too—a number of big collectors, mindless speculators, readers of art magazines, even our friends Balakian, Baxter, and a few other members of the Manhattan art cartel."

"Well, Horst, what can I say? It's open to the public."

On the staircase, a woman Turner didn't recognize raised a glass of champagne to toast him and smiled before continuing her ascent.

"Yes, of course," Wieselhoff went on. "I was simply wondering whether three lots in particular couldn't be withdrawn from auction to be settled privately between—"

"Don't say it, Horst."

The man smiled guiltily. "Ah, too bad. But I had to try, didn't I?"

Turner squeezed the man's shoulder, wished him luck, and started up the stairs.

Even though his name didn't appear on tonight's program, Turner was known in the Parisian art world and, as he moved through the crowd loitering on the fourth floor, was waylaid several times by friends and acquaintances who frequently seemed to find their own presence there obscurely confirmed by his. This, he thought, boded well.

His social obligations discharged, he entered the hall and made for his favorite seat, in the third row, against the wall. From there, he could position himself sideways to the room and see, without drawing anyone's attention, who was bidding in-house, whether the phone bank was active, and where the auctioneer's eyes, which missed nothing, focused their interest. It was never less than enlightening to study people's behavior when money was in play.

The remaining bidders began coming in and taking their seats. He thumbed through his catalog impatiently. Then something—an instinct, a tic, a trick of the mind—made him look up again just in time to see Max Colby stride by unaccompanied, headed up the middle aisle, apparently without noticing him.

At first Turner thought he must be mistaken. Odile would never have allowed this to happen; it could not happen. But a moment later, when Max was almost halfway to the back of the hall, he was accosted by a young woman seated on the aisle, someone Turner didn't know. She was blond, self-possessed, even bold, and when she stood to kiss Max hello, he noticed a tattoo on her upper arm, a finely delineated wheel of many spokes. She gave a short laugh of what seemed to be delighted surprise. The man she was with—older, charming in demeanor, well dressed in a boxy suit—rose to be introduced, smiling as though in anticipation of a rare and almost certainly instructive pleasure. He and Max shook hands vigorously—two men who'd been informed of each other's talents, which they'd now be able to judge for themselves.

Turner looked away, his blood gone cold in his veins.

Kukushkin.

WHEN ODILE GOT HOME, she knew right away by the faint scent of cologne that she'd missed Max, that he'd gone to the auction after all, and that later there would be things to discuss. She called upstairs for Allegra but got no response. Probably she'd already left for her party with Dominique.

Suddenly loath to be alone in the apartment, she went back out into the courtyard, no clear destination in mind. Passing the anarchists' door, however, she saw it was propped open a few inches with a cobblestone, and, as if this were a sign somehow meant solely for her, she stepped forward without thought or hesitation and knocked loudly. Chantal's face appeared, looking concerned at first, then brightening into a dazzling smile. "Odile! What a surprise!"

"Am I interrupting?"

"Not at all. Anyway, the others are out right now. Please, come in."

Odile nudged the cobblestone aside with her foot, and the door shut behind her.

"Would you like a beer," Chantal said, ". . . a beer?"

"Thanks, that would be perfect . . . perfect."

At first Odile thought the echo was the effect of their voices bouncing off the walls of the almost unfurnished room, but then she realized it was in her head—a symptom of fatigue, she supposed—and immediately it ceased. The computers, she noticed with some relief, were turned off.

"Make yourself at home," Chantal said over her shoulder as she took the stairs two at a time. Odile had just settled into a torn and tufted settee when her host rushed back down, now holding a six-pack of German lager and two mason jars. "Did you hear what happened at La Santé this afternoon?" she asked, handing her a jar and a beer.

"I heard the alarm and helicopter. What did happen, exactly?"

"Three prisoners escaped," Chantal said with demure satisfaction. "The media are keeping it quiet on government orders, because no one wants to look incompetent or stupid, you know? Pretty funny at this late date. Anyway, that's what I was told." She drank deeply of her beer.

"Incredible! But how'd these guys get out? I thought La Santé was supposed to be totally exit proof."

"It is. But underneath are all these tunnels and sewers and stuff—like the catacombs. Somehow these guys must've broken through the basement level and into the passages. My friend says they came out through a manhole cover in the middle of Arago, right into traffic. Can you imagine?"

"Now *that's* something I would've liked to have seen," Odile told her.

"Me too," Chantal agreed merrily. She finished her beer and opened another, while Odile sipped hers politely. "Ever been into the catacombs?"

"What for?" Odile said. "To meet tourists?"

"No, I mean the real ones. Three hundred kilometers of passages, chambers, loose bones, even a movie theater—right here under our feet. The underground Paris."

Instantly, Odile's mind played back for her at quintuple speed the slide lecture she'd seen when attempting to deliver Thierry to the Russians. Right away, without even wanting to know this, she understood that the catacombs were where Gabriella, and very likely Tregobov and Thierry too, were hiding.

"But I thought the police had closed up all the entries," she lied sheepishly. "You know, because of terrorists and so on."

Chantal laughed and gestured with her mason jar toward the room's far corner. The dining table had once again been relieved of its top, which was propped against the wall beside it. "You know the police will say anything that makes it seem like they're in control. Go on, have a look. And this is hardly the only one in the arrondissement."

The flared and ribbed wooden pedestal that ordinarily supported the tabletop was, Odile discovered, hollow at its core, leading to a kind of stone-aggregate shaft fitted with U-shaped rebar ladder rungs that descended into darkness and beyond. "How far down does it go?"

"Right here, only eight or nine meters. But then, if you follow the tunnels, you can go practically anywhere in Paris. There are many levels down—six, we think. Some of the passages are a tight squeeze, and you have to crawl, but a lot of them are not. You've heard the stories, no?"

"Of course. Not that I always know quite what to believe."

"How could you? The police also spread a lot of misinformation to make their job easier. But a lot goes on down there anyway." Chantal finished the second beer. "Tonight, for example, there's a big party, still secret, I hope, in the so-called Bunker, under a high school near the Jardin du Luxembourg. That's where the others have gone. Would you like to come with me?"

Odile froze, seized suddenly by the sense that events had been tending in this direction for a long time. Then she said, "Thanks, it's so nice of you to ask, but I'm supposed to go to a dinner at le quai de la Tournelle tonight. Some friends who own a houseboat are—"

"Le quai de la Tournelle? That's perfect! There's an exit right nearby, not the tourist one, but much better. I'll show you. Besides . . ." Then she paused.

Odile thought uneasily of the basement steps in her father's house, uneasily of darkness. "Yes?" she heard herself say.

"Okay, I probably should've asked you first, but the girls were so eager to go, to the party, I mean—"

"The girls?"

"Allegra and Dominique. They went with the first group, led by Fabien. You remember, the guy with the mustache?"

Odile sighed. "Oh, yes. Fabien." She ran one hand over her newly cut and just gelled hair. "Okay, let's go. Right away."

"You're coming? That's so cool!" Chantal jumped to her feet and, heading briskly up the stairs again, called down, "I'll just get our coveralls, boots, lights, and stuff. Five minutes max!"

Darkness was only an idea, Odile tried telling herself. Or possibly it was relative, on a continuum with light, which diluted it and kept it an idea. Or whatever.

Chantal returned with the equipment, which they donned silently, in somewhat military fashion. Once down the ladder, with miner's lamps on their heads and thigh-high rubber boots on their legs, they projected beams of light in the direction they were looking—crazily at first, as they got their bearings in the vaulted chamber where they'd arrived, then in parallel when they entered the surprisingly spacious tunnel connected to it.

They walked for awhile in silence. From time to time Chantal directed her headlamp at points of danger: fissures, pits, decades-old machinery. There was also garbage left by previous visitors: plastic water bottles, food tins, depleted batteries. Side passages ran off in all directions, but Chantal seemed to know her route.

"No map?" asked Odile.

"We're not going that far, and I've been there before. But there's a makeshift map in my pack, just in case."

"Ah, that's good."

Chantal laughed. "You know the one about the guy and his wine cellar?"

"I don't think so."

"This guy's looking for a particular bottle of Bordeaux, which he thinks might be at the back of the cellar, and then he sees a door he's never noticed. He opens it and discovers a tunnel completely new to him. Who knows what treasures might be found there? The house has been in his family for generations, and the wine cellar was once very famous. So, leaving the door open for a bit of light, he enters the tunnel. Within minutes, he gets lost. Not just sort of lost—completely lost. It takes him two days to find a path back out. He barely survives."

Odile shivered. "The rule of threes."

"The rule of threes? This I don't know."

"A human being can survive three minutes without air, three days without water, three weeks without food. At the maximum."

Chantal looked Odile directly in the face, momentarily blinding her. "Is this true?"

"I think so. My father told me about it. He knows that kind of thing."

"But that's extraordinary."

"Alas, no. It's very, very ordinary."

"Oh," Chantal said, "I see your point. It applies to everyone."

They said nothing more for some time.

Later, as the tunnel narrowed, Chantal took the lead and began to make a series of zigzag turns—left, right, left again—of which Odile soon lost track in her effort to keep up. Her old fears of subterranean darkness quivered at the edges of her consciousness like ghostly fingers, but she forced herself to concentrate on the glow of Chantal's headlamp to hold her fears at bay. Turning back, probably never a realistic option, was now out of the question. How often one had to relearn this simple truth. If indeed it was simple, or the truth.

The tunnels narrowed further, growing mazelike and inclining steadily downward, so that soon the two women were wading through water. At first there was just three or four inches of it, but as they progressed it deepened. Six inches, nine inches, a foot and a half. At two feet Odile began to panic.

"How much farther?" she asked, as coolly as she could.

"Don't worry. This is the hardest part, because of the water. Then we go up again, and there's a resting place. After that, maybe twenty minutes."

Over and over in her mind, trying to contain her panic, Odile rehearsed a litany of self-indictment: *How could I have let this happen? How? I knew Allegra was lying about the party. I knew. Everything's going to pieces. Everything. And what am I going to tell Max?* But before long, the words lost their sense completely, becoming little more than a means to regulate breath—which, she soon supposed, was as good a use for them as any.

The walls were limestone. At the tunnel intersections were brass plates, various in design, announcing the streets aboveground. Odile grew calmer.

"I come here to cleanse my mind," Chantal said apropos of nothing.

"It's so dark," Odile whispered, "so unbelievably quiet."

"Yes, that's it. You understand."

With two more corners turned, they found themselves at the foot of an ancient stone staircase that rose far beyond the reach of their headlamps' beams. Without a word they started up it, Chantal in front. It occurred to Odile that a stumble here could easily mean a broken ankle, and she tried to match Chantal's footsteps exactly.

They climbed for what seemed to Odile a very long time, and she was out of breath when they reached the top. The stairs delivered them onto a kind of extended balcony, a platform, really, whose features Chantal silently pointed out with her headlamp: stone benches carved into the walls on three sides; original graffiti, carefully dated, from the revolutions of 1789 and 1968; a stone bas-relief rendering of a castle, impressively detailed but undated; a rather large wooden flat in which someone was cultivating mushrooms, several species of them thriving nicely; and a table made from one of the great circular saws originally used to mine the limestone with which Paris was built. Then, as if by silent agreement, both women turned off their lamps and sank down onto the stone benches to rest. Complete blackness, silence, erasure from the world. Peace.

"Are you really an anarchist?" Odile said after a while.

Chantal sighed. "If you mean do I throw bricks through windows all the time and spray-paint everything black—no. But I *am* in solidarity with the great American statesman and friend to France, Thomas Jefferson, who said, 'Were it left to me to decide whether we should have a government without newspapers, or newspapers without government, I should not hesitate a moment to prefer the latter.' " She paused sadly. "As you see, we have a government, but no longer do we have a truly free press . . ."

A silence passed.

"By any means necessary?" Odile couldn't help but ask.

"By any means necessary," Chantal confirmed.

"Yes," said Odile after a time. "Me too."

The two women embraced but said no more. How her father would have loved to have heard this, seen this, been part of it, thought Odile. On the other hand—and here lay the true genius of life, what really made it worth the suffering and stupidity and apparent senselessness—none of this would ever have happened had Sebastien actually been present to witness it. And so one was called forward once again, against one's will, into a battle without tears or mercy—a war worth fighting, however impossible the terms. You went on with it because you were born to it. And that was enough.

A moment later, Chantal said, "I know you're worried about Allegra, but I promise you she's okay. Maybe we should get going, though. We're really close now."

They turned their headlamps on simultaneously. Blinking in the sudden light, they stood up.

"Close to what exactly?"

"It's called the Bunker. It was a German bomb shelter and communication center during World War II. That's where the party is. Just stay close to me."

Odile stayed close. Shortly they emerged into an extended area where each intersection was marked by a lit votive candle—at least a dozen flames visible in the distance. They followed this path, and before long Odile thought she could hear music, the same strange music she'd heard coming from Chantal's apartment last Friday during the dinner party. It had a funny-sad character to it, beaten-up and spare: the occasional looped piano chord, a bass line spaced so wide that Odile was continually surprised that she could still pick out the rhythm when the next notes sounded, a few electronic figures that might have come from another keyboard but probably didn't. Youthful voices half-sang their rhymes quadruple time in a Cockney English heavily inflected with African and Caribbean accents, working their hip-hop lyrics first against the music, then in time with it, then against it again. It took her a while to be sure the sounds were recorded, not live, but as they got closer, she began to hear live voices too, speaking French—the partygoers, she assumed. She could smell hash, though before she could say anything Chantal told her once more not to worry, Allegra was definitely fine. Much to her surprise, Odile accepted this reassurance without protest—her compliance, she thought, likely the result of having been guided such a long distance through the dark. Anyway, there was nothing to be done until they got to the scene of the action.

Which, sooner than she expected, they did.

"I'm sorry," said Chantal, "I forgot to tell you about this part. You're not claustrophobic, are you?"

"Not really," Odile lied.

"Good. Then everything will be fine." With her headlamp, she indicated a small crevice in the wall, perhaps two feet above their heads. "That's how you get in. What you do is, first, throw in your pack. Then I'll boost you up, you'll go in headfirst, pushing your pack ahead of you, and crawl through the passage, which is maybe four meters long at most. I'll push you from the back, then you're in. I'll be right behind you." She shook back her hair. "Okay?"

"Let's go," Odile said firmly.

Chantal took a preparatory breath, grasped Odile around the tops of her thighs, lifted her up, and pushed. Odile, with no more than six inches leeway on either side, wriggled forward along the passage, pushing her pack ahead of her, tasting dirt and lime. In less than a minute, the two of them were standing side by side in the Nazi bunker, with perhaps a hundred people dancing, drinking, talking, and smoking around them.

The party was very much louder inside than out, its roar muffled by the limestone walls, and at first Odile felt a little dazed. *I gave you / the doubt of /*

*the benefit!* a singer insisted again and again over a rising and falling triplet of . . . what? Digitized flute, maybe, or keyboards, along with bass, drum, and guitar samples. On the far wall an old metal sign read RAUCHEN VER-BOTEN, though this clearly wasn't stopping anybody.

"Let's find the girls first," Chantal shouted. Odile nodded vigorously, and they set out, following the room's perimeter counterclockwise. The crowd was multiracial, of varying sobriety, everyone obviously having a good time. Several smaller rooms stretched beyond this one but seemed empty.

They passed another sign, unmistakably authentic, that read RUHE! with a swastika emblem beneath it that Odile suspected was a later addition. Halfway around the bunker, she caught sight of Dominique, who was smoking furiously and swaying to the music, a water bottle in her hand. Assailed by misgivings, Odile hurried over to her. "You came!" Dominique said, dropping both cigarette and water bottle to throw her arms around her. "We really hoped you would!"

"Where's Allegra?" Odile asked in the calmest tones available.

"She's here somewhere. With that guy Fabien. Dancing, I think."

"Great. Perfect."

Odile's irony, though, was lost on the girl, who was glowing with sisterly goodwill. "Your haircut," she said, examining it closely, then touching it here and there with gentle fingers. "Very, very cool! May I ask who did it?"

But these words didn't even register on Odile, who was scanning the room for Allegra, panic rising in her throat. "How long ago did you see her?"

When Dominique failed to answer, Odile gazed into her eyes and, with dismay and sudden comprehension, noticed at once what she should have seen from the start. The girl's pupils, glistening liquid black, were dilated to the size of shirt buttons.

"DO I HEAR TWO FORTY?" cried the auctioneer. "Two hundred forty thousand francs for lot number two?"

Turner saw a man nearby tug twice, very gently, at the handkerchief in his jacket's breast pocket.

"Thank you," replied the auctioneer, without looking directly at the bidder. "We now have a price of two hundred fifty thousand. Who will go to two sixty? Two sixty?"

A woman at the back raised her paddle. "Thank you, Madame. Two hundred sixty thousand francs. Can we go to two seventy? Two seventy? Anyone? No? Fair warning, then. Going once at two hundred sixty, going twice . . . He waited for a moment, looked pointedly around the room, then brought the hammer down firmly. "Sold to Madame for two hundred sixty thousand francs."

It was a good price for so early in the game, and Turner was pleased. Still, it often happened that if the oxygen got sucked out of an auction too quickly, then the excitement disappeared with it, and later lots sold poorly or not at all. As with anything traded or desired, nothing, finally, could be guaranteed. Perhaps that was why the system worked—at least to the extent that it did.

While the porters removed the lot from the stage and replaced it with the next one, Turner stole a look at Max, Kukushkin, and the exceedingly confident blond girl he presumed to be Nikolai's—the word came back to him quite unpleasantly—consort. As a trio, they made a hard read. How could they possibly even know one another? And why, if not for the obvious reasons, were they actually here?

Either Kukushkin or Max or both could have come to confront Turner over their presumably distinct grievances with him. However, Max's apparently accidental encounter with the blond girl, and her clear, even deliberately stagy connection with Kukushkin, threw everything into question.

Maybe the Russian just wanted to buy some flags, and Max just wanted to see what his wife had retrieved from the fallen empire of the East. Possible, certainly. But unlikely. Turner felt a headache coming on.

The next three lots sold at similar prices, in comparable bidding, to different parties—all good omens, in his view. Lot number six, however, was particularly desirable and surely one of the three that Wieselhoff had hoped to buy privately for himself. In immaculate condition, the red velvet banner, fringed with braided gold and silver tassels of exceptional luster, depicted, not only the obligatory hammer and sickle, but also Marx, Lenin, and Stalin, standing at attention in a gradually receding line that placed Marx farthest away and Stalin closest. All three gazed skyward toward a vision of the future that seemed all the more palpable, even imminent, for being left to the viewer's imagination. The flag measured five meters wide, and Turner had decided on a somewhat aggressive pre-sale estimate of six hundred thousand to seven hundred fifty thousand francs. The hammer price on this one might easily determine the course of the rest of the auction, and he worried suddenly that the estimate was too high.

"Lot number six," said the auctioneer into the microphone. "An exceptionally fine piece, in most remarkable condition." He paused, as if reluctant himself to relinquish this particular work to the unruly forces of the marketplace.

*Good man,* thought Turner. *Must have a word with him afterward.*

"Bidding for lot six," said the auctioneer, "will start at . . . a hundred thousand francs."

Immediately several hands and paddles went up.

"Thank you. To the gentleman in back. Bidding currently at one hundred thousand. Do I hear one fifty?"

Again several takers, perhaps more than before.

"Thank you, sir. May I get two hundred thousand?"

The phone bank lit up—three ringless phones attended by three very young women in black silk dresses and pearl chokers. The frontmost girl blinked three times in the auctioneer's direction.

"Very well. Three hundred thousand. Bidding currently at three hundred thousand francs. Do I hear three fifty? Three fifty? Thank you, sir. Four hundred thousand? May I ask four hundred thousand? Who will say four hundred?"

Turner stole a look at Kukushkin. Kolya, leaning back in his chair, had his arms crossed over his chest and a pleasant but distinctly sardonic smile on his face. He didn't seem to have noticed Turner yet and appeared to be enjoying himself. His blond companion and Max Colby, meanwhile, were utterly absorbed in the spectacle, like children watching television in a dark room.

"Four hundred thousand to the gentleman in back," said the auctioneer, his eyes darting around the room. The pace of the bidding had begun to pick up. "Four fifty. Five hundred thousand. Five fifty. Six hundred thousand. Six fifty."

Realizing that Wieselhoff still hadn't placed a bid, Turner looked over and saw the inscrutable Swiss was following the proceeding very closely. It was clear he intended to acquire this piece and had a strategy for doing so, but as usual he did nothing to give himself away.

One of the girls at the phone bank raised an index finger to the auctioneer.

"Seven hundred fifty thousand," said the auctioneer. Most of the original bidders seemed to have dropped out, but Turner couldn't tell who actually remained in the running and who was only waiting for the right moment to join in. Things were going nicely indeed.

"Nine hundred thousand? Who will say nine hundred?"

A man unknown to Turner stood up, looking very convincing in his finely cut Milanese suit of black summer-weight wool, a trimmed mustache of matching hue, and a silver-and-black striped tie. "One million francs," he announced in an accent that indeed proved to be Italian. He sat down, creating a silence that shortly was replaced by a general whispering among the bidders.

*"Grazie, Signor,"* said the auctioneer, bowing his head slightly. "Your interest, I believe, is not misplaced."

There was another silence while all present considered the situation, many of them trying to get a look at the Italian. Then another flurry of bidding—both from people who'd previously dropped out and from others who hadn't yet been heard from. The auctioneer received each incremental price increase with deadpan unsurprise that bordered on piety. He was no longer having to persuade anyone. He named a price, chose among the bidders, and found the next price.

When the flag had reached a valuation of two million, five hundred thousand francs, another pause ensued. It resembled a kind of fear and was known in the trade as "the sighting of the precipice." Doubt and avarice, almost olfactory in nature, could be felt rising from the crowd.

"Two million five," intoned the auctioneer. "The current bid is two million, five hundred thousand francs." He seemed to contemplate the very nature of pricing, of sales, of ownership—a solemn business, he appeared to indicate, perhaps the only thing worth thinking about. Then, coming to himself, he leaned forward and spoke into the microphone with practiced restraint. "Who will say three million?"

Yet another silence, deeper than before. The auctioneer began to fiddle with the hammer. "May I hear three million? Will anyone say three million?"

Then, to Turner's astonishment, Kukushkin rose to his feet and said, in a voice neither smug nor falsely modest, "I will bid four million francs for this item." He sat back down again.

Excited whispers broke out across the room, and even the auctioneer looked momentarily stunned. Such aggressive bidding wasn't unknown— its purpose being to scare off the rest of the pack—but Turner had never before seen it used so casually.

The auctioneer recovered. "The bid is four million francs. Will anyone say four million five? Four million five?"

The silence was total.

"Fair warning then, at four million." He looked around the room. "Going once, going twice—" And then, just as the auctioneer was about to bring the hammer down, Wieselhoff called out, in a perfectly neutral tone of voice, "Five million even."

Everyone turned to look.

When Kukushkin recognized Wieselhoff, he smiled and shrugged, and the Swiss nodded his thanks. The auctioneer said what was required of him, although it was obvious now to everyone that the sale of lot six had reached its natural end. The hammer came down at a price of five million francs.

Turner discovered that he was perspiring. He wiped his brow with his handkerchief, then, not quite able to stop himself, turned to cast a glance at Kukushkin.

This time Kolya was waiting for him, his smile no longer the least sardonic. The two men locked eyes for several seconds before Turner nodded in what he hoped was a congenial fashion. Kukushkin nodded back. Then Turner, filled with foreboding, forced himself to look away.

# CHAPTER 30

"LOOK AT ME!" Odile commanded, shaking Domi-
nique by the arm. The party continued to swirl around them, a smear of
color and sound. When she'd gazed once more into the girl's eyes, she
thrust her away in outrage. "Ecstasy?" Odile cried. "Are you crazy?"

Dominique shook her head tolerantly and smiled. "It's just a party drug,
you know. Not like smack or anything."

"Allegra too, I suppose?"

With a shrug, Dominique attempted to explain. "It just happened, more
or less. When we got here, these three really nice guys asked us if we
wanted any of what they had. Everything just seemed so *right*: the timing,
the place, the—" Abruptly, her thoughts caught up with her words, and she
fell silent.

Odile looked around the bunker. New guests were emerging from the
entry crevice in a steady stream, and it was clear that the party would go on for
hours. "Fine, then. I'm going to think about this," she told Dominique. "Meanwhile, I want you to stay right here, where I can find you. Understood?"

"Of course, Odile. I promise." She laughed. "It's okay that I use your first
name? Because, you know, I just feel so close to you." Giggling. "Maybe we
were sisters in another life!" And with that she began dancing, holding her
hair up off the back of her neck with one hand and pursing her lips in a
pout that soon became a frozen smile.

Odile sighed with exasperation. "Stay here, okay? Don't move! I'll be
right back." Then she plunged into the crowd.

"You get it, don't you?" Dominique called after her. "We can never lose each other now! We're completely connected!"

She didn't look back. The number of revelers had by now increased sufficiently that she was forced to devise a new system for her search, passing first through the middle of the party, then prowling some distance along its edges before crossing the center again. The lighting, provided by miner's lanterns, flashlights, and candles, wasn't much help. Several times she thought she saw Allegra dancing with Fabien, but in each instance she was mistaken, deceived by shadows and her own anxiety. *I can't let this happen,* she told herself, pushing on. *I refuse.*

Minutes passed before, in an accidental synchrony of the party's movements, a channel of free space opened up, and she glimpsed Allegra, dancing with abandon—loose hair flying, arms raised high, sweat pouring from her brow. She was at the center of a ring of other dancers, both male and female, who were urging her on, and for a moment Odile found herself transfixed, as if this were a half-remembered scene from her own adolescence. Prancing out to the ring of spectators, Allegra teasingly chose a partner and resumed her dance, this time just the two of them. Then the crowd shifted again, abruptly cutting off Odile's line of sight. At once she began to press forward, squeezing between these total strangers.

By the time she got there, the music had changed and the dancers had re-sorted themselves accordingly. She quickly found Allegra and Fabien seated on a dilapidated sofa by the limestone wall, Allegra on his lap, the two of them laughing and trying to catch their breath. Since Odile hadn't yet decided what to say, she simply stood there in front of them.

When Fabien noticed her, he got to his feet so quickly that Allegra nearly fell to the ground. They displayed identical clenched smiles for a moment before he stepped politely forward to greet Odile. She ignored him.

"I hate to interrupt this no doubt *urgent* dialogue, but getting here was hell, and my patience is running low. So let's go, Allegra. I'm taking you and Dominique home immediately."

"Home? What for?"

"What do you mean, what for? You lied to your father and me about the party, you're on drugs—no, don't bother, Dominique told me everything—you've been crawling around in the dark and dirt with people you don't even know, risking your lives. So now I've come to take the two of you home. End of story." She grasped Allegra by the upper arm and began steering her toward the spot where she'd left Dominique.

"Wait! I can't believe this!"

"Believe it."

"And I didn't *lie* to you and Dad. Dominique and I just . . . we just had a change of *plans*." She turned to Odile in appeal, pupils dilated, face flushed. "Don't you ever do that? Change your plans? Your mind?"

"Save your breath, Allegra. We're going." To her relief, Odile saw Dominique, still some distance away, dancing by herself right where she'd left her. Now all that remained was to find Chantal, their underworld guide, and persuade her to lead them back to street level.

"I know you're not really mad at me, Odile. You have such a beautiful soul. I love you, don't you realize that?"

"At seventy-five francs a pop, everyone's soul is beautiful. Until you come down, that is. Then you pick up where you left off."

"Odile, it's not like that."

"Everything's like that," she surprised herself by saying.

They continued to edge sideways through the crowd. When they finally reached Dominique, the girls embraced as if they hadn't seen each other in years, squealing, laughing, talking. Odile had forgotten that at their age you could somehow speak and listen simultaneously, and she found the sight of them exercising this skill unexpectedly reassuring.

"Good," she said at last. "Now, you two will stay right here while I find Chantal and get us out of here. Understood?"

They nodded solemnly, looking for the first time somewhat frightened.

Odile set off. She hadn't gotten very far, however, before she saw exactly what she'd feared and hoped to see ever since leaving Chantal's apartment. Gathered in a shallow niche in the bunker's wall, not a hundred meters away, were Thierry, Gabriella, and Tregobov, locked in close conversation.

She hesitated. Then she thought, *Tonight's the night.* She was not sure herself what she meant by this. *Tonight has got to be the night.*

When she reached them, she stepped up and tapped Thierry on the shoulder.

"Hello," she said as casually as she could.

Both Thierry and the doctor turned to look at her in astonishment, but Gabriella seemed strangely unsurprised—part of her style, Odile thought. She decided to match this indifference of affect for the next several hours; and if it worked, she'd keep it.

"You were at the slide lecture, weren't you?" Gabriella said. "I was almost certain I saw you, but *he*"—she continued, indicating Thierry— "said that was impossible."

Odile ignored this question. "Right now," she said in her best faux-festive voice, "what I'd most like is a word with your leader. Alone, if that's possible."

"Alone in a crowd," said Gabriella, as if singing to herself, but she made no move to intervene. Meanwhile the doctor had assumed the expression of polite confusion with which, Odile had noticed, he tended to veil his true opinions. Thierry threw a quick glance at each of them, then stepped several feet to the side.

Odile joined him. "What would you say, Thierry, if I told you I can get the three of you out of Paris tonight? In total safety."

"I'd say, great, fantastic, let's do it. But what's the catch?"

She waited a beat before replying. "The catch, as you put it, is that I require the truth from you, the whole truth this time, with no inventive feints and flourishes. If you lie to me in one single detail—and I'll know right away if you do—I will pick up the phone and have the Russians on you so fast that your scheming little mind will spin until it stops for good. Which in this case shouldn't take very long at all, I'd imagine. What do you think?"

Thierry looked out over the crowd. The recorded MC, now female, was singing very fast, over and over: *Nu-oh / We'll never go / We'll never go / Cha-ching! / Cha-ching! / Nu-oh / We'll never go / We'll never go . . .*

Throwing a quick glance behind her, Odile saw that Allegra and Dominique remained where she'd left them. They were talking and hugging and giving off a glow. *Good,* she thought. The night, she was beginning to suspect, would be long. She turned back to Thierry.

"Why would you want to help us now?" said Thierry. "And what if you don't like the truth?"

"The truth is not to be liked or disliked. It simply is. I want to know it, and I want all the rest of this to disappear from my life forever. By dawn at the latest, I definitely will have made this happen in every particular. So, if you care at all for your safety or that of your friends, you'd better choose how you want to play it. Immediately. Right now."

Thierry produced a pack of American cigarettes and offered her one that she refused. He took it for himself. "As I said before," he reminded her, "the more you know, the more you'll be at risk. You understand this isn't about a few flags, correct?"

She waved his words and cigarette smoke impatiently away. "We've been through all this. Don't you get it? *I don't care.*"

He nodded past her to Gabriella and the doctor, smiling to indicate that all was fundamentally on track. "If you say so. But then how do I know you're not working for the other side now?"

"You mean the Russians? Because in that case I would've fed you to them long ago and washed my hands of this whole embarrassment. Besides, did I not bring you the thirty thousand?"

Someone was distributing glo-light necklaces, a gesture that lent the proceedings a suitable retro touch. As Odile surveyed the room, she saw that chemical goodwill was much more prevalent among the guests than she'd first thought.

"I like your haircut," Thierry said.

"I like yours," she answered evenly.

"So," he asked, scratching his neck, "how do I know this escape plan you're proposing is real?"

"You don't. But consider the alternatives."

"And what I tell you will remain only with you? Nobody else? Not even your husband?"

"You have my word."

He exhaled smoke lengthily, waiting out one last moment of doubt before he began. "All right. Everything I said at your house is true. Except there was no passport to be delivered en route to Moscow, not then. And the refrigerator unit really was a refrigerator unit."

"Containing human egg cells, perhaps?"

"Yes." He looked troubled, as though about to qualify what he'd just said, but he let it stand.

Odile inspected him closely. "Egg cells you were taking to your doctor friend, yes?"

Thierry sighed massively. "You really are too smart for your own good, you know."

"My own good's my own business. Tell me what the original plan was, *and* what it is now. Or, you know—or else."

"The plan." He scratched his head pensively. "Well, without getting too technical, I will tell you that Dr. Tregobov has perfected—"

"Get technical. As you said, I'm a smart girl."

"So you know what stem cells are, I assume?"

"Of course. Pluripotent cells is the technical term, I think, something like that. They're the ones capable of growing into just about any kind of human tissue. The idea is to use them for therapeutic purposes, organ repair in particular. Right now they're more or less the holy grail of genetic research. The big problem, as I recall, is how to direct them to grow into the exact kind of tissue you want—Nobel Prize guaranteed for whoever figures it out." She felt herself growing irritated again. "I do read the newspapers, you know."

"And you're familiar with the whole idiotic uproar over using human eggs, with their DNA replaced by someone else's, to produce these stem cells? The so-called moral dimension?"

"Of course," she snapped. "But all that was taken care of a year or two ago. When they figured out how to use skin cells, I think it was, instead of embryos to start a stem-cell line."

"No," Thierry said. "It wasn't taken care of. Because the truth is that the younger the starter cell, the better the results. And what's younger than an embryo?"

At that moment a black-clad kid, dancing wildly and wearing pink prism glasses, crashed into Odile from behind. Pushing him violently away, she shouted after him, "Fuck you, monkey boy!" She knew she wasn't contributing to the sought-after atmosphere of peace and tolerance, but she didn't care about that either. "Hurry up!" she told Thierry, who was laughing despite himself.

"Patience, my little horror, patience." He ran a hand over his scalp as if he still had hair. "The crux of the matter is that Dr. Tregobov has worked out a process for turning on and off the genetic material that has been added to the egg—whose own nucleus has been removed, remember—so that it will infallibly turn into stem cells. This is a first, a great discovery. But. The exact proteins required to make this happen must be adjusted to suit the cytoplasm, the denucleated egg cell. Unfortunately, not all cytoplasm works equally well with this process. So a two-step approach is required for each case. The doctor needs a first set of eggs from the donor, both to see if the cytoplasm is viable and, if so, to adjust his standard protein set for the woman in question. Then he can store the unique protein signature he arrives at, the essential information, on a gene chip—which these days can be nothing more than an ordinary DVD—so that, should he have to leave his lab suddenly, as Dr. Tregobov obviously did, he needn't bring the actual stem cell line with him. Instead he can re-create it from the DVD and a second set of donated eggs from the same woman. Are you with me?"

"Perfectly," Odile said. "Now tell me what you *don't* want to tell me."

"Kukushkin's idea was to have his fiancée donate the eggs. For this he promised to get Tregobov out of Belarus, a most disagreeable place, as I'm sure you would concur. Fine. But there's more: Kukushkin also wanted the doctor to share with this woman the worldwide patent rights to his incredibly promising, not to say staggeringly lucrative, scientific breakthrough. Tregobov agreed immediately, of course, the potential earnings from his discovery being virtually limitless." Stroking his chin dreamily, Thierry grew reflective. "It's very clever, the way Kukushkin works, keeping his own name at a distance from his various projects. One can always learn from him." He shook his head in what Odile took to be admiration.

She glanced back one last time at the girls. Allegra was braiding a love lock into Dominique's hair and talking nonstop.

"At any rate," Thierry went on, "my task, which you somehow deduced, was to drop off the first set of eggs at the Brest station so they could be tested. If their cytoplasm was found viable, their necessary protein signature would be worked out and put on a DVD. The dropoff went very smoothly. One of Tregobov's assistants met me at the station, where I gave him the refrigeration unit and returned to you. A walk in the park." Overhead, in the middle of the stone ceiling, an electric candelabra flickered dimly to life. A couple of boys on a stepladder had been working on it for some time, and there was scattered applause as everyone looked up to admire the fixture.

"But then, coming back," Odile prompted.

"Not so smooth," agreed Thierry. "I was supposed to provide Tregobov with that EU passport—his Belarussian one having been confiscated—and bring him back to Paris with us. But there was no one—not a soul!—waiting for me in the Brest station. So I had no choice, I had to stay behind and work something out."

"That's quite a commitment," said Odile. "What did Kukushkin give you for this extra initiative? Another thirty thousand francs?"

Thierry looked away, feigning distraction.

"Don't worry," Odile told him. "I already know you replaced Kukushkin's fiancée's eggs with Gabriella's." She tried, but failed, to suppress a triumphant smile. "Turner found out that Gabriella had been taking fertility drugs," she explained. "It was just a guess on my part that you had her eggs with you, in that container. But that's right, isn't it?"

Thierry didn't dispute the point. "And does Kukushkin know?" he said.

"I'm not sure. At first I think he was just upset when you didn't bring him the doctor. But then, when his associates discovered that Gabriella was your girlfriend, and *she* disappeared too . . ."

"Right."

Odile glanced away. Many of the dancers were chewing on pacifiers to avoid grinding their teeth—a hazard of the drug, she seemed to recall. "It's possible there are other elements involved," she said finally, "but I don't really know. What I do know is that if I were you, I'd plan for the worst." She watched him carefully, but he didn't flinch. "I take it Tregobov doesn't know you switched the eggs."

"No, but he couldn't care less. They're compatible with his process. Now that he's out of Belarus, his only concern is to get to England, which has laws very supportive of stem cell research. He's anxious to have the patent approved, so his discovery will be officially credited to him outside the usual professional journals. Money doesn't seem to matter much to him, except to fund his work, of course. He's a scientist. Whether he shares the patent with Kukushkin's fiancée or Gabriella isn't even on his radar. His only concern is that the cytoplasm be viable."

"Lucky for you." She was about to go on when she felt her waist suddenly encircled by youthful arms, sweaty and affectionate.

"I love you, Odile," said Dominique, "and this is so much fun. But we're really *hot*, and there's no more water."

"Don't worry. We're going to leave in a minute, sweetheart. Please, would you and Allegra go find Chantal? And I'll meet the three of you over there by that swastika sign, all right?"

Dominique looked suddenly anxious. "You won't tell my father, will you?"

"We can talk about that on the way." She gave the girl a hug. "Now, get going." Dominique hurried off.

"So that's my story," Thierry said. "What's your plan?"

"I want the three of you to meet me at midnight at le quai de la Tournelle. There's a houseboat tied up there called the *Nachtvlinder*. You'll see it. There'll be one blue light turned on at the top of the wheelhouse, otherwise nothing. Don't call out, just come aboard as quietly as you can. I'll explain the rest then."

He appeared to think about it. "You wouldn't set us up, would you, Odile? I mean, a boat is so much like a trap, when you think about it."

"Set you up?" She laughed in his face. "No, I just want to believe a new life is possible, even if not for me. Surely you can understand that."

Thierry suppressed a smile but nodded as though admiring an unusually deft bit of handiwork. "All right, then. We'll see you at midnight."

"On the dot," Odile added, though it made no difference if he arrived promptly or not.

"On the dot," he repeated, eyes sparkling, then he turned and rejoined his group.

Not much later, the girls showed up with Chantal, whom Odile asked to get them to street level. Their exit from the bunker was considerably less taxing than their entrance, but once back in the passages, they had to go down a couple of levels before ascending again, passing countless side tunnels—the real catacombs—piled three or four feet deep with human bones and receding immeasurably into the distance. At the mouth of one lay a pair of latex gloves. Allegra stopped to stare at them.

"What?" Odile asked.

"This," Allegra said. "I've seen it all before. Those gloves. The four of us standing here. The water dripping down the walls. Dominique twisting her hair and holding it up like that. The bones crisscrossed just like that. Everything."

No one could think of what to say to this, and in twenty minutes they were on the street. Odile flagged down a cab. As they lurched off, she took out her cell phone to see if Eddie Bouvier was home.

# CHAPTER 31

"THREE HUNDRED THOUSAND, then. Do I hear three fifty? Will anyone say three fifty? No?" The auctioneer brought down his gavel with a crack. "Sold, to the gentleman in the back row."

Since first entering the auction hall, Max had been on the lookout for Turner, though he hadn't settled on an appropriate course of action, if action was even what he wanted. Then he'd been almost immediately distracted by the unforeseen presence of Véronique and the Russian she was with, who was undoubtedly the business partner she'd told him about and most likely her lover. The two of them had moved down a place each, so Max was seated next to her on the aisle, and her gardenia-laced perfume only added to his distraction. He hoped she wouldn't flirt with him in Kukushkin's presence, but even as he entertained this thought she leaned one breast into the crook of his arm and whispered, "I never thought I'd see *you* tonight."

"Likewise," he replied as quietly as he could.

"Are you here to bid?" she asked.

"No. Actually, I'm looking for a guy who works here, somebody called Turner."

"Really!" She withdrew for a moment and whispered rapidly in Russian to Kukushkin, who nodded. Then she again put her lips to Max's ear. "That's him in the third row, over against the right-hand wall."

Looking, Max saw that it was.

"Lot sixteen," said the auctioneer. "Bidding for this item, a particularly fine example from the Brezhnev era, will begin at one hundred fifty thousand francs. Who will open the bidding? Thank you, Madame. One hundred seventy-five, who will say one seventy-five?"

When it came to marital infidelities, Max had observed, the wronged party invariably reacted in one of two ways—equally comic and devoid of logic—by blaming the betrayal either on the loved one or on the interloper. To his utter lack of surprise, Max fell into the latter category. It was the more practical position, he supposed, if reconciliation was your goal, but choice initially played no part; you reacted according to your nature, pure and simple. What to do about the situation, however, was another question entirely, one in which reason might conceivably be brought to bear, if you proceeded with care and discipline.

"Thank you. Two twenty-five? May I hear two hundred twenty-five thousand? Yes? The bid is now with the gentleman in the back."

Again Max felt Véronique's breast against his arm, her breath in his ear. "Turner," she whispered. "Wasn't he the one who hired your wife to bring these flags back from Moscow in the first place?"

He looked at her without responding. Maybe, he thought, there was a shape to the evening's events and accident didn't figure into it.

"Fair warning, then . . . Anybody? So, sold at two hundred twenty-five thousand francs.

Kukushkin leaned past Véronique to speak to Max. "In Russia, we have joke. We say, everything Soviet leaders told us about socialism was total lie. But at same time, everything they told us about capitalism was completely correct. This is the world we inherit, no?"

Max laughed politely. "You won't get any argument from me."

The porters were removing the sold lot from the stage.

"Véronique tells me you are filmmaker. I think this must be very expensive occupation."

"It can be. But I don't make Hollywood films. All I need is enough money to make the next film, although even that much can be hard enough to scrape together, believe me."

"Yes. I think Hollywood films must be like making war. Moving many people and much heavy equipment around for months and months—even years—with timing impossible, long supply lines, unpredictable results. Very costly. If you succeed, everyone is hero. If not, then you, the general, will be hanged in the streets like a dog."

Max thought this an odd thing to say to a new acquaintance, but since it was also perfectly true both he and Véronique laughed.

"Now Kolya's the king of capitalists," she explained. "But his background is a little different from yours and mine. So he brings a unique perspective to business affairs."

"I can imagine."

The porters brought the next lot in and placed it on the display easel. This was another of the prize pieces, featuring head-and-shoulder images of Lenin and Khrushchev, shown side by side at daringly equal size, shortly before the latter's fall from grace. The bidding began at a hundred fifty thousand and continued briskly until it reached three seventy-five. There was a lull, then a man who sounded unmistakably Swiss put in a preemptive bid of five hundred thousand. At the same moment, Max, caught up in the drama of the sale, felt Véronique's hand squeeze his thigh hard. She lifted her chin brusquely in the direction of the exit, where Turner, already halfway through the door, was making a hasty departure. The hammer came down on the lot. With a glance at Kukushkin, Max excused himself and, still lacking a clear plan, hastened after the man he believed to be his wife's lover. It had never occurred to him that Turner might actually flee.

The area immediately outside the auction hall was deserted except for security and another of the auction-house girls in black, her superior status indicated by a second pearl choker immediately above the first. There was no one on the marble staircase, and Max heard no footsteps on the lower flights.

"Excuse me," he asked the girl, "is there an elevator?"

"Certainly. Right over there." She pointed down the corridor.

But when he reached the elevator, the ornate needle above it indicated that it was already descending. He debated trying to outrun it using the stairs, but immediately saw that by escalating the level of physical exertion he'd be committing himself to an outcome that could only be more physical still. It would embarrass everyone and almost certainly prove counterproductive. As a compromise measure, and to regain some degree of dignity, he recalled the elevator, took it to ground level, and had a look around the street outside. Once convinced that Turner had eluded him, he went back inside, relieved that he'd avoided what surely would've been a fiasco. He reached the fourth floor just as the auction was letting out. *Reason, care, and discipline,* he reminded himself.

Kukushkin and Véronique emerged from the sale arm in arm, their expressions growing concerned when they spotted him. They made a handsome couple, expensive looking and substantial. "Apparently Mr. Turner was in unusual hurry tonight," Kukushkin said. "Perhaps because he made so much money."

"Yes, I lost him," Max admitted. "Is he a friend of yours?"

The crowd flowed around the three of them and down the staircase, talking excitedly. It had been a very successful sale—over ten million francs, twice the expected gross.

"Oh, I have small business with him from time to time. Besides, he is fixture in art world, well known in certain circles. And you, you know him well?"

"No," said Max. "I've only met him once."

The couple stared at him, waiting for him to say more. When it became apparent he didn't intend to elaborate, Kukushkin smiled at him in what seemed to be good-natured sympathy. "May I propose, in that case, you join us for a drink? Véronique and I would greatly enjoy the honor of your company, and my club is around the corner. You might find it amusing place." He leaned forward and added, in a melodramatic stage whisper, "Russian, *very* Russian."

Max hesitated, seized again by the sense that he'd stumbled into something much larger than it had first appeared, with his part already choreographed. But he brushed away his doubts. In times like these, forward was the only possible direction. "It would be a pleasure," he replied.

After walking a couple of blocks, they arrived before a massive oaken door with no windows and no apparent street number. Instead, it bore an iron-grillework peephole at eye level and, just below that, seven brass Cyrillic letters, Медведь, meticulously polished and set flush into the wood. Kukushkin, his fist poised to knock, turned playfully to Max. "Do you know what it is meaning, this word?" He pointed to the brass letters.

"Sorry, I don't have any Russian at all. But I guess it must be the name of the place, right?"

Kukushkin roared with laughter and began to pound the door thunderously, announcing his presence in shouted Russian for good measure.

"It means 'The Bear,'" Véronique told Max, as if apologizing for Kukushkin's failure to answer. "The bear, of course, is a symbol for Russia." She shrugged. "Sentimental—but really, these days, who cares?"

"Not us," said Max, testing his ground. She smiled—a little grimly, he thought.

Finally, the iron bar covering the peephole slid to one side and a pair of ice-blue eyes appeared at the grille. Then the bar slid shut again, the door swung open, and a blast of cigarette smoke and disco music escaped into the night. The three new arrivals filed in, the door closed loudly behind them, a deadbolt slammed shut. From several quarters, shouts of welcome greeted Max's host.

"You realize," Véronique whispered, "that when Kolya calls this place his club, he's speaking literally."

"You mean he owns it."

"Exactly. Along with many other things, of course."

They were standing beside a long mahogany bar that serviced the entry area. Set against the opposite wall was a red leather banquette with a dozen small zinc-topped tables positioned closely before it. A tall muscular man in a black suit and gray roll-neck sweater—the manager, Max presumed—came forward to give Kukushkin a crushing embrace and the traditional three kisses. He ceremoniously pressed his lips to Véronique's hand and shook Max's, then returned his attention to his boss, and they at once fell into serious conversation. At a glance from Kukushkin, Véronique took Max's arm and guided him past the bar to three broad steps that led down into the primary space. They stopped there at the threshold, as if their mission were purely educational, arranged for Max's benefit, as perhaps it was.

The club had two stories, with a mezzanine running around the three nearer sides and projecting a few feet over the main floor. Semicircular booths of black leather lined the walls, which were covered with flocked red wallpaper, while widely spaced tables occupied the center of the room. Beyond them, in the back, was a parquet dance floor on which six or seven conspicuously well-dressed couples were dancing in desultory fashion, colored lights playing over them from above. Finally, against the rear wall, on a shallow platform that stretched the width of the room, was a fifteen-foot-tall effigy of a bear, rearing up ferociously. Hollow and made from clear acrylic, it was filled with water in which a hundred or more goldfish swam contentedly. To either side of this extravagance, and effortlessly upstaging it, half a dozen improbably beautiful women, expressionless and perfectly naked, their pubic hair shaved into identical vertical strips, lent themselves to the music with neither complaint nor enthusiasm. Flower arrangements towered here and there about the room. Except for colored spots over the dance floor and those trained on the girls and the bear, the lighting was dim, but Max guessed there were maybe forty patrons downstairs, with another twenty-five on the mezzanine. It was a little past nine thirty.

"Yes," Max said after a time. "Quite Russian."

"It's not my favorite place," Véronique allowed, "but sometimes it has its advantages." She smiled at him. "Anyway, we have a private room upstairs that's very nice. I'll show you." With a quick glance over her shoulder, she added, "Kolya will be along any minute. We'd better hurry."

# CHAPTER 32

OUT OF THE AUCTION HOUSE and onto the street, Turner forced himself to slow down, turning corners randomly until he sighted an inconspicuous, mid-block *brasserie,* soothingly crowded. Squeezing himself in at the bar, even though a few tables remained free, he ordered a double whiskey and drained it at once. He ordered another and, despite the bartender's disapproving gaze, bolted it down too. He grew somewhat calmer. By the time his third drink arrived, he remembered that he was armed, that he'd just made a little under ten million francs, and that he was, for better or worse, in love. He made an effort then to behave more befittingly, sipping rather than gulping his drink and examining his surroundings in the mirror behind the bar as if considering, in a detached if not entirely theoretical way, what they might be worth to him should he decide to make an on-the-spot offer. Before long, he was himself again.

It was fear, of course, that had driven him from the auction floor.

He had lived with various kinds of fear all his life. About this he was undeceived and also, though he admitted this to no one, unashamed. It took a clear eye and philosophical cast of mind to see the benefits embedded in this accident of temperament, one which for him had been compacted into a kind of credo: *I fear, therefore I am.* It was that simple. So many had less.

And yet.

Lately—he couldn't say exactly when—he had begun wondering if this view hadn't outlived its usefulness, or worse, without his noticing, had ceased to be true at all. For instance, he knew quite well that he harbored little fear of Max Colby. Over the years, he'd had to deal with his fair share of disobliged husbands, and by now he knew pretty much what to expect from them and how to handle it. Even Kukushkin, whose threats and messages had been far from subtle, was no longer enough to inspire real terror, at least not face-to-face. It was clear that Kolya, despite his air of understated, carefully tended ruthlessness, wanted to maintain a healthy distance from whatever extralegal activities might be carried out at his behest. He saw himself as a gentleman and, for the most part, wanted others to as well.

So if what had driven Turner so precipitously from the auction was fear, it wasn't the kind to which he was accustomed. Two worlds he had believed were completely separate had just now collided, to effects unknowable at best. That the woman with the tattoo had seen fit to bring Max and Kukushkin together—their meeting seeming less and less plausibly accidental—both puzzled and alarmed him. The fear unfolding in him now, he saw, belonged to an entirely new order that rendered his old credo useless. He was afraid this time of losing something irreplaceable, he was afraid for someone else.

After paying his bar bill, he walked for some time without purpose, avoiding the larger thoroughfares. When he happened past a bus stop shaded from its streetlight by a chestnut tree, he sat down and, after several seconds wasted pointlessly in thought, called Odile's cell. To his surprise, she answered on the second ring—though still talking over her shoulder to someone else, as if to indicate she wasn't alone, not at home, not to be trifled with.

"Hi, it's me. Can you talk?"

"Hang on a minute."

He heard her walk into another room and close the door. Somewhere in the background children were laughing.

"So, Turner, my dear. How was your auction?"

"From a financial point of view, outstanding. We netted about twice what I expected—a little under ten million, after the house cut."

"We? Who might that be?"

"Well, you can have half of it if you like," he heard himself say.

She laughed. "Thank you, but no. This sudden wealth, I think, would be difficult to explain."

"Suit yourself." He took a deep breath. "But there were some other surprises, too."

"Such as?" Odile said quietly.

"Your husband was in attendance, for one thing."

After a small silence, she said, "He saw the article in *Le Monde*. He asked me to go to the auction with him, and when I said no, I guess he decided to go by himself. Did you talk to him?"

"No, but I think we can assume he knows."

"Yes, he noticed the watch, I'm fairly sure. And of course, if one puts that together with everything else . . ."

"But there's more. He was sitting with Kukushkin and a woman I don't know, probably his girlfriend. She knew your husband. In fact, she seemed to be introducing them right there for the first time."

"What? I don't believe you."

"I left before the end—to avoid Kukushkin, of course. But I do wonder what direction your husband and Kukushkin's conversation might've taken, especially given a discreet nudge by this very *enthusiastic* girl. Any ideas?"

There ensued a much longer silence. "What does she look like?"

"Late twenties, blond, some kind of tattoo on her arm. A wheel, I think."

"I don't know her."

"It seemed that she and your husband hadn't expected to run into each other, but I'm not really sure about that. Anyway, she was clearly with Kukushkin—his date, as it were—and she introduced them right away. Almost as if she'd already spoken to each about the other—favorably, by the looks of it—and their curiosity was sufficiently piqued for her to bring them together."

This time the silence was so long that Turner wondered if the connection had been lost. "Hello?"

"I'm here."

"Look," he said, "I need to see you."

She sighed. "That can't happen tonight, Turner. I've got to be somewhere."

"Somewhere?"

"A dinner party at Rachel and Groot's—you know, my houseboat friends. It was meant to make Max forget about the auction, though obviously *that* didn't work."

"But Odile, something's happening, something serious. I can feel it. Kukushkin, your husband . . . I'm worried about you."

"Don't. It's a waste of time."

"What's that boat called? It has a Dutch name, doesn't it? The *Nacht* something or other?"

"No, you're absolutely *not* to come down there! Do you understand? For any reason at all."

"But just in case."

Again, a pause. "What's that? I can't hear you clearly. You're breaking up."

"At least call me later, so I'll know you're all right."

"Hello? Hel*lo*? Damn these things."

The connection seemed perfectly clear to Turner. "Odile?"

"Shit! Now I can't understand a word you're saying. All I'm getting at this end is static. But I'm grateful for the alert, if *you*, by some chance, can hear *me*. Yes? No? Fuck, that's it, it's pointless to go on. We might as well be talking to outer space."

And with that the line went dead.

HER THUMB STILL PRESSED to the end button, Odile leaned up against the wall and closed her eyes for a moment while she caught her breath. "Bye," she said in afterthought, dropping the phone back into her purse.

She stepped over to the mirror and pinched her cheeks a few times when she saw how pale she looked, then returned to Eddie Bouvier's living room, where he and the two girls had started—and were even half attending to—a game of blackjack. All three looked up at Odile as if they'd been waiting for her for hours, though it hadn't been ten minutes since she'd swept in with Dominique and Allegra, fresh from the catacombs. The druggy glow still enveloped the girls, but Eddie appeared not to notice.

"Papa, can Allegra and I just go to my room and listen to some music?" Dominique asked. "I'm really not in the mood for cards."

"Go. We adults will do just fine without you and your moods." He gathered up the cards and shuffled them distractedly.

As she got up from the table, Allegra went over to Odile and whispered in her ear, "Remember what you promised!"

"Remember what *you* promised," Odile replied with a smile.

The girls vanished like cats. Eddie fanned the cards out before Odile and she took one, laying it faceup on the table. The queen of spades. He picked it up without interest and returned it to the deck. Then he wearily put the deck aside.

"Thanks so much for looking after Allegra tonight," said Odile. "Max and my plans got badly scrambled when they decided they didn't want to go to that party after all."

"Not a problem." Eddie settled back in his chair. "But I wonder what made them change their minds. Earlier, they were so eager to go."

"Oh, I don't know, they had some petty quarrel with the girl giving it, what's her name."

"Lili de Bassignol."

"Yes, Lili. Something to do with the guest list. Anyway, you can be sure that by tomorrow they'll have forgotten all about it. I remember being thirteen. It's not easy."

"On the other hand," Eddie said, "it's not so easy being my age either. Fewer surprises, less forgetfulness."

They laughed.

Odile folded her legs under her. "Speaking of surprises, how's your brother, the besotted bridegroom?"

"To tell you the truth, he's driving me crazy. It's his wedding plans. He calls me three times a day to ask advice: how this is done, how that is done, what do I think of this caterer, that florist—ad infinitum. Naturally, Gaspard's ghastly girlfriend wants a very grand wedding reception, highly visible. And in Paris."

"So I take it the detective turned up no skeletons in her closet?"

"Ah, the detective." Eddie's eyes went distant, and there followed a silence so lengthy that Odile grew uncomfortable. It was as if he'd totally forgotten she was there. Then, just when she was about to say something, anything, to reestablish her presence, he snapped back to awareness and smiled at her.

"Everybody has secrets; it goes without saying. And this detective found out a great deal about this Strasbourg girl, who, believe me, has more to conceal than most brides-to-be. But as your friend Rachel so sensibly predicted, none of this affected Gaspard in the least when I told him." Eddie shook his head. "I should've known."

"Love is blind," said Odile gently, her gaze fixed for some reason on the tabletop. "Otherwise, you know, there'd be so very little of it."

"Practically none," Eddie agreed, reaching for his glass.

They smiled at this reminder of their similar view of the world, one not always available or congenial to others, which was fine with them.

Odile said, "I've been meaning to tell you. Dominique's doing much better, I think. She still has her moods, but more out of habit than anything else. Happiness used to terrify her; now she's only suspicious of it. Like the rest of us." Odile laughed. "But she'll be okay, I'm certain."

"I hope you're right. These days, it's hard to tell."

Odile left a small interval, then asked, "Does she ever see her mother?"

"Her mother's running a bamboo tourist hotel in Bali, as I may have already told you. So the long answer, politely put, is no."

"Oh yes, I remember." Odile pretended to hesitate, then to make up her mind. "You know, Dominique and I are getting along very well lately. Of course, we've been seeing much more of each other since Allegra arrived. Anyway, tonight I told her that she should feel free to come by anytime to talk or just hang out, with or without Allegra. I hope you don't mind."

Eddie's face lit up. "Really? Are you serious? Odile, you're an angel!"

"*That* we both know to be a lie. But at least I'll try not to encourage her toward devil worship, all right?" She swallowed and tried to smile. Eddie's compliment had frightened her. It reminded her of what the night's business might yet entail. Already she was on her feet.

"Odile, I cannot tell you how grateful I am. She desperately needs a woman to confide in, a woman of the world like—"

"Forgive me, Eddie. I've got to run." She pulled her sweater from the closet and threw it over her shoulders, failing, in her haste, to allow him the courtly pleasure of helping her into it. "May I ask a favor?" she said instead. "Would you call Max and tell him the girls decided against the party, and Allegra's spending the night here, but that everything's fine?" Checking her watch, she added, "Better try his mobile, because I'm not quite sure where he is just now."

"Absolutely. I'll do it right away."

At the door, when they embraced, he drew back and looked at her with concern. "But Odile, you've lost so much weight!"

She gave him a crooked smile. "It's an experiment."

"An experiment? In what?" He followed her out into the hall.

The elevator was already there. She got in, drew the accordion gate shut, and, as she started down, called back up to him, "I'm fasting. I want to see what it's like not to eat."

THEY WERE ENSCONCED in Kukushkin's private aerie—a soundproofed, wood-paneled chapel of calm, fitted out with antique birchwood furniture from Saint Petersburg that over the centuries had been lovingly rubbed to a golden glow. Only a row of security video monitors and a window, mirrored on its other side, that looked out on the floor below gave any evidence of the club's more public revels, which had by now picked up noticeably.

Kukushkin removed an open vodka bottle from a solid block of ice and poured Max, Véronique, and himself another round. There had been many such rounds, requiring many lengthy toasts, but now that they were on their second liter things had become much less formal, the toasts more like token interruptions in the ongoing conversation. Other than this loosening of ritual, however, neither Kukushkin nor Véronique seemed at all affected by the alcohol. Max kept up with them—this, too, was obligatory—but was trying miserably to conceal his drunkenness.

They raised their glasses.

*"Za lyubov!"* Kukushkin offered with a glint in his eye.

All downed their drinks, then, as was customary, took a bite of the accompanying *zakushi*—pickled baby beets, stalks of wild garlic, caviar on black bread, and other delicacies—lavishly laid out on a silver platter.

"It means," Véronique explained to Max, " 'Let us drink to love.' " Then, to Kukushkin: "Max is one of the very lucky few who actually love their wives. He told me this almost as soon as I met him. And I believe it's true."

Kukushkin laughed. "Perhaps lucky because honorable, yes? Not every man meeting beautiful young woman in a café would be so quick to mention his wife, I assure you." Then, to Max: "You are honorable, Max?"

They stared at him with disconcertingly intense curiosity.

"I'd like to think so," Max replied. "And, yes, I do love my wife. But of course, deep down, like all men, I'm probably capable of anything, given the right circumstances. It's what you decide you can live with *afterward* that determines how far you let yourself go, assuming you're in control of your actions in the first place, needless to say. At least that's my opinion."

His listeners nodded encouragingly, waiting for him to go on.

"Well, for instance, to lie is dangerous, destructive, and often stupid. To lie to yourself is worse still. Both lead to chaos, misunderstanding, and wasted time, which I personally abhor. But not to lie at all can be just as dangerous, just as destructive and stupid. To use the truth as a blunt object with which to batter people over the head, who would say that's a good thing? So the problem becomes, where to draw the line?"

"Indeed," said Kukushkin, glancing quickly at the security monitors. "Very difficult problem. But to be in control of all actions: this is *central* problem. Precondition of honor."

"Yes, of course."

"So. I conclude you are honorable man after all, Max. Not Pushkin, maybe, but honorable man." Kukushkin inspected him closely, then roared with laughter. Max politely joined him, but Véronique looked away with undisguised discomfort.

"What about you, Kolya?" Max asked. "Also honorable?"

"This is subject not yet fully addressed," the Russian said gruffly, though amusement again rippled visibly through him.

Thinking about his moral pronouncement, Max was compelled to recall how easily a person might pass from liquor-fueled eloquence into incoherence of one sort or another, all equally unwelcome. And yet the present bottle, now that it was opened, would have to be finished if Max wasn't to insult his hosts, so he took advantage of the lull in the conversation to pour them each another round. After this, he estimated, just one more would be left. That would signal the end of their evening together. He'd enjoyed it, but enough was enough.

"*Na zdorovie!*" he said, raising his glass.

"*Na zdorovie!*" the other two repeated.

All drank, then reached for the *zakushi*.

Kukushkin had just raised a stalk of wild garlic to his mouth when something he saw through the window caught his attention, and he flung the morsel back on his plate, cursing softly. Following his gaze, Max saw that a fight had broken out on the dance floor—two leather-clad young men trading blows at an incredible, almost robotic rate. Both wore heavy gold rings, and there was already quite a lot of blood. Kukushkin picked up a nearby phone, spoke a few words of Russian into it, and immediately four security men, automatic pistols drawn, appeared downstairs to separate the men and escort them roughly out of the club. The clientele appeared unfazed. No doubt they'd seen it all before.

"Please excuse momentary unpleasantness," Kukushkin told Max, "but is inevitable, you know. Russians very passionate people."

"Famously so," said Max. "In your literature, in your music and dance, in everything requiring . . . *dusha. Dusha* means soul, right? If I remember correctly."

Again Kukushkin and Véronique studied him more clinically than Max thought suitable to the occasion. They seemed to be waiting for him to reveal something necessary, even crucial, to the fruition of interests as yet unspecified, and, worse, were making a quiet display of their patience. He felt a twinge of resentment. Had the three of them not exchanged nearly two liters' worth of cheer, friendship, personal confession, and moral speculation right here in this very room? Should trust not follow naturally from all that had been said and shared and sworn to for eternity and beyond?

What, otherwise, was the point? Were they not all bent on ascertaining the truth, however discomfiting, strange, or disappointing?

The truth! Only then did he realize just how hopelessly drunk he was, how inane. The truth. He'd dropped his guard, then lost it altogether. That wasn't like him, and quite probably he'd pay dearly for the lapse. But so be it. He'd proceed from here because this was where he was, and because so much remained to be done. Miles to go before he slept? Fine. He was up to it.

Kukushkin said, "I see you are cultivated man, knowledgeable in culture and arts. Also in deepest dramas of human heart. Love, violence, honor. Who knows, maybe even loss and grief, suffering. You know suffering?"

"As much as most men my age," said Max.

"Yes, yes. This too I see." Kukushkin's eyes were fixed thoughtfully on Max. "Allow me to tell you story. Do not worry, is not *War and Peace*, only short anecdote, personal in nature. Okay?"

"Certainly. I'm very interested to hear it."

Now Véronique was staring at Max with an intensity even greater than before, as if his reaction to what he was about to be told would determine the fate of her most cherished hopes, perhaps the very hopes she'd confided to him at one of their meetings, though at the moment he couldn't recall quite what those hopes were.

"My father, Ivan Kyrillovitch—this was in Stalin period, after war, but still very shitty time for Russia—had two great strokes of fortune in life. One, he was musical genius. Straight from childhood he played violin like someone not of this earth, full of that quality so rare, even in most technically accomplished musicians, that it cannot be named, only recognized. Is possible to call this quality depth of feeling or maybe soulfulness that can move dictators to tears. But I will tell you, it was more than that. Much more."

Kukushkin removed a pack of Turkish cigarettes from his breast pocket, offered them around, and, when he had no takers, took one for himself. He lit it and smoked for a moment or two in silence. Max looked at Véronique for guidance, but she, still studying him intently, offered no help.

"Fortunate stroke number two. He married my mother, poor girl from Odessa who came to Moscow to study ballet. Very beautiful, very hard-working, not egomaniac like most dancers. When he met Irina, she had just been accepted to join Bolshoi. One year later they were married, not rich but happy, and life goes on for some time. I am not yet in picture."

For a moment, Véronique's fix on Max wavered and, laughing softly, she said, as if to herself, "Imagine Kolya not in the picture. Would this be good or bad, I wonder."

Kukushkin smiled. "For my father, I think, it was bad, but this Max will soon decide himself. When Stalin died, people also asked, is good or bad? But that is different story."

"Perhaps," said Véronique enigmatically.

"Okay. So, for my father, there develops big problem: one day, after a couple years of marriage, suddenly his musical gift, his special way of playing, has been taken from him. Still he has technique, still he has job, still he can play, but: feeling is gone. He who played for only this feeling and its emotional effect on *audience*, okay? The spiritual *transports!* Music and my mother were twin joys of his *life!*" Kukushkin drew deeply on his cigarette, then slowly exhaled the smoke. "Meanwhile, my mother, career is taking off. Dancing more and more lead roles, traveling with company to Europe. She is celebrated, happy. And all this time my father grows more and more—what is word?—morose. Yes, morose is also big part of Russian temperament. Part of *dusha.*"

"Kolya, my love," Véronique interrupted, "please get to the point. I'm sure Max will have to leave before long." She touched his shoulder affectionately but returned her attention to Max, scrutinizing him as before. The effect, he decided, was a bit strange but not at all unpleasant.

"Yes, yes," Kukushkin said, releasing yet another cloud of blue smoke that Véronique hastened to wave away, lest it obscure her line of sight. "So, long story short, my father tries everything he can to regain gift, mastery. Works with concertmaster. Plays different, very *special* violins. Consults other very *talented,* even world-*famous* musicians. Nothing works. Finally he confides in best friend, tells best friend he is in despair, perhaps cannot go on, et cetera, et cetera. Friend is silent for long time. Finally he says, 'You know, Ivan Kyrillovitch, your wife has been spending great deal of time with principal dancer of ballet company. Is only my opinion, but maybe examination of this most *vibrant* teacher-student relationship—keeping intelligence and heart held close, of course, with benefit of *reason*—would put things back to normal. You never know with music. Its sources, such a mystery.'"

Max couldn't restrain himself. "So your mother was having an affair! Your father sensed it without realizing it, and that's what took the fire out of his music, right?"

"This is exactly so, yes." Kukushkin let some seconds pass in contemplation. "After making discreet inquiries, a few careful *observations,* he determined beyond all doubt that my mother had become the principal dancer's principal lover. Three, sometimes four times a week. It was true."

"And what did he do?" Max asked. "How did he handle it, your father? What did he do?"

Véronique's gray-blue eyes now bored into him with a harsh, expectant light that he ignored.

"Most important," Kukushkin continued, "is what he did *not* do. He did not confront his wife with what he knew. Why? Because then he would lose her, most certainly. This is axiomatic."

"Yes, I . . . I do see that. But what, then?"

Kukushkin shrugged and stubbed out his cigarette. "He waits until my mother takes trip to visit family, then goes to this man's house and shoots him dead while sleeping. Most effective solution. Permanent."

Max sat back in his chair, stunned. "But your mother must've been devastated."

"She was sad for a time, but she had no idea her husband was responsible. Crime never solved because no one ever tried—what but trouble could result? So after two, three months, my mother realized this was life, that she loved her husband, and wanted both to be happy." He paused. "Less than year later I was born." He laughed. "And here I am."

"What about your father's music? Did he ever get the magic back?"

Kukushkin smiled broadly. "*Da.* He stayed with orchestra one year more, then formed his own string quartet. When LP recordings become possible, they make many successful records. Interpretation in particular of Heinrich Biber's *Mystery Sonatas* is famous throughout Europe and Russia. Very difficult work. Sixteen short pieces, each has different tuning for instruments, not normal one. But he played these sonatas like a god. Now in Germany is plan to reissue recording on CD."

"Amazing."

"And yet it is also *normalno.* Because life is always—how to say?—more receptive, even *accommodating,* to those who know how and when to act." He turned to Véronique. "You agree, *dushka?*"

"Of course." Then, to Max, "Don't you?"

"Absolutely," he answered. "To know . . . and not to act is not to know."

And with that, at long last, Véronique seemed satisfied. More than satisfied. She seemed like a woman who, having bet everything on an intuition, had been proven almost supernaturally astute and deserving of the admiration that had, in any case, been hers all along. She had become, in the most complete sense, beautiful.

Reaching for the vodka bottle, she wordlessly poured them each the final round and replaced the bottle, upside-down, in its sleeve of ice. When all glasses were raised, she bestowed a lingering gaze on each man in turn and, with a smile that Max had never seen before, gave a toast: *"Nu, budem!"* She turned to him. "It means, 'And now, let us live!' "

The three observed a moment of thoughtful silence, then drank.

Going downstairs, Max stumbled a little—he was very drunk—and Véronique took his arm to steady him. While Kukushkin gave the club manager some parting instructions, she said quietly to Max, "I'm still looking for that man I told you about, the man who has something of mine, something personal. His name is Thierry Colin, should you happen to run across him, as you very well might."

"Why do you say that?"

"Because Paris is quite small in some respects. And because now Kolya and I trust you completely."

"That's good to hear. In any case, I'm glad I'm not Thierry Colin, not in this small place."

She threw a darting glance to see if Kukushkin was watching, and then, suppressing a giggle, kissed Max lavishly on the lips. "So am I," she said, her eyes glittering. "That would be highly inconvenient."

There was a limo waiting by the curb. Kukushkin offered him a ride, which Max politely declined. "It's such a nice night, I think I'll walk." There was a full moon and a gathering fog, which, in combination, made the sky an unearthly white.

"You are going far?" asked Kukushkin, affecting muted concern for Max's condition.

"No, no. Just down to the quai de la Tournelle."

"But that is *quite* far," protested Véronique. "Why don't you come with us?"

At that moment the chauffeur opened the door for her, and Max had the fleeting impression that he'd seen the man before, he couldn't remember when. "No, you're very kind, but I think I need the air."

"Excellent," said Kukushkin. He and Max embraced. "We are friends, yes?"

"We are friends."

"Good." They embraced again. "We will see you soon, then."

"Definitely."

Kukushkin got in, then the chauffeur shut the door behind him and drove them smoothly away, Véronique's arm waving a languid goodbye through the open window.

Only then did Max recall exactly when and where he had seen the driver before: he was one of the strangers who'd looked up at him from outside his studio on the day of Allegra's arrival. But he had no time to consider the significance of this coincidence, because he now remembered he'd failed to turn his cell phone back on after the auction and had missed his daughter's promised nine thirty check-in call.

In a near panic he switched it on. There were no messages from Allegra, but five from Eddie Bouvier. He punched in Eddie's number.

# CHAPTER 33

"YOU DIDN'T LISTEN to my messages," Eddie said reprovingly. In his profession, phone messages were an art form and not to be taken lightly.

"I forgot to turn my cell back on till now. When I did, I saw you'd called, but it just seemed faster to get back to you, to call you . . . directly."

"And you're drunk."

Max grimaced. He hadn't realized it was that obvious. "Okay, maybe a little, I was with Russians. *A* Russian. One Russian. But I'm fine. It's Allegra I'm worried about. She was supposed to call."

"Then you can stop worrying. She's right here, perfectly safe. The girls decided not to go to that party after all, so Odile brought them here for the night. They're in Dominique's room, planning how best to subjugate the male of our species."

"Can I talk to her? Allegra, I mean?"

After a moment's hesitation, Eddie said, "If I were you, Max, I'd wait until . . ."

"Oh, right, okay. Yes, I see what you mean." He made a mighty effort to clear the slurry of syllables from his anesthetized tongue. "And Odile?"

"She's at your friends' houseboat, I think. For dinner." After a pause, Eddie's voice took on a different tone. "So you really didn't listen to my messages, not at all?"

Max grew wary. "No, Eddie. I didn't listen to them."

"Because, besides letting you know that the girls were with me, what I wanted to tell you was . . . Listen carefully. You remember that detective I hired to investigate my brother's fiancée?"

"Yes, of course."

"He found out that the man she was seeing here in Paris, the one who died suddenly, was Sylvain Broch, your DVD pirate, so recently assassinated."

"I knew it!" Max blurted. "I knew it! You mentioned last Friday at dinner that this other man your brother's girlfriend was mixed up with, the guy in Paris, was at the same time seeing a woman whose husband had died—in a car accident, you said. This woman is Sophie Leclère, the late Broch's lover and partner in the real-estate business. I've spoken with her twice."

"Ah. I didn't put it together at the time." Eddie's voice seemed to float away into the realms of troubled thought.

Awaiting its eventual return, Max watched a trio of young women, fashionably dressed and alight with laughter, gain easy entry to the club. One of them, wearing a gardenia in her jet-black hair, glanced back at Max before the door slammed shut. "What is it you want to tell me, Eddie?"

Eddie sighed. "It turns out that Broch, at least as far as the counterfeit-DVD business goes, was more like a middle manager. He rented that loft, yes, but he had an underling actually turn out the disks—his cousin, someone named Thierry Colin."

"Are you sure?" Max had to laugh. "Thierry Colin?"

"Don't tell me you know him."

"No, but maybe fifteen minutes ago this girl asked me to keep an eye out for him, I'm bound to run into him soon, she said. Paris is a small place."

"And who was the girl?"

"The girlfriend of the Russian I mentioned earlier, guy named Nikolai Kukushkin. A banker, I think."

A silence. Eddie cleared his throat. "As you know, Max, I try not to be judgmental of people or their activities. It's bad for business and inhibits one's vision of what's possible. But I have to say, as someone with your interests very much in mind, that the company you've been keeping lately is doubtful in the extreme. Thierry Colin worked for Broch, yes, but Broch himself worked for the gentleman you just mentioned. Colin was only paying off a gambling debt, but Kukushkin . . . he's a known crime boss with many successful enterprises. Remember our talk about La Peau de l'Ours?" Eddie was seized momentarily by a coughing fit. "You do, of course."

"And all this you just found out now?" Max asked.

"In point of fact, it was the detective who found it out. As he explained it to me, this Strasbourg girl has three great passions—besides herself, of course. Music, cocaine, and the folkways of the Russian mafia. Apparently Broch let it be known that he was well acquainted with Kukushkin, who has the added advantage, in her eyes, of coming from a famously musical Russian family. His father, in particular, was a great violinist—a genius, I'm told. So together these things drew her to Broch—his contacts, the stories he was privy to, her expectation of meeting Kukushkin." Again Eddie sighed. "She's very talented, very beautiful, and a true terror. And not so stupid that she didn't guess who had arranged Broch's death. My brother could hardly have been unaware that he, Gaspard, was just her backup prospect, her second choice in love. Yet he got lucky all the same, at least as he sees it." Eddie sounded resigned. "One must have a very strong stomach to hire detectives, you know. Inevitably one finds out much more than one wishes."

"So Kukushkin *is* La Peau de l'Ours?"

"We were never able to determine that. There may be someone above him. However . . ." His voice trailed off.

"However?" Max prompted.

"I want you to sever all contact with these people and come to my office first thing in the morning. There's more to say, but not on the phone. We've been reckless enough already. Can I expect you at ten?"

"If you say so, Eddie. Sure."

"Good. I'll see you then, Max. And stay safe." He hung up before Max could reply.

Lowering his phone, Max stared at it for some seconds, as if it might somehow provide the information he required. Then he snapped it shut and began walking, as briskly as his current state would permit, toward the quai de la Tournelle.

Barely had he reached la Place Beauvau, however, a few blocks east of the auction house, when he stopped, thunderstruck, to stare up at the sky. The moonlit fog burned a pearlescent white that bathed the city in an uncanny, seemingly sourceless brilliance that illuminated everything, leaving no shadows. The effect resembled neither day nor night. It seemed to refer to something he'd once known quite well but had long since forgotten. He wanted it back.

Flipping his phone open, he called Jacques at home. To his relief, he answered on the second ring.

"Sorry to hijack you like this," Max said, "but I need you to bring the cameras and sound equipment down to the *Nachtvlinder* as soon as possible. No, wait, not down to the boat. Stay at street level, I'll meet you there. Take the Citroën."

"You can't be serious. At this hour?"

"Is that a problem?"

Jacques muffled the mouthpiece with his palm, and though Max couldn't make out the words, he knew his assistant was having a whispered but increasingly rancorous exchange with his companion of the moment. While Jacques preferred living alone, he had a rotating cast of women, about whom Max found it expedient not to inquire, precisely so that he could make sudden requests like tonight's. This unspoken arrangement, he suspected, also suited Jacques's social needs at least as often as not.

Some seconds later, he was back on the line. "This is going to cost me, you know."

In the background, the girl unleashed a steady stream of invective at Jacques and men in general, who, Max had to admit, from time to time probably deserved it. A glass shattered against the wall. Then what sounded like a bottle.

"But?" Max ventured.

"But," his assistant allowed, "it *is* becoming a bit claustrophobic in here, now that you mention it. I think maybe some time outdoors might do me good."

"As soon as you can, then." Max didn't want to lose the light.

"On my way, boss."

Snapping shut the phone, Max quickened his pace.

Not the light, not the moment, not anything.

# CHAPTER 34

DINNER WITH RACHEL and Groot, which for Odile consisted of nothing more than a glass of iced lime water and a few token artichoke leaves, had an unexpectedly bracing effect on her. The three of them sat topside, under moon-blanched skies, and while her hosts contentedly ate the calf's liver they'd seared in thick slices on the hibachi, Odile outlined her plan.

She had, she explained, met three people who desperately needed to get out of Paris before dawn. Though they'd done nothing illegal, they were being avidly sought by both the local authorities and various members of a Russian crime syndicate. All the main transportation hubs out of the city were being watched. In any other circumstance, she noted, she would've left them to their fate, but because she'd been convinced their case was special, with possible consequences far beyond what could now be known, she felt obliged to help them if she could.

"*Ja, ja,*" Groot said. "Go on."

So she reminded Rachel of the picture of the doctor that the CRS had shown her and, without going into detail, explained that the other two people were just minders, escorting this scientist out of the country because the French police wrongly suspected him of being a bioterrorist. The Russians were another story. But the point was that this researcher had made a rare medical breakthrough that might very well save tens of thousands of lives, maybe hundreds of thousands, even more. All he needed now was to get to England and safety.

Groot smiled. "This isn't like you, Odile. You've become a humanist, practically Dutch, one might say. Though without the hypocrisy, I hope."

"I have my own reasons for asking you this favor. Will you do it?"

"You want us to take these people to England?"

"Yes. I'm sure they'll pay." She laughed. "Actually, I don't know that at all. But Max told me you might be planning a maiden voyage, so I thought . . ."

Rachel frowned and turned to Groot. "Are we? A maiden voyage?"

"I was considering it. Though only if it would please you."

"But what about Max's film?"

"This would be part of it," Odile said. "He was going to tell you, but I guess he hasn't gotten around to it yet." Fascinated, she saw she was veering giddily into improvisation and reckless untruth. She had no idea what she might say next.

"So they're fugitives," Groot said. "How did you leave it with them?"

"They'll be here at midnight."

Rachel and Groot looked at each other, consulting silently. It occurred to Odile that they would very likely be getting married after all.

Groot pushed himself away from the table and stretched. "*Ja*, okay. I think we can do this. If Rachel agrees, of course." Stifling a yawn, he stood, laid his napkin beside his plate, and went below, leaving the women to talk.

"I know I'm asking a lot," said Odile, "but I have to live with myself."

"It's all right. These Russians, though, they're the ones who firebombed us?"

"Yes."

"And the three people who want to go to England. There's the doctor whose picture I saw. But the other two?"

"One is the guy I went to Moscow with to pick up the flags. The other's his girlfriend. They're all working together, more or less."

"Sounds complicated."

"Maybe, but not for us. As long as we get them out of here."

"I see." Rachel took off her glasses, polished the lenses on an edge of the tablecloth, and put them back on. Peering at her friend curiously, she said, "Anything else you want to tell me?"

In the distance, a lone siren bloomed.

"No," Odile replied. She glanced reflexively at her watch, then attempted a smile. "Not really."

·     ·     ·

MAX HAD BEEN WAITING no more than ten minutes when Jacques pulled up in the Citroën and got out. The two men stood wordlessly together, taking in the light.

"I've never seen anything like it. Will it photograph? Is it real?"

"A full moon refracted by fog," said Max. "No shadows. I've never seen this either."

"What are we shooting? Do we have a scene?"

"I don't know." Max threw his cigar into the street. "If not, we'll make one up. But let's get down there before anything changes."

They unloaded the cameras and sound equipment, then headed down the stone steps to the quai.

"I think the best idea is for you to set up right there, by the retaining wall, so you can get the boat as a whole. I'll take the other camera on board and see what's happening. Rachel and Odile were topside until a little while ago—I saw them from across the river—but they must've gone below, probably to join Groot. I'll roust them."

"Yes, this is good."

"But Jacques, I want you to use your judgment. If you think you've got enough from your angle, or if I can't get them up into the light soon enough, or even if you just see something good that I'm missing, come on board. Quietly. You'll know what to do."

Nodding, Jacques surveyed the scene, mapping it out in his mind. "And that blue light on top there? What does that mean?"

"It means that God is a camera," said Max, who'd forgotten he was still drunk.

On the quai, he watched Jacques set up his vidcam and tripod, then train it on the *Nachtvlinder*. After taking a look through the viewfinder himself, Max was satisfied. "Okay, ready?"

Jacques nodded. "Let's do it."

Going up the gangway, Max took care to make as little noise as possible. He thought it odd that those on board wouldn't be topside in this light—once-in-a-lifetime light, the light of rapture and unforeseeable outcomes. Of course, he couldn't expect others to see what he pictured, at least not until he put a frame around it. And even then, how many? But it didn't matter. Doing it was the thing.

Once aboard, he could hear Rachel, Groot, and Odile conversing softly below, and he had to stop for a moment to ask himself what, exactly, he wanted from them. So much of what had just happened—the auction, his encounter with Kukushkin and Véronique, his phone call with Eddie—had yet to sort itself out in his mind that he was operating more impulsively than usual, operating, it had to be admitted, like someone half drunk. Yet he thought maybe impulse was just what he needed right now. Forces larger than himself, whose true nature remained unclear, had allowed him a glimpse of the world as it really was, and all his instincts told him to pursue it with every resource he could muster. *I know more than I know,* he thought. He waited a little longer for something to contradict him—reason, perhaps, or ordinary good sense—but nothing did. He shouldered his equipment and descended the companionway steps.

The conversation below ceased immediately at his approach, and all three rose guiltily to their feet. Looking from one to another of his prospective subjects, Max saw an expression quite like shock on their faces. He decided to let the moment play out. Without comment, he considered his surroundings: the dimly lit compartment, the river-facing portholes brighter than the compartment, the nautical magazines neatly stowed in a bamboo rack, the map of the Seine framed and bolted flush to the bulkhead, the bank of wooden storage lockers, the pair of canaries in a cage not yet shrouded for the night, the cantaloupe rolling listlessly about in a bowl as the *Nachtvlinder* pitched in the wake of a passing boat. Max's eyes settled on Rachel. She looked stricken.

"I'm sorry," he said. "I guess I should've knocked."

Groot was quick to intervene. "No, no. You just surprised us. That's all." He made a move to help Max with his equipment, but Max shook his head fractionally and he backed off. "The light," Max said. "I thought maybe we could shoot a couple of—"

But now Odile stepped forward, quite composed again, and as she looked him in the eye something like a memory came hurtling back to him. Yet it was more immediate than a memory, it was her voice in his ear, saying, as it had that early spring afternoon, topside on this very vessel, when the two of them were in easy harmony still: *Enough. When the time comes, you'll do what must be done. I require it, and you won't fail me.*

To his immense relief, he understood that now was that time.

"Max," she said simply.

WHEN TURNER'S CONVERSATION with Odile came so abruptly to an end, he'd redialed at once, only to get her voice mail on the first ring. This he took to mean that her phone had been switched off, whether by herself or someone else, and as thoughts of the evening's developments ricocheted through his head, he commenced, in his agitation, to walk the moonlit city streets at random, oblivious to both direction and purpose. By the time he got a grip on himself, in the eighteenth arrondissement, a street sign informed him, even though he already knew, that he was on rue de la Goutte d'Or. He wondered briefly why there weren't more people around, especially given the extraordinary light, and in a neighborhood known for its night trade. Then he saw, and realized he'd been seeing for some time now, an unusual number of police on the street—plainclothes and uniformed, on foot and in squad cars, with the occasional riot van parked inconspicuously in an alley. He hesitated, tapping his forefinger against his pursed lips as he pivoted slowly to survey the scene. Then he headed south toward the river.

At first he kept to the main boulevards—Magenta, Fayette, Haussmann—but before long grew uncomfortably aware that the belt-and-tape holster he'd rigged for his gun was designed more for concealment than for access—a definite disadvantage, should there actually be a moment of need. He turned down a side street, then another, before sheepishly slipping into a half-darkened doorway.

Unbuttoning his shirt, he transferred the gun to the waistband of his trousers, in front, at the left, then buttoned his suit jacket over it. He knew he was behaving like a character in a movie but so now was everyone else—all over the world, every waking hour, without even thinking about it. The times encouraged people to magnify their view of themselves, and, like it or not, you had to accommodate. He stepped again into the street.

"Watch out!" cried a voice closing fast from behind.

Turner leapt back onto the sidewalk just in time to avoid being run down by a helmeted bicyclist in black leather.

"Moron!" the man shouted over his shoulder as he sped off.

"Asshole!" Turner called after him, then continued south.

If, as he sometimes suspected, there would come a day of deliverance for people like himself, people so rabid to live that they knew neither up nor down, right nor left, then maybe fear wasn't the survival mechanism he'd imagined it to be. Maybe, instead, it was the problem. A hindrance to what would otherwise happen. But how could you tell? Speculation did no good, that much was obvious. And in the end, of course, fear or no fear, the same fate awaited everyone. Or so one was led to believe.

Moment by moment, then, block by block, Odile seeped back into his thoughts until she eventually displaced all others. He grew more confident. Despite her efforts to discourage him, obvious from the start, he remained undeterred in his pursuit. He believed she loved him, even if she wished it were otherwise. And people floundered, they changed their minds, outside events intervened without warning. Why shouldn't he have a life with her? He felt it within his power to make this happen. Anyway, he had to try. He owed it to himself, a changed man, and he owed it to Odile, the woman who'd changed him. Nothing else would do.

Rounding the corner onto rue des Halles, he saw a group of police halfway down the block, taking counsel together, their vehicles obstructing the street. Unpleasantly aware of the weapon jammed into his waistband, he crossed the street to avoid the officers, one of whom called out to him.

He stopped in his tracks, and the cop dashed across the pavement to have a word with him.

"Good evening, Officer," Turner said. "Is there something wrong?"

"As a precautionary measure, there is a civil alert, yes, and that is something we must all take seriously. Your identity card, please."

Reaching into his breast pocket, Turner produced his wallet, removed his identification card, and handed it to him.

The policeman looked him over with care, his gaze lingering thoughtfully at the waist, where Turner's jacket was buttoned tight. Then, after a quick, hard glance at his face, the officer shifted his attention to the card. "Where are you going tonight, sir?"

"To my home. I live in—"

"I can see where you live," the officer said curtly, then handed back the card. "Go there directly, no stops."

"Yes, of course. As quickly as possible." Turner hesitated. "Should one be alarmed?"

For the first time the officer seemed to ease up slightly. He looked evenly into Turner's eyes and, with no suggestion of levity, replied, "Sir! One should never be alarmed. One should be alert."

"Well said." Turner glanced at his watch. "So, with your permission, I'll get going."

"That's a very good idea." His interest in Turner exhausted, he jogged back to where his fellow officers were gathered.

Turner hurried on and did not look back. But he wasn't going home.

TOPSIDE on the *Nachtvlinder*, temporarily united in their desires, Rachel, Groot, and Odile assembled for a scene that Max had yet to glimpse or invent. The fog was still rolling in and the light was brighter than ever, but with no idea when the moon might set, he couldn't bear to lose any camera time. Each wasted second hurt.

Turning toward the quai, he gestured for Jacques to keep shooting. From his assistant's vantage, the freshly painted boat would be blending more and more into the overall whiteness, even partly disappearing into it.

"Where do you want us?" asked Rachel.

Max led them to the river side of the boat, stationing Odile amidships, just out of camera range. Groot and Rachel he took closer to the stern, where the light was brightest. When he had them arranged to his liking, up against the railing, bodies half turned toward each other, he put the light meter to their faces, took a reading, and retreated behind the camera to frame the shot. Satisfied, he drew himself up in somewhat priestly fashion to address his principals.

"Okay. This will be a little different from what we've been doing, because I won't speak. I won't ask questions, and I won't be a factor. But don't let that worry you—quite the opposite. Once we start, you'll be free to do or say anything you want. You can even think of yourself as someone else, if that appeals to you or helps you get to where you need to be. What I do ask is that you keep things moving, physically and verbally, following your gut. Don't think, just let it out. Ignore me and accommodate to whatever seems real. Understand?"

He inspected each of them in turn. Meeting Odile's gaze, he experienced a thrill of complicity. Whatever happened now would happen to them both. They'd respond as one. And as things had been when the two of them had first met, so would they be again. The readiness was all.

"Two scripted moments only," Max went on. "First, Rachel, I want you to slap Groot as hard as you can on the cheek. The right one, since you're left-handed. Is that okay with both of you?"

They looked at each other for a moment, then nodded.

"Second, when I give the signal to Odile, she'll come into the action. Incorporate her however you like. Odile, follow your impulses. Other developments—and as you know, there will *always* be other developments—should be treated naturally. Oh, and I've got Jacques down there on the quai shooting too, in case we need some backup footage. He may come aboard later. But ignore him just as you do me."

Max, though hoping for no questions, left a short interval in which they might be posed. None were. "So, guys, that's it." He put his eye to the viewfinder. "Everybody ready?" He took their silence as assent. "Rachel, it's all you."

Inhaling deeply, she clenched her teeth and drew her left hand back, palm open. Max started to film. The slap, when it came, was much harder than anyone but Max had expected, snapping Groot's head around to face the camera. But he didn't flinch or move away. He didn't touch his cheek. Max slowly tightened the shot.

"Does that mean no?" Groot asked her.

"It means I wanted to slap you."

"Then do it again."

She did, harder still.

"Exactly," said Groot. "So this is what I think." He took her elbows in his palms to gentle her. "Odile, our friend, has asked us to help her. We have agreed, because the circumstances are unusual, and because she's our friend. But you don't really want to do what she asks. You want me, the upright Dutchman, to be the one to bear the bad news and say, 'No, what you ask of us is illegal. No, it would endanger our safety and maybe that of our boat. Besides, and for no particular reason, we don't *want* to do it.'"

Max zoomed further in until his subjects' heads and shoulders were tightly confined within the frame. He could tell that Rachel wasn't sure whether Groot was acting, telling the truth, or telling a truth he thought was hers.

"No!" she said. "Don't be ridiculous, putting words in my mouth like that. Even a child could see what you're up to. Pig!"

He smiled and, superbly, became one.

She lunged, but he easily fended her off. She lunged again and, slipping one ankle behind the two of his, pushed him over backward, onto the deck. His surprise, Max saw, was genuine. She stood over Groot, hands on her waist, panting, as he propped himself up on his elbows and forearms to contemplate her.

"Do you feel better now?" he asked.

"I don't know." She shook her head as if to clear it. "I mean, I've been wanting to do that for awhile, but it doesn't really make me feel any better."

"Love in its savage state," said Groot, getting to his feet. "So invigorating."

"What's *that* supposed to mean?" Rachel demanded.

With a slow roll of his hand, Max beckoned Odile into the action. She came at the pace indicated, a languid stroll suitable for a moonlit night on shipboard, but when she entered the frame, Max's heart inexplicably began to race, just taking off on him, up, up, and away. There was no time to wonder why. Instead, he reminded himself that, even if he wasn't entirely in charge here, his own receptivity, properly cultivated, would eventually reveal what he'd come to record.

Odile said, "I've just had the strangest dream."

Max moved in on their three faces until they were framed close, like clover leaves bleached silver by the moon.

"Tell us," said Rachel.

"It was in a railway station, I don't know where. Eastern Europe, maybe. We were in the main hall, all four of us—a place that had once been thought grand but now was like a ruin, very dilapidated, you know? And there was a huge crowd surging around us, people trying to escape some kind of disaster. A war, I think. There was artillery fire nearby. Anyway, we couldn't speak the language, and we didn't have any money or tickets. The last train out was due to depart at any minute. I thought, *We're trapped. We'll die here.*"

"That doesn't sound like you," said Groot.

"But what I sound like and what I am are often very different things. Surely you know that, Groot."

"Anyway," said Rachel. "The dream."

"Yes. So just as I was thinking these thoughts—of resignation, you might say—a great stillness came over the departures hall. I looked around me. Everyone but the four of us had all at once been frozen solid, like ice statues. In the blink of an eye. No one could speak or move. Only us. Max was the first to realize what this meant and he pushed forward, knocking people aside. Some of them, a lot of them, shattered when they hit the marble floor. We didn't care. We were also knocking over these frozen supplicants, almost as if it were a game. I wondered if this was death for them—breaking into a million pieces like that—or whether being frozen had already killed them. It didn't matter, though. I was completely detached. We made it to the window, grabbed tickets for ourselves, and ran to the platform. The conductor took our tickets, and we got on just before the train pulled out. We got away." She drew inward, speaking now to herself. "We escaped."

A short silence followed. Max made motions to proceed.

"This, I think, is quite positive," Groot said. "In adversity, we were resourceful together. Survivors amid the calamities of the world, which are always legion. You should be happy. *We* should be happy."

"But we weren't the ones who froze those people. That just happened." She deliberated further, then declared, "We weren't resourceful, we were lucky." She glanced at Groot to see if she'd offended him, then recoiled. "Oh my God! Your cheek, what happened?"

"Does it show?" He touched the inflamed area. "Yes, well, Rachel was expressing some dissatisfactions. And in this case I *wasn't* lucky."

"Liar," Rachel said.

"It had to do with the guests we're expecting," he told Odile. "Your friends."

"It had to do," Rachel corrected him, "with your putting words in my mouth." She turned her back to the others and, leaning on the rail, gazed moodily out over the river, into the translucent white.

"Listen," Odile said, "if this is about us getting those people out of Paris tonight, let's just call it off. I'll tell them—"

Thinking he'd probably end up running Odile's words in voice-over, Max panned left to focus solely on Rachel, whose sultry sulk was quickly taking on a power of its own. At precisely the same moment, however, a large white yacht ran by, very fast and close, throwing up great curls of frothy water that were nonetheless almost invisible in the fog. The roar of its engines drowned out whatever Odile was saying and the sudden swell cast the *Nachtvlinder* back against her mooring. As the houseboat rebounded off the quai, Rachel was in turn thrown hard against the rail. She held tight. Some seconds later, when the wake had subsided, she leaned over and peered down into the Seine—looking for something she'd dropped, it seemed to Max. But whatever it was, it was well and truly lost. She turned to the camera, and Max saw that her glasses were gone, her deep blue eyes as large and liquid as mountain lakes.

"That was my last pair," she said ruefully.

Max zoomed in slowly on her features and held the shot, waiting. When she blinked a second time, he cut. "That was great, you guys. First rate. Take five."

Groot drew Rachel aside. "Do you want me to get my mask and go down after them?" he asked.

"Thanks, but you've already had enough river toxins for a lifetime. I'm pretty sure I've got the lens prescription below somewhere."

Max stepped back to insert a new cartridge into the camera. Something about Odile's improvised dream account had caught his fancy, as if it contained a message for him, but he couldn't decipher it. He looked around to see if the light was holding. It was.

Then he heard Odile say, in a hoarse whisper quite unlike the voice she'd used to recount the dream, "They're here."

Looking to the gangway, Max saw Jacques backing slowly onto the boat, filming. He was soon followed by an athletic young woman Max had never seen before, then a fastidious-looking man with sparkly eyeglasses and shaven scalp, then by the man whose picture the CRS had shown Rachel shortly before Max received his punch to the gut. The doctor. As they came aboard, Jacques peeled off along the quai-side rail, still filming, but no longer an obstacle to Max's field of view. Unthinkingly, he turned his own camera a hundred and eighty degrees on its tripod, put it on automatic, and went forward, along with everyone else, to greet the new arrivals.

Odile gave him a dazzling smile, and he returned it. Quite possibly, he thought, he was the most inventive and daring filmmaker of his time.

"I am Groot Gansevoort, captain of this boat," the Dutchman said. "As I understand it, you want us to take you to England. This is correct?"

"Yes," said the woman, who didn't introduce herself. She wore a white denim jacket and carried a turquoise purse. "We would be so grateful. And we can pay you."

"This is Rachel, my first mate," Groot continued. "It will take us at least twenty minutes before we can get under way. I think the best thing would be for you to stay out of sight for now, and since I'll need Rachel's assistance, her friend Odile, whom you've obviously met, will escort you below."

The doctor whispered something into the other man's ear. Without hesitation, the latter addressed himself to Max. "Our guest of honor is a little worried about the cameras. Is it possible to know what they're for?"

"Of course," Max said. "We're making a short feature film about this boat, which has been recently restored, and its owners, whom you just met. I am Max Colby, and film is my profession. Your friend has absolutely no cause for alarm."

"Thank you," he replied. But his eyes remained fixed on Max.

Odile was already shooing the new arrivals below. When the one facing Max failed to respond, she called impatiently after him. "Thierry! Hurry up!"

At this, Max stayed the man with a hand against his chest. "You are Thierry Colin?"

He nodded almost imperceptibly.

"The person who went to Moscow with my wife, smuggled the flags, counterfeited my film, and vandalized its ending. Correct?"

Colin looked both surprised and perturbed, as if he were receiving this news about himself for the first time. But after drawing a long breath he said, "Yes, I'm afraid that *is* correct. All of it. Though if you'd allow me the opportunity, I would very much like to explain myself."

Max didn't respond.

Using the same hoarse whisper as before, Odile again appealed to the man to get himself out of sight belowdecks.

"She's right," said Max, lowering his hand. "Go. Do it now."

"But—"

"I don't want your explanations."

Looking thoughtful, Colin lingered a moment more. But no words came to him, and he went.

When they were alone on deck, Jacques gave Max a thumbs-up. "Let me be the first to say that I understand practically nothing of what just happened, but one thing is certain: we got every bit of it, sound and image." He pointed to the audio boom he'd propped overhead against the wheelhouse.

"Good work," said Max. "A decisive moment, for sure." He gnawed at a thumbnail, mulling things over. "Not that I understand much of it either. The doctor we know. Apparently he's about to flee the country on our very own *Nachtvlinder*. Tonight." He fell deeper into contemplation. "And that guy, Thierry Colin. You heard what he said." Max smote his brow. "Bastard! What's more, somebody just warned me to watch out for him, right before I called you. But I never imagined I'd see him *here*."

Jacques squinted westward with feigned indifference, his eyes running up the Eiffel Tower. It was still alight, if only for a few more minutes. "What does Odile say? I get the feeling she understands it."

"So it would appear, yes. Or part of it, anyway. But I can't ask her."

"Why not?"

Max smiled grimly and shook his head. "Such are the mysteries of matrimony, my friend. The less you ask, the more you actually find out. Besides . . ."

Jacques waited for Max to go on, but just then a dark thought intruded, abruptly quashing Max's need to instruct.

"Forget it," he said.

Nearby, unseen, a clutch of ducklings and their mother made the occasional small murmurings that waterfowl make when they sleep—to keep track of one another, it was said. Or for reassurance.

"One more question."

"Yes?" Max said sharply.

"What made you decide to step into the frame? You're in the picture now. A character."

Max softened. "I don't know, it just happened. We can always lose it in the edit."

"Sure. But I bet we won't."

"Really? Why's that?"

Jacques took off his baseball hat, smoothed some stray hairs back into place, and put it on again, visor in back, as before. "Because it works."

Max looked sideways at him. "You think so?" he said, chewing again at his thumbnail.

"Under the conditions, namely that we don't know what's next, we need all the flexibility we can get. With you out there in the action—your camera left behind, as before, on automatic, and me handling the other one as needed—we maximize our options, no?"

Max inspected him through narrowed eyes. "So you're telling me you want to take over as director of this picture, is that it? You're relieving me of my command?"

Jacques shrugged. "I just feel really on tonight, that's all."

Bemused, Max watched Rachel hurry past the two of them and down the gangway. A moment later she was at the quai-side hookup, beginning to detach the *Nachtvlinder* from her electrical feed and other assorted umbilicals. Groot was no doubt in the engine room. Things were moving fast.

"You're right," Max said. "And I'm feeling the same. So we'll try it." He took another small black cigar from his shirt pocket and lit it. "Now, Jacques, would you be so kind as to have a quick talk with Rachel down there? See if you can find out the order of business, technically speaking, for casting off?"

"Aye, aye, sir." Struggling to conceal a smile, Jacques turned on his heel and hurried down the gangway.

Max walked to the stern, his thoughts aswarm. He remembered the man who had called last Friday, during the dinner party, highly strung, asking for Odile without identifying himself, of whom Odile, when informed of the call, had asked, *French guy?* And indeed he'd been French. If, as now seemed entirely possible, the caller was Thierry Colin, and he, not Turner, was the one having the affair with Odile, then things were far more complicated than Max ever could have anticipated. *He has something of mine, something personal,* Véronique had said of Colin. And now the same man had just admitted to having appropriated one of Max's films. If his film, why not his wife, with an alternative ending for her as well? Impossible. Odile would never knowingly betray his work. Possible. *Paris is quite small in some respects.* And then there was Eddie, cautioning Max to sever all contacts with these people, say no more on the phone, come by first thing in the morning. *Stay safe.*

Out of the corner of his eye, Max glimpsed Jacques running up the gangway to get his camera. Rachel followed with an armload of cable. Max returned to the stern and put his own camera on automatic.

"Max?"

He wheeled round in surprise. "Odile." He hadn't heard her approach.

"You *are* with me on this, aren't you?"

He stepped forward so that they were both in the camera's field. "Of course I'm with you."

"Good. Because there's no other way, believe me."

"What's going to happen?"

"We're going to get the doctor out of here. Apart from that, I have no idea. But you and I are pooling our chips. We'll do what's necessary, no matter what."

"I know," he said. "Because you require it, and I won't fail you."

She laughed and embraced him. "By daylight tomorrow, everything will be fine." She rested her head on his shoulder. "You'll see."

But what Max saw over her own shoulder was Thierry Colin emerging from the companionway. Max watched him go to the quai-side rail and lean against it, watching them.

"This light is just exquisite," Odile said, unaware of Colin's presence. "Almost like the light of a new world, you know? A place where a new existence could really be possible for everyone. Wouldn't that be something?"

Meanwhile, Jacques had taken up position on deck, facing the quai-side rail and gangway, just out of range of Max's unmanned camera. He was shooting Colin, Max saw, from about a forty-degree angle, covering both him and the gangway's open gate. It crossed Max's mind that Jacques was allowing for the possibility that Colin might make a run for it.

"How well do you know this Thierry Colin?" he asked.

"Thierry?" She broke from his embrace. "He doesn't matter. It's the doctor we have to think about. His safety. Because—"

Max waited.

"No," Odile said decisively. "No questions. Even to ourselves. Otherwise, we'll fail to do what's ours to do, and everything will be lost. So, no questions."

Max didn't answer. When she looked up into his eyes and saw them fixed on the gangway, he felt her mood shift—radically, dangerously. "No!" she cried out, even as she was turning to see what had engaged his attention. But it was clear that she already knew.

"I told you not to come here!" she shouted. "Ever, ever, ever! Why are you so stupid?"

Turner, who'd been striding forcefully up the gangway, a man with a mission, stepped on board and immediately came to a halt. He and Colin looked at each other with utter distaste. Then Turner scanned the deck methodically, taking in Jacques, the two active cameras, Max, and, lastly, Odile, to whom he nodded with visible concern. An unhealthy vigor seemed to be animating his every movement.

"Good evening, Colby," he said, "I hope you enjoyed the auction."

"Probably not as much as you did. But there were some compelling moments, I have to say. And the company was good."

"This man," said Turner, pointing to Colin without taking his eyes from Max. "Do you know who he is?"

Max stole a look at Odile, who, arms crossed over her heaving chest, was just barely containing herself, a study in sheer will. "Pretty much," he replied. "True, I still have a few blank spots that need filling in, a few questions." *Reason, care, and discipline,* he reminded himself. "But I have the feeling you're about to fix all that for me."

"Thierry Colin works for a man," Turner said evenly, "who intends to have your wife killed. And me too, if that makes any difference."

Odile gathered breath for speech but before she could utter a sound, Max placed a palm gently across her mouth. "Don't," he whispered. "I told you I'm with you." Eyes shining, she exhaled a humid warmth between his fingers. When he removed his hand, she had grown calm again, her silence as sure and fatal as a vow.

"This guy you're talking about," Max said to Turner, "this guy who wants people killed, his name's Kukushkin, right?"

Turner looked guilty, worried, confused.

Jacques repositioned the camera and continued to film.

"Well, after the auction I spent almost two hours drinking vodka with Kolya, at his private club. He didn't mention wanting to kill you. Or my wife either, for that matter. But I guess anything's possible." He paused. "Right, Thierry?"

Colin shrugged. "Some things perhaps more than others."

"Odile!" Turner took a step toward her. "You've got to come with me! It's a trap. Remember what I told you on the phone? It means we've got to go now, before it's too late."

Max turned curiously to his wife. Cool, even arrogant, in stance and posture, she met Turner's gaze and shook her head no. This refusal left Max suddenly certain that it was Colin, not Turner, who was her lover. She was leaving Turner to fend for himself, having arranged Colin's escape.

"I won't leave you here," Turner said. And with that he began marching toward her, obviously intending to remove her bodily from the boat. Max's mind was still racing to grasp the situation when, halfway across the deck,

Turner slipped on a patch of diesel, skidded, and went down flat on his back. Simultaneously, an object spun away from him across the deck with disconcerting speed. When it came to rest and all present saw what it was, there was a moment during which no one reacted. Then Max and Turner and Colin dove for the gun.

Much later, Max would recall Odile standing against the river-side rail, arms crossed, watching them struggle over the weapon, and wonder at her calm. He would wonder, too, at Jacques's composure as he filmed. And at the absence of the others, still below. He would wonder at so many things. But all this came back to him only much later, when everything that mattered had been settled.

Now was only turmoil.

Turner, though hardly recovered from his fall, was the first to get his hands on the gun. Colin and Max grabbed him and worked methodically to pry his fingers from it—he had both hands around the grip—but when they at last succeeded, the gun slipped loose once more, sliding across the newly varnished deck like a hockey puck. Both men went for it, reaching it at the same time.

Max got one hand around the trigger guard, and Colin, who was stronger than he looked, had it by the barrel, gripping it hard and pushing it away from himself. Apparently, thought Max, his intuition had been correct: he and this man weren't at all on the same side. With his free hand, he made a fist and punched Colin repeatedly in the face. It took several blows before he finally relinquished the weapon, fell over, and, when back on his feet, retreated to the quai-side rail. There, curiously, he stood side by side with Turner, his accuser, who was still catching his breath. Training the gun on them both, Max backed slowly to the opposite rail, next to Odile, still impassive, watchful, dire.

"Are you all right?" she asked him.

He was panting for breath. "No questions," he managed to say.

Jacques filmed.

The fog was thickening, so the light, while just as bright, wasn't quite as limpid as before. Belatedly it occurred to Max that the gun hadn't gone off during the struggle. He felt for the safety and found it firmly engaged. So Turner hadn't come aboard intending to fire, at least not right away. Max switched the safety off and held the gun out at arm's length, aiming it alternately at Turner and Thierry. Neither man, fearful no doubt of drawing fire, made any attempt to escape. Finally Max's eye—and, with it, the pistol—settled decisively on Thierry Colin, who was dabbing at his bloodied nose with a handkerchief.

Time came to a stop, as if it had never been anything but a rumor. A nothingness inside a rumor.

From within that nothingness, Odile said, "No." She rested her hand lightly on Max's hand, the one holding the gun. "Not him." Then very gently, so gently, as if to correct Max with the least possible affront on a nicety of table manners, she moved his hand a few inches to the right until the gun was aimed squarely at Turner's chest. She released the wrist. "Him."

And Max squeezed the trigger.

## CHAPTER 35

*SO THIS IS WHAT it's going to be like,* Turner thought. He knew, the moment the bullet entered his chest, that he would die. Knew not because of the pain, vast and terrible though it was, but because already the pain was becoming a thing apart from him, superfluous and unclaimed. Knew not because of the blood, which was spurting from him in quantities he'd never seen or imagined, but because he understood he must leave it behind, wanted to and could leave it behind. And, above all, he knew not because he was alone now, aware that the others were standing deliberately apart from him, making no effort to help him, afraid of what they'd unleashed, fearful it might take them too. Rather, he knew he was dying because in life he had always been alone, like absolutely everyone else, in every possible place or time. And now that solitude was coming to an end.

The woman had betrayed him, but he felt no bitterness. His love for her only grew—touched, as it now was, by pity. Pity not for her, but for the innate clumsiness of the living, who meant one thing and did another over and over again, time after time, every moment they drew breath. Fleetingly, he wished he'd known as much from the start. But then that wish, too, fell away. Not just because its fulfillment would've done no good, though it wouldn't have, and not because, knowing, he would've lived his life differently, making different choices at every opportunity, though he would've done just that, and those choices, too, would've been clumsy and his life no better. The wish fell away because he was leaving the world of wishes, which now stood revealed to him as an empty series of inventions, desperate and comic, that helped a person believe more fervently in the illusion that better things lay just ahead, almost within sight, perhaps around the corner, if only one persevered.

Persevered.

And now, he was starting to see, better things *did* lie ahead, but things so different from what people ordinarily strove for that no foreknowledge of them could possibly make a difference—even the slightest difference—in something as random as a life.

He felt events moving faster now. The part of him that had not yet let go was angry that his death was being filmed by that boy with the baseball hat turned backward, who could only be working for Odile's husband, the filmmaker. To what possible end was his dying being filmed? Not one iota of what was really transpiring here, nothing even remotely important about his passage, could ever be made visible to these people or any others.

Or any others.

And now Rachel had a mop. She was mopping up his blood. Did they think he was *already* dead? For just a fraction of a moment he struggled to come back to their level, if only to correct them on this point. But he was going too fast, drawn with increasing urgency toward what before had been unimaginable but now lured him on and on and on.

He could move no part of his body, not even his eyes. Still, he thought he could hear sirens in the distance. Two, three, then several more. Converging. Had they been summoned for him? He certainly hoped not. He didn't want anything like that now, not at this point.

And it was precisely at this point that he passed through an invisible membrane, or maybe it was a baffle, since he knew he wouldn't be back this way again. A flash of regret. Gone. Then everything became clear to him.

Odile had loved him. She had struggled against it, but to no avail. And he, despite his fears, had loved her. Of course the verdict on fear was that, yes, it did keep you alive, or he wouldn't be dying now. But it was more usefully deployed on behalf of others. That much he'd learned, even if it had taken him this long. He had learned it at the last minute. Just in time.

And the sirens were not sirens, he realized, but music. He strained to make it out.

He was beginning to know everything. It was true that your whole life passed before your eyes as you died, but not like a movie, as people always said. More like a flashbulb going off.

The light from the flashbulb expanded, radiating outward to include other lives. He saw what lay ahead for the people on deck with him. Pity and love, love and pity—all his other feelings had fallen away from him like misbegotten, flightless birds that had clung to him until he could carry their weight no more. Or had forgotten how to.

And just as the dazzling, pearlescent white prepared to engulf him, making it impossible for him to tell up from down or locate himself in space at all, he finally recognized the music he was hearing: it was the passacaglia from Biber's *Mystery Sonatas*. He hadn't heard it in years. But it was right—and always had been—about the essential nature of things. All things. How he loved it.

So this was what it was going to be like. Deliverance. An event long anticipated by everyone, now finally about to unfold in all its alien splendor. And he was grateful in a shy, almost childish fashion to be part of the proceedings. To have been invited. Given a role. Included.

Odile had cared for him. And there was music.

It was enough.

# CHAPTER 36

GROOT TOUCHED TWO FINGERS to Turner's neck, at the carotid artery, and shook his head. Apparently, Odile thought, he, too, had decided to ask no questions. For that she was grateful.

Jacques filmed.

Rachel was still mopping up blood, her eyes wide with disbelief. Thierry, his hands trembling noticeably, lit a cigarette. Everyone avoided looking directly at Max, who held the gun loosely around the trigger guard, the barrel pointing at the deck. He was staring straight ahead at nothing.

Without a word Groot took the pistol from him, wiped it down with a rag, and heaved it overboard, some distance upstream from the boat. Only then did Odile remember that her own fingerprints had also been on the gun, artifacts of the night she'd taken the weapon from Turner and thrown it into his laundry basket. It occurred to her that she must now be in shock—something else to be grateful for.

"Hey, Dutchman!" It was the man from the neighboring boat. "Did you hear that just now? It sounded like a gunshot."

Noticing the bullet casing lying on deck, Groot picked it up and put it in his pocket. "Yes, I heard it. But I often hear things like that down here. Anyway, there's nothing to see."

"Good. Then I'll return with pleasure to my bunk."

Odile rolled her hands in a gesture to Groot, urgently signaling him to go on.

"Hold on a moment," he called. "I've been meaning to tell you. Now that we've got the engines working, we thought we'd take a shakedown cruise, to see that everything's shipshape, so to speak. We'll be gone a few days. So don't let anybody steal our berth, okay?"

"What do you take me for, Dutchman? I'll blow them out of the fucking water if they even try."

"Many thanks, my friend. Sleep well."

"I never sleep well." He spat into the river. "But I rest."

"That's all that really counts, isn't it. Good night."

The neighbor retreated, muttering to himself.

"Now," Groot said, turning back to the others. "I must remind you that I'm captain of this vessel, and you'll have to do things my way as long as you're on board." He waited for objections, but there were none. "First, I think we can assume the other passengers"—he meant Gabriella and the doctor—"heard everything that just happened. Still, that's no reason to bring it up or offer unnecessary explanations. The less said, the better."

Again no objections.

"Second, Monsieur Colin, will you please rejoin them now? I'm certain they'll find your presence reassuring."

Thierry tossed his cigarette overboard and went below.

"Finally," Groot said, "we'll have to give this unfortunate object"—he was referring now to Turner's body—"a head start on us. Otherwise it will trail us right down to Le Havre."

"But what about the nets?" asked Odile. "Aren't there underwater nets just outside the city limits, to catch debris?"

"The authorities had to take down the nets, because there was too *much* debris. Anyway, they'll find the body soon enough, once it begins to bloat. I myself have seen three since moving here." He turned to Rachel. "My love, will you please go get that big duffel bag from the storage locker, along with maybe thirty feet of nylon line? Thank you."

Max was going through Turner's pockets, laying out on deck his wallet, pen, phone, keys, magnifying loupe, notebook, business cards, and whatever else might identify him.

Odile came over and crouched beside him. "Max. Let me do that. You should be filming."

He looked at her in perplexity. "Filming?"

"The *Nachtvlinder*'s about to set sail. You don't know when you'll see her again, let alone your two costars. So this, as they say, is it." She scooped up Turner's personal effects in her arms.

"Odile?"

"Yes?"

"You're a pretty cool customer."

"Cool *customer*?" She frowned and wrinkled her brow in vexation. "Excuse me, I don't know this expression."

"I love you," he said.

"That one I know." She showed him a pallid smile, then headed off with Turner's possessions.

Max went to get his camera.

Dumping her former lover's personal effects on the hibachi grill, Odile began soundlessly to cry. Although she wasn't entirely sure why she'd done what she had, she knew it had been necessary. There were good reasons and bad reasons, as there were for nearly every action. As it happened, she'd come to believe in the doctor and the potential implications of his work. Of course it was convenient to tell herself that hundreds of thousands of lives would be saved at the sole cost of Turner's, and that such a trade alone must surely justify what she'd just brought about. Certainly everyone present—everyone but Max—would gladly agree without her ever having to utter a word. In fact, the time would most likely come when, *force majeure*, she herself would believe this explanation, or at least accept it. But she knew the truth was more complicated than that. At best, this was half the truth—not false, just incomplete. And then the memory came to her of how, shortly after returning from Moscow, still toweling herself dry from her first bath in days, she had thought, *Very possibly nothing happens at all until it happens again.* Nothing. And what would her life be like, really, had she not met Max that night when she was fleeing his predecessor? Nothing.

She didn't know when she'd stopped crying. Reaching for the can of lighter fluid, she lifted it high above her head and set about drenching Turner's items, watching the thin, clear stream spatter down upon the things that he'd carried with him daily, the things that constituted proof of his identity, of himself. When the can was empty, she found some matches, lit one, and tossed it on the pile. A fire leapt up, much larger, strictly speaking, than was needed, but at the same time one suited to the purpose. For a few seconds she watched it burn. Then she walked past Jacques's camera to join the others.

Rachel had just returned from below with the duffel bag and the rope. She'd changed into a black bathing suit. "Do we want weights, too?" she asked. "I'm thinking of your dumbbells."

"No. Unless the body is anchored to the bottom, it will surface in a couple of days anyway, because of the bloating. Besides, we don't really want it here, in our spot, do we. Better to let it float downstream."

Max had set up and was filming this discussion.

*Thank God the girls aren't here,* Odile thought.

Groot stripped down to his undershorts. Rachel went back to mopping up the blood. There was so much of it. How fortunate that the deck had just been revarnished. There would be no stain.

From below came the sound of a woman weeping. Gabriella must have realized it was Turner, her boss and unofficial mentor, who'd taken the bullet. Odile was wondering why Thierry didn't just shut her up, when, abruptly, the crying ceased. *Good,* she thought.

Turner's body, which had been driven back against the rail by the impact, had gradually slumped over sideways until it now lay faceup on deck. Taking it by the feet, Groot dragged it away from the main pool of blood in the vain hope they could pack it up without themselves being drenched in gore. Determined to see this grisly task finished as soon as possible, Odile unrolled the duffel bag, unzipped it, and laid it alongside the body. Then she thought, to her horror, *But he's too tall. He won't fit.*

Stripping to her underwear, she crawled along the top of the duffel bag, smoothing it out as she went. When she got to the end, she saw that her fears were unfounded. Those fears, anyway. The bag would do.

"Rachel," Groot said. "We need you here."

She threw the mop aside and came.

Max and Jacques were shooting the scene from different angles. Life was continuing.

"What we must do is roll him over on top of the bag and then pull it up around him. Rachel, you go there, by the shoulders. Odile, by the calves. I'll get the middle."

They took up their positions and, on the count of three, rolled the corpse. Though the physical exertion involved was slight, Odile felt faint afterward and had to rest. When she was ready, they pulled the edges of the bag up around Turner, tucking him into his riverine cocoon. Odile pulled the zipper closed along the length of the bag with a savagery that surprised her. Then she staggered to a chair and vomited as quietly as she could into the geranium planter.

Groot, taking up the coil of fluorescent orange rope that Rachel had brought from below, trussed the bundle tightly along its length in a zigzag pattern, which he finished off with a surgeon's knot. The pattern of the rope against the black nylon bag reminded Odile of something she'd seen before, something important, but she couldn't quite bring it to focus and soon stopped trying.

After about a minute, as if by prearranged signal, they all three went back to the bundle, picked it up, and carried it around to the river side of the boat. There they balanced it on the railing, at what would be the small of Turner's back, then quietly slipped him headfirst into the water. The bundle sank partway down and, still dimly visible, performed a slow-motion roll before the current carried it soundlessly, definitively, and miraculously away.

"We'll give him thirty minutes before we cast off," said Groot.

They cleaned what still needed it. It was decided that Jacques would accompany the *Nachtvlinder* to England after all, then fly back with his footage. They might need some transitions or postscripts. He and Max, taking one of the cameras with them but leaving the sound boom behind, went up to street level to get more video cartridges out of the Citroën.

Hugging herself, arms across her breasts, Odile walked slowly back to the river side of the boat and stopped there to stare into the whiteness. The lights on the Eiffel Tower had been switched off some time ago.

What she needed now, she thought, was to rest for a moment, find some small place of peace where she had no duties and no fateful decisions to make. She put her clothes back on over her bloodstained underwear and moved over to the quarterdeck, where the chairs were clustered. She sat down, a sigh escaped her, and, for just a second, she closed her eyes.

Then she was lost in a place where there was neither time nor even the memory of it, a place that was like a forest without paths. She pushed blindly through it, ignorant of all direction, determined only to keep going, heedless of the branches that tore at her face and forearms, undeterred by the half-buried rocks over which she repeatedly tripped and slid. Nearby, she knew, hidden among the trees, the people of this place were watching her in silence, wishing her neither good nor ill, simply waiting for her to be gone. The thought filled her with a bottomless sorrow that was like a kind of grief. *But where is Max?* she wondered. And then: *Am I fleeing something or chasing it?* Possibly it didn't matter. She pushed on. A wind sprang up, quickly gaining force until it hurtled through the treetops like a freight train. She was looking around for shelter—a storm seemed imminent—when, unexpectedly, she came into a clearing. Startled by the sudden openness, she brought herself up short, then froze altogether. Not fifteen meters from where she stood, a large animal snuffled through the underbrush, browsing for food. She fell back a few steps, but too late. Catching her scent, the bear jerked its head up to inspect her and immediately began to growl. The low, rasping sound, carrying with it intimations of far worse to come, frightened her very much. She tried to back away, but the brush seemed to have closed up behind her. *I'm finished,* she thought. *Done for.* She was still trying to make sense of her situation when the bear reared up, unleashed a terrible roar, and, with hallucinatory speed, launched itself directly at her.

Odile's eyes fluttered open. At once she was restored to herself—a woman in a deck chair, aboard an admiral's gig turned houseboat, set to depart for England at any moment. Whether what she'd just now experienced was sleep or some more esoteric synaptic event, she was at a loss to say. In either case, she now understood that one last bit of business was left for her to take care of, her and no one else. She got skittishly to her feet.

Jacques, emanating an air of deranged lucidity, bounded up the gangway with a canvas bag of fresh video cartridges. Rachel directed him to the companionway, and he disappeared below.

Odile had begun a slow survey of her surroundings when she sighted Max on the quai, setting up his camera. Everything was on track. The light had held.

Coming briskly around the wheelhouse, Rachel told her, "It's almost time. You'd better get ready to go ashore."

Odile could feel the blood sparkling in her veins.

"I just need a minute with Thierry before you go," she explained. "Would it be possible for you to send him topside for me?"

Rachel let her blue eyes linger on Odile's, then nodded and went.

Odile returned to the river side of the boat. Waiting there, she recalled a cryptic maxim—Maoist, she believed, dating from the time of the Cultural Revolution—that her father was fond of reciting. "If you are winning the race," the adage went, "it is not because you are winning the race. It is because everybody else has stopped." The thought, of course, was subject to a deliberately wide range of interpretations. She'd never quite been clear about which one Bastien himself espoused. Irritated by her own mind's workings, she pushed the syllogism firmly from her consciousness.

Moments later, Thierry appeared on deck, newly confident, his carriage verging on the cocky. Odile let him come very close to her before she spoke. "I thought you might want to thank me," she told him, "for saving your life."

He smiled. "You know quite well, Odile, that there can never be words enough to thank you for such a thing."

"I think you're mistaken about that," she said. "But let's find out, shall we?"

"With pleasure." He seemed genuinely happy, a new man alight with a new destiny. The slate wiped clean.

"I know, for instance, that you pirated my husband's film for DVD," she said, watching him carefully.

Thierry flared his lips and shrugged in a pantomime of contrition. "I offered to explain myself to him, but he didn't choose to hear."

"He has many things on his mind right now." Wisps of ghostly white fog floated by. "So why don't you explain yourself to me instead."

"If you like." He assumed the genial manner of a man recalling the details of someone else's life, an individual with whom he'd once been quite close. "As you somehow know, I had gambling debts. They had to be paid off. My cousin—"

"I read your notebook, Thierry. The one you keep in that briefcase at your apartment."

"You read my notebook."

"Yes. So can we please skip the preliminaries?" A swell of anger passed through her. "Why did you change the ending of *Fireflies*?"

For the first time since coming topside, he looked uneasy. "It's true I changed the ending, but not just of *Fireflies*. Several other films as well."

"Really? How very interesting, Thierry." With a fierce gaze, she began to circle the man. "So you're a director, then? Is that it?"

"No! Nothing at all like that!" He wheeled around, trying to catch her eye. "It was more a kind of private joke. No, not exactly a joke. More like an experiment."

"An experiment."

"Yes. I wanted to see if something as substantial and complete as one of those films could support a different outcome entirely and still be—still seem inevitable."

"Seem or be?"

"Be," he said.

There was a silence. His own answer seemed to surprise him, and, a second later, depress him utterly. But he forced himself to recover.

"What is La Peau de l'Ours?" said Odile, ratcheting up the pressure.

"It's many things. I probably know only some of its aspects." He'd begun to sweat. "But one *can* safely say that it is a conglomeration of criminal enterprises. The DVD operation was theirs, a relatively minor arm, I think, though very profitable. As you know, that's how I was paying back my—"

"But only the DVDs whose endings you altered list La Peau de l'Ours as the copyright holder. On the packaging."

"I needed a way to distinguish them from the others. I wanted to be able to track them. It was an experiment, I told you. Shit!"

"Who's in charge of this organization? Kukushkin?"

"Yes, him." Again he looked troubled.

"But?"

"But La Peau may be part of something much bigger, I don't know. From time to time I've had hints." He shook his head vexedly. "Only hints, though. I can't be sure."

Odile sighed at his performance, if that's what it was. But of course she couldn't tell.

Passing by, heading to the bridge, Rachel said, "We'll be starting up the engines in just a minute. I won't be able to engage the clutches until you're safely off the boat, Odile, and the gangway's back on board. Okay?"

"Sure. I'm almost done." She turned back to Thierry. Studying him unhappily, she couldn't shake the sense that, as witness to the killing, he now presented a new kind of risk. She swallowed hard and moved still closer to him, her face in his, his back against the rail, the river beyond, the white fog everywhere.

"Thierry, you saw what my husband did for me earlier. Of course you did, or you wouldn't be here now. He was all set to shoot you—and believe me, he would've done it without a qualm—but I told him to hit the other guy instead. Do you understand?"

"Of course. As you say, I wouldn't even—"

"And did you hear Max ask me why he should shoot that man rather than you? Did you hear him ask me anything at all?"

"No," Thierry admitted. "Nothing."

From the bridge, Rachel shouted down to Groot in the engine room. "Ready on starboard!"

Odile waited out the diesel lag. When the starboard engine rumbled to life, she went on with what she had to say, raising her voice just enough to be heard. "You see, Thierry, Max trusts me completely—loves me and trusts me, no questions asked. And I'm the same with him, naturally." She shrugged. "The point is that such trust presumes responsibility on the part of the one trusted. That's its nature."

"Indeed. But what does that have to do with me?"

She turned and walked a short distance away. After contemplating him for several seconds, she came back and resumed her former position in front of him.

"Your status has changed," she said. "You are now a witness to what happened on board tonight. What's more, of the six people present at the time of the shooting, you're the only one whose loyalties are—how to put it?—uncertain. From our point of view. So that makes you a loose end. Understand?"

Thierry's eyes widened slightly at this suggestion. "But Odile, you don't think . . . How could I possibly—I'm going to England this very moment, thanks to you, and I'm never coming back."

She stepped away again, waving her hand back and forth in the air between them as if to disperse an unpleasant smell. "Yes, yes, I'm sure. But I have to think of Max, and of how seldom, in the long run, 'never' really means 'never.' You know?"

"Listen. There's absolutely nothing to worry about, Odile. Why? Because absolutely nothing happened. I didn't see anything at all. Period."

"This is difficult," Odile said. "To trust you or not?"

"Trust me," Thierry answered firmly. "You have no reason not to."

From the bridge, Rachel again cried out to Groot below. "Ready on port!"

Waiting for the diesel particles in the port engine cylinder to mix with the compressed air and ignite, Odile reflected that nothing about the human heart was as impressive as its ability to deceive itself. Such resourcefulness, so much intelligence, all in the service of . . . of what? It was impossible to know.

With a prolonged shudder, the port engine kicked in. Odile made up her mind.

"Okay," she said. "That's my signal to disembark. So I'll say goodbye now, Thierry."

Not without sadness, she came forward and put her palms against his chest—a final gesture of camaraderie that began to change in nature as she increased the pressure she exerted on him, pushing him back against the rail until his footing on deck became precarious. *Can this be all it takes?* she thought, her surprise tinged with disappointment. *Nothing more?* Below, the Seine flowed ceaselessly seaward.

"Odile."

She increased the pressure.

"Odile! Please. I can't swim."

Looking him in the eye, she saw that it was true. For some seconds they continued to exchange stares, their faces so close they might have been about to kiss. "What a shame," she heard herself say. "You really should wear a life jacket, then. These channel crossings can be quite brutal."

And with that she took her hands from his chest and turned away. She heard him release the breath he'd been holding. Without looking back, saying nothing more, she left him there.

As she trotted down the gangway onto dry land, Odile found herself watching Max film. After a moment's thought, she looked back to see what, precisely, he was recording.

And then she realized that everything had happened in this way—exactly in this way—before. And now it had happened again. She blinked.

The *Nachtvlinder* had begun to ease from its berth into the river's main current, headed for the downstream lane on the other side of the Île Saint-Louis. In the moonlit fog, the boat grew increasingly indistinct. Moment by slender moment, it was fading away.

She blinked a second time.

Whiteness.

# CHAPTER 37

MAX SUBMITTED the finished film, titled *Bateau ivre* for French distribution, to Cannes the following year. It was accepted, screened, and, after quickly becoming the talk of the festival, won the Jury Prize. Rumor had it that the version shown was only one of three, each so differently edited as to constitute another film altogether. No proof of this ever surfaced, and Max, when asked about it in interviews, always dismissed the notion out of hand. But nothing was the same after that.

Isabelle H. called him personally and begged him for the female lead in his next project, regardless of what it was. She'd been going through a divorce the year before, and in retrospect saw that she'd been insane with unhappiness and ire. She hoped—in fact *knew*—he'd understand. And he did.

Eddie handled the negotiations. By mid-July, they had thirty-four million in studio backing and a crew handpicked by Max, the best people he knew in the business. Jacques, not unexpectedly, had declined the position of assistant director of photography in favor of a project of his own that, after Cannes, had quickly gathered momentum. Meanwhile, Max's new film was set to begin principal photography in mid-August, on location in Grasse. This time there was a solid script, and though Max wasn't sure if he'd follow it or not, Isabelle H. had promised him she'd do it however he wanted. She pronounced him to be the future of cinema and added that she, for one, had no intention of being left behind with yesterday's hucksters and starlets. Besides, the August light around Grasse flattered everything it touched, even in the narrow streets of the mostly working-class town itself. Perhaps, Isabelle admitted, she was still a little vain.

On the second Friday of August, Max and Odile, along with Allegra, who'd returned from New York to spend the summer in their company, were flown down to Grasse, where a renovated villa had been rented for them some distance north of town, on a steeply set parcel of land at the southern foot of the Alps. The place was flanked by two large fields of flowers—one of jasmine, the other of tuberose—cultivated for the local perfume industry. The combined scent was intoxicating, ceaseless, and a bit unreal. From the villa's veranda, looking down toward the sea, there was an impressive panoramic view of the French Riviera and its coastal resort towns.

After their arrival, when she and Max were done unpacking, Odile said, "I think, my love, that considering my present condition I'll allow myself a nap." Max kissed her, asked her how she felt, then left her alone. She was three months pregnant, easily tired, and definitely to be listened to. The pregnancy had been an accident, more or less, or anyway not a conscious decision, but immediately they'd seen the rightness of it, the eerie serendipity. Given all that had happened. Given all that hadn't.

"Well, *I'm* going for a walk," Allegra announced just as the kitchen's screen door shut behind her. She had lately developed an air of romantic melancholy, by turns ironic and not. It was well suited to the environs and even to the diaphanous clothes she had brought along. The year had changed her more deeply than that, though; she had grown harder or, Max sometimes thought, less expectant. As she'd predicted the previous summer, her mother had indeed married the proctologist, and Max thought it likely that his own position had been strengthened by comparison. While Allegra no longer bore him or filmmaking any discernible ill will, he knew he was still on probationary status and that things might change at any moment. Nevertheless, the respite was welcome.

Downstairs, on the villa's stone veranda, Max found the housekeeper had laid out a pitcher of iced tea and that day's *Nice-Matin* on a green metal table for him. With a sigh of relief, he sat down, poured himself a glass, and sipped it while gazing out over the downhill vista of fields, towns, coastline, and sea. After awhile he took off his dark glasses, leaned forward, and, for a minute or longer, considered more analytically the visible world laid out before him. Then he sat back and put his glasses on again. Isabelle H. had been right about the light, not that he had doubted her. Women who believed their faces were their fortunes took pitiless note of such matters and were, of necessity, almost never wrong. Even though Isabelle was an actress, not just a face.

So all the platitudes were true. And everything was flux.

He and Odile hadn't spoken once of that moon-scorched night in Paris. They had never spoken of killing Turner. They had never spoken of her affair, let alone with whom she'd had it. Nor had Thierry Colin's name ever come up. All that was behind them now. The *Nachtvlinder* had set out, as planned. Max had filmed it, as planned. Jacques had returned from England with some essential sequences of Groot and Rachel, who, after much equivocation, had gotten married in Le Havre before proceeding to cross the channel amid unseasonably rough weather. Perhaps predictably, however, nothing had been heard firsthand from either the newlyweds or their passengers. No one knew if Rachel had seen the film, but Max was certain she'd eventually get in touch. So things had worked out, after a fashion.

As for Turner, his body had surfaced three days after his death, just as Groot had predicted. An investigation was launched, but it had never come to bear even remotely upon those aboard the *Nachtvlinder* that night, the perpetrators, witnesses, and fugitives. The big story of the day had been the escape from La Santé of three prisoners, none of whom had been apprehended, and in the public outcry over poor security at the prison, many other cases had been pushed aside or forgotten. As usual.

Pouring himself another glass of tea, Max let his thoughts turn to the new film, tentatively titled *Scentless* in a not-so-oblique reference to Grasse's world-renowned perfume industry. The beauty of southern France was extraordinary, verging on the obscene, and he'd have to work against that to extract the most from it. No doubt he'd chosen the locale in part as an antidote to the ugly edges in *Bateau ivre,* but there was no surviving this business if you didn't please yourself at the outset, when you still had the chance. More worrisome was the thought that now, as a prospective father of two and a contented, though watchful, husband, he was at risk of succumbing to mere happiness. All he needed to banish this troubling notion, however, was to remember Allegra's infancy and the rigors it had entailed. Nothing, at least nothing he truly cared about, was predictable or easily contained by expectation. One might cite Odile in this regard.

She had recently announced her intention to expand her business once the baby was born, taking on a partner and turning out two carefully conceived clothing lines a year. Significant pieces of this plan eluded Max, most especially those relating to child care, but he knew there was nothing he could do about it except assume an attitude of cautious encouragement and then embrace it fully. Which is what he would do. And in the end, what would be, would be.

Perhaps, he thought, it was he who was becoming a Buddhist.

The faint but ceaseless buzz of insects, the narcotizing scent of jasmine and tuberose, the heat of the midafternoon sun, the taste of crushed mint on his tongue, the mere thought of *Nice-Matin*—all conspired to send Max into a light doze. He dreamed, blessedly, of nothing.

When he woke, twenty minutes later, it was to the sound of gravel crunching beneath radial tires. Isabelle H. and Allegra were tooling up the villa's semicircular driveway in a vintage sapphire-blue roadster, top down, and they were laughing like beautiful fools, actual tears streaming down their cheeks. In an effort to look directorial, he leapt to his feet, straightened his sunglasses, and put his hands firmly on his hips, as if he'd been awaiting them for some time.

"Look what I found," said Isabelle in English, laughing and wiping the tears from her eyes as she pulled up before him. She shut off the engine. Allegra, still in the grip of hilarity, opened the passenger-side door and raced past him up the stairs and into the villa. Shortly, Odile could be heard laughing too, with no more restraint than the others.

"Well," said Max, greeting Isabelle H. with a kiss on either cheek and a small smile, "I guess something's funny. May I get you a cool drink?"

"Thanks, that would be wonderful." She took a seat at the table, removed her broad-brimmed sun hat, finely woven of lavender flax, and shook out her famous blond hair. "But I can't stay long. I just wanted to see if you were really here."

"Yes, I'm here." He continued to inspect her. "I came. We'll see. You'll conquer."

"Really? Do you think so?"

"No question."

She laughed again: a sound like a handful of gold coins tossed carelessly down a stone staircase.

The housekeeper arrived with smiles and more iced tea. She recognized Isabelle H. without fussing over her, thus putting both actress and director at ease, then discreetly withdrew.

"But seriously," Isabelle said, once she'd drunk down half her tea. "I've now read the script five—no, six—times and not yet have I begun to exhaust its possibilities. We don't start shooting until Monday, yes?"

"That's right." Max lit a cigar and studied her. "Tell me," he said, "what's it about, this screenplay?"

She told him. At great length. In French.

For a long time he smoked without speaking, brow furrowed, considering her answer. Then, abruptly, he leapt to his feet and hurled his glass as far out over the sloping lawn as he could, tea spilling from the vessel's lip in a lazy amber skein. "You know nothing!" he shouted at her. "Nothing!"

"Yes," she told him calmly. "And I intend to know even less."

He looked at her with new interest. "Really?"

"Really. For this film, I want to be a blank slate, open to anything, without preconceptions." She tilted her head and smiled. "Like the characters in *Bateau ivre*, of course." After studying him for a moment, she laughed wickedly. "Max! You didn't take all that nonsense I just said about the script seriously, did you?"

Moving to her side of the table, he leaned down and kissed her respectfully on the cheek. "So, we understand each other even better than I thought. And I'm certain now—totally and completely positive—that this is going to be a very, very fruitful experience for both of us."

She smiled and returned her tranquil gaze to the vista spread before them. "But of course," she said. "Why else would I possibly be here?"


MAX, Odile, and Allegra had dinner that night in the villa's cypress-paneled dining room. The housekeeper's sister, a silent disapproving woman who departed as soon as the food was ready, had prepared artichokes, *fruits des mer*, frisée salad, and grapefruit granité. Allegra, the only one of the three not exhausted by the day's activities, wanted to know if it was really true that oysters acted as an aphrodisiac.

"It's disputed," answered Odile. "How many have you eaten?"

"Seven?"

"And do you feel like making love?"

Allegra considered this seriously. "Yes, I think so."

"Then don't eat any more. You're too young."

Smiling craftily, Allegra immediately downed another. "Aiee!" she cried out. "My ass! It's on *fire*! Quick, put it out, put it out! Anyone, please! It's unbearable! Help me! Help!"

Max closed his eyes and shook his head in refusal of the inevitable.

"Allegra," said Odile, "that's enough. Your father and I are too tired tonight for your antics."

"I know." She spoke as if privy to secret ironies, smiling to herself.

They ate for awhile in silence.

Halfway through the granité, they were startled when the living-room phone rang. As far as Max knew, no one even had their number.

"I'll get it!" cried Allegra, springing from her chair.

Max and Odile exchanged a glance of concern, but a moment later she reappeared looking somewhat deflated. "It's for you, Dad. Monsieur Bouvier. He says it's important."

Wiping his mouth with his napkin, Max went into the living room.

Odile gave Allegra a reflexive, uncharacteristically self-conscious smile. She'd postponed informing her of the pregnancy for all the usual reasons: fear that first-trimester complications would make the news superfluous; reluctance to announce her state publicly before her body did it for her; uncertainty, despite Max's reassurances, that Allegra would respond well to hearing she was about to have a half sibling; and, finally, a desire, as inexplicable as it was instinctive, to keep her condition a secret—one to be shared only with Max—for as long as possible. She supposed all women had this impulse. It was the beginning of the long custodianship that was motherhood.

Across the table, Allegra's honey-brown eyes were fixed on hers. The tilt of her head indicated both the intensity of her curiosity and her desire to appear casual about it.

It was time, Odile decided.

"Listen, sweetheart. There's something I want to tell you."

Allegra sighed and took a huge spoonful of granité, as if to forestall all possibility of having to respond to whatever was about to be said.

"Your father and I—"

But exactly at that moment Max reappeared, looking both agitated and strangely puzzled. "Quick! Where's the TV in this wretched place?"

Shifting her mouthful of granité to the side of one cheek, Allegra jumped to her feet. "You don't know? I mean, would you guys be totally clueless without me or what? Come on!"

She led them at a run to the wing of the villa that looked out on the swimming pool in back. Over her shoulder, she called, "It's a satellite dish, so we get, like, everything!"

"What's this about?" Odile asked Max quietly.

"No idea. Eddie only said—"

"And it's got a giant hi-def screen, really supercool!"

"—not to miss the BBC international news. Which down here, he says, starts any minute now. 'Something of personal interest to you and Odile in particular,' was how he put it. Those were his actual words."

"Sounds ominous."

"He wouldn't say more."

"Hey, are you guys lost?"

They found Allegra in a long rectangular room, one wall of which was glass. Incorporated into this wall was a sliding door that led to the pool and its cedar deck. The underwater lights were on—somewhat perplexingly, since as far as Odile knew, no one had used the pool since their arrival—and lent the air a turquoise shimmer. On the wall adjacent to this one was a huge flat-screen TV that Allegra had already switched on. She was now blasting fiercely away at it with the remote, the tip of her tongue protruding from the corner of her mouth as she concentrated on the succession of crystal-bright images.

"Which channel?" she asked. An intricately coiled rug of sisal rope covered the floor.

"BBC World," Max said.

He and Odile seated themselves on the chrome-framed, cream leather couch facing the TV as Allegra continued to scan stations. When the quaintly familiar orange-and-black BBC logo sequence appeared, Max stopped her.

"Oh, puke-orama!" Allegra exclaimed in disgust as soon as she saw that all this excitement was over nothing more than a foreign newscast. "Boring, boring, *bor-ing*." She tossed her father the remote and left the room.

"What's gotten into her tonight?" Max wondered aloud.

"Shh."

The anchorwoman, blond, attractive, but broad-shouldered and maternally stern in the British manner, had already begun her lead-in: "—so that what for so long seemed only a promise, at times hardly a hope, has at last been redeemed beyond all doubt. For more, we go now to King's College, London, and our science correspondent, Vikram Gupta. Vikram?"

"Thank you, Katty," said the slim young man, his eyes appearing very large in his tea-colored face. "Just two hours ago, right here in the staid precincts of King's College, an announcement was made which one can safely say will change the course of medicine, if not of human life itself, for all time."

The picture cut to a taped video excerpt from the press conference the reporter had been referring to, and immediately Odile knew what was to come. A middle-aged man at a lectern—the screen chyron identified him as "Director, Stem Cell Biology Laboratory, King's College, London"—was declaring in deliberately understated tones that, thanks to recent breakthroughs at the lab, his team was now able to attain a one-hundred-percent success rate in transforming therapeutically cloned human embryos into viable stem cell lines, cells capable of turning into any of the more than two hundred forms of tissue that make up the human body. Here, clearly mindful of the political and moral brush fires this announcement was certain to ignite, he raised a calming hand. A therapeutically cloned embryo, he reminded his audience, was nothing more than a human egg cell whose nucleus has been replaced with that of a cell belonging to the patient to be treated. "Thus," he added, "however one defines life, nothing of it—nothing whatsoever—is lost in this process. There can be no moral qualms, and for that we can only be grateful." He paused briefly. "But we have still more to report."

Max turned to Odile in astonishment. "Is this what—"

"Shh!"

The scientist adjusted his spectacles and continued. "While we have had some success in creating stem cells before—nothing like a hundred per-cent, of course, but some success—the real problem has always been how to direct these stem cells to grow into the kind of tissue required in any given instance, whether it be heart muscle for the cardiac patient, bone marrow for the leukemia victim, or brain cells for someone suffering from Parkinsonism. Today it is my privilege and honor to announce that, due largely to the efforts of one man—a brilliant scientist and recent arrival at our laboratory, our small band of devoted brothers and sisters—we are now able to accomplish this extraordinary task with the same one-hundred-percent efficiency attained in the stem cell production." He appeared briefly overcome with emotion—a good portion of it envy, only partly dis-guised. He turned to his left. "The man I am referring to is Dr. Aleksandr Tregobov. Sasha, I don't believe anyone has seen your face outside a labo-ratory in years. So would you please rise? Rise and be counted among the greatest minds of our time."

Looking very uncomfortable, Tregobov got up from his seat. He was wearing a white lab coat and the same black-framed glasses he'd sported in the photo Rachel had been shown by the CRS. At the sight of him, the press corps rose as one to its feet, shot a flurry of photos, then burst quite unex-pectedly into applause. Tregobov, looking if possible even more discom-fited, acknowledged this accolade with a brief bow before sitting back down. "Thank you," he said inaudibly.

The picture cut back to the science reporter, standing outside the lec-ture hall as he sketched out for his viewers the ramifications of this stun-ning development.

"I can't believe it!" Max said. "How much of this did you know back when—"

"I'm not sure," Odile replied. She'd moved so close to him that the entire left side of her body was pressed against his and her left leg slung over his right. Now she sought out his hand and squeezed it tightly.

"Odile, what's the matter?"

"Nothing. Let's listen."

"So," concluded the young reporter, "it is no exaggeration to call this development one of truly earthshaking proportions, its implications virtually unlimited. You can be sure we'll be hearing a great deal more about it—and the many vexing issues it raises—in the days and weeks ahead." He paused to sweep his straight black hair back from his brow. "Katty?"

"Earthshaking news indeed, Vikram," the anchor replied. "Thank you." Flashing an appropriately bedazzled smile, she reengaged the camera—and her viewers—before assuming a more solemn manner and picking up her end of the story. "Of course, with today's rapidly changing intellectual-property laws and the corporate sector's involvement in just about everything, from soup to nuts, it's no surprise that science and business have become ever more closely intertwined. Here tonight to help us understand this still-evolving alliance"—she swiveled in her chair to introduce her guests, whose images now filled the screen—"are two people in the very thick of it."

"Oh my God!" said Odile in a low voice.

"Him!" Max exclaimed. "And what's *she* doing there? I thought—"

"Mr. Nikolai Kukushkin and Ms. Gabriella Moreau, codirectors of the StemTech Corporation, based here in London. Thank you both for joining us on such short notice."

"So that's Kukushkin," said Odile to herself. "Unbelievable."

"It is our pleasure to be here," intoned the Russian, who, in addition to his usual boxy British suit, had donned a tie for the occasion. Beside him, Gabriella smiled fetchingly in a soberly cut turquoise dress.

"Ms. Moreau," the anchorwoman said, "could you begin by telling our viewers what StemTech does, exactly? Or rather what it will do, since I gather it's a very recently formed enterprise?"

"Yes, this is correct. As you perhaps know, Katty, it has for several years now been possible, under the Worldwide Patent Cooperation Treaty, to patent things not previously covered by copyright law. I'm speaking of genes and other living matter, whether 'natural' or 'artificial' in origin; the scientific processes that make them available for practical use; previously unknown applications for naturally occurring substances; and so on. Accordingly, all the processes announced at King's College this afternoon have been duly patented, as is common practice today, and StemTech was formed as the sole licensing agency for those wishing to make use of those procedures. The corporation, in other words, was designed to be the most efficient conduit to the patent-holding party, so as to minimize bureaucracy and quicken response time. We are very concerned about accessibility."

Katty, who appeared mildly dissatisfied with this answer, turned next to Kukushkin, and as she sought to formulate her question, Max said to Odile, "You never actually met Kolya back then, did you? Kukushkin, I mean."

She shook her head. "No. Just his minions."

"Mr. Kukushkin, your background is mostly in banking. What drew you to this project?"

"Such revolutionary advances, such exciting possibilities, who would not be drawn to them? Is for the good of mankind, and how often does one get a chance to be part of such work? But, speaking more personally, I have known Dr. Tregobov for a number of years, back when he was virtual slave to state of Belarus, from which he has now fortunately emigrated. The fact is this: he, like any true research scientist, is concerned only with his work and where it leads him. He does not want to be bothered by legal details and trivialities, of which there are bound to be an infinite number in this case. And so we may say it is only natural that he should turn to me, his loyal and admiring friend, at this critical time. Part of StemTech's mission, besides to act as conduit and licensing agent, will be to shield this great scientist from the countless distractions he must otherwise face, distractions that would likely be overwhelming and make further research very difficult for him, maybe impossible."

"But surely you would agree," said Katty, who seemed to feel her story slipping away from her, "that a great deal of money will be made from Dr. Tregobov's discoveries."

"Money will perhaps be made, yes. But it will go to the patent-holding party, not to StemTech. Profit is not a factor in this instance."

"Then why patent these processes in the first place? Shouldn't they be available to anyone who needs them?"

"This is not for me to say. But as previously mentioned, it has become common practice in recent years to patent such discoveries." Kukushkin could not suppress a laugh. "You know, Katty, there are genes in the bodies of all of us sitting here tonight that have been patented by the people who first identified them, people we will never meet and who will put them to uses we will never hear about. Whether, in future, this practice will stand up to legal challenge, I do not know. Is simply current situation."

"A brave new world, by any standard," said Katty, glancing quickly at the studio clock. "Ms. Moreau, in the few seconds left to us, is there anything you would like to add?"

"Only this," said Gabriella, her eyes flashing satisfaction. "That Dr. Tregobov's discoveries will save countless lives and can only be cause for celebration. Yesterday we were without these tools, which now will help so many. Today we have them. It is a kind of miracle."

"Indeed it is," said Katty, bringing the interview firmly to an end. "Nikolai Kukushkin, Gabriella Moreau, thank you for being with us."

"Thank you, Katty," replied Gabriella. Kukushkin, looking deeply into the camera, nodded once in grave farewell.

"In today's other top stories," said Katty, swiveling back to fill the screen with her indomitable presence, "mudslides in Indonesia have left more than three hundred dead or missing, as monsoon rains—"

Max hit the remote, and the screen went black.

Odile slowly disengaged her body from Max's. Getting to her feet, she walked over to the glass wall, arms folded across her chest, looked out past the pool, and brooded over what she'd just learned. Max remained where he was.

"It's a story of which we each must know quite different parts, isn't it?" she said, after awhile.

"No doubt," Max replied. "But you definitely know a lot more of it than I do."

A silence.

Then Odile said, "That night, the night of the auction and everything that happened after, you said you'd just come from having drinks with Kukushkin. At his private club, you said. Was that true?"

"Yes. I'd gotten to know his fiancée a little, more or less by accident, and when I ran into her at the auction, she introduced us."

"His fiancée," Odile repeated thoughtfully. "She wears a floral perfume, maybe? Gardenia?"

Max laughed. "That's right."

"I wonder what happened to her." Odile's thoughts drifted idly for a moment before she corrected course. "What's her name?"

"Véronique."

"Véronique." She mused over this answer, half aware of her own reflection in the plate glass in front of her even as she stared through it at the shimmering pool. "So I suppose Gabriella—" But she stopped herself in time. "My God, Max. All that seems so very, very long ago. Almost," she added, "as if it happened in another lifetime."

"It *was* another lifetime. Anyway, don't brood. It's bad for the baby."

Odile turned around, a wan smile on her face. "You're right. And it's completely useless. So I think I'll go take a bath, if anything so mundane can be had in a place like this." She kissed him in passing and went off in search of a tub.

"Keep an eye out for Allegra, will you?" Max called after her. Then, to himself, in a voice from an old movie: "It's quiet. Too quiet."

IN HER BATH, amid billowing steam, Odile found herself thinking about her father. Predictably, he'd refused to see *Bateau ivre* or comment on its success. But she thought she'd lately detected a softening in his attitude toward Max, perhaps because she herself had grown visibly happier over the past year. Soon she would inform the old Trotskyite of her pregnancy, for once telling him something he didn't already know, and Bastien would come around at last, accepting Max as his worthy son-in-law, co-custodian of the Mével genes. The thought pleased, but also amused her. In the end, she'd proven more stubbornly ascetic than Bastien, and now that she was sure of her victory on this score, she was content to let the competition fade away unacknowledged. Life required no less.

And life, as one was always being told, had its reasons of which reason knew nothing. Gabriella, for instance, who'd succeeded after all in having her eggs substituted for those of Kukushkin's fiancée, this Véronique of whom Odile until now hadn't heard a word, though she'd caught scent of her perfume on Max that night aboard the *Nachtvlinder*. Obviously, too, Gabriella was now co-holder with Tregobov of the patent rights to the various processes just described on the news, making her quite soon an unimaginably wealthy woman. Whether Thierry had found a place for himself amid these arrangements was hard to say, but Odile thought it unlikely. He'd already been rendered redundant the moment the doctor boarded the boat. Maybe the plan—or the counterplan—had called all along for Thierry to be jettisoned once he'd served his function, and from what Odile had gathered about Kukushkin, she could only imagine the worst. In any case, the Russian would now be getting his share of the licensing fees through Gabriella, whom he had perhaps even married in place of Véronique to give the deal more legal heft. Odile recalled with embarrassment her own envy of Gabriella's youth as, hiding in Thierry's closet, she'd watched her undress to try on the lingerie he'd left her as a gift. Folly and foolishness. Odile herself felt far younger now than she had on that day. Or, rather, younger *and* older. Renewed.

She didn't know how much Max had deduced or been told about all that she'd kept secret from him. It didn't matter. She didn't know, either, what or how much he himself had kept from her, nor how their separate silences had intersected to bring them to this new and unexpected place in their life together. But again, not knowing didn't matter, and she felt no need to find out. They had come this far, she and Max. They would go farther still.

She closed her eyes in weariness. From downstairs came the sound of the TV again, an old movie, American, undubbed. She distinctly heard Cary Grant say, "Yes, I *will* say you do things with dispatch. No wasted preliminaries." Allegra giggled at something Max said.

Some time later, Odile jerked up out of her own drowsiness, uncertain where she was. The water had gone cold. She got out of the tub and, taking a towel from the rack, stepped out onto the balcony to dry herself. She turned her face to the night sky.

From the southeast, a storm was approaching. Lightning flickered, and thunder followed more and more closely. Along the coast, the lights of Nice, Antibes, Cannes, and Fréjus shone like the precious stones of a necklace cast negligently aside after a long evening. The storm had yet to make landfall.

Putting on her old silk robe, Odile slipped quietly downstairs. She heard Grace Kelly say, "Let me do something to help you." But instead of joining Max and Allegra to watch the movie, she continued out onto the veranda and sat down on the stone steps. They were still warm from the heat of the day.

Below, along the coast, the storm came in hard and fast, blotting out the stars as far as she could see, from northeast to southwest. Lightning bolts, accompanied by teeth-rattling cracks of thunder, darted from sky to ground, sometimes in multiples or jagged forks, giving the air a pungent ozone smell. Then came the rain, which she could hear falling on the towns below and could feel as a sudden temperature drop rolling uphill like a runaway fog, but which she could see only by lightning flash. Sometimes the bolts were almost constant, but at other moments were separated by intervals of darkness during which Odile grew tense, anticipating the next burst of light.

She sat where she was, too absorbed to move, as the storm continued to roll inland. It came on so fast that there was a period, just before it reached her, when the lights of the coastal towns emerged from darkness, the bad weather already done down there. It cheered her to see the lights again, as if, in some childish game of wishes, she'd come out ahead.

Then, quite nearby, there was a tremendous flash, a shower of sparks and a violent explosion. In that fraction of a second, she saw that lightning had struck one of the rows of electrical pylons that ran up the mountain-side like gigantic, narrow-waisted warrior figures, abstractly humanoid in appearance. Knowing what must follow, she turned back toward the coast just in time to see the towns lose their power, each cluster of lights winking out in sequence in less than two seconds.

Then the hillside power failed too, casting everything around her—the villa, its neighbors, the flanking fields of jasmine and tuberose, things she was already trying to visualize—into total, placeless darkness.

She stayed where she was. Inside the villa she heard Allegra's half-pretend shriek followed by Max's teasing, coaxing words.

When he came out onto the veranda and sat down silently next to her, Odile rested her head on his shoulder.

The rain arrived, falling in sheets. They watched.

After a time she said, "I almost never think about the past anymore."

# ACKNOWLEDGMENTS

DURING THE WRITING OF THIS BOOK, I was aided immeasurably by the generosity of a number of people, most especially: Betsy Baker, Bertille de Baudinière, Natalie Bataille, Dajana Cesic, Zhenya Edelmann, Gary Fisketjon, Fran Gordon, Bruce Levine, Kathryn Maris, Arthur Perkins, Béatrice Pire, Anne Rochette, Wade Saunders, and Masha Yatskova. My thanks to all of them.

—TM

## A NOTE ABOUT THE AUTHOR

Ted Mooney is the author of three previous novels, *Easy Travel to Other Planets*, *Traffic and Laughter*, and *Singing into the Piano*. He was senior editor at *Art in America* for over thirty years and now teaches a graduate seminar at Yale University School of Art. His fiction has appeared in *Esquire*, *Granta*, and the *New American Review*, and he has received grants from both the John Simon Guggenheim Foundation and the Ingram-Merrill Foundation. He lives in New York City.

## A NOTE ON THE TYPE

This book was set in Janson, a typeface thought to have been made by the Dutchman Anton Janson. It has been conclusively demonstrated that these types are actually the work of Nicholas Kis (1650–1702).

*Composed by Creative Graphics, Allentown, Pennsylvania*
*Printed and bound by Berryville Graphics, Berryville, Virginia*
*Designed by Maggie Hinders*